THE AMERICAN GIRL

THE AMERICAN GIRL

A NOVEL

Monika Fagerholm

Translated by Katarina E. Tucker

OTHER PRESS

NEW YORK

Production Editor: Yvonne E. Cárdenas

Book design: Simon M. Sullivan

This book was set in 10.5pt Janson by Alpha Design &
Composition of Pittsfield, NH.

10 9 8 7 6 5 4 3 2 1

LIBRARY OF CONGRESS CATALOGING-IN-PUBLICATION DATA
Fagerholm, Monika, 1961–
[Amerikanska flickan. English]
The American girl / Monika Fagerholm ; translated [from the
Swedish] by Katarina E. Tucker.
p. cm.
ISBN 978-1-59051-304-0 (pbk.)—ISBN 978-1-59051-383-5 (e-book)
1. Teenage girls—Fiction.   2. Death—Psychological aspects—
Fiction.   3. Teenage girls—Psychology—Fiction.
4. Adolescence—Fiction.   5. Teenage girls—Sexual behavior—
Fiction.   6. Swamps—Finland—Fiction.   I. Tucker, Katarina
Emilie.   II. Title.
PT9876.16.A4514A8513 2010
839.73'74—dc22
2009041117

Nobody knew my rose of the world but me.

TENNESSEE WILLIAMS

CONTENTS

Contents

II.

*THE
AMERICAN
GIRL*

THE AMERICAN GIRL

THIS IS WHERE THE MUSIC BEGINS. IT IS SO SIMPLE. IT IS AT the end of the 1960s, on Coney Island in New York. There is a beach and boardwalk, a small amusement park, some restaurants, fun slot machines, and so on.

There are a lot of people here. She does not stick out from the crowd. She is young, fifteen–sixteen, dressed in a thin, light-colored dress. Her hair is blond and a bit limp, and she has not washed it in a few days. She comes from San Francisco and, before that, from somewhere else. She has all of her belongings in a bag she wears over her arm. A shoulder bag, it is blue and has "Pan Am" on it.

She walks around a bit listlessly, talks to someone here and there, answers when she is spoken to, looks a little bit like a hippie girl, but that is not what she is. She is not anything, actually. She travels around. Lives from hand to mouth. Meets people.

Do you need a place to crash?

There is always someone who asks.

And you can still live like that, even during those times.

She has a few dollars in her hand, ones she has just gotten from someone. She asked for them, she is hungry, she wants food. Really she is just hungry, nothing more. But she is happy otherwise, it is such a beautiful day here, outside the city. The sky is endless, and the world is large.

She sees a few kids who are pretending to sing in front of a machine where you can record your own song. They can still be found here and there even during those times, and exactly at places like these: "Record your own song and give it away to someone. Your wife, your husband, a friend. Or just keep it for yourself."

Like a small silly memento.

She steps into the machine just for fun and randomly starts feeding coins into it.

You can select background music, but she does not. She pushes Record and then she sings.

Look, Mom, they've destroyed my song.

It does not sound very good. It really does not. But it does not mean anything.

Look, Mom, what they've done to my song.

The words do not fit very well with reality. It is such a beautiful day out there.

And when she has finished singing she waits for the record and gets it.

And then she suddenly remembers that she is supposed to meet someone here.

She is in a hurry to get to the designated place, it is a park.

She is going to meet a relative. A distant one. Not the relative, but the distance to the place where the relative lives. It is a place on the other side of the earth.

That was the girl, Eddie de Wire. The American girl who was found drowned in Bule Marsh, the District, a few years later. A place on the other side of the earth.

IT HAPPENED AT BULE MARSH 1969–2008

―――――――

IT HAPPENED IN THE DISTRICT, AT BULE MARSH. EDDIE'S DEATH. She was lying at the bottom of the marsh. Her hair was standing out around her head in thick, long strands like octopus tentacles. Her eyes and mouth were wide open. He saw her from where he was standing on Lore Cliff, staring straight down into the water. He saw the scream coming out of her open mouth, the scream that could not be heard. He looked into her eyes, they were empty. Fish were swimming in and out of them and into her body's other cavities. But later, when some time had passed.

He never stopped imagining it.

That she had been sucked down into the marsh like into the Bermuda Triangle.

Now she was lying there and was unreachable, a distance of about thirty feet, visible only to him, in the dark and murky water.

She, Edwina de Wire, Eddie. The American girl. As she was called in the District.

And he was Bengt. Thirteen years old in August of 1969 when everything happened. Eddie, she was nineteen. Edwina de Wire. It was strange. Later when he saw her name in the papers it was as if it was not her at all.

"I'm a strange bird, Bengt. Are you too?"

"Nobody knew my rose of the world but me."

She had talked that way, using peculiar words. She had been a stranger there, in the District.

The American girl. And he, he had loved her.

. . .

There was a morning after night, a night when he had not been able to sleep. At daybreak he ran through the forest over the field over the meadow past the cousin's house, the two decayed ramshackle barns and the red cottage where his sisters, Rita and Solveig, lived. He jumped over three deep ditches and got to the outbuilding by the border of Lindström's land.

He walked into the outbuilding. The first thing he saw were the feet. They were hanging in the air. Bare feet, the soles gray and dirty. And lifeless. They were Björn's feet, Björn's body. Cousin Björn's. And he was also only nineteen years old that same year, when he died by his own hand.

They had been a threesome: Eddie, Bencku, Björn. Now it was only him, Bencku. He was left alone.

And so, he stood and screamed out into the wild dazzling nature of late summer, so quiet, so green. He screamed at the sun, which had just disappeared behind a blue cover of clouds. At a dull, calm summer rain cautiously starting. *Drip-drip-drip* in an otherwise total and ghostly calm. But Bencku screamed. Screamed and screamed, even though he suddenly did not have a voice.

He became mute for long periods of time. Thoroughly mute: he had not spoken that much before, but now he was not going to say anything at all. According to the diagnosis, a clinical muteness brought on by a state of shock. As a result of everything that had happened during the night.

Another child was also moving around in the District then. She was there at all possible and impossible times of day, in every place, everywhere. It was Doris, the marsh kid. Doris Flinkenberg who did not have a real home then despite the fact that she was maybe only eight or nine years old.

It was Doris who said she had heard the scream at the out-building by the border of Lindström's land.

"It sounded like a stuck lamb or the way only someone like Bencku sounds like," she said to the cousin's mama in the cousin's kitchen in the cousin's house where she gradually, after Björn's death, would become a daughter herself, in her own right.

"It's called a pig," the cousin's mama corrected her. "To squeal like a stuck pig."

"But I mean lamb," Doris would protest. "Because that's what Bencku sounds like when he screams. Like one of those lambs you feel sorry for. *A sacrificial lamb*."

Doris Flinkenberg with her very own way of expressing herself. You did not always know if she was serious or if she was playing a game. And if it was a game, in that case, what kind?

"One man's death is another man's breath," Doris Flinkenberg sighed in the cousin's kitchen, so delighted over finally having her own home, a real one. Only someone like Doris Flinkenberg could say "One man's death is another man's breath" in such a way that it did not sound cynical but, actually, almost normal.

"Now, now, now." The cousin's mama said to Doris nevertheless, "What are you actually saying?" But there was still something soft in her voice, in a calm and settled way. Because it was Doris who had come to the cousin's house and given the cousin's mama her life and all her hopes back after the death of Björn, her darling boy.

But who could have imagined then that only a few years later Doris would be dead as well.

It happened in the District, at Bule Marsh, death's spell at a young age. It was a Saturday in the month of November. Dusk slowly transformed into darkness and Doris Flinkenberg, sixteen years old, wandered through the woods on the familiar path down to Bule Marsh. With quick and determined steps. The growing darkness did not bother her, her eyes had time to get used to it and the path was familiar to her, almost too familiar.

And it was Doris Night, or was it Doris Day, or was it the Marsh Queen, or one of the many other identities in the many games she had already had time to play in her life? You did not know. But maybe it was not important anymore.

Because Doris Flinkenberg, she had the pistol in her pocket. It was a real Colt, certainly antique, but in working condition nonetheless. The only thing of value that Rita and Solveig had ever inherited from anyone: a distant ancestor who, according to rumors, had bought it in 1902 at the big department store in the city by the sea.

Afterward, when Doris was dead, Rita would swear she did not know how the pistol, which was stored hidden away in a specific spot in her and Solveig's cottage, had gotten into the hands of Doris Flinkenberg.

It would not be a complete lie, but also not entirely true.

Doris came to Bule Marsh and she walked up Lore Cliff. She stood there and counted to ten. She counted to eleven, twelve, and fourteen too, and to sixteen, before she had gathered enough courage to raise the pistol's barrel to her temple and pull the trigger.

She had already stopped thinking, but her emotions, they swelled in her head and her entire body, everywhere.

Doris Flinkenberg wearing the Loneliness&Fear shirt. Old and worn now. A real cleaning rag, that was what it had become by this time.

But anyway, in the space between two numbers the resolution had taken hold of Doris Flinkenberg anew. And she just raised the barrel of the pistol to her temple, and, *click*, she pulled the trigger. But first she shut her eyes and screamed. Screamed in order to drown herself out, to drown out her fear, and the shot itself, which she would not hear anymore, so that was even more absurd.

Shots, I think I hear shots.
It echoed in the woods, everywhere.

It was Rita who heard the shot first. She was in the red cottage about a third of a mile from Bule Marsh with her sister Solveig. And it was strange, as soon as she heard the shot she knew exactly what had happened. She tore her jacket from the wall and ran out, through the woods to the marsh with Solveig after her. But it was too late.

Doris was already dead as a rock when Rita made it to Lore Cliff. She was lying on her stomach, with her head and hair hanging down over the dark water. In blood. And Rita lost it. She tore and pulled at the dead and still warm body. She tried to lift Doris up, and how absurd was that, to carry her.

Carry Doris over troubled water.

Solveig had to do everything in her power to try and calm Rita down. And suddenly the woods were filled with people. Doctors, police officers, ambulances.

But. Doris Night *and* Sandra Day.

In one of their games.

They had been two, actually. Sandra and Doris, two.

Doris Day&Sandra Night. That was the other girl, she had also had many names, which they made up during their games. Games that had been played with the best friend, the only friend, the only only only, Doris Flinkenberg, at the bottom of the swimming pool without water, so far. It was Sandra, she was bedridden for weeks after Doris's death, in a four-poster bed in the house in the darker part of the woods that was her home. She lay with her face turned toward the wall, knees bent and pulled up toward her stomach. She had a fever.

A stained, worn nylon T-shirt under the big pillow. Loneliness&Fear: the other copy of the only two in the history of the world. She squeezed the shirt so hard her knuckles turned white.

If she closed her eyes she saw blood everywhere. She was in the Blood Woods, wandering there in the darkness, confused, like a blind person.

Sandra and Doris: it had been the two of them, they had been best friends.

And, only Sandra Wärn out of everyone knew this: Sister Night&Sister Day. It was a game they had played. And in just this game she had been the girl who had drowned in Bule Marsh many years ago. She who was called Eddie de Wire. Her, the American girl.

The game had another name as well. It had been called the Mystery with the American Girl.

And it had its own song. The Eddie-song.
Look, Mom, they've destroyed my song.

And all the words and peculiar sayings had also belonged to the game.
"I'm a strange bird, are you too?"
"The heart is a heartless hunter."
"Nobody knew my rose of the world but me."

But, *shadow meets shadow.* There, in the darkness, those weeks when Sandra did not leave her room, it happened sometimes that she crawled out of bed and stood by the window and looked out. Looked out over the muddy landscape out there, over the familiar, low-lying marsh, over the clump of reeds . . . but more than anything toward the grove off to the side. That was the direction in which her gaze was drawn. That is where *he* was usually standing.

And he was standing there now, looking at her. Her behind the curtains in the room with the lights out. Him out there. They stood there across from each other and stared at each other.

One of them was the boy, and he was Bengt. Quite a bit

older now. The other was the girl, Sandra Wärn. Who was the same age as Doris had been when she died, sixteen years old.

2008, the Winter Garden. Johanna is walking in the Winter Garden. And everything is still there, these many years later.

In Rita's Winter Garden, a park, a world all by itself. A defined space for entertaining, recreation, enchantment.

A world in and of itself, for games, also adult games.

But at the same time it is an intricate combination of public and private, conventional and normal, but also the secret, forbidden.

Because there are things in the Winter Garden you do not talk about, things you only imagine. Underground and above. Secret rooms, a labyrinth.

You can walk down there and experience almost anything.

All of the old things, in their own way. The District and its history are also in the Winter Garden. Like pictures on the walls, names and words, music.

Carry Doris over troubled water.
Death's spell at a young age.
Nobody knew my rose of the world but me.
I walked out one evening, out into a grove so green.
Shots, I think I hear shots.
Look, Mom, they've destroyed my song.
In the middle of the Winter Garden there is kapu kai, *the forbidden seas.*
Loneliness&Fear
Doris Night. And Sandra Day.

2008, the Winter Garden. Johanna is walking in the Winter Garden. She works here after school and on the weekends.

You have access here after the other areas are closed. Johanna can be alone here, she likes being here.

Johanna loves the hours when she rambles around on her own in the Winter Garden, with music flowing in her ears. The Marsh Queen's music.

She is seventeen years old, it fascinates her.

But she is also looking for something special. That room, that red room. It happened at Bule Marsh room. That which belongs to *kapu kai*, the forbidden seas.

What happened at Bule Marsh once, everything is in that room.

She ended up there once by mistake. She has looked for it but never found it again. And now she knows for sure that she has to find her way there again.

Because it was like this a long time ago, New Year's 2000 when the Winter Garden was inaugurated. It was that night eight years ago.

It was her and her brother. They were not supposed to be there, their mother Solveig had forbidden them.

But they went through the woods anyway, just the two of them, in the middle of the night, and they came to the Winter Garden.

The children came to the Winter Garden, which revealed itself in the woods, there where the Second Cape began. The ornate old-fashioned letters over the gate drew your thoughts to an old-fashioned garden in another country, with sphinxes on both sides of the entrance, and the light, most of all the light. A silver and metallic shine so strong that the children who had come out of the darkness of the woods were blinded.

It was so beautiful, so tremendous.

Stirring emotions the children had never felt before.

They walked in toward the clear, sharp light, toward the people and the party, to everything within it.

THE DISTRICT

Baron von B. liked to play poker. He was not always lucky, but he took the defeat like a man is supposed to. That is to say, he paid out without making a face.

In the beginning there was the District. The Second Cape and the First Cape and the great woods and something else too. In the beginning was the war, and the war, it was lost.

Certain areas caught the eye of the victorious nation, the great land in the east, areas that were highly desirable for future military exploits and just in general, and the country could keep its independence regardless.

One area was handed over to the victorious nation, for a time. The District was located in just that area. Consequently, the people were evacuated and everyone was forced to move, and later during the years that followed it was as though the area was closed off from the outside world.

It was during these tumultuous years that Baron von B., who happened to own almost all of the Second Cape and a significant portion of the woods and so on, sat down at the poker table. And played. And lost. And played. And lost.

Against the cousin's papa and the Dancer. They won everything.

The whole of the Second Cape, a significant portion of the woods, and so on.

And some years later when the occupied area was returned it was not the baron but the cousin's papa and the Dancer and his wife with their three children who came to the District. And settled there. Like a real clan.

And that is what they were in the beginning. But shortly thereafter the Dancer and his wife were killed in a car accident and the three children became orphans.

The three children: that was Bengt and the twins, Rita and Solveig.

I.

BENGT AND THE AMERICAN GIRL

(Bengt's story)

B*ENGT AND THE BUILDINGS, 1969.* AS A CHILD BENGT WAS fascinated by the buildings on the Second Cape. They were built on land the cousin's papa had sold for large sums of money. The Second Cape was a peninsula jutting out into the sea, one of the most beautiful places in the District. The area was divided into individual parcels of land on which houses were built, modern vacation homes for an exhibition of country living, one of the first public displays of its kind organized in the country. When the exhibition was launched one summer at the end of the sixties, the houses were sold one after the other, for the most part as vacation homes for people with money, the houses were not exactly cheap, and often to people without any ties to the District.

They were unique houses, utopian houses. Houses built in a bold, new architectural style. And Bencku, he knew about architecture, he knew those houses. He had studied their blueprints and discussed them with the architects, he had hung around the buildings while they were being built. So he was obsessed with them long before they were finished.

He also saw himself as being the expert on them; he knew more about them than their future owners, more than the architects who had drawn them. Because he was the one who was from the District, the only one who knew the houses in that environment.

And the surroundings, the District, it was his world: the Second Cape, the First Cape, the four marshes, and the long, deep woods that ended by the marshes in the east—there where the house in the darker part gradually came to be built.

And the entire District existed in Bencku's head in a truly unique way. That is what he drew on his maps. He would devote himself to these maps during the remainder of his youth.

Bencku and the maps. They were not exactly a secret. He spoke about them, in any case, with the people he knew well. But there were not many who got to see them, almost no one, so many thought it was just talk. That it was just Bencku who wanted to seem self-important, as usual.

But they existed. They existed in reality. Little by little Bencku drew in almost all of the houses, all of the places, everywhere in the District. But in his own way. He used pictures, codes, and his own names. Names that were a mixture of the traditional names in the District and all of the words he had made up or looked up in books. *Kapu kai*, for example, it means *secret ocean* in acronesian.

The names also served another purpose for Bengt. It is like this: he thought that regardless of who was going to come live and own the houses on the Second Cape, the houses were, by virtue of him being the one who had named them, his. *Just like everything was his.*

Bencku himself. He was thirteen years old then, tall, and looked considerably older. A surly and taciturn fellow, who kept to himself for the most part; except sometimes, when he was among people he knew, it could happen that impassioned, he opened up and held lengthy expositions about this and that and it seemed as though he was the only one who was interested. Architecture and crime, monochronics within landscape architecture, that sort of thing.

"Bencku is bananas," his sister Solveig would often say to her twin Rita when it was just the two of them in the red cottage.

"He has a screw loose," Rita would second. It was a time, at the beginning of time, *once long ago*, when the sisters had always been in agreement.

Rita, Solveig, Bengt: the three siblings did not have very much in common, though they were all tall. And that there was not much of anything else was something Rita and Solveig were really very careful about pointing out.

And all three of them were "cousins" in the cousin's house. They had been taken in by the cousin's papa and the cousin's mama, whom the cousin's papa had married when his brother and his brother's wife had been killed in a tragic car accident when the three siblings were little. The cousin's mama had a son of her own when she came to the house, he was Björn. And the cousin's mama, she was Superintendent Loman's daughter, and basically someone who stood with both feet firmly on the ground in all kinds of weather.

Cousin Björn shared a room with Bengt on the second floor of the cousin's house. Björn was eighteen years old, worked in the woods and might go to school to become an agronomist. For the most part he hung out in the barn on the cousin's property, tinkered with his moped or with junk which there was a great deal of in the cousin's papa's extensive collection. Bengt was often there with him; Bengt and Björn, they stuck together.

They were best friends despite the fact that Björn was five years older. And in some way they were a lot alike, for example both of them were rather quiet. Björn's silence was less noticeable than Bengt's, it was like Bengt was a bit more prickly. Björn was well liked and friendly, and easy to get along with.

Björn and Bengt: together they made an amusing, odd couple. People would sometimes say *the collected silence*. Bengt, thirteen years old, and half a head taller than Björn, the older, thoughtful one. The cousin's mama used to say "the apples of my eyes" about both boys.

. . .

So that is the way it was before Eddie came, before Bencku met Eddie and everything changed. And once everything started changing, everything happened very quickly. In less than one year everything that had been would be destroyed.

Eddie from the boathouse on the Second Cape, Eddie with the guitar and the thin, flat voice, but it did not matter. Eddie who spoke with a strange accent and with phrases that were sometimes very bizarre, but that still, and maybe just because they were so strange, made an impact on you.

"I'm a strange bird, Bengt," she said. "Are you too?"

Eddie, the American girl.

Eddie most beloved, but in the mire.

Eddie most beloved but gradually in the mire.

Private property. When the houses on the Second Cape had been sold, Bencku no longer had any right to them. The new owners moved in and took over the entirety of the Second Cape, made it theirs. In their eyes Bengt was an odd one, an intruder who walked on other people's property without permission.

You could see him between the stylish buildings on the stretches of woodland, in the yards and in the gardens at all hours of the day. Or on their beaches and on the jetties that were sticking out like tongues between the cliffs. It seemed like he was everywhere, and always in his own way. And there was no one who could stop him.

"Aren't you going to go home and play in your own yard?" someone might yell.

"The public beach is in the other direction. EVERYONE is allowed to be there."

"Doesn't your mother get worried when you're gone so long?"

Bencku did not answer, barely took any notice of them. And it was not outright frightening but certainly rather annoying. But among themselves the adults on the Second Cape did not speak out much about this nuisance. Despite everything, Bencku was just a boy, and a child.

Little by little signs with PRIVATE PROPERTY or NO TRESPASSING started popping up. Some properties were enclosed by fences that were painted a brilliant yellow or red in order to soften the impression of exclusion. Someone got a dog—of course not any gigantic beasts of the kind that would populate the District fifty years later, but rather those small and hot-tempered ones who barked incessantly and understood the most important assignment of all: to differentiate between those who were family and those who were not.

But it did not help a bit. Bencku was where he wanted to be regardless, furtive, quiet, and obstinate. And he was not exactly invisible, he was so tall after all. Walked a bit stooped over, with his head leaning to one side, and his light hair hung a bit loosely over his eyes, which were prickly and peering.

Sometimes it happened that he stayed away, sometimes even for several days. But sooner or later he was always back, and that was almost the most annoying thing of all. Just when you thought you had gotten rid of him he was there again. Almost in the middle of your garden, if he felt like it.

That is the way it went for several weeks before the children from the Second Cape got their hands on him.

Sea urchins. They would gradually grow into sea urchins: become sunburned, superior teenagers who would hang out only with each other. But they were still just children, a touch more brazen and maybe a bit more spoiled than others, but not in any noticeable way. They were the way most kids are, that is to say, in the middle of their own games. They were a group of seven–eight kids who hung out together and just this summer they had decided that they were the Lilliputs. The Lilliputs in their own carefully demarcated Lilliput Country, a country that by chance just happened to be the entirety of the Second Cape, neither more nor less.

And, of course, the Lilliputs were on the prowl for their Gulliver to torment to death. A giant was trespassing on their property. And it was as easy as anything to find him; they had actually had him under supervision quite a long time before they struck. And Bencku, he did not suspect a thing. He was so deep in his thoughts as he always was when he wandered around on the Second Cape, defiantly moody but with an endless self-assuredness. And when the attack finally took place in the thicket between the Glass House and the Red Tower he was, in other words, taken unawares. Bencku was easy pickings, maybe all too easy.

In just a few seconds the children had surrounded him and pushed him up against a tree trunk.

"Don't come don't come don't come don't come near me!" he had stood there and yelled, flapping his arms as if the much shorter children had been insects he should have been able to ward off. But it was his voice that betrayed him. It was filled with terror, thick with a real, unbridled fear, and the panic shone from his eyes, which had been filled with deceit only moments before. And in a strange way it was inciting, downright fascinating, and all of it increased the hot temperament that prevailed among the Lilliputs, who had been planning this for a long time.

It was early on a Saturday evening at the start of the summer vacation, clear skies and just the right temperature. At a distance, not so very far away, the adults were on the cliffs of the Second Cape, on their properties, and in their gardens. Calls and voices spread through the air; somewhere badminton was being played, croquet balls were being hit against fragile metal hoops somewhere else. A *clink* could be heard when the balls hit the hoops, there was in other words almost no wind, voices could certainly be heard. For those who wanted to hear them.

It was obvious then that this time the children would get to play their game in peace and quiet.

"Now we have you, Gull," the smallest boy hissed, a stocky boy with yellow-green eyes and a sharp look, almost as sharp as Bengt's could be but in other situations. It was Magnus von B., who years later would be like grease on bacon with the object of torture he now had in front of him. But for the time being he was the General of the Lilliputs with only one thing in mind.

"Now we're going to teach you a lesson. Gull is going to learn to stay away from here. To stay away once and for all."

It was a girl who attacked him first, with her nails. She also had soft-drink bottle caps around her fingertips, and she attacked him with these sharp tips, scratching him. His shirt was torn open, the buttons scattered, and the metal made deep gashes in his skin, the pain whistled through Bencku's head and there was blood. Bencku screamed and screamed, even though he probably understood no one was going to come to his rescue. They could kill him if they wanted to: there was no one on the Second Cape, no one in the entire world who would stop them from doing so.

No one can stop us, when we start our game. The playful children became even more excited by the blood and their own audacity and that Bengt so openly showed he was afraid. He who was so much bigger than them, and they also had something of their parents' irritation inside. "Do you want that kind of person sneaking around on your property?" Now you'll see! Here we come!

"Now we're going to tie you up and leave you here in secret to be humiliated and to think about your trespassing," said the boy. "And when we've come up with a suitable punishment for you we'll be back. A Peeping Tom like you should be punished so that he never again sets foot on our land."

"If you survive, that is," the girl added, the one with the nails and the blood. "Don't be so sure."

"And now we're going to cover your mouth. No screaming here. Just go jump in the sea, Gull, you won't find any help here."

And he was pushed over on the ground on his stomach, someone sat on his back and he felt how his face was being pressed against the ground; someone else wound tape around his wrists and legs. Wide, sharp-edged insulation tape that cut into the skin and it burned if he made even the slightest movement. His head was pulled up by the hair at the nape of his neck, some cloth, a handkerchief or something similar, was stuffed in his mouth, and then someone was there with the tape as well, his lips were going to be taped shut.

"Now Gull is a mummy."

It was madness. They were going to kill him, and they could kill him if they got it into their heads to do so. But at the same time, that and everything else, it was already slipping away. Far, far away. Because it was futile. He was no match for them. He was at their mercy now, they could do what they wanted with him. And because of that, he drifted away.

Like in a dream. And it was there, somewhere in that dream landscape, he suddenly heard someone calling for him. And it was her. Eddie de Wire. The American girl.

That is when she was there. She came running through the woods, small and thin in light pants and a light blue woolen sweater, with her half-long light hair flying around her head. She came from the Glass House, and with her jumps and her calls it was like she cut through the indifference that otherwise ruled in the presence of what was going on. And the kids became scared and surprised and scattered in all directions, like rats.

And suddenly, for just a brief moment, there was life and movement in other places on the Second Cape again. An adult could be heard calling: "What's happened? Has the boy fallen and hurt himself? Is it bad?"

Later, when Bengt went over everything in his head, and he would really go over it, again and again, he would of course be convinced of the impossible: that he had seen her coming to his rescue. He had been lying there with his face drilled into the hard ground. But it was a feeling, a dream that slowly became reality.

Later, when she was actually there and had turned him over on his back and started tearing the tape away from his mouth, it was very real then, their first meeting, a reality.

"Can you walk? Lean on me. Here. Take my hand. I have a knife at home, the tape is too tight."

And Eddie and Bengt, they had walked on the path farther in toward the Second Cape, the one that led down to the Glass House where the baroness lived. To begin with he had leaned against her and she had taken off her woolen sweater and laid it over his shoulders so that it covered his back, and then she walked close, close behind him so that his wrists, which were still taped together, could not be seen. But suddenly, again, it was completely empty: the Second Cape was a completely deserted place. All sounds of play and games and summer activity were gone, just like all the adults, all the children.

"Careful. Can you make it? Does it hurt a lot?"

Bencku had mumbled something that might have been a yes, but it is not certain. Because the pain, yes, it was there, just like the shock and the blood and all the rest of it, the indignation and the humiliation. But at the same time, that had also suddenly faded into the background, he almost did not feel it at all. The only thing that was really there was resentment and shame, pounding inside him: why, WHY, did he have to meet her like this?

Because he knew instantly, as soon as she came, as soon as he had seen her running toward him—which he had not seen, but still—that this was something he had been waiting for, something tremendous.

"I'm Eddie. And you are?"

. . .

She lived in the boathouse below the Glass House on the Second Cape. The Glass House, one of the most beautiful houses on the whole of the Second Cape; it was situated on a hill and all of the walls on the side facing the sea were filled with floor-to-ceiling windows. When the light fell on the glass panes it was reflected in the water and a game of color and movement arose, which was especially intense in the fall when the wind blew hard.

The boathouse stood on pilings in the water, a short distance from the last rocks on the beach. A short and narrow walkway made of boards led out to it. It was a small red cottage on the edge of the sea, in a traditional style, not at all modern. But the best thing about it was the veranda next to the entrance. It was a terrace with a ladder going straight down into the ocean— and the terrace did not face anything else. You saw only the sea, nothing else.

"Come in." Eddie opened the door for him. "This is where I live. But watch your head. The ceiling is quite low."

It was just one room. Almost the entire floor space was taken up by a wide bed. Next to the bed there was a table and in front of the table there was a chair. It was the only furniture in the room. There were a few books on the bed, a notebook, a guitar.

And then, she had dressed his wounds in there, and they had properly met. And while she was doing that she said something strange:

"I saved your life. Maybe someday you'll have the opportunity to do the same for me."

And after that they started hanging out together. Not together like a couple. Together like two people who spend a lot of time together, almost all the time they have.

And the sun went down, the moon came up. A large harvest moon against the backdrop of sea and sky that blended in with the horizon. It grew dark, it became night.

"I feel like we're soul mates, Bengt," said Eddie. "We belong together."

The conversations with Eddie.
  The Glass House. Shopping Mall Theory, America.
  If you're going to San Francisco.
  Mom, they've destroyed my song.
  And the maps (he showed them to her).

"Nobody knew my rose of the world but me. Tennessee Williams had a sister named Rose. When he left home to make it as a writer she became mentally ill. It had been just the two of them when they were children. The family moved around a lot, they had relied on each other.

"When Tennessee Williams left home she was suddenly alone. So alone that she went crazy. He never forgave himself for that.

"And Rosie became his cross to bear, *his cross to bear in the world*.

"He would carry his rose, his sorrow, tattooed inside."

With Eddie on the Second Cape, with Eddie in the District. Eddie, white against the background of woods, water, all of the buildings. She fits, thought Bengt. And something else, which sounded ridiculous when you said it but was true in the atmosphere that ruled then: a mood that would prove impossible to recreate.

He thought this mood was what everything was made for, everything new. The whole of the Second Cape. And then the amazing happened, his world became her world.

When Eddie was gone all of this would be turned against him. Eddie's mystique, the entire environment. It would be transformed into a dark, threatening force, one filled with questions. *Nobody knew my rose of the world but me.* But what did that mean?

And he would be surrounded by a desertlike loneliness: Eddie cursed.

And Bencku: something inside would turn against him. He would be defenseless in the face of the threatening and the inexplicable. What had existed? What had been real? What happened? Who was she, really?

And what did he mean by that? He did not know, would not know. Knew enough to know that he did not know. And going deeper inside, starting to learn and investigate, without Eddie: it was the same thing as disappearing deep into real madness.

Consequently, when Eddie was gone Bencku would remember very little of the conversations with her. What she said and he said, and so on. Likewise, words. When Eddie was gone there would be no words inside him for a while, none at all.

"What happened?" Solveig would ask when he started talking again in the middle of everything.

He would shrug his shoulders quite nonchalantly, say that he did not know.

And in part it would really be true.

But that nonchalance in him, that would be new. When he regained the ability to speak after the tragedy, it was as if he had become someone else, not an adult, but old enough.

There would not be rhyme or reason for a long time after Eddie was gone.

"I feel like we're soul mates, Bengt. We belong together."

"I'm a strange bird. Are you too?"

"Nobody knew my rose of the world but me."

And blah blah blah. Those sentences would be in his head like a pouring rain, rumble around in there like in a centrifuge. And no. It was impossible. He would not be in it anymore.

And also, about Eddie: what did it matter what people thought or did not think about her, who she was and what she said, what was a lie and what was truth? Correct, incorrect, right and wrong? Some never got the chance to grow up and mature, or just live long enough so they would have a chance to excuse themselves, or then, explain.

Give their point of view on the matter.

Some people were forever sheathed in the mistakes of their youth.

As the cousin's mama used to say, in other situations, like a joke. Some grew and came into existence. One time, several times. Some came into existence again and again and again.

Eddie became nothing. Obviously. She never got a chance.

Eddie's body in Bule Marsh. In the kind of raincoat she never used to use, too.

"Would you save my life?"

Yes. But obviously he had not been very good at it.

"She drowned. She just sank and sank and sank. Like she was sucked up. Slurp. She disappeared."

But first, nuances, before everything happened. How it started, that which was the change. And after the beginning the end came very quickly.

Sometimes Bencku waited for her in the boathouse if she was not there when he came. Maybe she was with the baroness in the Glass House, or out running errands. She did not say exactly what she was doing during the day, and Bencku had not asked. It was not important after all. The important thing was the boathouse, what existed when the two of them were there.

One night he waited in the boathouse in vain. For hours. He even had time to doze off on her bed and when he woke up it was almost dark and still she was not there, that had not happened before. He strolled off, in the twilight. Not angry, but certainly disappointed. He walked back over the Second Cape, through the end of the woods to the cousin's house, and he immediately noticed something was new and different.

Two orange spots in the opening to the barn, low voices. Music in the background, Björn's music. Bencku recognized it immediately but there was still something keeping him from walking up right away or calling to Björn from the dark.

He remained standing at the edge of the woods and he had seen. And when he realized what he had seen, whom he had seen, he wished of course that he had hidden himself completely.

"Who's there? Bencku! We can see you. We know you're there! Come here!"

And he walked over to them where they were standing with their arms around each other, smoking their cigarettes, almost swaying with the music. Eddie tried to make eye contact with Bencku, her shirt was red, he would remember that, and when he cast a quick glance at her she did not look the slightest bit embarrassed or apologetic.

Bencku sat at the desk and drew in the light of the desk lamp until late in the night. Björn finally came.

"Are you still up? What are you doing?"

"Drawing," Bencku said without looking up.

Björn dropped down on his bed.

"Aren't we going to turn the lights out?"

"Yeah." Bencku got up, carefully rolled up his map and placed it under the bed. Then he got undressed and put on his pajamas, crept under the covers and turned off the lamp on the desk next to his bed.

Björn was just lying there, still dressed, in the light of the bed lamp staring at the ceiling.

"Are we turning the lights out then?" Bengt asked.

"Mmmm," said Björn.

And added, suddenly with a loud and important voice, in a tone which, at the same time, was filled with both tenderness and amusement.

"Now she's here. The whore."

"What?" Bencku avoided looking in his direction.

"Well. The woman," Björn added. "In my life."

. . .

Bengt had not even said, "She isn't a whore," before he attacked Björn. And they fought. For real. Bengt had the upper hand at first because Björn did not take him seriously, but then, when he understood that Bengt was not giving up he got angry for real. The cousin's mama finally came up and separated them.

The next day no one spoke about the fight.

After the fight it was the three of them.

Eddie, Björn, AND Bengt.

And that was it.

The conversations with Eddie. Eddie came to Bengt at the marsh. She laid her hand on his shoulder: "What's happening to you?" And he felt how he was falling, literally. Into her, back inside. And they went back to the boathouse together.

The conversations with Eddie. Bencku and Eddie walked over the cliffs on the Second Cape, there was a hard wind. The sea was gray and foamy, it was cold and Eddie shivered in her short-sleeved blouse. Her sweater, she had left it behind somewhere else. Bencku walked after her with his hands in his jacket pockets, she was talking. Her mouth was moving and even though he strained, even though he tried to under-stand he was not at all sure that he heard what she was saying.

It was very windy, and it was difficult to understand in the wind. Eddie, she spoke so quickly and excitedly. She mixed in foreign words in her sentences, words that maybe he knew what they meant, but in some other time, in some other situation.

But he wanted to scream STOP WAIT.

STOP NOW!

"Sometimes I think . . . that it's so serious . . . I don't know if I can."

And then her voice died out again. Drowned in waves, foam, water, wind that had splashed and washed washed over them.

"One shouldn't eavesdrop," the cousin's mama said to Doris Flinkenberg who at this time was not living in the cousin's house in her own right yet. She was just the marsh kid from the distant marsh, she just was.

It was Doris who had made her way to the barn where Eddie and Björn had been. It was Doris who had huddled in the darkness and heard some things without being discovered.

"But I KNOW that they didn't notice me!" Doris Flinkenberg insisted.

"But you SHOULDN'T eavesdrop," the cousin's mama said decidedly and pulled Doris into the kitchen.

"Come and let's think about other things," she said in a considerably kinder tone of voice. "Come. We're behind closed doors now and we can do something fun together. Just the two of us. Should we do a crossword? Or put on the radio and listen to music?"

And Doris immediately started thinking about other things.

"Yes," she said attentively. "Yes. To all of it. First we'll do all of it once, then we'll do everything again. And then again."

And Doris was so happy that the cousin's mama's heart almost burst. Doris had such a hard time.

"Come now, Doris. Time to go home. I'll walk you."

"Don't want to!" Little Doris started crying.

"It doesn't help!" the cousin's mama had said and taken Doris Flinkenberg in her arms partly by force. "WE HAVE TO." She half carried, half dragged the hysterical Doris Flinkenberg up to the main country road on which you have to walk quite a few miles away from honor and integrity in order to get to the marsh hovel where Doris and her marsh mama and her marsh papa lived.

"My heart breaks," the cousin's mama would lament when Doris was not there. "It's so terrible."

The conversations with Eddie. They walked in silence. Along the path down to the boathouse. The last bit she took his hand in hers. Her hand was warm, almost hot and damp with sweat. Bencku cast a sideways glance at her. She was pale.

Then the end came very quickly. It was the morning when everything happened—or, when everything had already happened. For Bengt, this is the moment when reason and logic split, and once it started, it lasted several weeks.

It was early in the morning. Bencku had not slept at all. He was walking on the main road, the one that led up to the main country road or down to the Second Cape, depending on where you were headed. Bencku was on his way to the Second Cape, but he might as well have been heading in the opposite direction, toward the town center and the bus stop.

The sound of a car engine suddenly could be heard in the middle of that early morning. It was a Jaguar, one of those antique models, very nice, and it was white. It came driving fast and everything happened in a moment, he became so surprised that he stepped down into the ditch.

She was sitting in the backseat, her face pressed up against the window. He saw her, she saw him, it was going so quickly, but still. A moment. And presto it was gone. Presto the car had driven away and he was standing there alone. Alone in the District, alone in the ditch. Hand in the air—had he thought of it as a wave?

But this he was sure of, he remembered it for real. She had looked crazy. She had not been herself, not at all. He could not explain in what way. But that expression she had, one she had never had before. Frightened out of her wits.

And that was the last time he saw her.

Then he never, never saw her again.

But walk. Walk. Walk. Walk. Bencku walked over the far meadow toward the outbuilding on the other side. How much time had actually passed between the one and the other, the side of the road and the outbuilding, was not clear.

Slowly at first, but then he started running. Faster and faster. Over the fields until he got to where he was going.

He stepped into the outbuilding. Saw right away what was in there. It was Björn.

. . .

And Bencku became completely mute.

Now only he was left.

"Nobody knew my rose of the world but me."

"Am I your rose now?"

The District hates itself. He stopped going to the Second Cape. But he found himself on the outskirts of the woods more and more often, where he wandered around, far away from everything else.

That was how he found the house in the darker part. That was how he discovered it, where it stood in all its impossibility: an alpine villa on the low-lying damp ground by a turbid marsh. The nameless marsh.

The entire house was a staircase. A hundred steps leading up to the main entrance.

A staircase leading to nothing.

On the other side of the house, the one facing the marsh, there were panorama windows covering almost the entire basement wall. He looked in and made out a large, rectangular hole in the ground in the middle of the basement.

A swimming pool?

The future angel in the mud. This was reality.

Nevertheless he did go back to the boathouse on the Second Cape one last time. The key was in the lock. It was empty in there, but in a new way. And he was not surprised. That was what he had expected. Empty in the normal way: as if no one had ever set foot there.

Chair, table, bed. The same furniture. The same light blue bedspread. Some flowers in a vase on the small table. Large tropical flowers, disgusting. The vase was made of thick crystal, and the tablecloth laid under it was newly ironed.

Eddie had hated that vase, used it as an ashtray out on the terrace.

The guitar was hanging by a brown leather strap from a nail on the wall above the bed. It was new, both the nail and the strap from which the guitar was hanging. *That was the way the baroness had wanted it.*

He lifted the bedspread and looked under the bed. Nothing there, but that was no surprise. He went out and closed the door. Turned the key in the lock. Then he left the boathouse and walked up to the house.

"I came to get my maps." It was with the baroness up there in the Glass House that Bencku started talking again. "So you have a tongue in your head after all," said the baroness not sounding at all surprised, where she was standing there on the veranda, which she called her Winter Garden, and pruning her plants. She had planted them in pots that filled the entire veranda. The veranda was an extension of the glass façade, with its own roof, also made of glass. This was where she forced her strange plants to grow: frivolous flowers in different colors, lit by different types of lamps and heated with extra heaters. "Good that you came. I've been waiting for you."

She set the pruning shears down on a windowsill, slowly pulled off her yellow rubber gloves, came up to him holding out her hand. Only then, because he had to, did he dare to look at her.

They stood there in the baroness's Winter Garden and shook hands, he and she.

But at the same time, it was as if she wanted to say something to him now, the baroness, something kind and comforting. Something that did not go together with her nature at all. This rough, square, straight-to-the-point style that matched her clothes so perfectly. Linen pants and a dark blue shirt, shimmering silver hair that shone against her brown face. Patinated. Maybe sixty years old, fifty-five.

"Wait here." She let go of his hand and disappeared into the house for a while, leaving him among the plants in the Winter Garden that smelled so strongly. But the door was ajar so it was not as suffocating as it could have been.

"Beautiful." The baroness had come back with his maps under her arm.

"I took them from the boathouse. This is why you're here, isn't it?

"Interesting," the baroness continued. "Almost like works of art. You have an artistic talent, there's no doubt about that. But a talent does not develop on its own. It demands work. Discipline. One cannot be . . . lazy." It was as though she also had not opened her mouth for some time, and as if she was not very careful about what she let slip. Her thoughts were somewhere else entirely.

"May I get you a cup of tea?"

"No, thank you." He shook his head, took the roll of maps, and left.

She came looking for him that same evening, at the cousin's house. She came to his room where he was lying on his bed next to the desk in front of the window and determined what he had already determined many times before: this was the room he could no longer be in. Then the baroness had suddenly been standing in the middle of the room and she spoke to him. Looked straight at him, as if she found everything else around her completely meaningless.

"I was thinking that if you need someplace to be . . . I mean with your . . . painting . . . a studio. You always have." She hurried to add, "Not the boathouse. But the house. There are so many bright rooms there, which are fantastic to draw in."

Bencku went back the next day. He had been assigned one of the large, bright rooms on the third floor.

"You will certainly have a good perspective here." The baroness laid her hand on his shoulder in the same rough and plucky way she had when she spoke.

"You can certainly find inspiration here."

He shook himself free. What did she really want from him? Was there not that tone in her voice again that made you think she was just about to say something else? That that was why he was here, because she had something to say?

"Come and I'll show you where the key to the kitchen entrance is. You may come and go as you like. Don't worry about me."

And he followed her out of the room, down the inner stairs in light-colored beautiful wood that led almost directly to the Winter Garden. Yes, everything was so high and bright in here, so clean, just like he remembered it from the housing exhibition, and before. But Eddie had not had access here. She had been allowed to be here only when the baroness was home.

"You don't have to feel forced to keep me company," she said later. "I'm used to being by myself. Eddie . . . she was an episode. I mean, in the loneliness. I've lived alone almost all my life."

But then it was as if she had pulled herself together again and came across other thoughts. "Oh. What I am standing here telling you? The story of my life?

"Life must go on," the baroness said, low and serious. "I guess that's what I mean."

But he could not be in that room, he had understood that almost immediately. He stared at the white paper in front of him on the large worktable that she had carried in from somewhere else in the house. She had given him the paper also, he had never had nicer paper. He walked around the room. There were photographs there, lined up on a dresser, which was white, and in some way it gave him the idea that it was not a coincidence they were there, those pictures. That it was exactly this room he had been given in order to "draw and become inspired in." They were the type of family photographs of serious uncles and austere aunts in long dark dresses. Boys in sailor's outfits, girls in light-colored dresses, with thick, long hair with rosettes. Bencku thought: is this what she wants to tell me? Is this what she wants me to be interested in? Her relatives and family with all their peculiarities, her relatives who had also been Eddie's relatives?

But when it was not like that. Not a question of any of it. He was not interested. Not a bit. But still. He could not keep his eyes off of the pictures. He knew what he was looking for.

Her somewhere there. And of course he found what he was looking for.

A portrait. Showing a completely normal girl in a poorly taken photo. A school photo, or something similar.

She was looking straight into the camera, she was looking straight at him, with her scared, scared eyes. There was no obvious sadness in them, just, nothing.

He took the photo and left the Glass House for good. The baroness was in her Winter Garden when he left. He lifted his hand to wave. She gesticulated wildly with the scissors. There was nothing grand about it. Maybe she did not understand that he would not be coming back, but later when she eventually realized she let it go, she did not look for him all over again.

So, he went straight to Rita and Solveig in the cottage.

And after that, he filled things in on the map.

The girl in the marsh. Eddie's death.

A few days later he moved into the barn on the cousin's property where he insulated a room for himself. Sealed the walls with newspaper and rock wool, bought a Russian wood stove on a payment plan from the cousin's papa out of his warehouse. A bed, an armchair, a piece of plywood for a table. A bookshelf for books, maps, documents. Brought out Björn's record player and some records.

Three on the jetty. It was fall again, the time of the rats, all the summer guests had left. Rita, Solveig, and Bengt were sitting with their backs toward land at the very end of the longest jetty on the Second Cape, dangling their legs in the water and talking about something but you could not hear what it was.

And there came Doris Flinkenberg, over the cliffs on the Second Cape. Doris, with the tape player, the one she had gotten from the cousin's mama when she came to live in the cousin's house as a new cousin, a wedding present, she said herself, and when others other than the cousin's mama caught wind of that, it sounded quite ridiculous. Doris could be heard from a distance now, the music playing as she was on the move. When she caught sight of Rita, Solveig, and Bencku she immediately directed her steps toward them and called out, at the beginning of the jetty, a big and resounding "HI!"

No reaction. Not even so much as a movement. Doris was like air to them. But do not think that Doris let this stop her. She set down the radio cassette player (she was extremely careful with it, one of the few presents she had ever gotten from anyone, and furthermore, even more important, it was the visible confirmation of her new status: she was a cousin's child now too) and walked farther out on the jetty until she was fifteen–eighteen feet behind the others who were still pretending not to notice her. She held out her hand and her index finger and yelled:

"*Pang! Pang!* Now I shot you!" Then something amusing happened. Everyone turned around at lightning speed, almost instantly. And their expressions, they were priceless. There was fear in them, and surprise.

Doris Flinkenberg thought it was hilarious.

"The looks on your faces!" she called delightedly. "Scared out of your wits! It was just a finger, the Doris Finger here!"

Rita was the first to recover. She got up slowly and started walking toward Doris with that stiff face she had when she was really angry. Doris flinched.

But at the same time the cousin's mama was there: she had popped up on the cliffs by the sea behind them.

"Doris!" she called. "Are you coming? We're going to bake bread now!"

In the beginning that was how the cousin's mama was after Björn's death. She could not leave Doris Flinkenberg, the new cousin's child, out of her sight.

And Doris, who for a brief moment had been afraid of Rita and the others, relaxed.

"I'm coming!!!" she called to the cousin's mama. And then she turned back to the other three, just as brazen as before.

"Only guilty people turn around!" she said.

And:

"I know something you would just die to know. I know something that you would rather die than wish that I knew. I saw something."

Room for me in the lodge. When Björn had died and Bencku moved out to the barn, there was room for one more child in the cousin's house. And that was Doris Flinkenberg, the knocked-about trash. kid, who moved into Bencku and Björn's old room on the second floor.

"My girl now," the cousin's mama said tenderly to Doris. "Of course on loan."

"Not on loan," Doris Flinkenberg protested, her mouth filled with bread. "For your own."

Even though it could be trying to listen when Doris Flinkenberg and the cousin's mama spoke their strange jargon with each other, it could not be denied that it was thanks to Doris Flinkenberg that the cousin's mama got her lust for life back after Björn's death. If Bengt had not been so crazy at first, she probably would have gone crazy herself. That was not an option, she was also a mother of course, despite everything, the cousin's mama, she said to herself, and everything could not fall apart. And for a while her purpose in life became organizing a safe home for the trash kid Doris Flinkenberg. And she was successful.

"One man's death is another man's breath," said Doris Flinkenberg. "Then there was room for me in the lodge." She was the only one who could say it and not have it sound cynical.

Stories in the kitchen of the cousin's house. The story about Eddie, Björn, and Bengt faded away in the District. You stopped talking about it, life went on.

That is the way it was. Björn had gotten angry with Eddie, he had a violent temperament under that kind-natured surface, and everyone knew it. And there had been a scuffle at the marsh and she ended up in the water and it all happened so quickly, *the current in the marsh is so strong*, he had not been able to save her.

For a long time there was only one place where the story lived on and it was, strangely enough, the kitchen in the cousin's house. It was the cousin's mama and, more than anything, Doris Flinkenberg who kept it alive. There, surrounded by the smell of baking bread, among crosswords and dictionaries and newspapers, *True Crimes*, it was told over and over again from certain fixed points of view. Analyzed and commentated on by both Doris Flinkenberg and the cousin's mama in their own, particular ways.

"It's never good to get attached to SOMEONE like he was attached to her," the cousin's mama said to Doris Flinkenberg.

"Pretty girl," Doris Flinkenberg added, carelessly, with a voice unlike her own. Doris was good at imitating, both real people and familiar voices. Now she continued, as if she were an uncle or an aunt, far too sensible: "But probably spoiled by the men's attention already at such a young age. But," with a final rhetorical fling, "what would I know about that?"

No one answered that question. But the cousin's mama clapped her hands.

"After all she wasn't from here. I don't know from where, but not from here."

"Not from the District," Doris decided firmly, mouth full of a bread roll. "Didn't value what we value here. Thought she was remarkable. Something special. You made your bed, now lie in it. Isn't that true?"

But the cousin's mama did not answer. Sometimes Doris Flinkenberg had the ability to carry her strange, playful ideas way too far.

"It was almost painful to see," said the cousin's mama, but flatter and more serious now. She had stopped herself in the middle of happily solving her crossword, dropped the pencil on a photograph in the middle of the crossword, a photo of the teenage pop singer Agnetha Fältskog, who wore a jersey dress with a heart-shaped hole through which her navel could be seen, and was completely still, looking out through the window.

"Why painful?" Doris Flinkenberg hurried to ask.

The cousin's mama did not answer. A muffled silence spread through the kitchen. Sometimes the cousin's mama's grief still caught her unawares and all of the old stuff floated up, she floated away—

Doris reached out for an issue of *True Crimes* and randomly flipped to an article she started reading out loud in order to get the cousin's mama thinking about something else. Away from that, *you always travel on your own in the land of sorrow*, which she had said once, so solemnly it sounded like she was in church. It was terrifying not least because of all of the terrible things that had happened—Doris Flinkenberg had already, for better or for worse, experienced terrible things in her own life (she had for example grill marks on her body to prove it)—but also because it took the cousin's mama away from her, to a place where neither she nor anyone else could go.

"He killed his lover with fifteen hammer blows to the head," Doris Flinkenberg read aloud with her best Sunday school voice and later she said, innocently and surprised like the child she actually was, "Jealousy can cause all sorts of things, can't it?" and laughed, carefully glancing playfully at the cousin's mama, a small *rascal* who wanted to say: come with me.

And the cousin's mama came along. But not right away. She still had to sit quietly and be in her own world for a while.

Because sometimes it did not help. Sometimes nothing helped against the sorrow and the unavoidable. Sometimes you just had to wait, wait until the cousin's mama would become herself again.

"Dé-co-lle-ta-ge," she later said suddenly and pointed at the singer's navel. "But you're supposed to have that sort of thing on your neck."

Doris Flinkenberg brightened.

"Oh. That's not a décolletage. It's just a pop singer's belly button."

By the house in the darker part of the woods, he found himself there more and more. He had started going there instead. Found himself there more often. Forty steps of cold concrete in the front, the flat roof, the small holes for windows. Large windows only in the basement facing the surrounding jungle. And it was a jungle: ferns and secondary growth grew tall, cramped during the warmest months of the year. Ferns whose stems could grow three feet high.

Yes indeed. An alpine villa. It was true.

But he was there more and more often, in the bushes, at the edge of the woods.

And saw.

There was a girl there, at the top of the stairs. She was maybe Doris's age, in any case crazy enough that no one had to tell you she was the one who lived there. She would stand there and ring her own doorbell. Ring and ring. For which there was, you understood if you stood and stared for long periods of time (which he did), no intelligible reason. The doorbell played some kind of melody, and that was what she set off, over and over again. She probably had a key, you understood that—but it was not the most important thing. Sometimes she opened the door herself in the middle of the song (and then the music grew quiet), only to close it and ring the doorbell again immediately after. When she had been doing this for a good while her parents turned up, a relatively pretty woman who had a strange piercing voice when she yelled (and she yelled at the girl, it always ended with that) and a man who always wore sunglasses. They were angry with the girl, they scolded her, as you would scold a spoiled child.

And then they disappeared into the house and the girl was alone. She looked around, and then, after a while, she started ringing the doorbell again.

She turned around and looked at him. He looked back.

He could not control it. This was reality.

A bit later, in the fall, Inget Herrman and Kenny de Wire came to the Glass House.

They were Eddie de Wire's sisters, they came from America probably after being called about Eddie's death. One of them, Kenny de Wire, stayed with the baroness after this. The other one also stayed in the country. Just became—

Bencku did not meet either of them, not then.

Only once when he was standing at the farthest end of one of the longest jetties did he see one of them.

She was on her way down the hill from the Glass House, toward the boathouse.

A second, but only a short one, he shivered, petrified.

She was so similar. It was almost her.

The American girl.

She waved at him. It was, he would come to know later, the oldest sister. Her with the strange name. The one who was called Inget Herrman.

Listen to the house, it is an organism. Nevertheless he was back again at night, he heard a shot. He went closer.

Imaginary swimming, somewhat later. Bencku at the house in the darker part. He had walked up and was standing and looking in through the window into the lower floor, through the vast panorama window that faced the marsh.

He saw the girl.

She was running up and down in the swimming pool with no water. Her hands gesticulating wildly like swim strokes in the air.

Back and forth, back and forth, eyes closed.

THE HOUSE IN THE
DARKER PART OF THE WOODS

(Sandra's story 1)

LORELEI LINDBERG WANTED TO HAVE A HOUSE. NOT JUST ANY house, but an altogether specific one, which she had seen on an alpine slope at an Austrian ski resort during one of the many honeymoon trips she and the Islander had gone on during the twelve years their marriage lasted. A marriage that did not end in mature mutual understanding: there was nothing mature about Lorelei and the Islander's passion, it was heated and regressive and impossible to live in, in the long run, except in the classical way, where one of them abandons the other, but who still, nevertheless after a certain time, would be remembered fondly.

Lorelei Lindberg was the woman in the Islander's life. It was a fact that would remain. That is to say there would be other women: Yvonne and Marianne, Bombshell Pinky Pink, Anneka Munveg the famous journalist, Inget Herrman. And, of course, she who later became the Islander's second wife: Kenny, born de Wire. But nothing would change the fact that Lorelei Lindberg was and remained the woman in the Islander's life.

"It's an Ålandic quality," as the Islander used to say. "My stubbornness."

"I want that house," Lorelei Lindberg immediately yelled when she caught sight of the villa situated so beautifully on a snowy slope with trees with snow-covered branches that formed the perfect wide, clear Central European landscape. The house appeared as it would on a serving tray, or like a puzzle, "Alpine Villa in Snow, 1,500 pieces."

High mountains could be seen in the background and gray and blue Alps whose white tops stood out against the sky surrounding them in the sunshine.

Lorelei Lindberg, the Islander, and their little girl, and yes, she was harelipped, found themselves on a promenade about 150 feet from the house on the slope on the other side of a field. Dressed as they should be for jet-setters à la late sixties; and even, if you happened to be the little girl, even a bit fashion forward. She had a pair of real moon boots on her feet, at least five years before such boots became popular for a short time and were mass produced so they could be purchased for a reasonable price in regular stores too.

"Can be done," the Islander answered calmly, put his arm around Lorelei Lindberg's waist and squeezed, mildly but decidedly and filled with spirit, and a typical enthusiasm that sometimes bordered on madness but that he nevertheless could, in this moment, keep from running wild.

And it was a well-thought-out gesture, one of the Islander's many small displays with Lorelei Lindberg whom he loved recklessly—"like a bull a she-bull . . . what is that kind called? . . . it can't just be a cow, an ordinary Lindberg-cow?" And that sort of thing could happen, that they carried on like that and said those things to each other forever and it was quite unpleasant for an outsider to have to listen to . . . And Lorelei Lindberg, she knew her Islander's movements, phrases, and gestures. She knew his expressions of love so well, and of course usually would not be late in reciprocating them. She loved him too, there was no doubt about that.

Can be done. Now, for example, precisely in just this moment in the middle of Central Europe, Lorelei Lindberg knew that meant she would get it. And it mattered to Lorelei Lindberg that what she said she wanted, she got. And it was not only selfishness and there was certainly no calculation behind everything, it was just the way this love story was and would continue to be all the way until it ended. You gave and took, took and gave. With real, concrete things.

Can be done. With these words the Islander wanted yet again to show Lorelei Lindberg what he was made of. An Islander, a real one, from Åland made of the right stuff. Someone who could do the impossible. Turn dreams into reality. All dreams, especially hers. Someone for whom no contradiction existed between big words and big feelings. Someone who spoke AND acted.

"An Islander lives in our love." That was another thing he was in the habit of saying over and over again. And, to really give power to his words, he added an almost defiant, "I'm not joking."

Lorelei Lindberg had a relatively vague understanding of what an Islander from Åland was all about. In reality she had met only two in her life, they were brothers, but quite different. She had not even been to Åland. Even her and the Islander's wedding had taken place on the mainland and without any close relatives present. *I've never set foot on Åland.* That was how she used to talk, in the beginning, a bit happy and a bit childishly triumphant in order to tease the Islander. Little by little, above all later, when the marriage was singing its last tunes, with rising and open agitation: "So what's so special about Åland anyway?"

That would be during the time when even the Islander no longer had the desire to talk about anything in detail at all. He would be in the recreation room, keeping quiet, polishing his rifle. Sticking long, Easter-yellow pipe cleaners into the muzzle of the gun, swishing in and out. But that would be in the future, when what was between the Islander and Lorelei Lindberg would not longer have room for words.

"My own orangutan." Lorelei Lindberg cheered happily and gratefully, those many years earlier, among the Alps in Austria. She was not as verbal as the Islander but there was really nothing wrong with her ability to, for example, come up with stupid nicknames for her husband.

The little girl, her in the moon boots, did not have very many nicknames, almost none at all. It was a fact that she had the habit of devoting a lot of time to her so-called sulking, which she was preoccupied with despite the fact that she was not more than nine years old at this time.

The Islander, in the snow, laughed. And Lorelei Lindberg laughed. And no, it was not easy to reproduce all of these scenes and conversations loaded with apparent meaninglessness while the powers that be were at work.

Despite everything Lorelei WANTED a lot of things, despite everything the Islander WAS a man with a strong tendency to make good on his word. And that was not meaningless. It was, and it would show itself to be, fated.

And all of this was something she should have suspected, the ugly little harelip.

The girl in the snow. Thus far, the virile twosome the Islander–Lorelei Lindberg had reproduced only one child (and there would be no more either). The only child in more than one sense: senses that the girl herself, with a sometimes feverish intensity, would devote herself to naming and dissecting into elements in the stubborn, persistent loneliness that characterized her early childhood before she met Doris Flinkenberg.

A small cross and harelipped girl, gray mouse deformity. The knowledge that a certain degree of timidity and uncertainty is often entirely normal in children whose parents are part of the international jet-setter lifestyle could not comfort the girl. Especially not—though it was something she definitely kept to herself before Doris Flinkenberg—the knowledge that she was in some way *normal*.

For many reasons. Most of all because she did not want to be. Did not want to be comforted. She found a highly perverse but intense pleasure in this: being inconsolable. A Sandra

Stammerer, a paltry I. But then, let us settle for that, an I in big, capital letters. A parenthesis. Or even better (as she loved to call herself when she got started), a postscript. PS PS PS PS was written about her; but also this was written with very large letters.

PS PS PS PS. Her name was Sandra.

This sunny day at the Austrian ski resort where Lorelei Lindberg discovered the house that would become hers and the fate of the entire small family unit, Sandra, true to habit, was standing a bit off to the side in these enormous boots that she had, moreover, whined over when she happened to see them in the window of an expensive designer boutique that sold exclusive forward fashion, whined until she got them. They had looked ridiculous, she just had to have them and she had pulled on her mother's jacket arm and remained standing there . . . When the mother just continued walking up the street she produced one of her great and notorious crying spells. Then Lorelei Lindberg had turned around and followed her into the boutique and bought the boots for her. You could say that they really were not a foot-friendly model, most of all because your feet boiled when you had them on because they were made of a strange artificial material on the inside as well as the outside (this warmth was also to the detriment of the girl, who had a certain predilection for thinking of herself as being *frostbitten*). But consequently she was standing there now, the girl, thoughtfully studying the building.

Unbelievable, she could immediately determine that. Later, when it became important to pinpoint this feeling, she would swear that she had thought that at exactly the point in time when she saw the miserable alpine villa on the other side of a snow-covered field for the first time.

It was some kind of weekend cottage. Quite square, with a straight, brown roof. This brown was a wide copper band that, without reason, appeared to frame the entire building, just below the more or less insufferably flat roof. Different kinds of green vines were crawling on the outside walls so it was not possible to see what color the walls under there actually were. On the other hand, you could just guess about it: gray, plastered, disgusting, decomposing.

But still: it actually did not matter what was on the front of the building because what you saw, and the only thing you actually saw, so that it etched itself in your mind, was a staircase. One with long, wide steps leading up to what looked like the main entrance of the house on the second floor. Although it could not be seen all that well from where the little girl was standing and thinking her gloomy thoughts.

From the spot where the little girl was standing it looked more than anything like a staircase leading to nothing.

The girl started counting the steps. She really had time to do this because when the Islander and Lorelei Lindberg played together they were not in a hurry to go anywhere. Now for example they were Göran, the King of the Apes, and Gertrud, the Queen of the Chimpanzees, in the snow on the field in front of the house.

Forty-two. That is what she came to. But at the same time, while she was standing there off to the side counting, terrifying premonitions about woe and death welled up in front of her. These kinds of premonitions were, in and of themselves, not alien to her. Just the opposite. They were the kind of feelings she had a habit of wallowing in under normal circumstances, almost like a hobby. In the small backpack that Sandra carried with her everywhere (it was in the hotel room right now), she had a special scrapbook with clippings for that purpose; she glued pictures and articles in it that were about violent deaths and horrible accidents.

There, stories were often from the jet-setter's life: stories about men and women who, despite their success and all their riches, had met tragic fates. Stories about men and women in whose shoes, regardless of how high-heeled and glittery they could seem when seen at a distance, no one could pay you millions to be in. Fateful meetings with deadly outcomes. Stories with bloody endings.

Lupe Velez drowned in the toilet in her own home.

Patricia in the Blood Woods.

Jayne Mansfield's dead dog (a blurred photograph of a small white terrier who was lying dead among blood and shards of glass from crushed windshields and whiskey bottles after a car accident).

Over the course of time there would be many more stories and, in combination with Doris Flinkenberg's stories and *True Crimes*, more than just a bit interesting.

"I was also fascinated by movie stars when I was your age," Lorelei Lindberg had said once in her usual fleeting way when she had happened to glance in her daughter Sandra's scrapbook. It was something Lorelei Lindberg was a master at in relation to her daughter: fleeting glances, flightiness on the whole, a judgment that arose from Sandra's, the object of the judgment, own sharp-sighted but moody attention. Flightiness in addition to some well-chosen words for the situation itself, words whose main purpose was still to function as a shortcut to the most interesting conversation topic in the whole world, that is to say, herself.

"There wasn't a lot of time to spend on frivolous things when I was growing up," she had continued accordingly. "The circumstances were difficult when I was growing up. Poverty and destitution and winter eleven hundred months of the year. The wolves howled . . ."

But now, this afternoon at the Austrian ski resort in front of an unlikely house, which was a dream that would be realized (there was no reason to doubt it, Sandra knew that more than enough from experience), Sandra suddenly became worried and afraid in a completely new way.

This isn't something I read about or see in magazines, she suddenly understood. This isn't a story. This is for real. This is happening to Mom, Dad, and me. It's happening to us.

And she looked at her parents. They were, to say the least, unmoved. They had continued their snowball fight in the snow on the field, which was deep enough to play in and which spread out in front of the house. Laughing and noisily chasing each other and catching up with each other, chasing each other and getting hold of each other, over and over again and with even intervals, in other words, pretty much the entire time. They tumbled together in a heap, tumbled around each other in the soft snow on the ground. Then up on their feet again, moving on. There was some type of unconscious system in it. *Because they got closer to the house the whole time.*

The little girl watched it all like a movie, and very consciously. It also was not the first time, and definitely not a new perspective, that of the outside observer. But suddenly, and this had never happened before, all of the comforting and self-righteousness in a customary on-the-side perspective was blown away. Suddenly it was actually the perspective itself that was the source of the discomfort and the anxiety growing inside her these last senseless sunny minutes before the landscape grew dark all at once and the snowstorm blew in over them. The source of the angst and the fear battling with all common sense just welled up within her.

It was a thought she had no words for yet, she was so young. Now it was above all a feeling and it struck down in her with a deafening force. If she was an outside observer, who said that she was the only one? Who said that no one else had seen? Any others? And IF someone else or some other people had seen, who had then said that his or her or their gazes would automatically be kind? Even uninterested? Who had said that there was not anyone else in the background, someone with an intention?

For example the evil eye, if that was what was watching?

The evil eye was a concept the small harelipped girl had experimented with in her thoughts for long periods of stigmatized, harelipped loneliness. But, and exactly in this moment she understood this, yet not in words, mostly as an abstract idea. Like Santa Claus whom you no longer believed in but was still a concept you gladly held on to. Or like a game. An imaginary game.

Now she understood that it could be real. That the evil eye might exist and completely independently of her own thoughts about this or that. And right now just in this moment it was more than a little alarming when she knew that her and her entire family's future was being decided.

It was, quite frankly, as if someone had thrown a disgusting wet towel in the little girl's pale, cloven face.

And she was seized by an overwhelming love, a tenderness that exceeded her common sense. Still, it was so obvious, regardless of how ridiculous her parents were: she still loved them. Of course loved them. Those stupid laughs, the stupid snowball fight, *it was so stupid, but couldn't they just be allowed to be that way?* Two who loved each other, and three. Could they not just be allowed to be that way, forever?

And she started praying to God, there where she was standing, to make the evil eye disappear. Or, at least to move it. She did not know which. It is also possible that she only asked for protection.

My God my God my God keep them away from the plight that will befall them. Protect them from. Pain.

But her parents in the distance had almost reached the fateful house, still being noisy and imitating each other, still completely ignorant in the matter of the big battle between good and evil forces playing out around them. And the little girl was seized by something similar to panic, there where she was standing with her terribly hot boots, in the midst of her own powerlessness. When not even God seemed to hear, after all nothing was happening. And in order to do something herself she ran out into the snow, a task that, in other words, was not entirely easy in the enormous boots, threw herself on her back on the ground with an energy uncommon for her. Gesticulated wildly with her arms for dear life, up and down, up and down, in order to bring about an angel to scare away the evil eye. Or at least move it.

An angel's stare is terrible.

An angel is so beautiful, gentle, the universe sings when you look at it.

Or, quite simply: tit for tat, eye to eye. The girl pressed herself against the ground even harder and made her most terrifying harelipped face up toward the dark sky above her. It became an angry and bold stare lasting several minutes without blinking, and in turn produced for the most part a lot of tears that in the storm just froze in the corners of her eyes so that her field of vision just diminished even more and her eyelids were frozen.

She became completely powerless right in the middle, all the energy left her at once. The sun disappeared at about the same time and the sky filled with black, violet clouds. The snow started falling, a snow that was transformed into a tight whirl in the wind that blew to storm strength, this also happened in just a few moments. Sandra was lying in the snow, now petrified. Unable to move. Her body did not want to. The evil eye had nailed her there on the spot. Her head was spinning, and now she understood she was going to die. She could do nothing about it, she would be buried in snow.

"Help!"

No, it could not be like this. She did not want to die! Did not want to! And she became scared again and started calling for help for everything she was worth. She did not know whom she was calling to, she just lay there and screamed, screamed while the whirling snow tightened around her.

"Help!" Once she had started screaming she could not stop, simply could not. And that was suddenly the most terrible thing of all.

Then Lorelei Lindberg was there, next to her. Frightened and agitated she popped up in the storm, she had lost her leather cap, heavy clumps of snow hung in her flaxen hair and her eye makeup had run down her cheeks in long green streaks. Lorelei Lindberg had an ability to forget everything when she was playing, to really lose herself in the game.

"Little child." Lorelei Lindberg's face wrinkled with concern and sympathy. "What happened?"

But little Sandra could not answer. Could not get a word out, still could not move. How would she explain? How in the world would she get anyone else to understand? It was not possible. So she just lay there, face turned toward the sky, which could no longer be seen, like a stuck pig and screamed.

"My God! Stop it now!"

If there was something that irritated Lorelei Lindberg it was her daughter's crying spells, the quite-often-occurring ones. She had truly avoided becoming familiar with them, being able to tell the difference between the one kind of crying versus the other kind, and one thing was certain, she could not be bothered to listen to them for very long.

And now her patience ran out once again. With a determined and energetic anger she took a hold of her daughter and tore her up out of the snow. These were no gentle grips: she was forced to use all her strength since Sandra herself was so heavy and without a will of her own, completely numb in all of her limbs, like a rag doll. And as usual, which she had a habit of doing when her mother treated her a bit roughly, Sandra disconnected herself mentally, was present but at the same time was not. But this time she did not do it to keep away, or because she in some way should have felt sorry for herself. Just the opposite. She had gotten out of the snow. To be brutally plucked from the snow might have been the only way. The spell was gone. She was content and quite relieved.

But suddenly Lorelei Lindberg stopped in the middle of her angry outburst. She let go of her daughter—yes, she had regained her ability to move, she could stand on her own—and she stared at the tracks left behind on the ground.

"But what a beautiful angel! Have you made that all by yourself?" The pride in Lorelei Lindberg's voice could not be mistaken, it was as if her anger had vanished into thin air, and her enthusiasm was just as real and honest as her intense frustration had just been. Lorelei Lindberg looked from her daughter to the angel in the snow, from the angel to her daughter and back, and she sparkled with excitement. As if it were something unheard-of. And then she turned around and called out into the snowstorm, which had already had time to transform the beautiful landscape into a foggy and gray soup where you could barely see where you were going.

"Humptey! Come and see what Sandra has made! All by herself!"

And shortly thereafter he appeared out of the whirling snow, out of the whining of the wind that obliterated all other sounds. He was the gorilla in high spirits, slightly bent forward, forehead wrinkled in creases, and hands dangling listlessly in front of him, almost dragging the ground when he walked forward quickly. And with his sights set on Lorelei.

"Here comes the snow gorilla to get you!" the Islander roared. "Ugh! This is an attack! The ape is back!"

"Stoppp! Tjuuuh!" Lorelei Lindberg shrieked but it was too late. Before anyone knew what was happening the Islander had thrown himself at her and both of them had lost their balance and fallen over on the ground where they rolled back and forth, back and forth, wrestling, snickering, over the angel in the snow which, of course, was destroyed beneath them.

Sandra barely had her moment of triumph, then it was over. The angel had only just been made (and to what effect? that was something you could really ask yourself) and it was obliterated from the face of the earth.

Then Sandra was beside herself again. But this time in the usual way, in the way she had been beside herself in her parents' company so many times before.

"You've messed it up!" she cried and burst into tears. The tears sprayed out of her eyes, she squatted in the snow and just roared. Of course the moon boots did not tolerate this kind of shifting of body weight, so she just tumbled down on her back and ended up in an odd position half sitting on the ground; it was really uncomfortable and did its part in making sure the crying would not stop.

Finally her parents paid attention. They finally stopped with their games. Lorelei Lindberg ran up to Sandra and tried to put her arms around her but Sandra just flailed wildly and became even more hysterical.

"My goodness, sweetheart," Lorelei Lindberg tried. "Calm down. It was just a game."

But Sandra did not calm down, nothing helped now, certainly not what someone tried to say. Everything was already destroyed, Sandra was inconsolable. And the Islander and Lorelei Lindberg stood powerless beside her; and now they had to accept standing there, discouraged and bewildered in the cruel storm, like two fools.

But not for very long of course. If there was, as said, something Lorelei Lindberg was not blessed with it was an angel's patience and, above all, this applied to her only daughter's cries and howls, which were, as said, frequently occurring.

"My goodness, child!" she finally yelled. "Get it together! I said that it was only a game! I'm not thinking of standing here and staring at you one more second!"

And Lorelei Lindberg turned around and started with great determination to trudge back through the snow toward the promenade that led to the village from which they had come, the village with all of the hotels, restaurants, and the nightclub the Running Kangaroo, which was the gathering place for the international jet-setters. And with all of the people. Once Lorelei Lindberg had gotten started she went straight ahead without so much as a glance over her shoulder. And quickly, very quickly, she was swallowed up by the storm and the fog—just like the house, the woods, the Alps, and the entire magnificent puzzle game had just been swallowed up.

Everything that was wide open becomes a closed world again.

Now there was just snow, and there in the middle father and daughter. Sandra, who was really trying to calm herself down now and gradually managed to do so, and the Islander, who was so often standing on both sides of the fence. His daughter on one side, his wife on the other. What the hell was he supposed to do now?

No. Getting there using reason was not possible. And that was a good thing indeed because that kind of musing would not have gotten him anywhere. He would just have remained standing in the snow, stiff and frozen in place just like his angel daughter was a moment ago.

No, as luck would have it the Islander was, in contrast to his daughter, someone who WAS NOT endowed with a complicated inner life. One second's thinking was enough, then he had turned toward her again:

"Listen up, little Miss Sourpuss! It can't have been that bad! Look at Dad!"

. . .

And he had thrown himself on his back in the snow and started waving his arms up and down, up and down, a few quick strokes and presto he had created a new angel next to the old one, Sandra's angel, the one that no longer existed.

"SIMSALABIM! Who's been here? No one other than director Houdini!"

He jumped up and brushed off the snow, made a stupid theater bow at the same time as he once more, carefully, almost in secret, glanced in the direction where Lorelei had walked into a wall of snow, where she could no longer be seen. He pretended not to be bothered by it, but as was so often the case when the Islander was pretending, what he was trying to hide became that much more obvious. He put his arm around his daughter and pulled her a little, just a little bit, again almost unnoticeable but the message was clear. Now he wanted to leave.

"You don't understand anything!" Sandra hissed and tore herself out of her father's grip. She was calm again but truly angry. Now it was enough! With all of it! Everything!

And she started running. Ran out into the snow, ran and ran, even if it was toward the road because if you did not hurry now it would be difficult to find your way back to the village at all (in the Alps the snow could block off roads in a second, she had read about that in the hotel's brochure just the day before).

In other words she WAS NOT running after Mom. She was running away. In general. Out into whiteness. Away from Mom, away from Dad, away from the evil eye, away from the house, the ominous house.

Little Bombay. Silk rasgulla. An exclusive blend. Not authentic, but it hangs so softly, so softly.

Little Bombay, the winter, one of those half-dark days, and at dusk, no one in the store.

There was never anyone in the store.

In other words, no customers. Almost. Just Lorelei Lindberg, that is what we call her, and the little girl.

A small silk dog, who was wagging its tail.

Or just lying, under a table, panting by her water bowl.

And the fabric fell over the edge of the table.

The fabrics that Mom cut, sometimes.

Dupioni. Italian. It is the best, the one with the very highest quality.

Then follows, in that order, the Indian and the Chinese.

Little Bombay, all of the fabrics.

And, when you looked outside, a wet snow was falling against the dark asphalt, so wet that it melted before it reached the ground.

There were not any customers in the store. Or: sometimes someone came in and bought a zipper or fabric for a lining.

One person would want Thai silk, but the texture of the one they had suddenly was not good enough.

It was supposed to be two-ply, not four.

These people, what do they think of themselves? thought Lorelei Lindberg, but she didn't say it out loud.

She didn't say anything out loud. Why should she? She wasn't the one who lit a cigarette and reveled in ambiguity.

She did not even smoke.

She arranged spools of thread and made estimates in her notebook.

Sometimes she looked up and asked questions.

Sandra, little Sandra, what do you think the Islander is doing right now?

And they guessed.

That was before the period of constant telephoning.

He rarely called. Almost never. But he came to the boutique just before closing time.

It was her friends who called, girlfriends.

"And now we've chatted away another hour again."

Organza.

They played music. Her music.

The banana record.

Sometimes she put puzzles together. "Alpine Villa in Snow," 1,500 pieces.

They were never finished.

"I'm waiting for the man" was one song.

"Heroine."

Another.

And:

"Take a walk on the wild side."

You didn't understand what they meant, you didn't listen to the words.

It was like when Bob Dylan sang:

"To dance beneath the diamond sky with one hand waving free."

It wasn't the words. Of course it didn't mean anything.

Just rubbish.

But you understood perfectly.

The Islander came at closing time.

And he took her home.

Another song that was played a lot at that time:

"Our love is a continental affair, he came in a white Jaguar

I waited for him in my red raincoat because it was raining that day."

Was that how it went?

They stood in the rain outside Little Bombay and waited.

The mom, the silk dog.

And it rained.

And yes, it rained.

Shantung.

Little Bombay, the soft silk dog.

And all of the fabric.

But the girl's cheeky, independent objective to run away on her own did not last very long. She had barely gotten up speed in her wretched boots before she understood she was in no way alone, she had someone after her and someone quickly beside her, someone who was not going to give up, which was confirmed by a familiar and playful smack on the back. It was the Islander of course, who else?

"Now we're going to accelerate these machines!" he shouted. "Now we're going to catch up to Mom!"

As if everything was still a game. And Sandra realized again that it was incurably hopeless, all of it. But at the same time, she had to give up. She could not resist him either. He was so funny after all, so happy, her very own father the Islander, the charming one in high spirits. She could not do anything about it either, that the temperament was incorrigibly infectious.

It was impossible to be angry with him for long. Because in Sandra there was also a little dog, the soft silk dog, the one who wagged its tail, wagged and wagged because it also wanted to join in and play.

And they ran together and in the whirling snow someone howled like a lighthouse on a foggy sea:

"Lorelei! Guess what! Sandra and I just came up with a brilliant idea! Now all of us are going to run back to the hotel as fast as we can and then we're going to stay in the room and drink hot toddies all day long!"

A moment's silence, and then a radiant "my fantastic small super piglets!" could be heard in response.

And the snow dispersed just in that moment and she was standing in the middle of the road in front of them, Lorelei Lindberg, arms spread out as if to envelop both of them in her embrace.

"What a delightful idea, by the way!" she continued, lowered her hands and smiled so tenderly and devoutly. Nothing more was needed in order for the small, soft silk dog also to obey, run laughing toward Mom, so playful and so eager, nosing against her mother's stomach and wagging her tail.

Little Bombay.
   They argued over whether IT was silk taffeta or habotai.

They argued, believe me. We prefer habotai. It's so thin and light. Like a veil.

"*Waiting for the man.*"

So porous, as if it wasn't fabric.

As if it almost didn't exist.

"*Little Sandra, what are you going to be when you grow up?*" *Lorelei Lindberg asks Sandra Wärn, her little girl, in Little Bombay, among all of the fabrics.*

"*I'm going to be a silkworm. A cocoon so soft so soft.*"

"*Ha ha ha,*" *said Lorelei Lindberg.* "*I don't think so.*"

"*Or a silk dog.*"

And to the Islander, so soft and light:

"*She says she's going to be a silk dog when she grows up. Isn't there something special about her? Isn't she wonderful?*"

And to Sandra:

"*I think, sweetheart, that you're going to be a clothing designer when you grow up. Wouldn't that be fun?*"

Silk chiffon and silk georgette. Two thin, thin materials that cannot be confused with each other.

We prefer georgette. Because a really nice georgette is difficult to find.

"*But we have this one, you can see on this sample.*"

"*Feel.*"

And it was in Little Bombay, among all of the fabrics.

Said and done. The family stayed indoors at their hotel the rest of the day. First in the bar and later in the restaurant and after a pass by the jet-setters' nightclub the Running Kangaroo to their own hotel room again, with room service. It rocked, rocked. Sandra Wärn would not have many memories of that evening and that night and what followed after, a few days. Mostly gaps, hallucinations brought on by the alcohol, she would became very sick from the alcohol she drank in secret and could not tolerate.

But from these gaps the following would, in any case, stand out. The image of Jayne Mansfield's dead dog among the shards of glass after a car accident that was fatal for everyone involved; the movie star and the dog, and also a small, crushed whiskey bottle would remain lying on the asphalt. In the end that was the picture she threw up on, when there sort of became too much of everything. Then it was already night and it finally dawned on her parents that something had gone wrong. And there was a quick end to the festivities.

In the hotel room: the Islander and Lorelei Lindberg "discussed." When they had "discussed" they started arguing. The Islander and Lorelei Lindberg loved to fight but had a silent agreement that this fact should not be revealed. If you did not fight for real then you could not make up for real afterward. And the best thing about fighting was making up. And then no one was allowed to bother them.

It was just when the fighting had reached its culmination that the nauseous feeling that could not be stopped welled up inside the little girl. And then hallucinations brought on by the drunkenness and the hangover, followed in a state between sleep and consciousness, a pounding headache and stomach pumping at a hospital where black-clothed nun-nurses with troubled expressions kept watch over the little harelipped girl.

But still, this was in any case indisputable. One morning, not the next one but maybe the one after, the storm had abated and there was sun and it was clear again and it was probably pretty late although Lorelei Lindberg was still lying in bed, asleep. The Islander shook Sandra, waking her where she was lying on the sofa in the big room that was almost a suite ("It's ALMOST a suite" was, among other things, the sort of thing her parents had the habit of arguing about). The Islander indicated she should be quiet and get dressed quickly and come with him. And out with the girl again and before she knew it she and the

Islander were back on the wretched promenade again, this time in a real taxi.

"This is going to be our home," the Islander said and pointed over the field at the same house whose magic power had not been banished.

"Here?" Sandra asked weak at the knees and for a moment she thought, despite her young age, she understood all of those people who drink themselves into a stupor to avoid coming face-to-face with reality. And she tried to put all the hesitation and all the resistance she could muster in this little "here?" But it was obviously not much. Her head continued to pound in the sunshine, her angel had been buried for good, her angel, other people's angels, everyone's angels, and now a completely neutral sun was shining from the clear and soaring sky again, a sky that was extremely indifferent toward them.

"Not here," the Islander said impatiently. "In our home country of course. Come, let's go and ring the bell. I need to take some pictures."

They had waded through the snow, first the Islander, then his daughter. Sandra had straggled behind anyway, perhaps deliberately. Everything was crazy, all of it, and it was spiraling in her head and her stomach was knotting up too. She saw how the Islander ran up the long stairs and rang the bell. And what was it? Some kind of alpine march suddenly started playing loudly in the idyllic nature. In other words, it was the doorbell.

Thrilled, the Islander yelled from the landing where he was standing, "What a gizmo!" down to his daughter, who was not the least bit enthusiastic. He waited and waited, the song died out, no one opened.

The Islander had to manage with the camera by himself as best he could, so it turned out that he captured only the outside of the house on his roll of film.

And soon he was busy with the camera: *click, click, click,* and *click.*

The girl closed her eyes because of the dizziness, and suddenly, she saw an alpine villa next to a muddy marsh in front of her. A house with a decomposing façade and a long staircase. And a woman who fell down the staircase, rolling violently down all the gray, concrete steps. Then coming to rest on the ground like a dead person.

Driven to the hospital, stitches in the neck with a stitch called butterfly.

And inside the house, in the basement, a swimming pool without water. And there was someone who was running in it, back and forth between the two short sides. Running and running, arms making swimming strokes in the empty air in front of her.

Imaginary swimming. That she was the child, she saw that too. And in the background SHOTS. *Pang.*

Though *pang.* Maybe it was just snapping in her head because the girl had gone down on the ground now in the alpine sun, she could not stand upright in all her day-after weakness and she knew that she was about to faint.

But then the Islander was there shaking her, holding her, and everything was okay again.

"Am I not an Ålänning worth the name?" the Islander said in a brilliant mood in the taxi on the way back to the hotel. "A damned impressive one with captains in the family going back generations?"

"Mmm," Sandra said because that was the way she had the habit of answering when he was going on like that.

"I mean the house," the Islander clarified in the sunshine. "Won't it be phenomenal?"

"Yes," Sandra answered slowly. And she knew then, in the same moment she heard her voice, that everything was so irreversible.

"This seals our union," the Islander also said. "Now we're sharing a secret. Remember. I'm counting on you. Not a word to anyone."

And then she also understood something else. She could no longer get out. She was involved now, whether she wanted to be or not. And it was no hallucination. It was nothing less than reality, which, despite her current dazed state, was more than ever before completely clear.

Little Bombay

Pashmina was invented more than four hundred years ago when Nur Jahan, wife of the Emperor Jehangir, asked her weavers to present a woolen fabric that was "as light as a cloud but as warm as a tender embrace."
    And she got it.
    Many are the finesses and secrets of pashmina.
    Silk is, should we say it directly, second class.
    We're talking about silk in pashmina, in other words.
    Real pashmina wool comes from the belly of sheep.
    Or was it the hindquarters.

"This is what it looked like. A room with bolts of fabric, two tables, and shelves.
    "A table and a chair and a record player in the back part of the room.
    "A water boiler. We always drank tea. A certain type of tea."

But she could also become angry. "Why didn't anyone come?"
    "And you ask as if business was going well."
    "Business is terrible."
    And all of the needles fell out of her mouth, she was so angry.
    And clink clink *the needles fell on the floor.*
    Little Bombay—
    Little Bombay, Köpmansbranten 42, in a suburb in the western parts outside the city by the sea, open between eight and six in the evening.
    A fabric store, "for silk. Can anything be more idiotic?"
    The puzzle in the back room, on the little table.
    Alpine Villa in Snow.
    And all of the fabrics.

". . . And the Islander. What is he doing again? He's hardly ever at home . . ."

And one day the door opened and an acquaintance stepped into the boutique:
"When you speak of the devil."
It wasn't the Islander, but the Black Sheep.

"Long time no see. But remember this. That it isn't always so wonderful to see what your dreams look like in reality."
The Black Sheep, the eternal student of architecture. The Islander's brother.
Always on the go, always busy.
Like the Islander. Yet so different.

And so it was, a time later. More like the time that it takes for a baby elephant to be ready baked in its mother's stomach.

"Here comes happiness from a lucky roll of the dice!" the Islander yelled and shuffled a large, square package into the bedroom of the apartment in their native country. The package was almost as tall as Sandra, covered with silver-colored paper and a wide red silk ribbon tied in the shape of a playful tropical flower right on top. Sandra knew. She had already seen everything, but later when it happened in real time she lay and huddled on her mother's bed, under her mother's quilt. Squeezed her eyes shut, held her hands over her ears and *la-laed* to herself to shut out what could not be shut out.

And then glitter confetti rained over the bed, the package, the room, her.

A few days before Lorelei Lindberg's birthday, it was just when you thought he had forgotten about all of it, in any case just when you yourself had forgotten so that you had eagerly started concentrating on other things in life, that the Islander had come into Sandra's room with a plastic bag in hand. Lorelei Lindberg was at Little Bombay, the fabric store, and Sandra was lying at home in bed suffering the last sweat of the first childhood disease (was it chicken pox or German measles? she did not remember). He closed the door securely and then dug around in the plastic bag and pulled out a rather large object that he unwrapped in front of her from the brown paper.

"Look, Sandra! What do we have here? Ring any bells?"

Sandra did not understand anything. Or well. When she saw the object, it was a bell, a front doorbell of quite a unique type— then she suddenly understood far too much. The Islander meant: "Do you remember?" Of course she did, she had immediately recognized the bell so she knew exactly what it resembled. The doorbell by a front door to a certain house that they had seen in the Alps, a long time ago.

And an Islander, as has been mentioned, never forgets a good idea once he has come up with it. And he was a man of his word, damn it, too, an Islander, not to mention woven from a rare, stubborn cloth.

The doorbell looked like a cuckoo clock and apparently worked the same way. You wound it by pulling on two metal strings on which two heavy clumps, supposedly representing pinecones from the forest, were hanging, these were also made of metal . . . When you rang it (pushed a button) a terrace door in miniature opened on the alpine villa in miniature that the bell was carved into, and some red and tipsy alpine men and alpine women with foaming beer mugs in hand marched out at the same time as the alpine march started playing. The nausea welled up inside Sandra yet again, a sick feeling sort of imitating the nausea during her hangover in the Alps, and there it was again, the peculiar taste of complete hopelessness and rotten rum in her mouth.

Nach Erwald und die Sonne. Die Sonne. Die Sonne. Die Sonne. The bell sounded. How in the world would she have been able to forget that?

"You have no idea how difficult it was to get this bell," the Islander said, pleased. "It was almost harder than building the whole house!"

Sandra listened to all of it, almost speechless with despair.

"But I managed!"

And she nodded. Once or twice, but otherwise she was mute, just mute, though as usual the Islander did not notice her play-acting. He was, as said, not the kind of person who devoted his time to analyzing expressive silences, uncontrolled chatter, and all the possible hidden meanings in them, etc. and etc. Everything that somehow had a double meaning.

"In other words it's done now," he clarified as if there was still some uncertainty on the subject. And added, filled with his own enthusiasm:

"In other words that's what has kept me occupied all these days. As we know Rome wasn't built in a day. And it takes two years for a baby elephant to become ready baked in its mother's belly."

After a closing remark like that, which was not funny at the time, just stupid and silly, the Islander communicated that it was the day after tomorrow, on Lorelei Lindberg's birthday, that it would "happen."

"And now the two of us are going to conspire a bit more on the topic. This was of course both our idea from the beginning. And of course we want it to be a tremendous surprise for her, right? The surprise of all surprises. To her from both of us!"

And the Islander put on his sunglasses, which at that time he almost never took off because in secret he imagined that he looked like a certain popular French movie star when he had them on, and of course he actually did. Maybe he also had the idea that it would remind Lorelei Lindberg of the jet-setter's life that they had lived more intensely in the past before this life and their child and the everyday and the, for the time being, bad business when there was currently considerably less of that commodity. And then of course it was not exactly cheap to buy land and build a house.

He put on the dark sunglasses so you could not see his expression. And sometimes—in moments just like these—Sandra became absolutely certain that what the Black Sheep in a certain white Jaguar had said would hold true: that there was nothing wrong with the Islander in and of himself, "aside from the fact that he isn't in full possession of his senses. Just ask me, I'm his brother after all."

Or, *a few bricks short of a full load*, which you said in the District where they would soon be moving. Behind the dark sunglasses it was filled with emptiness.

Little Bombay.

Don't let it dupe you. The finest pashmina is not a silk blend.
    Pashmina with silk is cheap.
    Not completely worthless, but not the finest and most exclusive, which we are now looking for.
    (Little Bombay, and all of the fabric.)
    Lorelei Lindberg was speaking with a girlfriend on the phone:
    "I have a child who cries so much."
    "When my daughter cries: Which my daughter does so often. Then I lose faith in life. Almost.
    "Then I lose my hold, my courage, my . . . everything."

Turned "Heroine" off and the radio on.
    This streamed from the radio instead:
    "Our love is a continental affair. He came in a white Jaguar."
    There was no one who escaped that hit during that time.
    "How it is . . . I don't know," said Lorelei Lindberg on the telephone.
"It's just a bit . . . I don't know . . . tricky. A strange mood."

. . .

Polyester has been created as a refined copy of the real thing.
    Advanced polyester is confusingly similar to real silk.
    But tell me then, what is the point?

*And the silk dog came out from under the table, turned off the radio
and on with "Heroine," again.*
    The door opened—the Black Sheep came in:
    "Sniff. Sniff. Mmm. It smells like MOUSE."

The birthday that took place a few days later started with Sandra coming into the bedroom where Lorelei Lindberg was lying alone in the big double bed (the marital bed, as it was also called) waiting to be told happy birthday while pretending to sleep. She was well aware of what day it was and carefully prepared for all of the antics that awaited her on this day. Lorelei Lindberg loved birthdays, most of all her own. Sandra had the birthday tray in her hands and was singing happy birthday alone in her thin, small voice: *In a cabin in the woods little man by the window stood saw a rabbit hopping by knocking at his door,* which was the only song she knew almost all the words to. Lorelei Lindberg opened her eyes pretending to be surprised, but bounced up spiritedly in a sitting position, stretched like a cat and laughed like the birthday child is supposed to. But at the same time, though she did everything to hide it, she was looking around furtively. But where was HE with all of her presents? All of the real packages, the real presents? Because on the tray Sandra was holding in her hands, next to the cup with scalding Lapsang souchong tea and some sandwich crackers with orange marmalade, there was just Sandra's own present, which was small and such a strange shape that you instantly knew what it was. An elephant, a small one, made of ivory. The kind of elephant Lorelei Lindberg had said she could never have enough of, and she probably had ten already.

But no Islander anywhere, which—though of course Lorelei Lindberg did not know it—the Islander and Sandra had agreed on ahead of time. The plan was for Sandra to tell her mother that the Islander unfortunately had had to go out of town on an urgent business matter early that morning and therefore would not be home at all on her birthday so unfortunately mother and daughter would have to make do with just each other.

This was in other words what Sandra was supposed to explain to Lorelei Lindberg after she had finished singing the miserable birthday song while the Islander would be standing behind the door, waiting for a good moment to interrupt the whole thing— and it would be just that moment when Lorelei Lindberg really started believing what Sandra was saying and had sort of given up hope so you could hear it in her voice as well. This surrender would be the signal for the Islander to *PADAM*, throw open the door and stand there in person in the opening with his Veuve Clicquot champagne, his cigarillos, which he smoked only in honor of her birthday and, most important, the present, the magnificent present and his shout: "Here comes happiness from a lucky roll of the die! Here you go!"

But in the middle of the birthday song Sandra become so discouraged and on the verge of tears over what was about to happen that she abruptly stopped in the middle of the song and saw no other option than to jump straight into her mother's bed, curl up tightly next to her mother's body, squeeze her eyes shut, and utter only weak whimpers of powerlessness to herself.

"My goodness, child, what's wrong now?" Then Lorelei Lindberg had in turn moved suddenly and the cup of tea on the tray, which Sandra had only just had time to set down on the nightstand before the sudden dive, tipped over and boiling hot tea had sprayed over both of them. Though most of all over Sandra's left arm and it had really stung. If it had not been Lorelei Lindberg's birthday, Sandra probably would have had a crying spell, though she managed to ward it off for the time being in honor of the day.

But so, sucking the spot on her skin that had been burned, Sandra had been held in the bed and thus made sure she got as far under the covers as possible, not to mention with her head first (like an ostrich who thinks it can escape from danger by sticking its head in the sand). Without seeing, without hearing, without doing anything. Only her tongue, her own small and hesitant tongue played over the tender, newly burned skin on her arm. Disgusting blisters would surely gradually pop up there, blisters that she would amuse herself with hollowing out holes in them or picking at them in general so that maybe they would become infected and she would be forced to go to the nurse's office at the French School. She could, if she really tried, already hear the school nurse's voice:

"If you touch it one more time you'll get scarring you'll have to carry around for the rest of your life. Do you really want that? Do you really want scars like that, you who've just had surgery on your lip? You who've just been given a normal mouth. Normal like all other children?"

Normal. The nurse at the French School had normal on her mind. But on the other hand, she had carried on so about Sandra's newly won normalcy that the effect had almost been the opposite. So you might think the school nurse, when all was said and done, still was not as convinced about Sandra's normalcy as she let on. Maybe she wanted to convince herself by carrying on like that? Sandra liked that, like a game.

And later in life, during the best times, those which were spent in the swimming pool without water together with Doris Flinkenberg, Doris would become a completely splendid school nurse in one game. Just like that she would understand the character and secrecy of the nurse at the French School; the game would be called the School Nurse's Secret.

"I was the first one who saw through her," Doris Flinkenberg would say with a voice muffled and oh so similar, in the swimming pool without water that would become their haunt in the house in the darker part. "SandraIdiotHarelip. An infernal liar. Putting on airs for all she was worth. I saw through her, I did."

Though this was nevertheless important information (and it was true). That now, this morning in the beginning of the history of the world, a fate was sealed, *the harelip not harelipped anymore*. Sandra had been in her second year at the French School when the diagnosis was made, and an operation was carried out soon thereafter. "We'll quickly send a referral in this matter," the school nurse had said proudly, as if this initiative was only her own and Sandra's. Little Sandra really had not done much to correct the delusion. In reality, Sandra had done nothing at all since the delusion itself had sort of been the whole point.

"One might think that your parents should have intervened a little sooner," said the school nurse who contacted the mouth specialist who immediately set a date and time for the operation on his calendar. "Have your mother and father really not said anything at all?"

"No," Sandra lied calmly and gently.

The school nurse just shook her head, the kinds of parents there were these days. Like so many others, she also had a lot of prejudices against the superficial party lifestyle, which in her eyes these jet-setters lived, and the fact that Sandra's parents, the Islander and Lorelei Lindberg, in Sandra's own portrayal also belonged to this group, had not changed it.

"Mom and Dad think it's fine the way it is." Sandra stoked the fire. "They think I look funny. They like laughing at me. Though they mean well. They just have such a phenomenal sense of humor. They don't mean it in a bad way."

And that had made the school nurse even more beside herself with anger.

"That wasn't nicely done," she said, and her voice almost shook with indignation. But then she had continued more determined than angry, downright triumphant, "It's good that I've taken matters into my own hands. And not because I have an opinion on the matter, *I wash my hands of it*, but I must say that personally I don't think you should laugh at a child."

It was of course lies, all of it from beginning to end, but if you had come this far in your lies you could not reasonably pull yourself out later down the line, of course the little harelip understood this instinctively, even if it was to the detriment of herself. In other words, the subsequent operation in question that was an inevitable result. "No pain, no gain," she tried to comfort herself with on the operating table where she shortly thereafter lay bound among knives and other instruments that existed solely to carve into her. But she had not been able to control herself and at the last second screamed, "I don't want to," but it had already been too late; the terrible ether mask was pressed over her face and she fell asleep and in a horrible ether nightmare she saw angry, chubby yellow guys dancing cabaret and woke up vomiting violently eight hours later.

In fact, the Islander and Lorelei Lindberg had taken Sandra to a whole slew of doctors and mouth specialists. Even in Little Bombay Sandra had sometimes been forced to give someone a closer look at her mouth, a customer or some other child-friendly soul who had good advice to give, someone who knew a plastic surgeon or had a relative who had suffered the same affliction.

"It's just a matter of cutting away and sewing together," the man in the white Jaguar said laconically, and it took a while for Sandra to identify him as the Black Sheep, the Islander's brother, because when he came to Little Bombay all of it, the clothes, the car, were so new.

"Cut and sew together!" That was the worst part. Not on your life! And the suggestion, expressed so bluntly, had just resulted in Sandra becoming even more stubborn. She had gradually, with her notorious crying spells as a weapon, simply refused to go to the doctors' offices. Just refused. And God help the one who did not respect her decision. Then . . . UAAAH! In other words, it was at the time the nurse at the French School was having her eyes opened to Sandra's harelipped state.

And this refusal, where did it come from?

Was it because as a child she was already dead set on cultivating this split as an attitude toward life, as a powerful OTHER perspective in favorable situations in any case? Unfortunately not.

She was scared to death, that was the truth. Afraid of the operating knives, afraid of the anesthesia, of the mere thought. A normal, petty fear. She was almost ashamed of this fact when she contemplated it herself.

But with the school nurse at the French School it had been about something else from the very beginning. In the beginning, Sandra had gone to her mostly in order to have something to do during the breaks and the study periods. In order to kill time. She was bored, had almost no friends. In itself, not having any friends at the French School was not very agonizing because there were so many students who were like her—reserved, self-centered, and scared to death of everything. Some of these children knew no French or any, as it sometimes seemed, other languages. They had traveled around the world so much they had not properly learned a single language at all.

But Sandra went to the school nurse because she noticed that she liked to have someone to talk to about her afflictions, imagined and real, and be taken seriously.

The school nurse could do nothing else. It was her job and her employers were not just anybody. The French School was a private school with an exclusive student body, which was not necessarily the same thing as talented but rather students with parents who were diplomats, employed in the international business world, and the like. So the everyday school nurse was a spirited, robust, and sufficiently primitive element in that environment. As long as she lived up to that role: one of those small, genuine people among the bigger, smarter ones.

But even simple people have secrets, even though they can be quite small. And that was what Sandra had done: she had picked up on the school nurse's secret. It was quite simply that the school nurse despised the teachers and above all the parents of the students at the French School, those who always, also in their absence, used their money and their influence to decide everything. But she liked children. Normal children: despite the fact that there was a certain lack of this kind of child at the French School, children who suffered from normal childhood afflictions such as flat feet, or bleeding gums as the result of a plain diet or quite simply malnutrition. And in the French School she attached herself above all to the ones who had some hint of a disability, and preferably because she was so practically inclined, a visible one.

This is what Sandra had seen and been moved by.

"Here comes happiness!"

PADAM! Back to the apartment, Lorelei Lindberg's birthday, reality. The door to the bedroom had been thrown wide open and finally there was the Islander with the champagne, cigarillos, and the enormous box that almost had to be pushed in. And with his happy yell. "Here comes happiness!" Lorelei Lindberg brightened up and was like a child again, the way she was when she got presents. She quickly jumped out of bed in her baby doll nightie and threw herself at the box. Tearing off the silver paper, throwing aside the ribbon and the bow without giving them a second glance, and in no time she got out . . . a die. Exactly that. Light yellow and enormous, a very enormous one, made of plastic.

A few days earlier the Islander had asked an acquaintance from his hunting league if he could have it, a league he had, before

Lorelei Lindberg, been an active member in. An acquaintance who coincidentally happened to be the director of an entire ice cream factory. Sandra, the unlucky accomplice, knew everything about this as well; furthermore she had been present at the transfer in the office of the ice cream factory. The enormous die with lid was an advertising model from the previous season and had originally been used during a failed launch of vanilla ice cream portions packed in small, small plastic dice in different colors. The advertising die had been in the director's office for a long time already, as an almost unlucky reminder of the unpleasant faux pas in the marketing. A true businessman does not like to fail; not a lot of convincing was needed from the Islander's side in order for him to be given it for free. Sandra, on the other hand, she got ice cream, and as much as she could eat too. She had eaten from this *blood ice cream*, eaten, eaten, eaten. And now, when she was lying under the quilt on her mother's side of the marital bed, she promised herself that she would never never eat ice cream again.

"Is it a diamond?" Lorelei Lindberg asked, filled with happy expectation while she eagerly pried at the plastic lid. When she had gotten it open she let out such a loud and high-spirited shriek that Sandra just had to look out from her hiding place and then glitter confetti rained over her as well.

Silver confetti over the entire room, everywhere. That was what the Islander had filled the entire die with. And for a moment Lorelei Lindberg was occupied with just the confetti. The Islander too, of course. They threw it around and yelled and became monkeys again, they were orangutan Gertrud in a yellow lace nightgown and chimpanzee Göran in a captain's suit and dark sunglasses. The Islander opened the champagne bottle, *ploff!* the cork flew across the room. Veuve Clicquot, and little Sandra crept out of the bed over the floor after the cork like a well-trained dog because she collected the small metal plates on the top of these corks on which the same grouchy lady was always pictured. Sandra had quite a few already, but that was of course exactly how it was supposed to be in the real life of a jet-setter.

The small, soft silk dog was hunting again. The confetti was mixed with sticky champagne that flowed and flowed and so, yet again, another of Lorelei Lindberg and the Islander's passionate chaoses was a reality.

But Lorelei Lindberg gradually calmed down and discovered her present anew. Lifted the die up in the air with both hands, turned it upside down, and shook out the rest of the confetti over the floor. Now she knew what she was looking for: *plop* it fell out among the last of the glitter dust, the small, small box. Sure enough, a box of matches that originated from the nightclub the Running Kangaroo, which they had visited many times at the Austrian ski resort where Lorelei Lindberg and the Islander and Sandra (the little silk dog) had spent their honeymoon, their seventh, eighth, ninth . . . and it just happened to be one of the very finest examples in Sandra's matchbox collection (yes, she collected matchboxes too). Not long ago when the Islander, during the planning of the birthday surprise, had asked his daughter to get out her collection and pick out a really nice box, he was the one who had laid eyes on it.

"Ha-ha!" Lorelei Lindberg yelled and pushed out the box. "A diamond," she repeated, certain of victory. She liked guessing what presents she was going to get, and for the most part she was usually right.

But now it was no gemstone she had unwrapped from the soft, white cotton that Sandra had laid in the box as a bed, but a key. A completely ordinary key, a Medeco.

"What's this? Where does this go?" she asked a bit hesitantly, a bit nonplussed, but yet not exaggerated. There were, after all, so many fun boxes and drawers and cabinets that had locks in them where such a small, phenomenal, as-ordinary-as-could-be key could fit.

"Get dressed now!" The Islander tore the quilt off of the bed where Sandra was still lying. "Both of you! We're going!"

"I burned my arm!" Sandra whined slowly, but of course there was no one who had time to notice her wailing now.

Out to the car with all of them, the Islander behind the wheel, they drive off.

That was how they came to the District. That was how they came to the house in the darker part of the woods.

Because the house. It became an anomaly. It was built in the darker part of the woods, in the District behind the woods on a piece of property that lay by a shallow, muddy marsh, and only in his wildest dreams, which the Islander sometimes could be good at when things were getting out of hand at work, could he call it a beachfront property—though it had been sold as one.

On the outside, the house was square, a rectangle in grayish-white brick and cement. It had a flat roof that was bordered by a wide copper-colored edging, there were some porthole-shaped holes in the façade that were supposed to represent windows splat splat splat splat four in a row right under the border. But it was the staircase that was the most striking. About forty steps, twenty to twenty-five feet wide, in clean, gray cement. Crumbly, unbearable.

The Islander had stopped the car on the hill above the house, which was located in the glen next to the swampy marsh, just before he let it roll down the road that led up to the stairs. And from that perspective, up on the hill, it looked like the entire house was a staircase. A stairway hanging in the air, leading to nothing.

"A staircase up to heaven," the Islander said to Lorelei Lindberg in the car while they were still on the hill. "This is where we're going to live." He added, just as if it was not enough already: "Everything is yours, Lorelei Lindberg. Just yours." Only then did he ease on the brakes and let the car roll down the hill.

Lorelei Lindberg was silent, completely silent. She stepped out of the car, she stood next to the lowest part of the house, she looked up. She looked at the long, tall gray stairs. Then she looked around. She looked at the Islander, at Sandra. There was no one else there in the woods, but still it was as if Lorelei Lindberg had looked around like someone who was surrounded by an audience of thousands. Like someone, to borrow an expression from Doris Flinkenberg who comes into the story quite soon, *on the big glitter scene*. But for once it was not about finding an outlet for an extreme need to make a spectacle, but to, well what? To save face? In that case, for whom?

For herself. To hide her own confusion in the presence of herself. How she was taken unawares. *My dream, did it look like this?* Then it was easier if you were playing a role like someone who is performing on stage, in the beam of the floodlights, in the presence of a million faceless faces in the dark.

Lorelei Lindberg said, "Fascinating." Her voice was flat and toneless the first time she said it. Then she said "fascinating" a second time, a few seconds later. The second time she had already gotten a tiny bit of color in her voice, even if which color, which mood, was something you could not determine for sure and maybe she could not either.

And Sandra looked around. She looked at the house, the copse, and the marsh. The Nameless Marsh, so small and petty that, as it would turn out, it did not have a name on Bencku's maps. Though it was winter she could still vividly imagine the many different kinds of insects that would come to live around the house. Spiders, different kinds of *creepy-crawlies*—just the word caused shivers to run down her back. Mosquitoes, ordinary ones as well as the special kind of bullymosquitoes that seemed to exist only at the Nameless Marsh and nowhere else in the world. Small, so small, that they could barely be seen but still capable of leaving four-inch-wide pimples on your skin if they were able to bite you. Thankfully Sandra's skin type was the bloodless kind, the kind of skin mosquitoes do not like. Super-sized rainbow flies. Beetles. Lots of beetles. Beetles with hard shells, clicking beetles, flying beetles . . .

The Islander had taken off his dark sunglasses. Now he held his hand out to Sandra, who was so engrossed in her own thoughts that she was not able to get away in time. *Gooberhead, didn't he understand anything?* Obviously not. The Islander's hand landed on her shoulder and started clapping it. Pat pat pat. This was the way he wanted it: *demonstratively conspiratorial.* Now he would show Lorelei Lindberg that there had definitely been two of them involved in this. The entire rest of the family. He and their daughter, Sandra Wärn.

But Lorelei Lindberg did not see them, not then. She was looking up, still. And she started walking up the stairs, step by step. After five or six steps she turned around for the first time and said, looking behind at her husband and at her daughter, with a voice that really was not hers, hesitating, veiled:

"And you've kept this a secret from me?" Took a few more steps and when she turned around for the second time she turned not only toward them, the family members present, but to the entirety of her imaginary audience *on the big glitter scene.*

"So this was the surprise," she said. "Fascinating." One's dream: Had it looked like this? Was this really what she had meant?

A stairway to nothing.

But so again, aware of the thousands of pairs of eyes that were watching in her imagination, but aimed at only one in the entire world, she said, with a voice that they had never heard her use before. It was thin and childish, but so honest and so fragile. She said:

"Thank you."

And those tiny, tiny words, which were not meant ironically at all, marked at the same time, in a creepy way, the end of her marriage to the Islander.

Later did she turn toward all of the others:

"I've never gotten a house from anyone. What do you say? You have to say: Thank you."

And she took the remaining steps sideways, tottered and almost lost her balance so that she had to steady herself on the outside wall and then she happened to touch the doorbell, which started ringing—or playing—its light-hearted alpine tune in march time. *Nach Erwald und die Sonne. Schnapps, Karappff. Bier. Bier.* For a moment the melody divided the compact silence in the woods.

Lorelei Lindberg just stared at the clock, frightened, as if she had seen a ghost. The Islander started laughing. Lorelei Lindberg cast a quick glance at him again and one moment it was as though it was possible to discern something so unthinkable as fear in her otherwise mischievous eyes.

Fear for her life.

Regardless, the moment was quickly over because later Lorelei Lindberg broke out into a rippling laughter that welled out into the quiet world that surrounded her. And then, in that moment, Sandra was one hundred percent convinced that her mother was playing a role for all she was worth. *That she was on the glitter scene again.* But now the performance did nothing. The main thing was that everything was fairly normal again.

The Islander and Lorelei Lindberg laughed. That was also normal. But it was not fun. It was just sad. All of this was so desperately depressingly saddeningly inscrutably sad.

The music stopped playing. It became quiet again.

Lorelei Lindberg, at the top of the landing, put the key in the lock, opened the door, and walked into the house.

. . .

"Everything is yours," the Islander whispered again at the foot of the stairs. His voice was thick, he was moved by Lorelei Lindberg, moved by himself, moved by their love. Now he let go of his daughter and started following his wife up the long, long staircase, like someone hypnotized.

"A staircase to heaven," he whispered. "Everything is yours."

This long, long midmorning and the girl was still on the stairs, still below the house, still on her way up. Now Lorelei Lindberg and the Islander could be heard from inside the house, they sounded like they always did again. "Interesting," Lorelei Lindberg said, that was what you heard, "interesting." The front door was ajar, the horrible bell had stopped playing, the metal chains with the pinecones in the forest on the ends were still swinging back and forth, hitting the brick wall, *dong, dong, dong.* In other words, it was quiet otherwise. Desolate. Not a gust of wind through the trees. The type of silence that does not exist anywhere else but by the house in the darker part of the woods, by the Nameless Marsh: Sandra would get used to it, she would even learn to love it, but now it was the first time she experienced it and it was mostly strange, as if there lay a quiet threat in it. Was it the calm before the storm? Or the calm in the eye of the storm?

Eye. Then she felt it on her back again. Maybe she had been feeling it for a while already, but she became aware of it now when she was alone outside the house. She turned around, had to force herself to do so because actually she really did not want to turn around at all, actually she wanted everything to just be normal.

That was when she saw him.

He was standing at the edge of the wood, in a glade on the right side, between the first higher branches of the wood, next to a rock. A boy maybe fifteen years old, maybe a little older—tall, skinny, wearing a brown jacket and blue farmer's pants. But the eyes. They were small and penetrating and they were looking, maybe they had done so a good while already, straight at her.

And she looked back, she forced herself to see. But he did not turn away either, not an inch. And when she had stared at him for a while she suddenly became scared for real, turned around and rushed head over heels up the stairs into the house.

But once inside she did not stay with the adults on the upper floor; instead, with her heart pounding, still in a state, she continued straight down to the basement. As though led by an impulse that was, strangely enough, calming. Straight down the stairs at the other end of the narrow corridor that started by the entrance, and yes, it was dark in there, the small aperture windows in the rooms, which lined the corridor with the beige wall-to-wall carpet, were even smaller than they seemed when you looked at them from the outside. The stairs were a spiral staircase, modern, one with slits between the steps and large spaces between the posts in the railing.

It was brighter on the lower level. That was due to the large panorama window, there was glass almost from floor to ceiling and for the most part it made up the entire wall on the back of the house that faced the marsh. Right now the window was so stained with dirt from the construction that you could see nothing through it. Later toward the spring and summer tall ferns and other overgrowth would burst forth from the ground and form a high and impenetrable jungle on the outside. But at certain times during the year, falls, winters, springs, it would be relatively light and very open down there.

Most of the furnishings on the ground floor were rather half finished, only the sauna area and the dressing room and the den, which was called the "rec room" in the house in the darker part, were ready to be used. But all of that, that was secondary and that was not what the girl was drawn to, but to the hole in the ground that in the future would be tiled in order to become a swimming pool. Still just a raw, black hole in the ground, foul smelling and rather damp. The girl stood at the edge of this hole and looked down into the darkness of the earth. And it suddenly bewitched her, the hole, the silence, the house itself, everything.

The voices from the upper floor, Mom, Dad, disappeared again. And Sandra immediately understood, completely calm and without drama, that she was going to stay here. That the house in the darker part of the woods was hers, *but not like a possession.*

Like a destiny.

So whether or not she got on well was a trifling matter, just like anything she thought. Because this was about necessity, the inevitable.

Here comes the night. So cold, so roaring, so wonderful.

And like a lightning bolt in her head she saw the following with her inner eye: she saw two girls in a swimming pool without water, playing on the green-tiled bottom among silk chiffon, silk satin, and silk georgette. And among all other things, which they would have so many of in their bags. Two backpackgirls among all of their things, the contents spread all over the bottom of the pool, mixed together and with the fabrics. Sandra's scrapbooks, Jayne Mansfield's dead dog, Lupe Velez's head in a toilet bowl, and so on, and Doris with all of her old loose issues of *True Crimes. The midwife's assistant Ingegerd, lacking moral scruples, and the nine incubator babies in her hands. He killed his lover with fifteen hammer strikes to the head.* Young love and sudden, violent death. And the Eddie-things, the story about the American girl, Eddie de Wire.

Death's spell at a young age. And pang. Sandra also saw how Doris shot the doorbell at the entrance to the house in the darker part to pieces that last summer when everything ended. The last year the last summer the last month the last last last before that moment when the summer has had enough of you and wants to get rid of you for good.

"Yet every wave burns like blood and gold, but the night soon will claim what is owed," which were the words of a song that played in Doris Flinkenberg's cassette player.

And also, a ways away from the house, in the bushes, an ill-humored one. The boy, always the boy. The same boy as before, at a proper distance, staring at the house as though he was convinced that it would decompose or sink down into the ground like Venice as a result of the power in his eyes when he looked at it.

"Disappear. Down into the ground. Sink."

But alone, she would be and continue to be a while longer, all the way until that day when Doris Flinkenberg got into the house and into Sandra Stigmata Princess of the Thousand Rooms (furnished with aperture windows, almost without oxygen).

She, the princess, who would nevertheless cease to exist in just that moment when Doris Flinkenberg started asking her stupid questions that she would answer before you had a chance to open your mouth.

"What are your hobbies? Mine are crossword puzzles, listening to music, and *True Crimes*."

"I don't know," Sandra would answer, but carefully, also because she was afraid of saying the wrong thing. "Though I don't have anything against firing rifles."

The house on the inside.
Sandra's room. The kitchen. The parlor. The small corridor.
The Closet.
The pool without water.

. . .

Above all the fact that the house was a work of hatred.

The Black Sheep in Little Bombay.
When they came in he was lying on the sofa in the back room snoring.
He sat up.
A shiny white Jaguar.
A red raincoat.

Little Bombay.
At first he was a threat.
On the other hand Lorelei Lindberg was happy when he showed up.
After the first surprise.
On the other hand she was also happy when he left.
So it was ambivalent.

He was lying, sleeping in the boutique when they came there one morning.
He had opened the door with his own key, why not, he was the landlord.

"What do you think of the house?"
"I thought I would show you what your dreams look like."
"Filled with nothing on the inside."
"I know WHERE they speak like that."

"A matchstick house for matchstick people. Have you thought about that? That it's about fitting into that shape?"
Asked the Black Sheep in Little Bombay, he spoke only to her—it was as if the silk dog didn't exist.
Huddled over her water bowl, under the table, and heard.
In Little Bombay, with all of the fabrics.

Lorelei Lindberg. Pins fell out of her mouth. Ping. Ping.
Pins with glass heads in different colors.
And the dog, she picked them up.

But Lorelei didn't ask her to help because her eyes were so bad.
Not that time.
"It's never easy to fall into the hands of the living God . . ."
"GOD?"

"You know," the Black Sheep explained to Lorelei Lindberg many times, "the game where the cat plays with the mouse until it gets bored. And becomes a light morsel to chew up."

"It's not a game. It's serious. It just looks that way."

"Exactly. That was what I was going to get to. We were two brothers. We had two cats. One's cat and the other's cat . . . but only one mouse came up out of the hole. And the mouse, that was you."

Doris Flinkenberg. In the beginning she ran away from her. The strange, slightly plump girl who sometimes used to follow her from the bus stop where she got off by the main country road when she came from the school in the city by the sea. Sandra knew who it was of course, one Doris Flinkenberg, who lived a bit closer to the capes.

She did not want to play with her.

So she ran away. And she ran fast. She held the girls' record in the sixty-yard dash at school, a talent for running that surprised even herself. So she certainly got away from the other girl, there was no question about that.

But the other girl, Doris Flinkenberg, she ran after. It was rather comical but also humiliating, for both of them.

And up the stairs to the house in the darker part, key in the lock, door open, into safety. Quickly close the door and stand inside the door and take a breather.

Quiet. Everywhere. Quiet like it could be only in the house in the darker part.

Until the doorbell started playing.

Nach Erwald und die Sonne. And playing. The stupid melody, over and over again.

CAN'T SHE GO AWAY?

Until Lorelei Lindberg, if she was home, came out into the dark, narrow corridor.

"Why don't you open?"

Sandra shook her head.

"Oh, you don't want to?" Lorelei Lindberg just said then and walked off.

Farther into the house. And Sandra followed her.

Much later. One Saturday morning in the house in the darker part Sandra woke up late, as she had a habit of doing when it was not a school day and she could sleep as long as she wanted to, but with the distinct feeling that something special was going to happen just this day. With sensual pleasure she stretched in the marital bed, which was hers now. It had been a few months since the marriage between Lorelei Lindberg and the Islander had ended, and the bed, which had been moved into Sandra's room some time before the absolute end, was still standing there where it had been placed one time after the last waves of passion in anger. It took up almost all of the space in the room, but the arrangement looked as though it would become permanent as the bed was undeniably comfortable. But now, in other words Saturday morning, the beginning of what appeared to be a normal day: the Islander at work in the world of business, and Sandra in her bathrobe, a kimono in silk brocade that smelled faintly of Little Bombay still a few months after the boutique had been cleared out. Through the whole day if she wanted. Saturday, the best day of the week. That plus an entire Sunday before it was time to return to the French School, which Sandra was still attending. And she knew as soon as she woke up that now, this Saturday, something new and interesting would happen.

She got out of bed filled with expectation, cast a glance out the window. No, then it was not the weather that was going to surprise her. A normal November day, gray and low, not to mention unusually gloomy, especially right here in the darker part where, at a certain distance, the high water in the Nameless Marsh this time of year made the house look as though it was floating around among reeds and other rotten vegetation. But it was not at all dangerous, soon the ground would be covered with snow, merciful snow. Sandra shoved her feet into her morning slippers with white muffs on top and three-inch heels (she had gotten them from her mother because they were too small and uncomfortable for her) and pulled her bathrobe a bit tighter, and then it happened, that which still happened during contact with the fabrics, that it ran through her, Little Bombay.

Lorelei Lindberg. *Mom.* Whom she sometimes found herself missing so much it felt like stabbing pains in her stomach. A longing that when it could not be stopped had to have a story created around it so that it could be somewhat overcome. And Sandra had created one in her imagination, which she could find herself in when she was alone and the mood was right. She was the child of the knife thrower in the story. A circus girl whose mother succumbed to a deadly illness (a version that she later changed to: fell down from the high wire one rainy circus evening in a provincial hole where no one went to the circus anymore because everyone only wanted to stay inside and watch television; only a few people saw her crash into the asphalt, the story was true, it was acrobat Rosita Montis's fate) and she was thus the little daughter who became her father's, the knife thrower's, assistant at a very young age. The temperamental, unpredictable, and otherwise also crazy father, but after the mother's passing, practically insane with grief, she allowed knives to be thrown at her every night in the extremely poorly visited circus tent they traveled with from place to place to place.

In certain moments that was what it was like for Sandra to be without her mother, to miss Lorelei Lindberg. But sometimes, when she was in another mood, missing her mother did not call forth strong emotions, occasionally none at all.

But an end to the fantasizing. Now Sandra went out into the narrow corridor that led to the kitchen and then she saw that the door to the basement stairs was open. Not ajar, but wide open. She stopped and cocked her ears. Could strange sounds not be heard from the basement?

Her heart started pounding, the adrenaline shot up into her temples. She was scared, but still at the same time it was a bit strange because the feeling of expectation did not leave her. The door to the basement usually was not open. It was not supposed to be. It was strictly forbidden. Ever since Sandra and the Islander had become alone in the house in the darker part of the woods the Islander was extremely careful about the fact that the basement door should be kept closed, and preferably locked at night. Under no circumstances was it allowed to be open like now.

"I can't afford to lose both of you," the Islander had sniffled by the pool without water where Sandra would sometimes play on the finished tiled bottom, also before Doris Flinkenberg. Sandra had given no response to that, just squeezed her eyes shut and tried not to hear, but she wished so desperately that everything would go back to the way it was.

The reason the door to the basement stairs should be closed was moreover Sandra herself. She had said that she walked in her sleep. It was not true, rather something she had made up a long time ago when a lie like that was really needed. It had been during the last turbulent time while Lorelei Lindberg was still in the house and a lot of messing around and fighting grew worse, fights without reconciliation after, fights that were gradually fought without thinking about reconciliation and Lorelei Lindberg who fell down the long staircase and came to lie on the ground below like a dead person, but got up again like a cat with nine lives. The bed was moved into Sandra's room and the adults themselves slept, when they did that at all, in different places in the house, impossible places, for example one in the Closet, the other on the sofa in the rec room. If you were Sandra on the sidelines, it had been a matter of paying attention then. To be able to move between different places sort of legitimately, but not like a grass snake. And Sandra had seen the bit about her walking in her sleep as a white lie. And after everything, when it became calm again, after Lorelei Lindberg, the lie had remained hanging there anyway and it started living its own life and before you knew what was happening it had become harder to untangle yourself from it than to let it remain hanging, as it was. And besides, it probably would not have been a good idea to start explaining too much about this or that to the Islander. After Lorelei Lindberg the Islander was in no shape for any explanations or protests, either his own or anyone else's. He was fragile like porcelain that could at the slightest movement fall to the floor and break into a thousand priceless pieces. A thousand small grainy pieces: due to the damp, everything inside the house was almost wet and porous, pieces, not even proper fragments. Piece it together later. Oh no. She could not afford that either. Not in the position they found themselves in now after Lorelei Lindberg and the Islander. Just the two of them, no one else but the two of them.

The Islander crying at the side of the pool, it had been awkward and terrifying. Sandra had sat on the bottom of the pool among her things, the fabrics, the scrapbooks, the dress-up clothes, and wished she was a thousand miles away.

And so, when he disappeared into the rec room in order to continue falling apart there, she really did not want to follow him in order to provide hugs or comfort or the like. In the beginning he had stayed there for many days and nights, with his mixed drinks or his pure schnapps, talking out loud to himself sometimes, strange sentences that were horrid not only because of the meaning of the individual words (he talked a lot of crap) but also because there was no point to them, not the slightest. Words and sentences here and there. "I'm singing in the rain," the Islander hummed. "Our love was a continental affair, he came in a white Jaguar." The like. The last-mentioned song certainly would not become a better song by being played over and over again also by Doris Flinkenberg in her spinning radio cassette player of the brand Poppy, manufactured in the GDR. "Really great song this one," Doris would say but Sandra would just roll her eyes. It would be a point, one of the few in any case to begin with, on which Doris and Sandra would not be in agreement.

The Islander in the rec room, Sandra in the pool without water, hands over her ears, making herself as small as possible, virtually insignificant. The last thing she wanted was to go into the rec room and provide comfort or hugs or the like, which one often did on television when family catastrophes took place. Hug and jug, as if anything at all would become better from it.

Sandra's only wish during a long period of time had been that the Islander would become normal again. And start doing normal things like, for example, polish his rifle.

"Hey. You want to go and do some shooting?"

One day in October, when the leaves had fallen and it was clear and cold in the world outside the great panorama window again, it had happened. Normalcy was back, the Islander had suddenly been there at the edge of the pool again fully dressed and newly shaved looking down at her. He had the rifle too and pointed it at her but she had not been scared at all, it was just a game after all. She had immediately understood that instinctively, an eagerly awaited mood that she recognized especially because nothing had happened in the house for a long time. And how she had longed for it during the time in between. Longed for monkey magic, tricks, shouting, anything.

And yes then. Of course! Sandra had jumped up in the air like a bouncing ball and dropped everything she had been doing, all her solitary stupid playing on the bottom of the pool. Oh, how she was sick and tired of it.

"Yes," she had answered with unusual determination. "It's about time I learn how to shoot a rifle too."

Then she and the Islander had gone to the shooting range together and there she learned to handle, in any case be of assistance with, pistols and rifles. And to her own surprise too, she noticed that she liked shooting, even if she was no fast learner. Unlike, for example, Doris Flinkenberg who in a short time sometime later would turn into a master markswoman. But Sandra was also surprised by how much she liked the shooting range itself, being there. That was actually the main thing, what fascinated her most of all. The special mood of concentration, silence, and resoluteness that existed there. Its own world.

The Islander's world. Her father's own world.

Like Little Bombay, the fabrics and the telephone calls and the particular music (the banana record was never brought to the house in the darker part of the woods), everything that had been Lorelei Lindberg's world. And it was strange, but that is the way it was: in the grand passion these two worlds had been incompatible.

It was in and of itself a rather general insight, that passion is often difficult to merge with an ordinary everyday life. But another thing, which was more important and harder to understand and accept, a helplessness, it was only when the contracting parties in the great passion had been separated that you could see them as they were in their respective worlds. That it was then that you could get to know them.

When Lorelei Lindberg was still there the Islander had not fired at the shooting range or hunted in the woods or sailed the seven seas like he loved to. Nor had he devoted himself wholeheartedly to that playboy lifestyle in the international jet-setter's life that was one of his goals; when the passion had still been young he had explained to Lorelei Lindberg that he intended to do that. Mostly he had run around and made better and worse business deals, but with a concentration level significantly below the one he would have after Lorelei Lindberg. And Lorelei Lindberg and the fabrics, had she even liked them?

With respect to the playboy lifestyle, it was actually after Lorelei Lindberg that the Islander to some degree would make a reality out of his ambitions in that area. In any case later in the summers with the women in the house on the First Cape and during the hunting season in the house in the darker part of the woods. There would be many women around him then, for example Bombshell Pinky Pink, the striptease dancer who made a philosophy out of striptease dancing—and it was actually Bombshell Pinky Pink whom the Islander and Sandra just seemed to happen to meet that first day when they were at the shooting range together, father and daughter, *pang pang pang*.

Not at the shooting range itself, but afterward. It was in the restaurant where they ate bloody beef, father and daughter across from each other at a window table for four. The place was half empty because it was still only early evening. Then, *PANG*. She had shown up, like an explosion. The Bombshell. And just like it had been an event. As if it had more or less not been written on her forehead (and on the Islander's as well for that matter) that this was a haphazard occurrence of the haphazard kind that was agreed upon beforehand.

"Excuse me?" So unforgettable even then, in her pink, very short spandex skirt, pink angora sweater with the low neck under which both large, round breasts were really popping out, glittering silver knee-high stretch boots that in some way got the white skin all the way up to the hemline to shine extra playfully but certainly so daintily because it was covered by only a thin membrane of nylon panty, which was noticeable only at a very close distance. Her big blond hair, it was actually enormous and teased, worse than Jayne Mansfield's even, but that was COOL. Just the right amount of cool and, yes, it was not exactly modest, or civilized, but it was the lovely and strangely delightful thing about it. "Excuse me?" she said in other words. "But is this seat taken?"

Bombshell Pinky Pink with her harsh but soft teenage girl's voice, a bit drawling as if some chewing gum had been forgotten in her mouth, sort of an eternal chewing gum that reminded you of another time (and that was the point), a younger, happier, and more innocent one. Quite as if it were an occurrence as said. The Islander had pretended to be surprised but politely invited her to sit down. This obvious spectacle performed for Sandra had not mattered to the girl. She would have enjoyed it in any case. And everyone had enjoyed it. Pinky had sat down at the table and the Islander had been in an excellent mood again. *A man has to do what he has to do* the Islander had been saying over and over again between the verses in the so-called conversation, which was about water and wind and the latest complications in an adult TV series called *Peyton Place*, nothing more than that, but the evening had been a complete success anyway, the first successful evening in ages and Sandra had also been cheerful and in some way eternally grateful to Pinky. Then the Islander had gotten drunk so it was Bombshell Pinky Pink who had to be the chauffeur in the car the whole way from the city by the sea to the house in the darker part.

Bombshell Pinky Pink on the large stairs in the house in the darker part of the woods. How she had run up the many steps like a happy child, up and down, up and down, taken striptease-dancing steps and the like so that you rolled your eyes and of course it had been silly and stupid but in some way like a, forgetting about everything else, sudden great delightful and silly laugh in the middle of the horrible, depressing world.

All of it had also had an effect on the Islander, he was satisfied and had quickly pulled the bombshell into the house with him.

But the fractured face of a harelip is truly dreadful.

Though Sandra had time to make a fool of herself again, at morning tea. She said something, sort of in passing, and almost managed to get the Bombshell to cry. Tears had gathered in Pinky's eyes and Pinky had nervously scraped the tabletop with her inch-long pink nails.

"I'm not a whore," the Bombshell said to her. "My profession is that of a striptease dancer."

And Sandra, she regretted it later of course.

But now, this novembersaturdaymorning a few weeks after the day at the shooting range, Sandra was standing on the beige wall-to-wall carpet in the upper corridor in the house in the darker part of the woods in her bloodred kimono with white butterflies and high-heeled morning slippers, listening. Yes. Then she slowly slowly crept toward the drab opening to the basement stairs. Carefully stepped out onto the spiral staircase, as soundlessly as she possibly could, pressed herself against the white plastered wall like a terrified woman on the cover of an old detective novel, and shuffled downward. The adrenaline continued to rush to her head, like at the shooting range in the moment before you fired your shot. There was something down there. Or someone.

Because Sandra had already heard something similar before. Quite simply the sound of someone lying and sleeping. Someone's deep, heavy breaths, but in such a high decibel that it sounded as though it could have been a giant or something of the like. A giant who snored, driving his hogs to the market.

Sandra had never heard anything like it. It was absolutely clear it was no one in the family. Only the Islander's brother, the Black Sheep, could snore like that. The Black Sheep (despite the fact that he had never finished his architect studies, had designed the house in the darker part of the woods, though that hardly had anything to do with the situation at hand) could snore so that the walls literally vibrated. Once when she and Lorelei Lindberg had come to Little Bombay, also a Saturday, he had been lying on the sofa in the back room of the boutique, snoring.

But that had, which was also very obvious now, been more adult noises. Sandra had immediately understood that the sound coming from the pool was not an adult sound but that of a child. A child of some sort, possibly a giant giantchild. *A mammoth child* flew through Sandra's head and oh how Doris Flinkenberg would laugh when Sandra described it to her afterward.

And sure enough. The strangest of the strange. A person was lying down there on the bottom of the pool, sleeping. A small person, though not so small in size, but a child. The child had spread out her sleeping bag among all of the paper, newspapers, and fabrics in which she was now curled up and sleeping, and she was sleeping deeply. Snoring with her mouth open and as said it could definitely be heard. Though the sound level was also amplified by the fact that the sound was bouncing against the empty walls and echoed farther out into the emptiness of the whole pool area.

Who the child was. She was not hard to identify. No one other than the strange, persistent kid, Doris Flinkenberg.

Earlier Sandra had run away from her, but now, now it was something else, Sandra understood that right away. That it was time, the right time for the first meeting, one of the most important of all meetings in Sandra's entire life. Because now it was the most obvious thing in the world that Doris Flinkenberg should be there.

And a laughter bubbled forth in Sandra with a speed that almost surprised her. It was an exhilaration without equal, a happy mood of a kind she had never felt before, not in ages anyway. So, instead of calling her father at work or the police to complain or to call for help or just climbing down into the pool and waking the intruder—because it was clear that Doris Flinkenberg had broken into the house—Sandra Wärn remained standing at the side of the pool, so quiet, so quiet, and watched Doris Flinkenberg with devotion and curiosity, at the same time as she tried to figure out how she was going to wake Doris Flinkenberg in the most unforgettable way possible. And suddenly it was important. Not explicitly the part about making an impression but to sort of show who you were, like the opening of a game, and with emphasis. Mainly so that all the possibilities that existed in the game would be obvious. Not only who you were but also who you could be.

Sandra took a few steps forward so she was standing right in front of the sleeping Doris in the pool, the still wildly snoring Doris. She stretched out her index finger like a pistol and said with a loud and authoritative voice:

"*Pang!* You're dead! Time to wake up now!" In other words, she did not yell, just spoke a bit louder than normal. But still, she had barely uttered the words before Doris Flinkenberg sat straight up in her sleeping bag with a jerk and drowsy and frightened, she looked around with the gaze of a terrified animal. It was a look Sandra would never forget. In the future Sandra would often think about how Doris slept, it said so much about everything about Doris Flinkenberg.

Like a cat on tenterhooks even when deep in the deepest sleep. Which of course went together with what she was and which she gradually, mostly at the beginning of their acquaintance (what a word for the ever revolutionary!), would explain in detail upon detail: a child who early in life—before she was taken in at the cousin's house—had learned in some respects the world is, to put it bluntly, a hellish place, that adults cannot be depended on and they do not mind hurting you even though you are a small child who cannot defend yourself, that if you want to survive and live on in a somewhat acceptable way you have to be on your guard and protect yourself as best you can. There is no absolute security anywhere.

Doris Flinkenberg, the mistreated child. And she would pull down the waistband of her pants to prove it: disgusting red-brown marks on the side. "This is where she grilled me. Her, my marsh mama. Or. She tried."

But so, in the pool, Doris caught sight of Sandra and quickly recovered. Let out a bemused laugh with no trace of fear in it, almost the opposite: a big and daring laugh dazed with sleep, no excuses here and no explanations either.

"Do you think I look dead? Then you have a problem with your pistol."

And there would have been and should have been a lot of amusing responses for that. But suddenly Sandra could not come up with a single one; she had suddenly been overpowered again by both the joy over the fact that Doris Flinkenberg was really there but also by her own shyness, which had the habit of playing tricks on her in situations, so she was careful not to drag out the show but at the same time say what she felt was necessary to say now so that Doris would not disappear off somewhere.

"Get up now," she said. "You're probably hungry. Should we eat breakfast first?"

And then you could see how Doris Flinkenberg relaxed, and a big, daring smile appropriate for the situation had spread across her entire round face.

"I am extremely hungry," she said then in the cleanest and most articulate Swedish, as if she were reading a verse out loud at the end of school ceremonies, "terribly *Dorisly* hungry. I could eat a house."

"Come on then," Sandra said nonchalantly and started walking back up the stairs. And then for the sake of appearance Doris simply had to hurry to crawl out of her sleeping bag just as nonchalantly but with an eagerness that was difficult to conceal. But it did not matter. Because this was how it was supposed to be, both of them knew that.

And up in the kitchen it began in record time, it did not take more than maybe twenty minutes, the process through which Doris and Sandra got to know each other better and became best friends, inseparable. The one AND the other, everything.

And so it would be during the years that followed up until the point that Doris Flinkenberg, on a dark November day a lot like this November day when they met for the first time, walked up onto Lore Cliff, had the pistol (the real one) with her, held it up against her temple and pulled the trigger.

They did not drink Lapsang souchong for breakfast that first morning in the house in the darker part of the woods, the tea with the smoky taste that Sandra usually always had—she had also been very particular about that. If the right kind of tea was not in the house, if Dad—or Mom, while she was still living there—had for example forgotten to buy any, Sandra had stubbornly refused to eat breakfast at all.

"What's this?" Doris Flinkenberg shouted with horror when she took her first gulp from the mug Sandra had handed her. "Perfume? I said COFFEE!" Doris resolutely spit the mouthful of tea into the sink. "We always drink coffee in the cousin's house! Bencku wins pounds of it for us. At the lottery, in other words, he has such *screamingly funny* luck," Doris added, as if she had been reading out loud from her crossword puzzle book. "Though in games," she continued lightheartedly and did not notice Sandra flinch. Before Sandra met Doris Flinkenberg she did not know very much about the District and the people there except for a few things and one of them was, of course, that the boy in the woods and Bencku were one and the same. "You know of course who Bencku is? You've seen him haven't you? The idiot in the woods? We come from the same house if that's not clear already. The cousin's house. He's an adopted son there and me, I'm a foster daughter. Oh boy, Sandra, if you only knew: my real roots, they're definitely nothing to brag about." And when Doris said that she rolled her eyes in the way that Sandra would gradually also learn was Doris-specific, and of course Doris mentioned a lot of things as she babbled along, things you wanted to stop at and ask more about (for example, the idiot in the woods, whose name was Bengt) but at the same time in just that moment, the first minutes when they were getting to know each other, it was unnecessary. "Now you have to tell everything about yourself," Doris Flinkenberg continued resolutely. "What are your hobbies? Mine are"—and here Doris paused before she continued, reached for another sourdough sandwich with a Balkan sausage, which Sandra had set on the table on a plate between them, and kicked the leg of the kitchen table as if to provide rhythm and an expression to her words—"listening to music. Solving crossword puzzles. *True Crimes.*"

So Doris just talked and in the beginning it had been rather difficult to get a word in edgewise. But, Sandra realized when she was listening to Doris, it did not matter. She did not have a problem with it. And more than that, she understood again in this strange predestined way that this is what she had been waiting for for so long: Doris's talk, Doris being there, Doris—everything with Doris. That in some way this is what she had been going around waiting for most of her life.

"Hellooo! I asked a question! Is anyone home?"

"Hm," Sandra carefully answered. "I don't know but maybe fabrics. Certain kinds. Not all. And then I also quite like shooting with a pistol. Though I'm not terribly good at it."

And she had said that and then she did not even dare to look at Doris, instead she was busy listening to her own crazy sentences echoing craziness in the air between them. And she just had to change the topic, fast.

"But now it's my turn to ask some questions. How did you get in the house? And what are you doing here now anyway?"

Doris Flinkenberg left the first question hanging, but on the other hand she spent a lot of time answering the other one in great detail. The evening before, she had suddenly gotten the idea that she could not stand one more moment in the cousin's house, that it was time to run away from there. That purpose hit her like a bolt of lightning, she explained: to just leave and never come back. So Doris had packed her backpack and left the cousin's house with her sleeping bag under her arm. Then she walked far away, along the road and on different paths. But while she had been walking there in her thin outdoor coat against the wind, in the cold, the irritability slowly disappeared and she had rather quickly started thinking about other things as well, like, for example, had she really taken everything she needed for the rest of her life, for example, she had forgotten the radio cassette player and all of the cassettes. So after not such a long time there on the road she had come to her senses again and turned back. But it had been about time for her to regret it because she had gotten quite a way away from the cousin's house, far too far, actually, to be able to make it the whole way back.

That was how she had arrived at the house in the darker part of the woods.

It had been closest then. You did not know for sure if she was speaking the truth or not, most likely not, all of it was quite absurd, not least with respect to the house in the darker part being where it was, not close to anything at all. In addition to everything else, everything in the whole District, the whole world just about. And there was really only one real road plus a few other paths in the woods that led there.

But whoever pays attention to such details now is an idiot. There was, for Sandra, as said, so many other things that were more important. This was the meeting of soul mates and it was a feeling that Sandra would never, for the rest of her entire life, experience so intensely. It could certainly be imitated but never recreated. There would only be this remarkable, one hundred percent harmonization with Doris Flinkenberg. Which only the two of them saw and were conscious of. Already from the beginning, even while they were young like now, and were not even capable of carrying on a sensible conversation.

And this harmonization, it had nothing to do with any external features. There were any number of differences. Sandra was, for example, at this point in time, small and skinny, had lanky, light-colored hair, and wore headgear at night. Again, Doris was rather round and the color of the main country road, not just her hair but sort of all over too. And she had what you could call an overbite. And these ENORMOUS feet, size nine or ten.

And always wearing the same large, leather boots.

"And of course I'm crazy for wanting to run away from the family I now have the privilege of being a member of," said Doris Flinkenberg who, after many digressions, had finally reached the moral of the story. "I mean the cousin's house. And the cousin's mama. Whom I love more than the earth, more than anything.

"My dear, dear foster mother. Oh boy, Sandra, you wouldn't know what rabble I originate from, biologically speaking. Marsh mom and marsh dad. Sandra, I'm probably," Doris whispered importantly, "a proper bastard."

And Doris had laughed as if liberated but then later she became hesitant and in her thoughts she went back to the cousin's mama.

"Though she's probably quite worried now, the cousin's mama. The idea wasn't to fall asleep down there in your swimming pool. The idea was just to rest."

And *prrrt*. Was that the sound of a telephone cutting through the air?

And it was the cousin's mama of course, who was wondering where Doris was.

"But now we have to hurry if we're going to have time to play before she comes here," Doris said when she had hung up the phone. "I mean. I was probably thinking about playing later too. But it's not exactly the same thing. Should we go down to the basement again?"

And Doris might as well have asked, "Will you marry me?" because Sandra would have answered yes all the same.

"Yes," Sandra said thus. "Yes."

And following Doris's lead the girls returned to the basement and crawled down into the swimming pool without water. Doris caught sight of Sandra's little backpack.

"So you're also a girl with a backpack. Open yours and I'll open mine and then we'll see."

And it was Doris with a backpack and Sandra with a backpack: two backpackgirls who emptied out the contents of their bags on the green-tiled bottom of the swimming pool so that everything mixed together. So that new connections arose and new, unexpected combinations. The one with the other, ideas, whims, big and small.

In Sandra's backpack there were, for example, strips with silk samples that came from Little Bombay, the scrapbooks, there like Jayne Mansfield's dead dog, Lupe Velez, and Patricia in the Blood Woods, and all of those living their own lives between the worn, blue covers of three-ring binders. There were also some matchstick boxes from hotels and nightclubs from the jet-setter's life, a plastic die with a lot of silver confetti inside. In Doris's backpack, which was not nearly as expensive as Sandra's and much smaller, there were cassettes with a lot of *Lasting Love Songs for Moonstruck Lovers* (Doris's intolerable music, her favorite), a few copies of *True Crimes* (a magazine), a few books, *Kitty Solves Another Mystery*, *The Woman's Role in Love Life*, and *The Crossword Book*, as well as a letter from the English royal house, addressed to B. Flinkenberg, Saabvägen. In that letter it said in English, Doris narrated at great length, that Prince Andrew, whom she had tried to start a pen pal exchange with, was reluctant to correspond with anyone who was not part of the family, or was, as it also in some way said, "comparable with." And so on.

The one backpack and the other backpack and everything inside them, games and stories, stories and games, games that were stories, would occupy Doris and Sandra for many, many years. And would be elevated, little by little, into another reality.

And beyond, almost into adulthood.

But now, for the time being, a relatively long time also, everything was still just fun. A joy and a humor that also spread to the others, those who were not directly involved.

The cousin's mama, for example, when she showed up at the house in the darker part a bit later that same day, she could not help but become infected by the happy mood down there in the pool without water. She became so happy that she also wanted to stay, so happy that she looked around and saw how dusty everything was. And when the Islander and Bombshell Pinky Pink showed up a little while later, a big cleanup was under way in the house in the darker part of the woods.

It also made the Islander happy, and he instantly hired the cousin's mama as the permanent housecleaner in the house in the darker part of the woods. This was, parenthetically speaking, the beginning of Four Mops and a Dustpan, the cleaning company that would gradually make the cousin's mama into a real businesswoman.

But Pinky, she rushed straight down to the basement and the pool without water and let out a childish yell.

"I want to play too!" she yelled and climbed down to the girls in the pool. And she became so eager that her breasts almost popped out over the edge of her tight, glittery top and she stumbled in the long silk that Doris, the Lady of the Harem, had wrapped herself in.

"Good day," Doris Flinkenberg said and held her hand out to Pinky.

"This is Bombshell Pinky Pink," Sandra said politely and now she wanted to be careful about not hurting Pinky again and therefore presenting her in a dignified way. "Profession: striptease dancer."

But then Pinky looked at Sandra again haughtily.

"Dad's girlfriend. And nothing else."

"But striptease," Doris urbanely got stuck on. "So interesting. It must be a truly demanding job. Tell me more."

And that became the start of a group project that Doris Flinkenberg would carry out in school without a group: Profession: striptease dancer. It was a project that later on would cause Doris Flinkenberg to be banned eternally from being in the same homeroom as Sandra Wärn who would rather soon transfer from the French School to the very ordinary junior high school up in the town center.

And this is how it was, just about anyway, when Sandra and Doris met, became friends and playmates. Moreover the best of playmates, in their very own little world.

They would have many games, long games. And no outsider would understand a bit of it.

But some of the games would deviate, regardless. There would be two big games, two main ones. One would be Sandra's game, the one founded on her life story. The other would be Doris's game, and it would not exactly be based on Doris's life, but on something rather close to it. Something that had happened in the District once. A terrible story.

The games would not be played at the same time, but in turn. The first game would be the Lorelei Lindberg and Heintz-Gurt game, the other would be called the Mystery with the American Girl.

And everything would be based on reality. Everything had to be true.

The first game, the Lorelei and Heintz-Gurt game, it started like this:

"And where is your mom then?" Doris Flinkenberg asked Sandra another day, one of the very first days they were together in the house in the darker part of the woods. They were in the kitchen then, eating a snack—Doris Flinkenberg always needed to eat snacks—in dress-up clothes from another game, an old game, which was already starting to get a bit boring.

"What happened?"

"There was someone who came and got her," Sandra answered vaguely.

"An angel?" Doris Flinkenberg asked expectantly.

"Hm," Sandra said ambiguously.

"An angel of death?" Doris added helpfully. "Liz Maalamaa?"

"Shh!" could be heard from the basement stairs where the cousin's mama was busy polishing the steps shiny and smooth again, shinier and smoother than they had ever been when Lorelei Lindberg lived there.

"It's forbidden to eavesdrop!" Doris Flinkenberg yelled toward the stairs. "She would so very much like to listen," Doris whispered, giggling so only Sandra would hear.

"I'm going to close the door NOW because this only concerns four ears all together," Sandra called in turn loud and clear so it echoed through the house. And even locked the door from the inside in order to guarantee peace and seclusion.

And so the game started. And it started like all of the best games, with a rather long story.

"He came and got her," Sandra began softly, with what she had never told anyone before and would never tell anyone else, ever. That which was so private that Doris Flinkenberg was the only one in the wide world who would get to take part in. "From here. In a helicopter. It landed on the roof."

"Who? Her lover?" Doris caught on immediately.

"Quiet now," Sandra said impatiently. "Don't interrupt. Otherwise you won't get to hear anything. But yes, her lover. You can also look at it that way. And he was secret, of course. Because that's what lovers usually are. But they had known each other for many years. They met at a nightclub in the Alps while living the jet-setters' life, the one that was called the Running Kangaroo. Here's the mug in any case, it's from there. I've drunk hunter's tea from it, you know, tea with rum . . ."

"Have you been drunk?" Doris Flinkenberg fingered the mug on which a kangaroo was pictured and was now so affected that she started rolling her eyes again.

"Quiet now, I said." Sandra held up her hand. "Yes, of course. I saw it with my own eyes. That they met, in other words. I was there. It was before we moved here to the house in the darker part . . . We were quite the jet-setters then. Well, anyway. He picked her up from here. The roof on the house is so flat, it's incredibly easy to land on.

"It was one day in the middle of the heat wave, last year. You know what it can be like on a day like that . . . completely still. And quiet. So quiet. The only thing to be heard were the insects that were buzzing and creeping around on the ground. All of those strange creepy-crawlies found in the marshes around here. Bullymosquitoes and fern ticks, the ones that tick when they move. *Tick. Tick. Tick . . .*"

. . . And Doris had nodded in agreement while Sandra disappeared farther and farther into her story . . .

"And heels. Her heels. *Clomp. Clomp. Clomp.* That day. So nervous. So filled with restlessness. Heels that moved from upstairs to downstairs to the bedroom, from the kitchen to the bedroom to the Closet and back, and then down again. The pool section, walked around the pool. Round and around. You know, Doris, what it's like when you're waiting for someone. And that was what she was doing. Waiting. Though you did not know that until it was too late . . . down by the pool. And then *clink* . . . She had taken off the ring she had gotten from the Islander, it had a ruby the size of a tablespoon set in it. And it fell out of her hand and rolled down into the pool. And that was when she called for help. She called for me because there wasn't anyone else in the house right then. 'Sandra! I've dropped the ring in the pool and I don't have my contact lenses in! Sandra can you please come and help me look!'"

Sandra had probably heard Lorelei Lindberg calling for her, but she had pretended not to hear. Had not made her presence known in the slightest, instead she had snuck out of the house, run down the stairs to the grove next to the house where she had the habit of spending time—*which was the place of the evil eye, where the boy had the habit of being sometimes*—but of course she did not say a word about the boy to Doris Flinkenberg, it was too complicated. There was a rock that was good for hiding behind. And maybe it was then already that she heard the strange noise in the background for the first time even if it had not forced its way into her consciousness yet. The helicopter. A buzz in the back of her head . . .

And no. Of course it was not that she had not wanted to help Lorelei Lindberg look for the ring—or any kind of ill will that she could feel sometimes, she was not a nice child, not really . . . it was just that she did not have the energy to stay in the house. Lorelei Lindberg's anxiety was so immense it infected everything, there was no place where you could be left alone. And especially when the Islander was not home it became intensified, almost electric—and Little Bombay did not exist anymore. There was only this: Lorelei Lindberg looking out through the window at the overgrown marsh and sighing. Not one person— threw a glance at her little daughter—not a sensible person anywhere. One time when Lorelei Lindberg had looked at her like that Sandra had almost started crying, but that was earlier. She did not cry any longer; she was older now and there were no more tears.

And this day, just this day: Lorelei Lindberg in a neck brace and her head shaved. A few stitches were visible on the bare spot on her head of the type that in medical talk was called butterfly. She had fallen on the long stairs, that was a few days ago. The Islander had hit her so that she lost her balance, and she had fallen, fallen, and rolled down the many, many steps while the horrid doorbell played in the background the whole time: *Nach Erwald und die Sonne. Die Sonne. Die Sonne . . .*

But afterward, when the Islander had been so sad he just cried and cried—and Sandra had never seen her father cry before; it was rather unpleasant. But then he had left and come back home again and had the ring with the tablespoon-sized ruby with him.

. . . When the sound that Sandra had been hearing in the back of her head for a long time became stronger, gradually completely deafening and a great shadow had sunk down over the bright summer day, Sandra threw herself behind the rock next to the house. She did not believe her eyes: it was a helicopter and it was flying so low that it almost grasped the treetops with its horrible insectlike legs creating an air pressure that pressed the grass and ferns and all remaining overgrowth, which there was of course a multitude of, down, down toward the ground. Sandra herself, mute from fear in the presence of the incomprehensible, but her eyes just as wide open in the presence of the same, just stared at how the silver-black helicopter sank down toward the house and landed on its wide, flat roof.

At the same time, in another place, but not far away (but probably far enough), on a highway: the Islander was driving at least a hundred miles an hour in order to make it home. Suspicion had grasped hold of him: if the worst happened, then! Then he had to hurry! Now! He must not come too late, just could not! And he had floored it.

But already, at the house in the darker part of the woods: Lorelei Lindberg had come out on the roof. She was dressed entirely in white, a white dress, white scarf around her head. She stood there and called to the man wearing a pilot's cap with ear flaps and aviator glasses, leather jacket, boots, and light beige aviator pants, calling out as if to outdo the rumble of the helicopter—she had looked around and discovered her daughter Sandra, who had now stepped out from behind the rock where she had been hiding. The fear had left her in a heartbeat. Now she was standing there next to the rock, in case Lorelei Lindberg had happened to forget, like a reminder.

"*Das Mädchen*," Lorelei Lindberg called to the man, who was Heintz-Gurt, her secret lover, who had, in other words, come to take her away. "The girl," Sandra Wärn translated for Doris Flinkenberg. "In German." He was impatient to leave, he tried to push Lorelei toward the helicopter door—a scuffle almost arose up there on the roof of the house in the darker part.

"*Das Mädchen nicht! Nicht das Mädchen!*" he yelled back and looked at her as well. "Not the girl," Sandra translated for Doris Flinkenberg. "Not the girl at all, in German." For a moment both of them looked at the little girl, Lorelei Lindberg and Heintz-Gurt. The adults on the roof. The girl in the woods. A moment.

And then the moment was over. Lorelei climbed up into the helicopter and before disappearing inside completely, she turned around—of course, the classical—one last time and looked at the rock by the edge of the woods and then, in that microscopically short moment, it was only the two of them in the entire world.

In case she happened to forget . . .

She looked so helpless.

And then, when everything was over and it was too late, Sandra lifted her hand—it was heavy like lead—to wave to Lorelei Lindberg one last time.

And the helicopter rose and was gone. Just a few seconds and the great silence and paralysis and the heat had settled, quivering and quiet over the house in the darker part again.

A car drove up, a door was slammed. The Islander, white in the face, came rushing toward his daughter who was sitting at the very bottom of the stairway up to nothing, on the last gray and decomposing step.

And the Islander instantly understood that he had arrived too late. Everything had already happened, it was irrevocable. Father and daughter, on the bottom step, alone in the peculiar silence that had always surrounded the house in the darker part. They had gotten up and with arms around each other in an odd way, started walking up the steps back inside the house.

"I went down into the pool that night," Sandra finished her story for Doris Flinkenberg behind the closed door in the kitchen in the darker part of the woods, just in time to hear an audible cleaning and poking about on the other side of the door.

It was the cousin's mama of course, who was knocking on the door, and she shouted in a very friendly but also decided way, "Girls, girls! Now you're really going to have to let me in girls! I want my coffee break too!"

But the ring. "I looked and looked." Sandra lowered her voice, they were in the room now, her room, had climbed up into the bed that was still called the marital bed even though there was only a wan girl who slept in it alone and it was so big it took up almost the entire room. "Later. At the bottom of the pool. And—I found it. Though it really wasn't easy to see. In other words. Tablespoon-sized. In that case it really was a rather small tablespoon that had been the model for it. And I . . .

". . . I took it and hid it and never told the Islander."

"I want to see it," Doris Flinkenberg hissed.

"Shh." Sandra hushed. "I said it was top secret. We have to wait until we're alone again."

And in the pool, later: Sandra took out the plastic die from her bag, the small one with the silver confetti inside, and there it was, at the very bottom. The ring. With the ruby. Well. It was not like a real tablespoon, not quite so big.

Doris squeezed the small plastic die in her sweaty hand.

"Here comes happiness," Sandra said softly and with meaning and reached out for Doris's hand, and Sandra slid the ring on Doris's finger.

"I would very much like to marry you, Heintz-Gurt," Doris Flinkenberg said and looked Sandra Wärn sincerely in the eye.

"That's very good," Sandra Wärn said in German, "because I think that's a rather good idea too."

"And then," Doris sighed happily with the ring on her finger, "they lived happily every after. In the Alps. In Austria.

"But," she added fatefully, "what happened to the little girl? The one who was left behind, alone?"

"Well," Sandra said dully and seriously, "it was probably so. That she was left behind, alone."

"Shall we," Doris said then in another tone and quite eagerly, "have the wedding kiss later?"

"What's going on here?" Suddenly, in the middle of the most intense game of games, Bombshell Pinky Pink was standing there at the edge of the pool in her bright pink clothes, the miniskirt made out of plastic-coated fabric and the light red blouse made out of polyester, which was low cut and so tight that there was not enough room inside and the contents were being pushed up toward her neckline.

And immediately she, Pinky with her X-ray eyes, caught sight of the ring. "What a rock!" she shouted. "That's what I call a diamond."

And she was already on her way down into the pool because as said, which she had said in other situations, "I have an instinct for rocks, especially ones that are shiny and glittery," and help, what were the girls supposed to do now? Pinky must not get a closer look at the ring. No. It must not happen. "Erhm," Doris interrupted her then, got up and stood in her way, but with the indisputable professional authority of someone who is dealing with a very serious matter. "Could I ask a favor? An interview?"

And then Doris explained as seriously and irresistibly as only Doris could when she pulled out all the stops, that it would be an honor if Bombshell Pinky Pink would assist with "a valuable firsthand testimony" for the research for her group project Profession: striptease dancer in school, a rather solitary group because Doris Flinkenberg had always been so peculiar that no one really wanted to be "a group" with her.

"It would be a great honor," Doris Flinkenberg finished and Pinky had forgotten all the diamonds in the world for a moment on the glitter scene and immediately said yes.

But the ring, Doris kept it on her finger. But only during grand occasions in the pool without water, and of course, only when Sandra Wärn was there.

Lorelei Lindberg and Heintz-Gurt. It was a story that took off then. Heintz-Gurt became a person, and Doris Flinkenberg, she would be such a perfect Lorelei Lindberg.

It was madness.

But one more thing. Lorelei Lindberg. That was Doris's name for her. Doris's invention. Lorelei, that was namely the most beautiful name Doris knew.

Lindberg. That was what you were called, there in the District.

La vie emmerdante/The cursed life. Sandra's last essay at the French School, rendered in print.

The famous movie star Lupe Velez was tired of life. She wanted to die. The man whose child she was carrying had left her. It was not Tarzan who had been her greatest love. To top it all off it was another love, one that had been secondary.

The famous movie star had partied with Tarzan in Paris, London, Mexico, and in her home in Hollywood, and in the end their tremendous passion had drained both of them of their strength. Both of them had pulled away, millions of miles from each other, like two wounded animals. And once you have burned a bridge it is not a matter of building it up again just like that.

This man now, who had left her, he was secondary.

The famous movie star Lupe Velez gathered all the tablets she had in her home. There were quite a lot, enough for a truly fatal dose. Then she called her friends and invited them to a fare-well dinner. Though she did not tell them this directly. She ordered her favorite meal from catering. Chili con carne. Strong.

They ate and drank champagne and spoke badly about men, love, and life. They reminisced about bad days, in order to get in the right mood.

The guests went home and the movie star was alone. She took one last bath, washed herself clean. After the bath she put on her very finest nightgown of silk, the one Tarzan had given her once. The bed was made with the finest linens, silk these as well. She did her evening ablutions, did not forget to brush her hair with fifty hard pulls.

And she took out the tablets. Poured them out over the night-stand, sat on the edge of the bed, started popping them in her mouth and swallowing them with champagne. When she had taken all of them she lay down on the bed, adjusted her body in a suitable position, just right, not exaggerated, elegant. And then she closed her eyes and waited for sleep and death to come.

She woke up and knew right away that it was not heaven. Her stomach was churning, she dragged herself to the bathroom. The chili. She barely had time to get the toilet lid up before it came out. But at the same time she slipped and lost her balance and hit her head on the cold porcelain of the toilet bowl. She lost consciousness, all dams burst. And her head ended up in the toilet bowl. That was how the famous movie star Lupe Velez would be remembered. As the one who drowned in the toilet bowl in her own home.

Passion, it is just devilry.

La passion. C'est vraiment un emmerdement.

. . .

Sandra turned in the essay, packed up her things, and stopped attending the French School. Then she headed straight to the ordinary junior high school in the town center, in the District, and was admitted as a student in the same grade as Doris Flinkenberg. Not in the same class, as said, but in the classroom next door, in the parallel class.

Lorelei Lindberg above the small washbasin in the back room in Little Bombay, had grasped the fluorescent lamp above the mirror with both hands and FSSSST for a few seconds the current flooded through her in one great shock. One second, only Sandra saw it, Lorelei Lindberg blinked yellow, hissing, electrical. The world stood still FSST and in one's memory that second became an eternity.

No, you're wrong, she had said to the Black Sheep.
   But I'm afraid.
   Of him.
   There is something strange about the house.
   And the boy, there is a boy wandering around.
   And yet I know that it's abnormal. That boy, he's just a child.
   There are rumors—that he's done something terrible. You don't know.

The Black Sheep:
   "That it isn't things you choose for yourself. The mouse doesn't choose to be a mouse."
   "I understood what you meant," she said bitterly.
   And silk georgette.
   And chiffon with polyester.
   My God it's melting.
   This wasn't real either.

But later she was happy again. Silk georgette. Organza. And shantung.
   Shamo silk—it's too wonderful.
   And chiff—

. . .

Then
  Suddenly
  Everything
  Was
  Over

The store had gone bankrupt.
  The Islander and Sandra emptied it.
  Loaded fabrics into the car and drove them to the house in the darker part of the woods.
  Little Bombay, all the fabrics.
  "We're leaving because nothing's happening here," she muttered and she wasn't the silk dog any longer. To herself. No. It couldn't be said like that.
  It wasn't like that.

"Let us call her Lorelei Lindberg," Doris had said at the beginning of the game. "Everyone in the next county over is called Lindberg and since she wasn't from here you can assume she was from there."
  Doris's way of reasoning. But it had helped.
  She could hide other stories in her heart—no stories.
  There were holes in the garden of stories—a well, dark like a cavity in the earth to stare into.

Belonged to the kind of hard things in the soul from which nothing could be woven.
  Viscose rayon pulp and nothing.

Little Bombay, all the fabrics—
  And the puzzle, 1,500 pieces, "Alpine Villa in Snow," half finished, it was still lying on the table.

"It's so empty. I shoot flies with an air rifle." The Islander shot empty rounds with his rifle in the rec room. Drank whiskey. Maybe it was his attempt at building up the courage to load the rifle with ammunition

and just make an end to everything. To himself, everything, the little girl in the pool.

You wanna implode your mind with the Exploding plastic inevitable?
   Little Bombay, all the fabrics.
   No. All of that was over now.

Imaginary swimming.
   The girl ran in the pool. Back and forth between the short ends.
   The Islander had gotten up and walked out to the pool area on unsteady legs, with the rifle.
   The girl who ran and ran as if she hadn't even seen him, eyes closed, back and forth, back and forth.
   Imaginary swimming. He had raised the rifle and aimed it at her.
   Then she had stopped suddenly. Looked up at him with big, defenseless eyes.
   He had fallen, crumpled together, the rifle had fallen out of his hand, he had started crying.
   Belonged to the kind of hard things in the soul from which stories cannot be woven.

The most beautiful story ever told

DORIS WAS THE ONE WHO TOOK SANDRA OUT IN THE DISTRICT. Sandra got to know the District in a new way. Until she had met Doris Flinkenberg, Sandra had mainly roamed around the house in the darker part of the woods without aim or purpose. Maybe followed in the boy's footsteps, in daylight of course, and when he definitely was not in the vicinity. Come to different places, Bule Marsh for example. She had also seen the cousin's property before, and a few other places, but they had not meant anything. Her head had been filled with strange thoughts that had nothing to do with the concrete reality surrounding her in the darker part of the woods, so full that she had not really had the energy to see anything outside of herself, or had room for anything else in her consciousness.

She had, in her aimless wanderings, mostly been occupied with thinking about whether or not someone was following her, if she was being watched. Was the evil eye there, all of that—the boy in the woods, and so on.

"Ah Bencku," Doris said when Sandra brought him up, "He's bananas. As bananas as a . . . BANANA," she continued. "What do you mean?" Sandra whined, but Doris just shrugged her shoulders. "You'll probably see later. Yourself." Which had not exactly calmed Sandra's anxiety. See what? Though it had not been possible to continue asking questions then because Doris Flinkenberg had, true to habit, bubbled on about a bunch of other conversation topics which, according to Doris in her own opinion, were much more interesting.

"Behind the marsh." Doris pointed at an especially brushy direction in the woods. "That's where I came from. In the beginning. Oh, boy Sandra. You should just know what lunatics I descend from on both my mother's and my father's side."

And again Doris pulled down her pants a bit and revealed a terrible dark brown but very visible checkered scar on her left thigh. "Do you know what this is?" she asked and Sandra just shook her head. "The work of idiots. They're over there. Beyond the marsh. Or, were."

"We're not going there, are we?" Sandra asked anxiously.

"Are you crazy?" Doris fastened her eyes on her. "I'm never setting foot there again. Never ever! Now we're going to turn off the path here and go in the other direction. To where civilization is."

And with these words they came to the cousin's house, which Doris Flinkenberg exhibited for Sandra like a museum of a happy home. Here was the kitchen, so shiny and clean, with the household assistant who was kneading the dough so conveniently, and there was the transistor radio from which the weather report came, and the Poppy radio cassette player—which could not be used as a radio because the antennas had come off a long time ago—with Doris's own music: *Lasting Love Songs for Moonstruck Lovers*, "Our Love Is a Continental Affair," and all of Doris's other songs on cassettes, just as unbearable.

And there was the cousin's mama with her crossword and her dishes and her cooking and all of her *True Crimes*. And next to the kitchen on the first floor of the cousin's house was the cousin's papa's room, though you were not allowed to go in there. He kept to himself in there and the best thing to do was to walk as quietly as possible past the closed door. Doris snuck by on tiptoe, with her finger to her lips.

"He keeps company there with his demons and phantoms," Doris hissed to Sandra on the stairs going up to the second floor when they could speak freely again. "And you're not allowed to disturb him. Though he's not dangerous. Not in that way. Not anymore now when he's past his prime. Meek like a kitten."

"What's a phantom?" Sandra asked when they came up to Doris's room, the nice and bright and spacious attic room where the daylight streamed in between the clean white apple-patterned curtains and you had such a pretty view over the entire cousin's garden below.

"A fantasy ghost," Doris Flinkenberg answered and sat down on her bed, on the bright yellow bedspread. "Ghosts that come from ancient times. There was a woman he loved but she's dead now. Anna Magnani, or the breasts from the working class. That wasn't her name really, but that's what Bengt says."

And when Sandra gave her a questioning look, Doris shrugged her shoulders impatiently.

"Oh," she said. "That's not important. We might get to that later."

It was rather cozy, really, in Doris's room on the second floor of the cousin's house. Such a pretty picturesque little attic room, perfect for two little girls to play their games in. But still it would never be like that, never a place where Sandra Wärn and Doris Flinkenberg hung out. There was already something else that they were disciples of. The house in the darker part of the woods, and most of all the basement and the pool without water was already theirs.

This room, Doris's room in the cousin's house—it was, yes, too normal. No room for Loneliness&Fear or for Sister Night and Sister Day.

"Come . . ."

And then they went out again, and over the cliffs to the Second Cape. They saw the elegant houses that had once been part of the housing exhibition for country living in the future, where the summer guests and the sea urchins now lived and there were Private Property signs almost everywhere. But of course you did not care about that, now in the fall when everything was deserted and *there was no season*, as the summer guests had a habit of expressing themselves. They saw the Glass House, the most beautiful of all the houses on the Second Cape, and it was one of those fantastic sparkling fall afternoons when the different colors of the trees shone in the sunlight and were reflected in the water that reflected in the glass windowpanes so that a game of colors arose and it actually looked a little like the house was moving, as if it were on fire.

And finally they went up to the house on the First Cape, which sat on a hill next to it, but a little on its own, surrounded by a pointed beach in three different directions. It was an old green villa with three stories, or almost four because the fourth one was a tower with a tower room.

And surrounded by a garden, now rather overgrown, which subtly crossed over into the real woods that continued a good way to the west until you came to the end of the woods, to the dark marshlands where a certain alpine villa had been raised.

The house on the First Cape had been empty for many years now already, and they got inside—it was as easy as pie, it was just a matter of walking in—and they went up in the tower and looked around at everything, everything that was around them.

And then down to the floor below where there was a large living room still with certain old pieces of furniture in it, not very well preserved but not entirely destroyed. And there, in the parlor, Doris stood in the middle of the room, closed her eyes and opened them again, and then looked straight at her friend meaningfully, as only Doris could, and said:

"A lucky house, what good luck that I was here." And made an expressive pause before she continued. "This is namely where the bastard was found. And the bastard, that was me."

And Doris curled up on the plush-covered sofa and waved to Sandra that she should sit down next to her.

"Come and sit here and I'll tell you about my happiest story. There are many good things about this story . . . but the absolutely best thing of all is that it's true. All of this happened for real!"

The story about the house on the First Cape/
Doris's happiest story

THE HOUSE ON THE FIRST CAPE WAS ONE OF THE FEW HOUSES in the whole of the District that had escaped destruction during the occupation after the war. When the area was returned the house was completely and, to top it all off, almost newly painted; the original furniture was still inside the house and even some of the other things. Some important person must have lived there, people thought, someone who had the power to prevent the vandalization that had otherwise been carried out more or less systematically in order to hide the traces of military and other activity in the area. And someone who had liked the house, someone who had been content there: even the garden seemed to have been cared for.

This stirred bad blood in the District, especially among those who had their former homes burned down, disrupted, soiled. And that the rightful owners of the house on the First Cape had not been in touch made everything that much worse.

To leave the house adrift. After everything. That was almost worse than doing what the cousin's papa had done, just showing up with his clan one day during the first period after the area had become free with that eternal but certainly completely legal document of Baron von Buxhoevden's confounded bad luck in poker games.

The house was empty. It would continue to stand empty. During many years it was a place where people came and went and hung out for shorter and longer periods of time. Very nearly every person in the District had either lived in the house on the First Cape or had known someone who had lived there—that is the way it was in the end. But still, the house would prove impossible to take possession of. There were always the original owners who dug their heels in somewhere in the background even though they never showed up themselves in the house on the First Cape. The women who would live in the house a while in the future were the first ones who would have a legal rental agreement to show. And for a time after that when the Backmansson family, descendants of the original owners, would finally move in.

The cousin's clan had also hung out in the house on the First Cape when they first came to the District. Very first in other words, when the cousin's papa's brother and his wife were still alive, them plus the twins Rita and Solveig and the oldest, the son Bengt. They had lived on the First Cape while what would later become the cousin's house was built below.

It was rumored that the cousin's papa actually had never given a thought to leaving the house on the First Cape. That he walked around miffed over the fact that the First Cape was located just outside the area he had won in the game. Sometimes he even tried to claim that the First Cape really was his too, but according to a verbal agreement. He tried to dismiss the fact that he had no papers to prove it as a meaningless technical detail. It did not work of course. But the clan stayed in the house anyway, contract or not. They probably would have continued staying there too since you really did not want to mess with the cousin's papa when he was in his prime. He had that brother too, in other words, the one who died, who looked like a testy bull, never said a word. But that nickname, the Dancer, in combination with his appearance and everything else you had heard about him sent chills down your spine.

But still, one beautiful day their fellow citizen Loman stood on the property of the house on the First Cape with an eviction notice in hand, this more or less on commission of the house's actual owners who, like always, remained invisible.

But paradoxically enough it was probably just this eviction attempt—plus of course the car accident shortly thereafter, in which the Dancer and his wife Anna Magnani or the breasts from the working class, which their only son Bengt would gradually call her, died—that caused the cousin's family to finally be accepted in the District. It was the last straw, you thought, about the owners who stayed away, to send out a compatriot as a lackey. Not to mention up there. Where you would rather not set foot—and it did not matter if you were a cop or not.

But so, at the same time, sort of another fate was also being determined in passing.

"One man's death, the other man's breath," as Doris Flinkenberg had a habit of saying at this point in the story in the cousin's kitchen in the cousin's house where she had the cousin's mama tell it over and over again.

It was namely so that Loman, who had received the commission to convey the warning about the imminent eviction to the cousin's papa, had a daughter. "Let us call her Astrid." That was how Doris Flinkenberg always described it to Sandra. Let us call her Astrid. This Astrid had a boy, his name was Björn. And Astrid, she loved children. And here, exactly at this point, Doris usually had to pause because she became so excited; her eyes twinkled and her voice became utterly soft.

This daughter happened to be present when countryman Loman set out for the house on the First Cape in order to have a serious talk with the cousin's papa. Maybe as some kind of protection: as said, the cousin's papa was known as a hothead with a violent temper, and this was as said while he was still in his prime before all of the tragedies befell him and he became docile and distant and locked himself in his room. Astrid together with her boy Björn had stood a bit off to the side as countryman Loman conveyed his errand. And she, Astrid, there was probably nothing special about her. She probably made no impression at all. That is to say as a woman, so to speak. She, Astrid, was a like a gray mouse. No one you paid any attention to. In comparison to Anna Magnani . . . the Dancer's wife . . . as if on cue rumba tones and thuds from dancing could be heard from inside the house, and they had in and of themselves been rather exhilarating and rhythmical tones, but at the same time there was something truly threatening about them.

Nothing had been decided then, with regard to the house or anything else. The cousin's papa had his shotgun of course, but maybe the presence of a woman, not in and of herself, but as in women-and-children (Astrid and Björn), had kept the cousin's papa's violent temper in check.

And maybe some seeds had been planted anyway.

A few weeks later and everything had been utterly transformed due to the tragedy of fate.

The Dancer and his wife died in a car accident on the way to a dancing spot in the inland area of the country.

And the clan, that is to say what was left of it, the cousin's papa and the three now orphaned children, left the house on the First Cape with a vengeance.

"In the end there was no need to evict them," the cousin's mama had a habit of saying at this point. "They certainly went voluntarily, after all. And"—with a slight giggle—"I got married." That's how the cousin's mama had explained it to Doris Flinkenberg in the cousin's kitchen so many times with the same light laughter in between, which Doris Flinkenberg was also very good at imitating. "And got all the kids at once. I who love children. And sometimes, dear Doris, it goes so well that you get more than you ask for."

"One man's death, the other man's breath," Doris Flinkenberg had the habit of saying again at just this point because she was already preparing herself for how the story would continue.

"Well, well, well," the cousin's mama had a habit of saying then, probably a bit frightened, even if she had already started getting used to Doris Flinkenberg's somewhat peculiar way of expressing herself. "Well, well, Doris. Maybe not exactly like that."

But now we are getting closer to the definite climax of the story: during this time, little Doris Flinkenberg had her very own mother who, among other things, had burned Doris Flinkenberg with a fish grill so that she would not be so "obstinate" all the time. And her own father, who every now and again was angry at this mother, we can call her marsh mama, and had therefore set fire to the ramshackle cabin that the little family lived in over by the beaches of the Outer Marsh. Two whole times besides, and neither time by accident, but it was after the second fire that the police came. Both times were at night and the mother and the child, who was Doris Flinkenberg, had been lying and sleeping inside the cabin—though both times Doris Flinkenberg had woken up and at the last minute managed to save herself and her marsh mama from the flames.

At the police station the marsh papa had made no secret of the fact that it had been his intention to kill his wife and that that intention still remained. In that respect he also did not distinguish between the mother and the daughter. "Like mother like daughter," he had said in marsh dialect, which had, of course, rendered him even more jail time.

At the same time, before during and after all of this was going on, the marsh mama was after her daughter, Doris Flinkenberg. Burning her and hitting her and carrying on, in various subtle ways too, so that Doris, who would otherwise have no problem using a bunch of peculiar words, did not have the slightest desire to provide any details. Sometimes Doris Flinkenberg was half unconscious because of the abuse, sometimes she dozed off right in the middle. And when the marsh mama went after her daughter she was also careful about leaving marks on places that could be concealed under clothes and she also had the utterly diabolical habit of exhibiting desperation afterward. Then it often happened that she took little Doris Flinkenberg in her arms and rocked her and cried and tried to get Doris to understand that she must not utter a word to anyone about what had happened. "Otherwise they'll come and take you away from me." Then the idea was for Doris to comfort her. That Doris was supposed to feel sorry for her and promise her, "Dear Mother, I'll never tell anyone about this." The strange thing later was that Doris Flinkenberg had actually promised her that. And she also had not uttered a word about it to a single person. But on the other hand, whom would she have had to turn to? And to whom would she have told and what? Who would have listened, so to speak? It was already obvious after the first fire that one would rather turn a deaf ear when it really mattered, so to speak, with everything.

Doris had promised. Promised and promised and promised. "Dear Mama. Everything will be okay. I won't tell anybody anything." Even up until the time the marsh mama had taken the hot grill, or, possibly, something else before, maybe something before a thought started growing inside Doris Flinkenberg, quietly, quietly, but decidedly. It was quite simply a thought with the laconic message that she would die here with the marsh mama, or, not die directly, then just succumb in some other way. She could no longer think clearly (also, this thought took several days as long as years to formulate), she could not get any peace or be exempt from fear anywhere. And not to mention, everything looked like it was just getting worse. Already after the first time the marsh papa had tried to set fire to the house and its occupants it was as if the marsh mama had only become more eager in her enthusiasm to knock the "obstinate" out of her.

It was as though the marsh mama could sense that something was happening to Doris Flinkenberg, that Doris was about to drift away from her, so the last few times, above all the last time it was time for a beating, the marsh mama went after her particularly hard and with extreme force. It was also the case that

Doris Flinkenberg had started being gone a lot, for real. That was when she had started hanging out around the cousin's house and the capes to the south, sometimes she did not come home at night either, it was summer of course so you would not freeze, you could sleep outside. The marsh mama did not understand any of this but it was not necessary either: she saw "obstinacy" and threats and that was enough.

Then, after that time when she was almost beaten to death, Doris Flinkenberg shuffled from her home by the Outer Marsh after her marsh mama had finally fallen asleep for the night, never to return.

That night Doris wandered around through the woods until she came to the southern parts of the District, where the cousin's property and the First and the Second Capes were. She got into the house on the First Cape and lay down in a corner of the big room and waited to be found. Later, she lay there and prayed to God that the one who found her would be the cousin's mama and no one else. She knew that it was possible of course because the cousin's mama had a habit of being in the garden early in the mornings since she had obtained special permission from the real owners of the house to pick gooseberries and black currants in the garden.

Doris prayed to God and Doris's prayers were answered.

At dawn it was the cousin's mama who showed up in the house, the cousin's mama who came and saw and called an ambulance.

Doris was taken to the hospital and while she was lying in the emergency room the cousin's mama had made her decision. Doris would be saved; Doris would get a real home. That became the cousin's mama's purpose for the time to come, and at the same time it was also what got her back on her feet again after her Björn's death and everything else that had happened at Bule Marsh a short time before that, which had shattered everything and made her powerless with grief. The reason she had not gone mad was that Bencku had been even crazier.

.   .   .

Bencku. Sandra had paid attention. The boy. Again.

"Wait a minute," said Doris. "I'll finish telling this now. We'll get to him later."

And now Doris was at the climax in her story, the story that was the most beautiful of all. And it started in the hospital where Doris had been lying and she made the decision that she would never become well again. Not healthier than she was at that moment anyway, which according to the diagnosis was "in stable condition." She did not have any pain anywhere anymore and the burns were healing as well as they could under the disinfectant bandages. And, oh, how nice it had been just to have peace and quiet and be taken care of. Escape the fear, not having to be on her guard. And the best thing of all: having the cousin's mama next to her bed, watching over her, both during and after visiting hours.

And so one time, it was an afternoon when it had been only the two of them in the hospital room, the cousin's mama had gotten up and leaned over Doris in her bed, taken Doris's little hand in hers and asked in a whisper, like a proposal:

"Do you want to be my girl, Doris Flinkenberg?"

Then the tears had welled in Doris's eyes and she was so moved that at first she could not get a word out. That was unusual because otherwise Doris was, as said, rather quick-witted, for the most part all the time, everywhere. Which had also been one of the marsh mama's hundred thousand excuses for beating her daughter with the grill iron, kitchen spoon, or just her fists: "Now, Doris, I'm going to hack that great stubborn big mouth out of you."

But suddenly Doris also understood that it was important to be quick. This was her opportunity of a lifetime and it might never come back. And she grappled after the words almost in a panic and finally got out "yes." And caught her breath and repeated, "Yes. Yes. Yes. Yes."

"Then, sweetheart," the cousin's mama replied in turn when she had gotten her tongue back again for her own sake because she was almost sobbing too, but softly now, so that no one else would hear them, "I promise to do everything in my power to make it so. Everything, Doris Flinkenberg, I promise. There is one thing you should know, Doris Flinkenberg. A lioness will stop at nothing when she's fighting for her young. And I am a lion, Doris Flinkenberg, when it comes to my children."

Doris had nodded solemnly in response, whereupon the cousin's mama lowered her voice to a whisper that was even softer:

"But first you need to promise me two things, Doris Flinkenberg. First, all of this and everything that follows has to be kept between the two of us. You and me. Second, Doris Flinkenberg. You have to trust me. You have to do what I say. E.x.a.c.t.l.y. Can I trust you? Do you promise?"

And these two questions were aside from the wonderful *do you want to be my girl, Doris Flinkenberg* the two biggest and most important questions Doris Flinkenberg had ever been asked in her life.

Doris had not been late about answering either. And she answered "Yes. Yes. Yes. Yes. Yes."

Shortly thereafter the marsh papa was sentenced to jail and prison and the marsh mama was also sentenced to jail and prison for check fraud, breaking and entering, and other lax morals. Yet not for having beaten her child; that sort of thing was so difficult to prove and it also would have meant that Doris would have been forced to testify against her mother. Instead it was the cousin's papa who had testified. Strengthened with a bit of schnapps, he testified and testified and testified and testified. It was the cousin's papa's last big appearance before he finally locked himself in his room next to the kitchen in the cousin's house and stayed there. Some people also said that everything the cousin's papa testified to had not been true—but it played a minor role because justice had prevailed and Doris got a home and that was the main thing.

"I live HERE now," Doris had said over and over again the first days in the cousin's house her new home that she had been allowed to come to when she was discharged from the hospital. At first she was a bit obstinate and a bit angry, as if it had been important to convince the surroundings that they would not get away with anything when it came to her, above all trying to get her out of there.

Little by little, when she felt safer, in order to convince herself. Was all of this really true? Or was she dreaming? To have a real home, was it this wonderful? And to have a mother, her almost very own? A cousin's mama who promised to take care of her her whole life and never never leave her?

"I live here now," Doris said but more to herself than anyone else, like an exhalation. "This is MY home now."

And Doris Flinkenberg had sat with the cousin's mama in the cousin's kitchen and solved crossword puzzles and played music that was playing on Doris's new radio cassette player that the cousin's mama had given her as a "homecoming present" (though Doris said "wedding present" a rather long time afterward) when she came to live in the cousin's house. "Our Love Is a Continental Affair" and the like, and sometimes she looked up and out through the window where the house on the First Cape could be glimpsed through the trees and other vegetation.

"A house of luck," Doris had sighed. "If the house hadn't been there you never would have found me," she said to the cousin's mama. "I would never have become your daughter here. In this house. How lucky that I was there."

"We are two castaways," the cousin's mama whispered in turn to Doris Flinkenberg and took her in her arms. The cousin's mama had lost her dear boy Björn, but she had gotten Doris Flinkenberg instead, even if only on loan. And the cousin's mama had hugged Doris, the borrowed child, hard.

. . .

"Where were we then?" said Doris Flinkenberg. "With Heintz-Gurt?"

". . . When the war was over Heintz-Gurt returned to Austria where he married a very ordinary Austrian girl with whom he had children, but in the long run the girl and family life became boring. He was a pilot after all and in Brazil he met a stewardess whose name was Lupe Velez and he moved to her home country with her and lived there with her until she grew tired of him and he had to return home to his wife with his tail between his legs. Then she was already so angry at him that she had decided not to say a word to him for the rest of her life. He tried to live amid this painful silence. And it was not very easy, so shortly thereafter he found himself living the life of a jet-setter, wandering around at the ski resorts, searching for adventure and more fun. That was how he met Lorelei Lindberg at a nightclub called the Running Kangaroo at that swanky ski resort . . ."

And Doris and Sandra walked back from the house on the First Cape, through the woods to the house in the darker part. Down to the basement and the pool without water, that place in the world which was theirs, their headquarters.

THE WOMEN AND THE WHORES
(Sandra and Doris's story 1)

———————

1. *The women*

"HERE THEY CELEBRATE THE WILD LIFE," DORIS FLINKENBERG said to Sandra Wärn where they were hanging out on their own in the shade in the garden outside the Women's House on the First Cape. "They don't let on that there was a yesterday here in the District. A yesterday filled with blood and murder.

"Dancing over corpses." Doris Flinkenberg smacked her lips at Sandra Wärn up in the dark branches of the sea apple tree or in the neglected rose bower that had at one time certainly been elegant and resplendent. Off to the side of the parties and the other events in the garden, not too far away but at just the right distance, thereby having the right overview of everything that was happening.

And there was always something going on in the garden next to the house on the First Cape during this time. Because it was those years when the women were there and the parties billowed around them, spread out over the entire District, almost everywhere. That was *the happy time*.

The summer women and the winter women—the whores in the house in the darker part. A few summers, falls. Then it was over. The women were expelled from the house on the First Cape and a completely ordinary family, they were called Backmansson, moved in. They were the real owners of the house, rightly said the direct descendants.

"Mmm," Sandra answered a bit impatiently because Doris had been carrying on like that for quite a while, walking like a cat around hot porridge. But still certainly smiling at her friend in that special way they had practiced together in the house in the darker part of the woods, a smile that signaled understanding and devilry and many ambiguities. *Our crafty fiendishness*, Doris Flinkenberg had said; that was what these expressions were supposed to demonstrate.

But also, not insignificant on Sandra's part, a smile that was intact. Two straight rows of teeth on top of each other could be glimpsed from between two normal lips. It had been a few years since the cleft palate surgery had taken place, the one that had released Sandra from a visible harelip and now, since a few months back, with a successful adjustment to her bite—one that had lasted since early childhood involving her teeth being pulled and two different kinds of braces, one for nighttime use the other for daytime. A lot of money had been spent in order to achieve the final result of a healthy and normal child's mouth.

"But tell me now, then," Sandra gradually whined more and more persistently at Doris Flinkenberg up in the sea apple tree or in the shadowy bower. But Doris only held a finger up to her lips. "Shhh, not yet," though there really was no one who heard her in the middle of the noise from the party. Also her face broke into that same smile, but when Doris smiled it revealed what you might call an overbite. There was no one who had bothered straightening her teeth and now it was too late; Sandra and Doris had both turned thirteen now.

But still, though you did not hear what the girls were saying to each other there where they were in their private shade off to the side in the garden, did you not discover, just by looking at them and their facial expressions, something muffled and alarming so to speak, something nevertheless a bit terrifying in the middle of all the light, summer, and fun? Something at least a bit ominous, which cast somewhat longer shadows in the bright day than what was normal.

Maybe so. Just tell the girls. In fact, it would have made them proud and interested to hear it.

Sandra Night&Doris Day, Doris Night&Sandra Day. Two girls in identical black shirts on which LONELINESS&FEAR stood in green paint on the stomachs. Long-sleeved nylon T-shirts in the middle of summer, but, and that was the most important thing, articles of clothing of which there were two identical ones in the entire world. Sandra had sewn them for their games, mostly just for fun in the beginning, but gradually a deeper message and content started taking shape inside them. For the time being mostly unarticulated, like a tone.

Now it was Doris's turn to lead the game, her turn to start. That meant that you had to follow her lead and have patience. A lot of patience, that was starting to become clear.

"Tell it now!"

Doris Night&Sandra Day, Sandra Night&Doris Day: those were their alter egos' identities for the game, to which the smiles they had practiced in front of the mirror at the bottom of the swimming pool in the house in the dark part also belonged.

"We're two sixth-sense siblings," said Doris Flinkenberg. "That's what we've become as a result of tragic circumstances. The phenomenon poltergeist. Do you know what that is?"

Sandra shook her head but looked expectantly at Doris, rain or shine the crossword solver with dictionary at the ready, who continued, "That's when the innocent child has had more than enough horrible things done to it and it has developed supernatural abilities in order to survive. The ability to see beyond what is," Doris Flinkenberg clarified. "See what no one else sees."

"You and I, Sandra," Doris hammered down. "We've certainly been treated badly enough. Me with my scars and you with your tragic family background. Heintz-Gurt, Lorelei Lindberg, all of that. You and I, Sandra, we know what it means to suffer.

"And the suffering has developed a hidden power in us that makes it so that we can see what no one else sees. See what others maybe should see but don't dare. The forgotten or what has been pushed away. Often"—Doris Flinkenberg made a solemn pause before she continued—"terrible things. Horrible crimes. Violence and passion. This is our starting point in any case.

"And," she added, "what we're investigating is real. It happened for real."

"I don't understand anything," Sandra said impatiently. "Get to the point."

"Shh." Doris put her finger to her lips. "Soon. But right now we don't have time because now we're going to a party."

A living room in the grass. And they headed up to the house on the First Cape where there was almost always something going on inside the house or outside in the overgrown garden. There with the kind help of Bencku and Magnus von B. the women had carried out the entire parlor furniture set, what was left of it anyway. A long table, curved white chairs, even the worn sofa with the plush cover. "Our living room in the grass," the women said and fastened white tent cloths over everything as protection against bad weather.

Bencku and Magnus von B. were also helpful in the garden in other ways. They cut the grass, they grilled bittyfish and green sea apples on the stone grill and when the women went to the city center in their light red bus *Eldrid's Spiritual Sojourn* in order to do some shopping, the boys were there and helped carry the shopping bags. "Bencku fell in love will all of them at once," Doris Flinkenberg established in the cousin's kitchen. "Maybe Bencku will get married later too," she went on to say, but to the cousin's mama and when Sandra was not there—she and Sandra had more important things to talk about when they were together and besides, Sandra always acted so strangely when Bengt was brought up.

Thus up in the garden, right up into the middle of the party where the girls took their places in the sea apple tree, which had its name from the fact that the cousin's papa, while he was still in his prime, had had Bencku and Rita and Solveig pick apples from it, certainly completely ordinary half-hard, wind-beaten junk that they had then sold to the summer guests as *sea apples*. The apples had been rapidly consumed since there were quite a few summer guests who were crazy about everything related to the *sea*.

And the women thought it was fun having two moody girls in the tree or in the middle of the rose bower. "Our mascots," said Anneka Munveg who was a news reporter and the one who was always the first to make the "scoop" wherever she went, in her crass and humorless way. "Our house pets," someone else filled in, one of the less colorful women, someone you would not remember afterward. "What was it they were called again, those chipmunks in Donald Duck? Wasn't it Chip and Dale?" That lit a fire under Laura Bjällbo-Hallberg. "The small imperialistic nibblers," she hissed. "Never in your life! Now that there's definitely an absolutely genuine Soviet counterpart." Life for Laura B-H during these years was a matter of finding the absolutely genuine Soviet counterpart to everything.

But when no one had come up with what the Soviet counterpart to the two chipmunks could be the girls quite simply became the "Soviet counterpart to Chip and Dale." And when that chant became too long to get out, it was gradually shortened to just the "*Soviet counterpart*," short and sweet.

And the women, as said, also allowed themselves to be entertained by Doris and Sandra's muffled serious behavior toward everything, that which belonged—of course they did not know—to the game Sister Night&Sister Day. The expression-less faces, the distorted smiles, and the enormous long-sleeved nylon T-shirts in the middle of the summer heat. "Sourpusses," the women burst out delightedly. "But maybe you're also needed in some way," she determined, the one who was the most deli-cious of the delicious, her with eyes the size of tea saucers, whom Doris and Sandra were in love with in their secret, innocent way. "Maybe you're needed in some way," Inget Herrman said ac-cordingly. "*If nothing else than like the darkness that gives depth to happiness.*"

The women on the First Cape had arrived in the District one Sat-urday morning in April. They came in a light red bus on which it said *Eldrid's Spiritual Sojourn* in fuzzy yellow letters along the sides. The bus drove over the cousin's property, not to mention almost straight across, but it was no one's fault because it just so happened that was where the road easement that led up to the path that led up to the First Cape was located. The bus stopped, the doors were thrown open, and the women burst forth from it, far from all of the women who would come to live in the house on the First Cape during the time that followed, but quite a few. A large enough number in any case so that inside the cousin's house you became speechless with surprise. Doris and the cous-in's mama who were busy in the kitchen with a musical cross-word and the first baking session of the weekend, the cousin's papa inside his room behind the wall, who otherwise during this time of year had the habit of lying in bed and drinking schnapps six weeks in a row—he was maybe into the fourth week that Sat-urday morning when the women showed up in the District—but now you could actually hear the noise from a chair being pulled over to the window on the other side of the room.

And all of these women were themselves a surprise, but also the following: who was it who just seemed to pop out of no-where there next to the bus? And who started to put on airs and act like it was the most natural thing in the world that a bunch of women had suddenly arrived in a light red bus that was parked next to the end of the easement road on the cousin's property where the path up to the First Cape started? If not—those inside the cousin's house could not believe their eyes, but it was true—Bengt.

The bus hardly had time to stop before Bengt was out of his barn, dragging his feet as usual, but it had little to do with the fact that he was not in a hurry rather that at this point in his life he had decided that this way of walking, dragging his feet, that is, made him interesting. Dressed to the hilt in his own apathetic way, in clean farmer's pants, a clean blue shirt, and a horrible red scarf tied around his head. Though it should be conceded that, aside from the thin stubble on his chin, he looked relatively decent.

In other words, Bengt with his tongue hanging out of his mouth, figuratively speaking of course, and this picture were in agreement with Doris Flinkenberg who, not exactly at this moment but certainly later, would become good at interpreting in different ways with words. She was talented with the richness of words after all. But now, right now, Doris was not analyzing at all, she was too astonished.

"Bencku picked up a scent," she said, rather weakly.

"Now, now, now, now," said the cousin's mama, just as distantly.

And Bengt, he was not looking at them of course, he did not look at the cousin's house at all. The women unloaded their bags out of the bus: bags, bags, their this and that, hundreds of things, while Bengt stood there and put on airs, filled his hands, let them load him up with stuff. And later they slowly started moving up toward the house on the First Cape, the house that had stood empty for so many years that you almost had time to get used to the idea that it would always be like that. They moved forward like a curious train rocking quietly, like a safari expedition in the swampy interior of the jungle. And of course, the peculiar scene had sound. Voices, laughter, and the like. But regardless, inside the cousin's house it was as if everything had played out in silence, which maybe quite simply was due to the fact that Doris Flinkenberg had kept quiet for once.

The women on the First Cape: there were eight–nine of them in the beginning, between the ages of about twenty and fifty-five. Also a few children were along, but for the most part they ran around and made noise and drifted together into a shapeless mass even while the women were there. The number of women was often higher, especially in the middle of the summer when the parties really got started. But of everyone there were still some who stood out more than others, like chosen ones, and most of them were already there on that first Saturday in April when the women took possession of the house on the First Cape—besides, they had a rental agreement to show, the first of its kind anyone had ever seen for the house on the First Cape. You would remember who these women were long afterward, even if the memory would blur amazingly quickly.

Consequently it was Laura Bjällbo-Hallberg, the one with the Soviet counterpart to everything; it was Anneka Munveg, a rather well-known news reporter who wrote a series of reports called "The Everyday Life of the Working Woman"; it was Saskia Stiernhielm who was a painter and who lived in something called the Blue Being—the blue room—in Copenhagen during the winter. If you wanted to reach her you had to address the letter to the Blue Being, Copenhagen and then one way or another it would get there. And then there were those names you remembered best because they were so funny, like Dolly Dreamer and Gaffsi and Annukka Metsämäki, but otherwise there was nothing special about them. Nothing conspicuous in any case, sort of lasting and worth remembering that a child demands in order to really be able to commit them to memory—

like her, the most delicious of the delicious, the one with eyes like teacup saucers, the one who was called Inget Herrman.

Whom both Sandra and Doris were a little fond of: "I think about her all the time. I think she's delicious delicious," Doris said to Sandra, and "jinks" said Sandra, that they were thinking and feeling the same way about something. And Doris rolled her eyes like a striptease dancer is not allowed to do and muttered, "Absolutely exquisite. I could die for her."

But *Eldrid's Spiritual Sojourn* on the bus, what did it mean? Not to mention that you would make a fool of yourself by asking. That question and a bunch of other questions, just as stupid. A club? Or: Eldrid, who is she? And so on. Of course you would not get an answer to any of this nonsense, and you would also gradually realize how unnecessary such questions were—such answers. The point was, as Inget Herrman expressed, *it is not a meaning that can be fixed, it just is.*

Trips, for example: trips out into the world, trips in geography, to cities, other countries, out in the world in other words, that which existed, the known and the unknown. But also other trips, the made-up trips, trips in your fantasy. And trips in your physical space—all unconscious outings you could make in feeling, thought, body, and mind, here and there.

Trips to these kinds of places and worlds that were created just because you were traveling through them.

The universe is a new flower.

Or, as Annukka Metsämäki carefully read in the garden one evening so shyly that it could barely be heard, "Now I'm going to read a poem that I've written all by myself." She started so softly she was almost whispering. "Louder!" someone yelled and so she raised her voice for the time it took to read *I am a white negro, there are no rules for me* whereafter she became so quiet so quiet again because someone yelled, "That's PLAGIARISM," and then the exchange of lines was a fact. Saskia Stiernhielm literally hissed to Laura Bjällbo-Hallberg like a snake, "Then you should always be there and know and decide everything."

"What do you want it to mean, girls?" Inget Herrman asked the girls. "Here. Take. And write. On the bus." And she handed them a small bucket with green paint and of course it made you happy, but still, once you actually had the brush in your hand you were really completely drained out of nervousness from the fear of making an even bigger fool out of yourself so nothing got written on that bus at all.

But gradually, slowly, still, with brush in hand, you started understanding what it was all about. A feeling. A power. Possibilities, openness. *That it was moving forward.* And then it was as easy as pie to steal the brush and the small bucket and use them for your own purposes: take them to the house in the darker part and paint Loneliness&Fear on your newly sewn polyester T-shirts for everything you were worth.

But consequently, it was above all the parties that the women in the house on the First Cape would become notorious for in the District. One party after another sometimes without a break in between; a party flowed over into another almost imperceptibly—and gradually the parties started moving to other places too. What had started on the First Cape radiated out over the entire district, even all the way out to the Second Cape. Not to every house of course, but to certain ones, quite a few actually; during the entire time the women were living in the house on the First Cape it was in fact only the Glass House where Kenny and the sea urchins were hanging out that remained so to speak untouched through it all. The baroness came out only a few times that summer; there were rumors she was seriously ill. But the First Cape, the women, anything else—none of it was in the Glass House. For real. Maybe something then, but in that case only as a relief against which the house's own, the white, would shine clearly and purely.

"Mom's new bordeaux-colored Nissan Cherry," Anna Sjölund from the Second Cape said for example. "I would really like one like that."

Here you find yourself. Ones who were like you. Confusingly similar. Almost yourself. Here you were occupied with each other and with yourself and with each other. The special mood that was created when you were together, skin against skin.

The time when the women were living in the house on the First Cape constituted entirely new possibilities, but also for those who were not there at all, that is to say not anywhere. For example, the cousin's mama now had the chance to expand her moonlighting, that is to say her cleaning business. Suddenly she had an entirely new customer base in addition to the Islander and the house in the darker part and a few of the more well-to-do families in the District. Quite a few of the summer guests on the Second Cape got in touch now too when their houses needed to be picked up after parties, and the word spread, and gradually Kenny was also there and wanted to hire her because when the baroness came out during the summer it was supposed to look like nothing had been going on in the Glass House before her arrival. And besides, all of these people, they also had permanent homes in other places. In the city by the sea, for example.

This meant that the work now became a real business in one fell swoop. Little by little the cousin's mama could start her own company and have employees and so on. Employees like Bengt for example. And Solveig. And Rita (reluctant, but still). And Doris sometimes, while she was alive, but more for specific tasks due to her young age (the house in the darker part, in the fall, after the hunting parties; more about that later). The company was christened Four Mops and a Dustpan. "The dustpan, that's Bengt," Doris confided to her best friend Sandra Wärn. "But don't tell anyone—it's a corporate secret."

. . .

But the parties spread, a tiny, tiny bit more. Finally, when they had carried on and carried on spreading all over both of the capes they somehow found their way to one of the narrowest and darkest paths in the woods, the one that led to the house in the darker part of the woods. There where the Islander was standing, at the top of the stairs, white shirt flapping, sloppily tucked into his pants, the buttons unbuttoned all the way to his navel just about, furnished with sideburns in accordance with the current fashion and with a gold medallion shining against his dark chest hair, glistening with sweat in the sun. Like the captain on a ship—

"Everyone on board!" is not what he yelled but he could have. And the similarity, no, it was not so crazy after all because look at the women who are coming toward him in masquerade clothes on the path up to the house, how they are drawn to him and the house like sea rats who curiously draw closer to a ship with one, let us say an interesting turn, toward port, down toward the mud—and really, it was Anneka Munveg and Inget Herrman who were in the lead.

Then, from the back, not the very back of the line of dressed-up people on the path, but in other words even farther behind than where Doris and Sandra were dragging themselves forward, the following could be heard:

"Sinking. Sinking." And Sandra turned around instinctively. It was the boy who was saying it of course. Their eyes met. He looked straight at her, but also, in a strange way through her.

"In other words this is where she died," Doris Flinkenberg said at Bule Marsh. "Fell down in the water, was sucked down into a dreadful whirlpool, never came up again. Is lying on the bottom, maybe she'll float up sometime. It's terribly deep here, the dredging didn't turn up anything. But you know she's lying here, that the water became her grave. There were witnesses."

In other words it was here, at Bule Marsh, that Doris Flinkenberg finally started her story. Midsummer Eve, still an early one.

Suddenly, in the middle of the party that was slowly getting started in the garden on the First Cape, Doris had done what Sandra had been waiting a few weeks for already. Given the go-ahead: The Game starts now.

"Come," she had whispered in Sandra's ear and pulled her away, far out into the woods, and little by little they had turned off on the winding path up to Bule Marsh.

And here they were now, at the marsh: the branches of hardwood trees hanging in a ring around a dark, still water. Opposite the highest cliff, that was Lore Cliff, there was a small sandy beach like an opening in the woodwork, which Doris Flinkenberg explained had once upon a time been a public beach. It was a short while, shortly after the new houses in the housing exhibition on the Second Cape had been bought up and the strip of beach next to the sea where you used to go swimming had become inaccessible. But later, after what had happened at the marsh only about a year later, no one had wanted to swim at the marsh and the public beach had been moved yet again, now to a real, sweet water lake in the western part of the county.

It was a strange place, it really was, even in the middle of the warm summer. Half dark and filled with mosquitoes at almost all times of day, and calm even when it was blowing fiercely in other places. You almost needed a storm in order to get the water on the surface of Bule Marsh even to ripple. And it was deep. Doris Flinkenberg looked down in the water. "Probably three hundred feet deep."

"That's impossible," Sandra Wärn said to her friend.

"He saw her here," Doris Flinkenberg continued. "That's how he drew it on his maps anyway."

"That's impossible," Sandra Wärn repeated. "Who?"

"You don't know?" Doris Flinkenberg asked and it was hard to hear if the question was part of the game or if it had truly surprised her.

"Well, him. The idiot in the woods of course. Bengt himself."

. . .

"And her name was Eddie," Doris Flinkenberg continued while the sun set behind the clouds and the mosquitoes crowded around them, two pale girls who, as luck would have it, both happened to be endowed with that rare kind of complexion that mosquitoes were not attracted to so that they could sit more or less undisturbed almost in the middle of the swarm in the small crevice just under Lore Cliff's highest point, which Doris had chosen for them, two very serious girls also, as said, with their homemade Loneliness&Fear shirts on. "She came from nowhere. You didn't know much about her. She wasn't from the District in any case because she spoke with a strange accent that wasn't familiar to anyone. People referred to her as *the American girl.*

"One spring she was just there, in the boathouse below the Glass House on the Second Cape, with the baroness. That's where she lived. Not like a daughter of the house, or a domestic servant, but like a guest of some sort, no one really knew. A distant relative, something like that. Sometimes the baroness said 'the boarder,' especially toward the end. They didn't really get along, Eddie and the baroness. There were rumors flying around Eddie about this and that, that is to say while she was still alive. Eddie was of the troublemaking kind, you couldn't rely on her. I heard it with my own ears. The baroness said it to the cousin's mama in the cousin's house where I was already spending a lot of time then. 'That girl is such a disappointment to me,' she said, many times. And consequently in the end in a rather upset state. She came to the cousin's house to warn the cousin's mama about Eddie de Wire. That's how I understood it anyway.

"So she lived in the boathouse. She was allowed to be in the Glass House only when the baroness was home. The baroness also explained all of this to the cousin's mama, so it wasn't a secret. Not directly. But it wasn't something that everyone knew. I guess that's the way it is," Doris Flinkenberg established worldly and omnisciently at Bule Marsh, "that for some people it's important to save face. In some way it was extremely important that no one find out about the problems she was having with the American girl. It was after all, she always said, still family.

"But later, Kenny, Eddie's sister, came. They were a better fit. I think the baroness became more content then. She stopped complaining about everything in any case. Though she never came to the cousin's house anymore. But there was a reason for that of course."

"Because if you're wondering what the baroness was doing in the cousin's house shortly before Eddie and Björn died, yes—so Björn was the cousin's boy in the cousin's house. That is to say before I came. They were together, Eddie and Björn, they were going to get engaged, it was very serious. So the baroness was going to do the cousin's mama a favor, she said."

"But Eddie, what a fascinating personality," said Doris Flinkenberg. "She spoke so strangely, not just with the accent, which she lost pretty quickly. But she said a lot of strange things. And it made a real impression on him.

"On Bengt that is, not Björn. For a while it was the two of them. Bengt and Eddie. Then Björn came and they were three."

"But in other words, fascinating," said Doris Flinkenberg. "You could really fall in love with her. And that's what he did. Head over heels. So in love that he didn't know left from right. You know what it can be like, right? We know. Young love. A violent end."

And yes, Doris did not need to say any more about it. If there was something Sandra and Doris knew quite a lot about it was that. When the contents of the two backpacks are united . . . It was the bitter midwife's assistant Ingegerd who had killed the seven incubator babies after being rejected by her lover, it was Lupe Velez who fell headfirst and drowned in a toilet bowl, it was the woman who had murdered her lover with fifteen hammer blows to the head, it was . . .

"And then"—Doris Flinkenberg suddenly shrugged her shoulders rather nonchalantly—"it went as it went. Death and woe became the result. Björn hanged himself in the outhouse by Lindström's land, and she, the American girl, drowned. Sank to the bottom of the marsh, like a rock.

"In any case that's how people think it happened, and so far there haven't been any reasons to think otherwise.

"And this is how it happened: they argued at Bule Marsh, and Björn, who was known for being the nicest person in the world, pushed her in the water out of anger. And by mistake. And then everything happened so quickly, so quickly. There's a hole in the bottom of Bule Marsh. She was sucked down into the deep. He couldn't live with it so he went straight to the outhouse and hanged himself.

"Just eighteen years old and he took his own life," Doris finally added.

"Loved her more than himself. That sort of thing is never healthy."

"But," now Sandra joined in with as steady a voice as possible. She struggled to remain calm and businesslike because she had her hands full trying to hold back the images that were popping up in her head again, facts that were mixing with fiction in a horrid way. The boy, who showed up again. A voice somewhere at the very back, Lorelei Lindberg's voice, from Little Bombay: *They say that the boy has murdered someone, I wouldn't go so far as to believe something like that, but there is definitely something unpleasant about him. How he sneaks around the house.*

So from this marsh a bit of this and a bit of that, old, new, truth and lies, she forced out her own voice and said as clearly and soberly as possible:

"But what's so unclear then? How is the mystery, so to speak, UNSOLVED? He pushed her into the water and she drowned. Everything was a mistake: he loved her so much he couldn't live without her and then he went and hanged himself. There isn't anything strange about that. I mean, there isn't a mystery about that, is there?"

She also shouted the last part and heard how her voice sounded hollow in the emptiness by the marsh.

"Well, of course," Doris Flinkenberg said impatiently. "It's not just that in and of itself. There is a factor X."

Factor X. And there he was of course. But not alone. On the beach opposite. They had come up there with their bags of beer and their cigarettes, their talk and their sour teenage excitement, which was now being spread across the marsh and with a slap disrupted all of the excitement and the magic. It was a small group on the tiny beach in the opening, maybe sixty–seventy feet away, but you could almost hear what they were saying to each other across the water since it was so quiet otherwise; Doris and Sandra had quickly crept down lower in the crevice so as not to be discovered.

Though they had nothing important to say, it was mostly one big raucous. It was Rita and Solveig and the brothers Järpe and Torpe Torpeson who often hung out together as a foursome during this time, and then there were some others in their wake. Rita Rat was in a bad mood as usual, and you could hear it. Rita managed to spread her irritability for miles around. Solveig stayed calmer, that is how it always was. Besides now she and Järpe Torpeson had their arms around each other as if they were married: Järpe daubed her ear with his tongue, lick, lick, and Solveig let out small small cries that were supposed to represent indignation but that expressed nothing other than some kind of bored enchantment. "That crazy Järpe he can never keep his hands in check." And it was Torpe, off to the side, who was sitting on the sand and drinking beer from a bottle. And Magnus von B. from the Second Cape, former general of the child army the Lilliputs on the Second Cape, but nowadays like grease on bacon with Bengt, and yes, he was there too of course.

Factor X.

Bengt was standing a bit off to the side, away from the others. He had walked all the way up to the edge of the water, he was smoking a cigarette and looking around. His gaze wandered about as usual, but suddenly it looked straight over the water, straight to the other side, up against the cliff where Sandra and Doris were hiding, stopped, focused, and saw.

Rita Rat came up next to him. Rita and Bencku spoke with each other, but so softly that you could not hear what they were saying. Plus Järpe and Torpe and Solveig and so on were talking the hind legs off a donkey in the background. Midsummer Eve. Such splendid fun. Torpe smashed the empty beer bottle against a rock. *Crash.* Finished another bottle. *Crash.* Smashed that one as well. And another and another and another.

But factor X. He looked across the water. Straight at the girls.

Though Doris and Sandra were no longer there. They had headed off through the woods, Sandra first, Doris after. Sandra ran as fast as she could, heart pounding, temples flushed, when she tripped over rocks and roots way out in parts of the woods where she had never been before. It was the deepest wood, where there were no paths at all, the part that lay closest to the marshlands where the marsh people whom Doris descended from had lived up until only a short while ago—now the area had been fixed up and would become an outdoor area for the county residents.

"Wait!" Doris puffed behind her. "What's wrong with you? Stop! I can't keep up!"

And little by little actually Sandra calmed down, with Doris safely behind her and with the growing distance to the marsh and Lore Cliff. She slowed down and there, suddenly, the woods opened into a glade. A soft, green moss spread itself out invitingly and she threw herself down on the ground, rolled around on her back and lay there and panted with exhaustion. Doris had ended up a good distance behind but when she caught up with Sandra she threw herself resolutely on the ground and in doing so landed so close to Sandra that she almost fell straight down on top of her. Then, instead of pulling away Doris put her arms around Sandra and they rolled around on the soft mat together, completely entangled like two wrestlers in a match or, well, like two people who are hugging. A completely normal hug. And that was what it was.

Doris, suddenly so merry and filled with laughter, giggling and soft, and if there was a game then Sandra was drawn into it at once. Also because she wanted to get away from the fear and the panic she had felt at the marsh a little while ago, and this was something else, something important. "Hey, what happened?" Doris laughed, whispering softly while she continued hugging Sandra, not to mention harder, and Sandra, she undeniably hugged back. "What happened?" Doris Flinkenberg whispered again but no longer as a question that should be answered but as a mantra, an affectionate and soft one, she was suddenly a purring kitten, so small and so soft.

She had hidden her face against Sandra's neck, nibbled on the Loneliness&Fear shirt with her teeth, sniffed Sandra's hair and stuck her tongue deep inside Sandra's ear and played with it there so that she had a prickly and tickling feeling in her stomach. So, what were they doing? What WAS happening? And what was Doris really whispering? Did she whisper *happened* or *hands* now?

Did she mean what had just happened at the marsh, that which had gotten Sandra to take off, or the other, that which was happening right at this moment?

But, an end to the puzzling. Because in the middle of the thought that barely had time to be thought, Doris's lips landed on Sandra's lips and all the uncertainty was dispersed in one blow. Because what it was could not be mistaken.

It was a kiss. A wet and true one, teeth against teeth and a rather lively tongue that wriggled in after, not to mention rather determinedly. Bursting from a relatively unorganized mouth to a highly well-regulated one, like a greeting from the one kind to the other. But who was visiting whom? Because what was it that was circling around the Doristongue if not another tongue, a Sandratongue? Not to mention that it seemed happy, just as enthusiastic.

So, a short moment, but just that, there was seriousness in the middle of the game.

The seriousness spread between the girls, so proud and, yes, so serious.

Sandra felt a real sensation and it was both true and interesting and important, but decidedly not amusing, not at all.

Because what did this mean now? Was this the step into adulthood? That moment when everything changed at once and became something else? The moment when the story about Doris and Sandra took another road? But in that case, then which one?

Was it the road toward the definite and the limited, which also had a name? That which was not so open to all possibilities like the winding road they were now on?

If it was like that, in that case, did you want to take that step? Already now?

Suddenly she felt decidedly that no, she did not even want to think about it now.

She did not want to grow up. Not yet. Not now.

But Doris, what would happen to her then, in that case? Would she be alone with the feeling and the d-e-s-i-r-e and so on? In that case it also was not any fun at all. Doris was supposed to come *along*, wherever you were, whatever you decided to do. That was the idea so to speak, the idea with everything.

But delightful relief, maybe Doris Flinkenberg was thinking the same way. Because the seriousness in the kiss had barely started and it was over. During that hundredth of a second in which the seriousness remained Doris Flinkenberg lay on top of Sandra Wärn and looked her in the eyes and Sandra looked back. Unfathomably.

A wee bit. And that was that.

And during the remaining hundredths of that second everything became normal again. Doris opened her mouth and said, suddenly with a voice that unmistakably resembled the voice it was supposed to resemble:

"I'm factor X. My name is Bengt."

And then Sandra was back to reality. She shook herself free and sat up on the moss like someone dazed with sleep.

"Hi," said Doris. "It wasn't anything. What's wrong with you? It was just a game."

And Doris, she remained lying on the ground. She looked up at the sky and now she was talking again.

"Sandra, when you're as lonely as I was. You know. Long ago. With marsh mama and marsh papa. Then you see. A lot. I saw, Sandra. All kinds of things. Both this and that.

"And what I saw? A lot of stuff, which I don't understand what it was, of course. I was so young. It was terrible for me. No place to be. No home, not a real one. I used to go to the cousin's house, to the Second Cape, and to the house on the First Cape. Those trips almost cost me my life later when marsh mama was going to punish me for them though I've already told you about that. But, in other words. I was quite young, but I remember what I saw. Absolutely certain. I saw factor X and the American girl. In the boathouse. They were together then and were doing things with each other even though she was probably five years older."

"Like what?" Sandra asked nonchalantly in order to conceal the lump in her throat.

"Well," Doris said seriously, "pretty much what we were just doing in the moss. And even more."

"And what's so important about that then?" Sandra blurted out hurriedly and mechanically.

"Don't you understand?" Doris got up from the grass filled with impatient energy. "That's what almost nobody knows. That she wasn't just with Björn. She was with him too. He was thirteen years old. As old as we are now. And she was nineteen. She lived two lives. Björn didn't know anything about it. Not in the beginning in any case."

And Doris's own thoughts lit a fire under her as well.

"Come. Now we have a chance! I'm going to show you something!" Doris flew up out of the moss. "We're going there now." She started walking again, quickly and with determination, with Sandra behind her. Of course Sandra had no choice even though she already suspected what Doris was thinking, where Doris was going. She did not want to go there, not for anything in the world. But she did not want to be left here either, in the moss, in the woods, which was also filled with evil eyes that were watching her when she was not with Doris Flinkenberg.

Still she was a bit surprised when she realized how close they were to the cousin's property. They were not at all as lost as she had thought; in reality they were not lost at all, just a few hundred feet from the cousin's property, where they were now walking up to the back corner of Bencku's barn. Again Sandra was struck by how much Doris actually knew about how you could move around in the District unnoticed, that she really knew a lot of places no one else knew. Despite the fact that it was a result of Doris's horrible past over in the marshlands Sandra could not escape feeling a pang of jealousy; suddenly she saw the difference between them so clearly. Personally she was the small, spoiled one, the one you barely needed to breathe on and she had fallen over and hurt herself and started crying. *Fall down, death die.* They had incidentally played a game like that on the bottom of the pool in the house in the darker part, she and Doris Flinkenberg. Sandra had fallen, fallen, over and over again, but then of course they had always had pillows under. And all the fabric, the suddenly almost so silly silk fabrics that had once been in Little Bombay.

She, the little harelip, while Doris had been out in the world, been moving in it, making it hers.

Here from the corner of the barn you could see the entire cousin's property without being seen by anyone else. You could see up to the First Cape too, not right into the garden but certainly far enough so that you could distinguish life and movement, music and voices. The Midsummer Eve party that they had left a few hours before now seemed to have gotten going for real. It was the kind of party that everyone in the District would seek out little by little. Also Rita and Solveig and Torpe and Järpe and them; they would pass by the house on the First Cape anyway in their search for the ultimate fun, which would not exist anywhere else, but they would still keep going. And Magnus von B. and Bencku. It was unavoidable. They would show up and then they would not be in a hurry to go anywhere.

And if you could see from the barn to the garden you could see from the garden down to the barn—and help! Sandra did not even dare think that thought through to the end.

"Come on." And now Doris Flinkenberg was already standing in the door opening and hissed, "Quick!" But Sandra dug in her heels and stood as though frozen in place and just shook her head. Did not want to. No. *Not in there.* N-e-v-e-r.

Doris almost genuinely surprised.

"You're not saying you're afraid? Of Bengt?"

Doris cleared her throat as if it were something extraordinary. Sandra did not answer, she just continued shaking her head.

"Idiot!" Now Doris became impatient for real. "This is our only chance. Now Bencku might be a murderer, but he really isn't that dangerous!" And with these words whose ambivalence Doris herself did not reflect further on because they were pressed for time, Doris Flinkenberg took a resolute hold of her friend and pulled her into the darkness of the barn.

Into the darkness, the damp, solitude.

It was the first time Sandra was in here and it was not really what she had imagined, that was immediately clear. But at the same time, she did not really know what she had imagined or expected. If someone had asked it would not have been certain that she would have been able to explain it.

It was rather normal, in fact. High ceilings like in an ordinary barn, in certain places there were spaces between the roof boards, which were in pretty bad shape. Creaking and cracking and a soft and sweet smell hung everywhere, one that even a jet-setter's kid could identify as a barn smell, highly normal. Sawdust, junk, and wood in piles. A chopping block with an ax in it in the corner. But not even in one's wildest fantasy could this ax be turned into a murder weapon; it screamed wood chopping. Nothing stranger than that. An old bicycle, a few steel bed frames, and then all of those rusty gadgets you do not know the names of.

His room was at the other end, in a corner. There was only a partition with leftover veneer panels making up the interior walls, there was a piece of cloth hanging in front of the entrance, which was not even closed. It was empty. No one there. And thank goodness for that.

And of course it was the room they were on their way to, with Doris in the lead, and it was easy enough to see that this was not exactly the first time she had been here on her own and snooped around without permission. Sandra followed her, still hesitant, but the fact that it was so normal in there got her to perk up noticeably, and she actually even felt a tiny bit of curiosity welling up.

Later inside the room there was only a bunk under a small window with endlessly dirty glass, you could barely see through it. A Russian wood-burning stove and a large drawing table that was a wooden panel on top of two wooden trestles, an old bookshelf with a few books. And everywhere elsewhere clothes, books, magazines, empty bottles, ashtrays, and so on.

The map. It was then, in the middle of the most ordinary of ordinary, that Sandra caught sight of the map. It was tacked to the wall opposite the bed, in the small corner that started where the bookshelf ended. And Sandra, she saw right away what it represented.

"Isn't it beautiful?" Doris Flinkenberg had tumbled down onto the bed with a crash, and no, it was certainly obvious, Doris was not afraid of anything in here. While Sandra withdrew again.

"He has several. They're the District. He makes up everything on them and still it's true. Quite clever.

"But," Doris continued, "we don't have time for this now. That's not why we're here. Look at this."

And Doris had stuck her hand behind the books on the shelf and fished out a key, an old, large one, and then, with movements just as practiced, she quickly pulled back the orange-colored rug on the floor, and there was a trapdoor in the floor with a lock, which Doris put the key in, unlocked it, and pulled the trapdoor open as if she had done it many times before.

She lay on her stomach next to the opening and rummaged around in the hole and pulled out a rather large bundle that she, with a short but certainly triumphant glance at Sandra, lay on the floor and waved to her friend that she should come closer. Sandra came of course, though she really did not want to, though again she feared the worst.

Doris Flinkenberg paid no attention to Sandra's hesitation, she was already in the process of unwrapping the bundle, a light blue blanket with holes, and revealed a bag, a shoulder bag in leather, light blue like the blanket, and it had Pan Am on it. The name of an airline, below the familiar logo.

Sandra just stared. She was scared again, of course, almost scared to death, but at the same time still fascinated. Extremely fascinated somewhere, so that it was almost burning in her body. But the fascination also made her afraid; all of it was so sick because she knew what it was. Doris did not need to say anything more. Doris did not need to say anything. But of course she could not stop herself:

"Her name was Eddie," Doris Flinkenberg started, like at the marsh a while ago. "She came from nowhere. She had everything she owned in a bag."

And without looking up Doris had started emptying the bag of its contents. She took out item after item and lay them out on the floor between them.

A few books, a booklet with guitar music. A 45 RPM record in a brown envelope without any text anywhere. A white woolen shirt, rather thick. A scarf, white-red-blue, a small purse, two wide, white plastic bracelets (which was almost the worst, it was so concrete), an alarm clock. A small case from which Doris fished out a photograph: "This is her. Look." And she handed the photograph to Sandra who accepted it mechanically so to speak, like a sleepwalker, the discomfort was still causing her to be too upset and too petrified really to be able to look at it, but she also accepted it with a tickling curiosity and fascination. And an alarm clock. A big one that you needed to wind at the back with a huge butterfly key, and Doris did. And for a moment the clock's resounding ticking filled the entire barn and at last Sandra had the desire to yell: "But quiet now, he can come at any time."

She checked herself in any case, Doris held the clock up to her ear.

"Listen to how it sounds. Like a bomb. A time bomb. Memento mori."

"A what?"

"Sometimes I set the alarm for Bencku. So that he'll remember that he's also just an ordinary mortal. In fact it's Latin and means remember that you're also going to die. Listen, listen to how the clock is ticking under the ground. Memento mori."

"Stooppp," Sandra hissed. "What is this? What are they doing here?"

"He's taken care of them. I guess he thought they were his."

Sandra fingered the girl's things. The book with the chords to simple songs to sing and play on the guitar, and those books, whose contents Inget Herrman would later explain to them in detail. *Breakfast at Tiffany's*, a book about shopping mall theory, and *Teach Yourself Classical Greek*, a volume that did not exactly look very worn. That small record in its thick brown paper, you wondered what was on it? No label in any case, but later they saw on the cover. "This is your own music. This song was recorded by . . ." and on the dotted lines you were supposed to fill in the name of the person who was singing and the date. And which song.

But of course Sandra did not have the peace and quiet to investigate anything in detail, not now, there would be time to meditate over that later. Now she just sat there and stared, and the songbook opened to a really fateful page as if on request.

"Hang down your head, Tom Dooley. Poor boy, you're bound to die."

"Factor X"—Doris lowered her voice to a whisper—"fell in love with her. So in love that he didn't know up from down." And then she repeated the same thing she had already said at the marsh, but now, here in the barn, with all the things, it sounded even more fateful. "We know what it can be like. Young love, a violent end." And Sandra nodded again, dreamlike, while chills ran down her spine, chills that yet again had a tiny bit of that terrible sensual pleasure in them. The unconscious midwife's assistant Ingegerd, Margarethe who loved only one . . . poisoned her sister with snake venom . . . and all of the others who sliced open their arteries in bathtubs and pools because of unhappy love and desperation, stuck their heads in gas ovens in musty kitchens with poor ventilation, started cars in garages . . . and left or did not leave behind more or less dramatic messages. "Good-bye, cruel life." *Adieu à la vie emmerdante.*

Kiss my ass I'll be damned now you cheated on me again and it was the last time I said.

"Said and said." Doris had, in another situation, once objected to such farewell letters when it was a question of suicide. "Just as if it makes things better by saying this or that at that stage, when everything is already irrevocable. I certainly wouldn't write a stupid farewell letter if it were me."

Recognizable, yes, but still so different. Because this was no story, this was real and you could feel the reality of it all right here in Bencku's barn, among the American girl's things.

It was a living person who had owned them, a living person who had used the scarf, read the books, tried to interpret the music, and so on. The American girl. Eddie de Wire.

And it was a completely different thing. Suddenly you became so excited by it that you could almost hear your own heart beating in the silence, in a race with the wretched alarm clock that was ticking so deafeningly *tickticktocktock*. Memento mori. You really would not be able to believe that there was a cheerful party going on somewhere else, basically in every other place, since it was Midsummer Eve after all, and right at this exact moment.

Loneliness&Fear. Sister Night and Sister Day.

"I'm a strange bird," Sandra heard herself say. "Maybe you are too."

It came out almost automatically, she would have been able to swear to it after the fact. Doris jumped and looked at her friend, amazed.

"But Sandra. Say it again. It's similar."

And Sandra repeated the strange string of words, Doris's eyes shone; she took the American girl's scarf and tied it around Sandra's neck and for a brief moment Sandra felt so strongly that she was the American girl Eddie de Wire.

She took the photograph in her hand and looked at it. The girl, the blurred girl. But still, in some way, acquaintances.

It was her, now it was her.

And the boy . . . her blood chilled.

"But what's with you? You look like you've made a fortune and lost it all . . ."

"But . . ." Sandra started. "Him."

"Aha." A glow of understanding broke out across Doris's face. "Of course you think it's him. That he was the one who committed the murder. Bengt in other words."

And it looked like Doris was going to burst out laughing over the absurdity of the thought. But she saw Sandra's frank need, where she helplessly fingered the photograph, regretted it and became serious again.

"Yes, there are people who believe that. That's what you'd think if you haven't believed how it happened for real, that Björn became angry at her and pushed her into the water. That that boy . . . so strange. And he was always together with them. What did he do that night? But Sandra. It's not him. I KNOW it."

"Come here and look." And Doris went over to the map on Bencku's wall.

"Here. Come and see."

And Sandra saw.

"She's lying here. You see. At the bottom of the marsh. It's certainly her."

Sandra gasped for breath. Yes, she saw. And saw.

"If he had drowned her, would he then have her on the wall? On his own map?

"I mean," Doris continued, "so that everybody sees."

"Bencku is certainly crazy," she established then. "But there are also limits to his craziness.

"Then I think it's probably Björn," said Doris, the twin detective. "When Björn became angry he became angry. One time he twisted the handlebars of the cousin's papa's bike out of position and hung the bicycle in a tree on the cousin's property. The cousin's papa's! Not even the cousin's papa dared go after him when he was angry. It didn't happen often, but when it happened, so."

"But," Sandra peeped when she finally got her voice back, "shouldn't these be given to the police? All of these things? Isn't it important evidence?"

"But Sandra, you don't understand," Doris said calmly. "The police have had all of this. That's where it comes from. Bencku got it from the cousin's mama. I know because I was there then. When she gave it to him. Because you know that the cousin's mama is the daughter of superintendent Loman, from the neighboring county, he was also the police chief in the District before the police districts were divided."

"Now I have to say it, Sister Night," Doris said grandly with such a hushed tone in her voice that for a short second Sandra got the idea that Doris was thinking about confessing to something terrible, such as "call the police now, it was me." Sandra stared at her and Doris stared back.

"The one who did it then?" Sandra stammered, rather helpless.

Then Doris relaxed because she had expected just that question.

And for a moment Sandra stood there rather bewildered and waited, like an idiot, with the photograph of the American girl in her hand.

But Doris Flinkenberg changed her tone of voice and continued in more everyday terms.

"Nah. But I think we have the solution right in front of us. Here." Doris pointed at the photograph of the American girl.

"I think she's the one we need to turn to. That she's the key to our riddle. Only her. The American girl. Eddie de Wire.

"We need to know who she was. Because there was something about her that didn't add up. It was as if she was deceiving us the entire time. Maybe Björn knew it, but in some way, he didn't want to. He didn't want to know. He wanted to be deceived. That's the way it is with love," Doris added, the last bit with all of the collected worldly wisdom she possessed.

"I think that we need to get to the bottom of this right here," Doris continued. "Find out who she was. Create a picture of her. Get to know her. *Walk in her moccasins*, as the Indians say. You don't know someone until you've walked in her moccasins for a few days."

Doris pulled up the scarf and pressed it against Sandra's face:

"Smell. Her smell." Sandra smelled. She did not smell anything. A bit marshy maybe, but it could just as well be because the scarf had been in storage under the floor for so long.

Doris touched Sandra. She caressed her cheek, and a moment's closeness—but of a completely different nature now than earlier in the moss.

"Now you're her and I'm him," Doris Flinkenberg said.

"Him who?"

"Oh, factor X of course. Say it one more time."

"What?"

"The bird."

"I'm a strange bird," she said like Eddie de Wire. "Are you one too?"

She had barely said it when the alarm clock started ringing.

"Memento mori," Doris said fatefully.

"Remember that you're also going to die," could be heard from somewhere in the darkness behind them and two of the women from the house on the First Cape stepped out of the darkness.

. . .

"When the cat's away the mice will play," said Anneka Munveg, who was one of the women. "And WHAT is going on here?"

But the girls stood as though petrified. There were moments in life when even a chatterbox like Doris Flinkenberg was quiet. This was one of them. Remember that you are going to die as well. For the one who was standing at the very back, her with the quiet voice and the literal translation, was no one other than Tea Saucer Eyes: Inget Herrman in other words, and she was looking straight at them.

With something mysterious in her eyes. There was not, when she saw the objects around the girls, any more laughter in them either.

"Two defenseless girls in the lion's den," Anneka Munveg continued as if nothing had happened, she had not picked up on the strange mood. Instead she was now looking around with all of her senses on alert like a real journalist is supposed to do when she comes to new places, always with the idea of a new scoop in the back of her mind, new experiences—and preferably the first to report them. Naturally Bencku's map on the wall opposite the bed caught her eye and she let out a delighted cry.

"But look at this," she called enthusiastically. "My God, so interesting. It's almost like a map over the Mumin valley!"

That is how Anneka Munveg continued her own bumbling show. *Bum bum bum bum* she carried on by the map though not for too long but certainly long enough that she would not be aware of what was going on next to her in the meantime. That the world stopped spinning for a second. Everything stopped. That is to say for the two–three other people. For Sandra it would remain a bit unclear if Doris Flinkenberg really had been as surprised as she claimed. "I should have understood," she would say. "But I had forgotten."

In other words it was this: the feeling of familiarity and

recognition. The one Sandra had felt for a brief moment when she had seen the photograph of Eddie de Wire for the first time. Now, in exactly this moment, the source of the feeling was discovered with a shudder.

Also Inget Herrman, who normally was not far behind Doris Flinkenberg when it came to how easily words flew out of her, became quiet. *Metaphysically quiet, so to speak.*

These seconds during which she in turn also understood, took hold.

The photograph of the American girl had fallen out of Sandra's hand during the first surprise. Floated over the floor where it now lay between them where everyone could see it. A moment, before, thank goodness—because right then Anneka Munveg started suspecting a scoop in progress behind her back—Doris's foot quickly covered it.

But they saw, all three of them. Eddie in the photo. The American girl. Inget Herrman. It was her.

Eddie risen again. A similarity so great that it just could not be a coincidence.

So quiet that you would have been able to hear a pin drop, *ping ping* like when the pins fell from Lorelei Lindberg's mouth in Little Bombay once a long time ago when she started talking without remembering the pins in her mouth.

"*Sandra! Help me! I can't see!*"

"What was it you were going to show me?" Anneka Munveg turned around and interrupted the whole thing, all of her senses on high alert now, when she noticed that her enthusiasm over the map on the wall had disappeared into thin air.

"We're out of drinks," Inget Herrman said to Doris and Sandra as if nothing had happened. "Where is Bencku? He said he had several cans left."

"In the woods getting drunk," said Doris Flinkenberg nonchalantly. "But I know."

"Doris, Doris," both of the women feigned again. "Is there anything you don't know?"

Sister Night, Sister Day. "That's her sister," Doris had said to Sandra while they were picking flowers a little later, flowers they were going to put under their pillows and sleep on so that later they would dream about who they were going to marry when they grew up. "I'm afraid I forgot to say that. I wasn't thinking clearly. I hadn't really put two and two together. Memento mori," Doris Flinkenberg repeated and laughed. "But it was actually rather exhilarating to remember it, for me too.

"So," Doris continued. "And now I'm picking my last flower. Then I mustn't say another word this evening. Otherwise there won't be any interesting dreams tonight!"

And Doris picked her last flower, a lesser butterfly orchid though it was endangered. And Sandra picked her last one, a lily of the valley, and in silence they walked back to the house in the darker part of the woods, down to the basement, where they rolled out their sleeping bags on rubber mattresses, crawled down inside them, and laid the flowers under their own pillows.

But Sandra did not dream about any man she was going to marry when she grew up. She lay awake a long time and went over the events of that strange evening when so much had happened. And now something else floated up.

The map. On Bencku's wall. She had seen what had been on it. The house in the darker part of the woods. The enormous stairs, millions of steps, and where? Up to heaven? Out into nothing?

And in the middle of everything a swimming pool. A figure there on the bottom. A girl? A woman? Who was it? Lorelei Lindberg? Or herself?

It also confirmed what she had known about the boy the whole time, even if it had never been said. He had been in the area in any case. He had seen.

And she had chills. Of course, she was certainly scared. But at the same time a strong will was born inside her, a normal will, to get to know the boy and speak with him. In the barn she had also understood that maybe there was nothing THAT strange about him, really. He was, after all, a completely ordinary person too.

Not just factor X. That was reassuring.

And not long thereafter the girls were walking with Inget Herrman over the cliffs on the Second Cape, and Inget Herrman told them about herself, about Eddie and Kenny, the three sisters who grew up on a property called Ponderosa once a long time ago and one time long ago also scattered across the world, "some are like reeds in the wind," Inget Herrman stated, "others less so."

Chantal de Wire, she explained, that was her, in another life. Chantal who set out for San Francisco and became Nothing there, Nothing Wired, more exactly. Inget means nothing, she explained, and that was how the name Inget came about. Plus the last name: the result of a quick unsuccessful marriage with some Sven. Sven Herrman, Inget Herrman's ex-husband. But no one Inget Herrman wanted to waste more words on at all.

"Girls, I'm not," Inget Herrman explained to Sandra and Doris, "exactly known for my good taste in men."

And they continued and came to the boathouse, the girls and Inget Herrman, sat down on the deck in front of the sea, only the sea there in front of them, and nothing else. It glittered of course and surged, of sea, it was so beautiful, *such a beautiful, beautiful day*. Inget Herrman with a girl on either side of her, feet dangling over the water's surface, all three. Inget Herrman told them how all three of the sisters had ended up here, in just this part of the world. Eddie who had gone away to visit the baroness, their mother's sister, or how it was; and how not so long after Inget and Kenny in different parts of the world as well, had received the terrible news about what had happened. "The District?" "The baroness?" They had not understood anything.

Inget Herrman told them about Eddie too. About Eddie's things in the bag; she explained them to the girls as best she could. The books *Breakfast at Tiffany's*, a so-so novel; *Teach Yourself Classical Greek*, which Inget Herrman smiled at, one of those a-big-smile-extends-your-life smiles; and the book about shopping mall theory and practice. That got Inget Herrman to gasp for breath, "Eddie, she tried so hard.

"Eddie, little Eddie, who was so young and confused," Inget Herrman said. "But still she wanted to do big things. Build worlds, build houses. A shopping mall. '*The future of consumption is consumption*,'" Inget Herrman quoted from that book. "Yes, I've read it myself. It was my birthday present to her. One time, when we were much younger and I thought there was still a chance that something might become of her."

Inget Herrman talked about Eddie, said all sorts of things like that, and all of it was interesting, it gave a certain scope to their own project at hand. "We need to walk in the American girl's moccasins," as Doris had said in the barn, but it provided nothing more. Meat on their bones maybe, but still, Sandra felt and Doris felt, so so strongly that they did not even need to talk about it afterward, that the mystery would not be solved with this information. That is to say with the knowledge about which books someone read and that sort of thing.

But still, it was so beautiful sitting with Inget Herrman on the terrace of the boathouse, where the American girl had once been herself, sat at exactly the same place, with the same fantastic sea in front of her, *exactly right here*. And that was something to hold on to, that, strangely enough, meant more.

And when Inget Herrman later spoke about greater things in connection to Eddie, more overarching, that was when you really felt you were on the right track.

"We didn't know each other all that well," said Inget Herrman. "Life can be like that. Even with your own sister. All three of us were separated pretty early. We were separated like reeds in the wind . . .

"It was actually first after Eddie's death that we were reunited. Me and Kenny anyway. We heard what had happened. On the other side of the world. We were both in America at the time, Kenny and I. But in different places, for a long time back. But we traveled here together. And then we just stayed here. Kenny with the baroness and I . . . I just. didn't get away from here. I didn't have any plans. Then. I just stayed here—

"But," Inget Herrman continued, "Eddie. It's a pity about Eddie. She was so alone. So very, very alone. We're all alone," Inget Herrman stated. "But Eddie, she was so alone you could smell it. And it was attractive but also pitiful. All the loneliness," Inget Herrman stated again, "rests on a secret."

And she had barely said it when Doris Flinkenberg filled in.

"I know what it's like to be alone." And, with a glance at Sandra, "We. We know."

It was such a spiritual moment, it would be remembered years after they had stopped solving the mystery of the American girl, that mystery and all other mysteries, when you did not want to know about any mysteries at all. Remembered later, later, when you were alone for real, what it had been like to talk with Inget Herrman about loneliness, abandonment, on such a fantastic, beautiful summer morning on the terrace of the boathouse.

"The sea was never so shimmering as when you walked by my side," as it played on Doris Flinkenberg's cassette tape player.

And Inget Herrman, who spoke about love, she was the only one who did not raise her eyebrows at the fact that it might have been Bengt and Eddie who loved each other most, despite the age difference, despite all the strangeness in it.

"A young boy. A half-grown girl. Who had nothing in common. What did they have in common?" Inget Herrman reasoned.

"In common," she later snorted. "As if love. Would be about that. Having something in common.

"I'm going to tell you about love," said Inget Herrman. "You don't fall in love with someone because that person is nice or mean or even because of that person's thousand good qualities. You fall in love with someone who brings something inside you to life."

And the very last thing she had said, which was almost the best:

"In the fall, girls, I'm going to invite you to the city by the sea. Then we're going to make some study visits to art exhibitions and see good movies and good movie theaters and really talk more about this."

"Now we have quite a few suspects," Doris Flinkenberg said when they had left Inget Herrman that morning and wandered, though quite energetically, toward the house in the darker part of the woods and the bottom of the pool in the basement where they had their headquarters as always.

"Not her? Inget Herrman?"

And Doris Flinkenberg turned toward Sandra and looked at her as if she were an alien.

"Of course not her, gooberhead. Are you crazy?"

Of course they had put the American girl's things back in the bag under the floor in Bencku's barn on Midsummer Eve, the bag back in the hole under the floor, wrapped in the blanket so that it would not look like someone had been there and snooped.

But one of the things did not really get put back, which so to speak mesmerized them: that record. They had not mentioned it to Inget Herrman either, maybe because "to walk in the American girl's moccasins" was still something they were going to do on their own. They had taken it with them, in other words, and the next time they were alone in the house in the darker part they listened to it; Eddie's thin, raspy voice rattled through the house in all the rooms where there were speakers.

A magical effect. Because it was her voice. This was a record that Eddie herself had recorded once a long time ago, at an amusement park in America. She had put a coin in the machine and walked into a stall and sung her own song into the microphone, and a while later the record had popped out of a hole, like photos from a photo booth.

A voice says more than a thousand bits of information. Because it was here now.

The American girl's song, a weak, out-of-tune, and distant whine.

Look, Mom, what they've done to my song, she sang. *It looks like they've destroyed it now.*

In English of course, it did not sound good, but it was her.

"Look, Mom, they've destroyed my song," Sandra hummed afterward.

"But Sandra," Doris Flinkenberg exclaimed, "it's fantastic. So similar."

And Sandra sang and when she sang she felt it so clearly and strongly, she was not pretending to be the American girl, she was her.

And in Doris's company she continued singing to her heart's delight.

But she would also, later, continue humming when she was alone and in entirely different situations.

For example, when she was alone in the house in the darker part of the woods, looking out through the window. Looking out into the woods, out toward the boy who might be there. Be Eddie in front of him, not for real, but like in a game.

And she was still afraid of him, she was. But not in the same way as before. Everything was different now, he had become more real. He had taken on new characteristics for her now, almost *become* a person to her.

Factor X who loved the American girl. The boy in the woods. Bengt.

Women in a state of emergency

WOMEN IN A STATE OF EMERGENCY. THESIS PRO GRADU. RESPON-
dent: Inget Herrman. Opponent: Inget Herrman. Adviser: Inget
Herrman.

It was up in the garden by the house on the First Cape when
the women were there; Inget Herrman was lying on the plush-
covered sofa under the canvas cloth in the shade talking about
her master's thesis. Talking and talking. And it was interesting.
The girls, *the Soviet counterpart*, up in the sea apple tree, and
with all of the other women around. "Proposal for an aesthetic
of resistance," Inget Herrman explained, taking another gulp
of wine, and of course the girls in the tree did not understand a
bit of it, "essentially" as Inget Herrman also said, but certainly
a lot of excitement and it was nice.

It was nice up there in the garden, so nice that if you happened to laugh at everything you saw and heard, both while everything was going on and maybe sometime afterward, you did
not laugh because it might have been funny in a stupid way. So
to speak ridiculous and meaningless.

Because there was something important there—you would
really understand how important later, when it had disappeared,
gone. Not only when the women themselves had left the garden
and the house on the First Cape, but gone altogether. "Everything that was wide open becomes a closed world again," as Lill
Lindfors sang on one of the records that were always playing up
there.

And that everything would be over, gone, so quickly. It was
something you had not foreseen while everything was going on.

It would be missed. And truly.

. . .

Bengt and Magnus von B. who were grilling bittyfish and green
sea apples on the stone grill, Inget Herrman with her generously
filled glass at her side. She was happy then, Inget Herrman, always happy when she had a very full glass of wine at her side.

Inget Herrman who drew a picture of "the woman's path and
other paths" on the tablecloth with a pen. A figure that maybe
slightly resembled the figures on Bencku's maps but mostly in
the intention, so to speak. Not in how they looked, in the aesthetic itself. They were not good-looking in any way, instead
rather streaky and straggly.

The woman's path and other paths: it was a straight line that
shot up out of the ground like the trunk of a tree, thick and
determined; it was, Inget Herrman explained, "a woman's path
of tradition and custom." But already almost from the beginning, from the root so to speak, other lines also extended from
these, out, this way and that way, thinner, just as thick, in certain places thicker than that straight line that just went straight
on and on.

On the one hand the figure became something of a rather entangled bush, but on the other hand you could also see it, if you
wanted to, like rays from a sun. Like lines of glitter, individual,
separate, all sparkling in their own right.

It was beautiful.

And Inget Herrman exulted:

"And what do we say about this? If it's also like this?"

And took a big gulp from her glass again, and added
thoughtfully:

"I think I'm also going to put this in the folder for my research material."

It was her thesis she was talking about.

And it was Laura B-H, who was writing a novel up in the tower
that summer, a novel about women that would later bring her

honor and fame. Though she did not know it then, she was just sitting and writing.

"About a real woman's life for real. That's important, I think."

Laura B-H who was lying down on her back on the ground in the garden one day, in order to read a poem that she had written once and had never finished. "It was in Ljubljana," it started, and it had a thousand echo effects that she really could not manage keeping straight. "It was in Ljubljana," and it described one of her own, personal experiences. How she had been out traveling, as "a lone woman in the world," and suddenly just grown tired of how you were not allowed to be alone (in peace) anywhere, how there was always some guy there reminding you of who you were, smacking his lips in your ear and grabbing hold. In Ljubljana she had had enough. She had laid down right by the steps to the train station and yelled to everyone, "Come on then. Touch me. Walk over me."

But in her own mother tongue. No one had understood. And it had of course been, explained Laura B-H, her good luck.

Because then the police arrived and she was arrested for disorderly conduct.

She read that poem and it was hideous as a poem. Most of the women up there thought so too, but the ordeal itself, the experience was true. It existed.

And you saw nothing of it then, it was something you would think about mostly later. That all of those people in the garden, everyone who had come here, who spent this time with the women in the garden, they all had something in their past that caused them to be right here at right this moment in the history of the world, and not anywhere else.

In the garden in the middle, for the girls, for Magnus and Bencku, for the women themselves, but for others, still: on the side.

In the garden in the middle, but still off to the side.

The garden in the middle, but only for a while.

The women would leave the house on the First Cape barely a year later, and that bus, *Eldrid's Spiritual Sojourn*, would not start. While the women hung out in the garden, the light red bus *Eldrid's Spiritual Sojourn* would stand parked below the hill and slowly rust away.

"Now we have to get to the bottom of this," Doris continued in the house in the darker part. "Take everything from the beginning. Leaving no suspects out."

Look, Mom, they've destroyed my song. When Doris and Sandra were not in the garden with the women they were occupied with their secret mystery. They listened to the record, the Eddie-record, when they were alone, over and over again. Sandra hummed and spoke like Eddie had spoken; she was quite good at it now.

"Nobody knew my rose of the world but me."

"The heart is a heartless hunter."

And the very best:

"I'm a strange bird. Are you one too?"

And she was wearing Eddie-clothes (it was a specially designed outfit that the girls had come up with, all on their own, and after coming up with this idea, Sandra Wärn had sewn it for herself using the sewing machine).

And Doris rolled her eyes.

"But Sandra. It's so good. It's just right."

And added:

"Can I be factor X now?"

Sandra nodded.

And Doris was factor X and came forward and then they did everything they imagined Eddie and factor X had done. With feeling of course. But it had nothing to do with the embrace in the moss, the one that had taken place on Midsummer Eve, once quite a long time ago.

It drifted away now. For the time being.

. . .

"Eddie," said Doris. "She stole. Things. From the baroness. It drove the baroness mad with despair. 'She is such a disappointment to me,' she said to the cousin's mama. It could very well have been a motive for murder."

"Mmm," said Sandra, in the middle of the Eddie game.

"Sandra, are you listening?"

"Yeah."

"But still. I don't really believe it. It was . . . family. And besides. Why would she invite the girl here from America just to kill her here?"

"It's not really convincing," Doris said and shoved Sandra who was humming her Eddie-song again.

"And the cousin's mama," Sandra said.

"What about her?" Doris asked viciously.

"She couldn't stand Eddie de Wire. I'm not saying she did it but we were going to look at everything, leaving nothing out. Maybe she was jealous. I mean, Bencku and Björn, they were the apples of her eye. Her children. And then the American girl came out of nowhere and took them away from her. Both of them, at once."

This had made Doris Flinkenberg deliberate for a moment.

"Yeah," she said carefully. "You're right. But I don't think so . . ." Doris thought for a while in order to come up with a real argument. "Once while Eddie was alive and was with Björn out there on the cousin's property, she said, 'That girl, Doris, is a theatrical performance.' But later when everything had happened, she regretted it terribly. 'I have such a hard time living, Doris,' she said, 'because of everything I've said. It's too terrible. Certainly this is a tragedy, it breaks your heart. Young people, that they have to suffer so much.' Sandra," Doris asked, "do you think someone who had committed murder would talk like that?"

Then Sandra became doubtful.

"No. Definitely not."

"And besides," Doris suggested, "just because you don't like a person doesn't mean that you want to kill her. Right? Not even the marsh mama wanted to kill me, directly. I was just so to speak—"

"Sorry, Doris. I didn't mean it. I don't think that it was the cousin's mama either."

"What do you think then?"

"I don't know."

"Things in motion," Doris Flinkenberg continued. "That's what Eddie, the American girl, said to him. It made an impression on him. He fell head over heels in love with her. For a while it was just the two of them. No one knows how serious it really was. It was one of the secrets about them. I saw."

"And we're there again," Sandra said and grew tense.

"Yes," Doris said in a sober tone of voice. "With factor X. With Bengt."

"So you're sure it wasn't him?" Sandra asked softly, as if she wanted to reassure herself again.

"Bencku." Doris laughed again. "No. Not Bengt. Then I would probably prefer the version everyone believes in. That it happened the way it looked like it had happened. Björn got mad at her at Bule Marsh and pushed her in the water and then he went off and hanged himself. It was the easiest so to speak."

"Yeah," said Sandra. "But Doris. Why all of that? I really don't understand any of this. Why are we going to solve a mystery if there really isn't a mystery?"

And Sandra was calm and started pretending in the Eddie-clothes, glancing through the window as well, maybe one too many times because Doris was of the attentive kind.

And Doris got up and climbed out of the pool.

She went out into the rec room where the record player was.

And came back, with the Eddie-record in her hand.

. . .

One last time. She stood at the edge of the pool with the record in her hand.

"A little bird whispered in my ear," she said happily, "that the American girl might be—"

And then. She broke the record in half.

"Alive."

Sandra saw the broken record. THE RECORD!! with Eddie's voice, the highly unique—and she was beside herself.

"What did you do?" And she became so angry that Doris was struck dumb.

"You destroyed it!"

"Yeah and so! We have other things to do than to lie here in the pool and pretend for strangers."

"Damn you, Doris!" Sandra screamed and ran away from the pool and up to her room and closed the door. Threw herself on her stomach in the marital bed and lay there and cried and screamed, cried and screamed, until little by little she did not understand why she was so upset.

That record, Eddie. The American girl. All of it was so stupid. So damn stupid.

Alive? Dead or alive. What did it matter? She was tired of this now, of the whole game.

Doris. Where was Doris now?

Had Doris left?

But Doris had not left. She had not left the house. She had waited loyally outside the locked door to Sandra's room. Standing there, occasionally knocking, furtively.

"Sandra. Let me in now. I'm sorry."

And then, gradually, with Doris outside the door, and the crying that had stopped, the anger left her, Sandra calmed down. It was just a stupid record. In a game.

And she crept over to the door and opened it.

And there Doris was standing in her Playboy outfit, authentic according to the girls' understanding about it all. A short skirt and rabbit ears on her head. It was too funny.

"Now, Sister Night, we're going to leave this for a while. Now we're going to a party. There's a masquerade in the garden on the First Cape. This is my outfit," said Doris, as if it were news: Doris always wanted to have the same outfit if there was a masquerade. "And that's your outfit. You can wear the Eddie-clothes. Is it even, then?"

Women in a state of emergency (and the party culminates).
And it was off to the garden, as always.

"What is a thesis pro gradu?" Doris Flinkenberg asked Inget Herrman, now that she was bolder.

"You'll find out later," said Inget Herrman. "When you're older." Because it was a bit later in the summer and Inget Herrman was not talking about her thesis so much anymore. "Believe me," said Inget Herrman, "there will come a time when you'll wish you didn't know. That you hadn't known at all.

"When you realize that you felt better when you didn't know," Inget Herrman said and looked at the clock.

It was a few minutes before noon.

"It would be nice with a glass of wine," Inget Herrman said, testing.

"Not before noon," Sandra said urbanely.

"That's something Sandra learned from the jet-setter's life," Doris explained to Inget Herrman. "During the time when she was there. With the Islander and Lorelei Lindberg. It was hot and passionate—"

Then Sandra had elbowed Doris, quiet now, it's enough now.

But suddenly all words were unnecessary. The clock struck twelve and the sun was at its zenith, the middle of the day.

"Erhm." And suddenly he was standing there in the garden,

no one other than the Islander himself. "There's a party in the house in the darker part of the woods," he said, almost shyly. "And all of you are welcome there."

And then they had wandered through the woods to the house in the darker part, the women, the girls, Magnus von B., and Bengt.

And they had come to the house, where the Islander was standing at the top of the stairs like a captain.

And it was then that Bengt, who was behind Sandra, had said, "Sinking, sinking," though very, very softly, so that just about only Sandra could hear. And she turned around and looked at him. And he, he looked at Sandra too.

And the high point of the party was reached.

At one point the Islander and Anneka Munveg were sitting on the stairs and they talked and talked. Anneka Munveg talked about her interesting job as a reporter, and everything in the world you could report on to everyone. The Islander nodded and caught on because Anneka Munveg was also so sexy, with her big light-colored Afro and her sober, black clothes. And Anneka Munveg told the Islander about "the working woman's day" and all of that. And the Islander nodded, again, at the same time as his fingers hesitantly fingered the hair at the back of Anneka Munveg's neck, these fingers were demonstrably there. Sandra saw, and she did not push them away, she acted like she did not care at all.

But then Inget Herrman was suddenly there asking the Islander to dance.

And the very last memory of that evening was how Inget Herrman and the Islander had danced something they called the "cowboy dance" at the bottom of the pool without water.

"Didn't I say that she would seduce him?" Doris Flinkenberg whispered from somewhere in the background.

. . .

AND THEN EVERYTHING WAS OVER.
   SMACK.
   SUMMER BECAME FALL AND IT WAS HUNTING SEA-
SON AGAIN.

2. . . . and the whores

"THE FLESH IS WEAK" HAD BEEN ONE OF THE ISLANDER AND Lorelei Lindberg's mutual hits during the time when Lorelei Lindberg was still there. One of these many mutual hits, when it had been some time since the passion was over, admittedly remained in your head. But so to speak disconnected, like a ballad whose specific significance you no longer could grasp.

So when the Islander started humming it when it started becoming fall you understood accordingly, if you were Sandra, that it meant something, but not exactly what. You recognized it but at the same time you did not. It was old and at the same time new.

Variety is the spice of life. Maybe it was that simple. *Now Pelle has finished his dinner and is ready for dessert—an ice cream would taste pretty good.* That way of seeing things, that philosophy of life.

This was in other words a brief paraphrasing of the fact that when the fall came and the hunting season started the Islander became restless and started humming these old songs—and polishing his rifle.

And then one day Pinky was there.

"Hey, princess, are you sleeping?" She was suddenly standing at the end of the pool in the basement in a red Lurex jacket and with a pink heart-shaped bag, glittering so in silver shoes with four-inch heels.

And the Islander, in a phenomenal mood, was right behind her. "And where do you have the cocktail shaker?"

It was the sign that it was now fall and the hunting season had started. Another time. The memory of the summer and the women in the house on the First Cape: it faded.

. . .

That early Saturday evening when the Bombshell showed up in the house in the darker part of the woods again Sandra was lying sure enough at the bottom of the pool without water. But she was not asleep, though it might have looked that way. She was lying with her eyes closed, on her back, she was thinking. A lot of images flew through her head, new impressions. There was a man whose head was a glass ball filled with water in which a golden yellow aquarium fish was swimming, with long, multilobed fins. It was a slum in the outskirts of Rio de Janeiro, built in miniature like a toy village on a gray hillside. Small, small shacks in rows, people in poverty, people in real shit. It was more real than real.

Then the fishermen's pub. Where she and Inget Herrman and Doris Flinkenberg had spent the rest of the day after the art exhibit. "An examination of what is going on in art around the world right now," as Inget Herrman had stood and said on the steps of the art museum.

"Rather dreary, actually," Inget Herrman said in the bitter wind. "Come on. Now I'm both hungry and thirsty. I'm going to show you a real fishermen's pub."

"Is this what it was like living as a jet-setter?" Doris had whispered to her best friend Sandra Wärn.

"Sleeping Beauty, are you sleeping?" Pinky continued. "In that case it's time to wake up now!"

That was before the real hunting parties. But like a preparation for them.

The women in the house on the First Cape were certainly still there. A few of them stayed over the winter, but they were the more sinister and less striking ones. The ones who had planted sprouts that had, of course, already withered away at the beginning of October just a few weeks after they had been planted, dyed paper and fabric with paint made from plants that they had boiled themselves and then called it "my art" this and "my art" that and talked about it and analyzed it in various expert ways.

They also talked about getting hens and goats but were so hopelessly impractical and slow with everything that they did not even have the energy . . . just talking about it tired them out. Sometimes even Bencku pretended he was not home when one of them came down the hill and knocked on the door to the barn or on his small dirty windowpane.

"Bencku might have too much bite," Doris had determined laconically in the cousin's kitchen and the cousin's mama was just about to reproach her "now, now, now" when Doris had already opened the kitchen window of her own accord, stuck her head out the opening, and helpfully yelled:

"He's probably there. Just knock hard. Sometimes he doesn't hear well."

But the other women, the real ones, they were somewhere else. The more unforgettable ones anyway. For example Laura B-H who had finished writing her women's novel and had gone on tour with it; Saskia Stiernhielm who was back in the Blue Being, you wrote to her and had your letters returned (if you were Bengt, that is, but only Doris happened to know that).

And Inget Herrman then, who had to stay in the city due to the extensive work of gathering material for her thesis. The work was really advancing, it had received a new title.

"The material is still alive," Inget Herrman said in the fishermen's pub. And then she started telling them about the new title, which was a working title, and it was interesting but . . . the girls still did not listen to it.

"Is this what it was like as a jet-setter?" Doris then whispered to Sandra Wärn so softly that only Sandra would hear, but Inget Herrman snapped it up and wanted to know more. When Doris could no longer keep quiet she started telling Inget Herrman about the Islander and Lorelei Lindberg and Heintz-Gurt and the whole story . . . and she probably would have blurted out everything if Sandra had not started jabbing her under the table, shut your mouth.

Inget Herrman had looked at Sandra, amused, but said nothing more about it.

"But the Islander then," said Inget Herrman. "Dad. How's Dad?"

It was awkwardly clear that Inget Herrman still had the Islander on her mind somehow even though the summer had been over a long time ago and she was engrossed in gathering material for her thesis. Doris was also attentive, and when Inget Herrman went to the bathroom she whispered worriedly, "She hasn't thought about seducing him has she? Again?" And when Sandra had not answered because what did she know about it, Doris had said, "But Pinky . . . Bombshell Pinky Pink?"

"How's your dad?" Inget Herrman asked accordingly several times during the girls' study visits to the city by the sea even before she started showing up again at the house in the darker part of the woods.

It was somewhat later in the fall and late Saturday nights and she sometimes arrived in a taxi in the middle of the hunting party after she had sat in the fishermen's pub and drunk some wine in order to build up some courage.

"Good," Sandra replied.

"Doesn't he feel a bit lonely in the house?"

"No, maybe," Sandra answered truthfully right then because the day Inget Herrman asked the question was also the same day Bombshell Pinky Pink showed up for the first time. In the evening, after Sandra and Doris's visit to the city by the sea.

The summer, the women in the house on the First Cape. That party had culminated.

All of that was so far away now.

. . .

Anneka Munveg, the famous news reporter. You could see her on TV during the newscasts and different programs dealing with topics of current interest. Once a bit later in the fall when the Bombshell was already feeling quite at home in the house in the darker part on the weekends, both before, during, and sometimes also a while after the parties (except during the week when it was a regular weekday and no Pinky anywhere) and all three of them had lain on the bottom of the pool and watched TV, Sandra and Doris and Bombshell Pinky Pink. They had dragged the television from the rec room to the edge of the pool and it was rather fun to lie there and relax to your heart's content among the soft cushions from the sofas in the rec room and among the fabrics from Little Bombay, among the magazines and music cassettes—Anneka Munveg had suddenly been there reading the news in the newsroom and then Doris and Sandra yelled at the same time, "We know her!" not to mention that they gushed with pride.

"I see," the Bombshell said trying to appear unaffected. "Is she . . . nice then?" The last part had come a bit hesitantly too with a very frail and whiny voice that was completely different from the Bombshell's normal hoarse, grating, and deep one.

"She is." Doris Flinkenberg had taken a deep breath and looked around so that you would understand she was about to say something incredible. "Fantastic. Indescribable. Delightful." But at the same time she noticed Pinky's increasingly uncertain and sad expression, and that had almost been the worst of it, that it in some way seemed like Pinky had expected to hear just these things, and that it also made her even sadder. Then Doris Flinkenberg stopped herself, let her shoulders slump listlessly, and added rather nonchalantly, "Oh. She's okay. I guess." And then she turned toward Pinky all over again and studied her with admiration. "Can I touch your hair, Pinky? What kind of hair spray do you use? Can't you do the same hairstyle on me?"

Then Pinky brightened and cheered up again.

"No. It's not possible. It's a hairstyle that is unique to just me."

"A unique striptease dancer hairstyle," Doris Flinkenberg clarified loud and clear in an unmistakable Doris way, whereupon she got up and walked over to the television at the edge of the pool and positioned herself under the screen on which Anneka Munveg's magnified serious face was talking. Then Doris took a few dance steps of the kind the Bombshell had a habit of doing on those occasions when she was seriously demonstrating for the girls what she called the striptease dancer's trade secrets, *what every striptease dancer should know*, and so on. And the girls, especially not Doris Flinkenberg, had never done anything in these situations to conceal their great thirst for knowledge on this subject.

"Please, Pinky," Doris begged while acting like a striptease dancer in front of the television screen. "Can't you please do one *almost* the same for me?"

Said and done. Pinky had not been able to resist such a Dorisplea. And the television was turned off completely shortly thereafter and the girls, with whom Pinky was included on these long Saturday afternoons, were thoroughly occupied with dressing up Doris Flinkenberg as the ultimate "erhm, working girl," and it was this playful activity and its visible results in the basement of the house in the darker part that would later lead to Doris Flinkenberg being forbidden from entering the house on all Saturdays, starting in the late afternoon, throughout the entire hunting season. This is because just as Doris on *the big glitter scene*, which consequently for this purpose was the edge of the pool, was performing her "erhm, working girl's" striptease dance show with her own "especially daring" choreography, the cousin's mama in her brand-new Four Mops and a Dustpan cleaning overalls happened to come into the house via the door to the basement, which for the most part was used only in the fall in connection with the hunting league's meetings since it was a convenient entrance/exit for the cleaning and catering personnel. "But cousin's mama!!" Doris yelled beside herself. "It was just for fun." But nothing helped. Doris Flinkenberg's fate was sealed. "Now you see to it that you get home immediately!"

That is how Doris and Sandra came to take over the cleaning in the house after the hunting parties. Doris was not allowed to be there, but she was so curious. So every Sunday morning after there had been a hunting party, Doris came to the house in the darker part of the woods and Sandra and Doris put on their Four Mops and a Dustpan overalls, the new ones, specially designed for the new business.

"It really smells like a brothel in here," Doris Flinkenberg whispered delightedly.

The flesh is weak. In other words it was now that the notorious hunting parties were launched in the house in the darker part of the woods: Saturday evenings, Saturday nights, and sometimes even up until early Sunday morning. Then the house in the darker part was invaded by the hunters from the hunting league. Not by all of them of course, but quite a few, above all the ones who, after a long and wild day out in the countryside, were in the mood for a long night filled with pleasures just as wild.

With the striptease dancers, or "erhm, the working girls," or whatever it was they were supposed to be called. "The catering," the Islander said, but obscurely.

"Erhm, the working girls." This *erhm* originated by the way from Tobias Forsström, one of the teachers at the school up in the town center. He was the one who, in connection with a certain essay that Doris Flinkenberg had written a hundred years ago, the one called "Profession: Striptease Dancer," had stirred tremendous commotion and made it impossible for Doris Flinkenberg and Sandra Wärn to be in the same homeroom in the future, had taken Doris Flinkenberg aside and kindly explained that you were not supposed to say striptease dancer *but call the phenomenon by its proper name.*

"Maybe I shouldn't be saying this but it's called, erhm, working girl." And a moment's silence had followed during which Tobias Forsström had taken in what had been said, what had come out of his mouth by mistake. "Erhm, I mean prostitute . . ."

From one marsh person to another. Tobias Forsström took on as his special task to take Doris Flinkenberg under his wing. That is to say he originally came from the same marsh. We marsh people, we have to stick together. That was what he had said.

Doris had not really listened all that much to Tobias Forsström's explanations. She was mainly happy about something else: that she now had TWO words for the same phenomenon, if not three. Prostitute . . . working girl . . . tehee tehee . . . she could barely wait to run over to Sandra and tell her.

But the whores, when they were in the house in the darker part of the woods: in general they were all easily recognizable but at the same time hard to tell apart. In high heels and short skirts, so that, as it were, you did not notice any distinctive features or their different personalities. One had black hair, another was a redhead, a third was blond, and so on, and there was nothing in between in the nuances, rather clear, strong colors that mattered.

A fourth did not look like an "erhm . . ." at all, rather like a prim version of the school's primmest girl whose name was Birgitta Blumenthal and wore a pleated skirt and blouse with lace. But the difference between the former and the latter was that the former were wearing rather detailed undergarments under their skirts and blouses. Underwear in red and black—

And in general, on all of them, tops over their breasts. Tops in spangle lamé and gold lamé and silver lamé. And socks and panty hose with holes in strange places, or nets, panty hose that were like fishnets. Sometimes no panty hose at all. No underwear. No *underswear* as you said in the District.

They blended together. All of them but Pinky. Because Pinky, she was an individual, specific. Pinky in pink from top to toe: Pinky in the polyester satin jacket with the white edging, the one that was t-i-g-h-t-f-i-t-t-i-n-g.

Doris and Sandra and Bombshell Pinky Pink. On the days, those times when the girls were not in the city visiting movie theaters, art exhibits, or the fishermen's pub with Inget Herrman, they were often lying on the bottom of the swimming pool not doing anything in particular. Talking, watching television, flipping through magazines. Fashion magazines: old issues of *Elle* and *Vogue*, "French" *Elle* and "Italian" *Vogue*. They had taken them from the Closet.

It was Pinky who had found them once when Sandra had taken her there.

The magazines had been there the whole time, but on a shelf high up on top of the fabrics and all of the rest, and Sandra who was quite short had never been able to reach the top. But Pinky, in her eighteen-inch silver glitter heels, was enthusiastic. "It's just how it's supposed to be," she called, delighted. "*French Elle* and *Italian Vogue*."

Not, that is, American or English or anything like that.

"There aren't many people who are aware of it," Pinky said importantly. "But this person, she . . . was that your mother?" Pinky asked Sandra.

"Is," Doris filled in absolutely sure. "It IS her mother."

"I mean," Pinky said, for once a bit impatient with Doris Flinkenberg, "*was* in the sense that she isn't here now."

Because Pinky was like that sometimes, she said things like that, like those about the magazines and some others, that sometimes in her mind Sandra mistook the person a little bit and started talking to Pinky in the way she had sometimes, a long time ago, spoken with Lorelei Lindberg in Little Bombay. It was, of course, when Doris Flinkenberg was not there; Lorelei Lindberg in Little Bombay had never belonged to their games.

Besides it did not fit in. The Lorelei Lindberg who existed in the games they played was different, and that was not stupid either, not at all, but as a game. And the name, Lorelei Lindberg, which had come about in Doris's mouth a long time ago, it fit there. And maybe also here, when it was a matter of Little Bombay, but in another way. That name, it was most obvious then, was needed like a kind of protection. For Sandra herself, protection for something that should still be protected because it was still there, in her, somewhere. The delicate and the difficult, all of that. The name Lorelei Lindberg, as an incantation, a formula for all that *belonged to the kind of hard things in the soul from which nothing could be woven.*

And one time among the fabrics in the Closet where Sandra had been with just the Bombshell, it happened that Sandra started asking Pinky a lot of things that Pinky had not been able to answer, on the whole she spoke in a serious way, which she had never done with Pinky before or even Doris Flinkenberg.

"What kind of Dupioni do you prefer? With which kind of weave? Do you like taft or eighteen-millimeter habotai? I have to say that my great weakness is really thin silk habotai."

Of course Sandra instantly realized her mistake, but it had still been too late. You could truly see how Pinky became uncomfortable where she was standing listlessly, leaning against a shelf while Sandra was rooting in the piles of fabric; Pinky in silver glitter shoes with mile-high heels, in the polyester jacket and in a miniskirt made of plastic-coated fabric suddenly demonstrably chewing on that chewing gum that was in her mouth like always, whether it was or not.

And what had suddenly come out of Sandra's mouth was a language she did not understand, it was just silly and artificial . . . habotaidupioni what kind of drivel was that? And when Pinky did not understand she became irritated and dissatisfied on the whole, started rolling her eyes in the way that a striptease dancer is not allowed to roll her eyes, except in her free time and preferably not even then since bad habits can imperceptibly take hold so that they pop up in other situations as well.

"Does a man want to look at someone who squints? There's nothing teasing about that," Pinky had once pointed out to both girls. "Tease. That means playfully seduce in English. And that's what a strip dancer should do. Tease."

"Tease with what?" the inquisitive Doris Flinkenberg had of course asked that time even though she definitely knew. But Doris had not been after information, instead she wanted to see and hear how Pinky Pink explained it.

"Well, if you don't understand then—" Pinky had stood up on the edge of the pool and wiggled her backside in the small pink skirt and stuck out the one body part and then the other as belonged to her profession. "Senses. Certain ones. Do you understand now?" Pinky stuck out her chest.

All three of them had laughed. It was so funny, but at the same time it also struck Sandra in moments like these, but in a good way, like a surprise, how strange the understanding that so suddenly and so strongly existed among the three of them, the Bombshell, Doris, herself, these early Saturday afternoons when the hunting league was not back yet. Sometimes it was like there were not two girls and one adult but three who were best friends and almost the same age. And actually there were not so very many years between them. The line between them, it arose later, when it became evening, Doris's ban took effect and a party gathered again.

And right then, in the Closet, that time when Sandra and Pinky were there just the two of them and Pinky started rolling her eyes at something strange Sandra had said and Sandra became so sad, so very infinitely sad so that she was not able to hide it, a lot of noise could suddenly be heard from the yard. A glance out the window in the Closet and there, the hunting league had gathered on the stairs after the day's exercises in the woods and a moose that had been shot on the ground (it was waiting to be lifted into Birger Lindström's van).

Pinky, in the Closet, had started thinking about other things. She stopped rolling her eyes over Sandra also because now she saw how sad that had made her. "Hey," she said and touched Sandra's cheek. "I didn't mean it, sorry. I say and do stupid things sometimes. It's just that I don't know anything about that sort of thing. And when I don't know I get insecure and angry with myself but don't want to show it." And then, with a glance out the window and back at Sandra, as if she had discovered Sandra for the first time in a new guise, she exclaimed:

"And think about what you know. I mean about all of those fabrics. I think you're becoming a real woman."

And Sandra, she had blushed again and become a bit speechless, but in a new way—speechless from embarrassment but also from bizarre pride that she both wished and did not wish that Doris Flinkenberg had been there and witnessed just then. Woman. Like a task. For a second Sandra felt chosen, floating so to speak lightly on a cloud in the face of the task she had ahead of her.

On the other hand, she could also imagine what Doris would say then. "Sandra. Woman. Hmm. An interesting thought. But God, so entertaining." And Doris would then start laughing and Sandra would also start laughing. Because they really did not want to become anything, either of them, just be together, like they were.

"But come on now!" Pinky had woken Sandra in the middle of her dreams in the Closet. "We have time to see *Happy Days* before they're finished cutting up the moose or whatever it is they're doing."

And Pinky had taken off her high-heeled silver glitter shoes and then they ran down to the pool again and turned on the television and they had just enough time to finish watching Saturday's episode of *Happy Days* before the hunting league took a sauna and the "catering girls" started dropping in. Everything was set up for dinner in the parlor on the upper floor and little by little everyone gathered at the long, laid table where silver candelabras with lit candles were standing. The Islander took his place at one end of the table and Sandra, who was of course the daughter of the house, at the other.

But still a detail, down there in the Closet. It was something Pinky had said just before she took off her shoes and Sandra took off her shoes and they raced down to the basement barefoot. "Then I would never have left this," she said suddenly.

And she had spoken about Lorelei Lindberg of course, Pinky, her voice was low and serious. A quick glance through the window toward the yard where the Islander in a red knit cap was, as it is called, "chatting happily" with the remaining members of the hunting league in the middle of the long, tall stairs below where the moose that had been shot was lying, ready for further transport in Birger Lindström's van, but still smelling of all the life that had recently left it.

"Some people never get enough," said Bombshell Pinky Pink. "Some people just need to have and have. More and more." And Pinky had looked around among the fabrics and the other things in the Closet one more time, the remains of what had once been Little Bombay. "As if this wasn't nice enough and beautiful enough for her. As if this just wasn't good enough."

The evening turned into night, and even more night. The dinner was eaten, the party got going for real. It was, of course, a completely different kind of party than for example the women's parties in the house on the First Cape, but a party all the same and as such it was fascinating in and of itself. Sandra liked parties, as said, above all the part about being a bit off to the side and studying the party carefully. Furthermore it was now a matter of being especially watchful since Sandra had the special task of reporting to Doris Flinkenberg; this report would be submitted the following morning during the cleaning, when she and Doris Flinkenberg, dressed in their brand-new Four Mops and a Dustpan cleaning overalls, would tear through the house like torpedoes with vacuum cleaners, rags, and cotton cloths and different kinds of fresh-smelling disinfectant solutions. Doris usually had a thousand questions and she expected answers to them. Doris was extremely careful about being able to form a detailed and meticulous picture of everything that had happened.

The hunting parties were actually even more fascinating compared to the parties on the First Cape. It was, for example, because everything changed and became something else for a while. For example, the closeness you had felt to Bombshell Pinky Pink earlier in the day was gone like a stroke of magic. Pinky outgrew you and became someone else and if there was someone whom Sandra was a bit embarrassed to see during the party's continuing evolution it was her, Bombshell Pinky Pink. But Pinky also avoided looking at Sandra, almost pretended like she did not know her. And it was a relief in some way, it truly was.

But during the party, what happened: of course what you knew was going to happen. The hunting men's jokes became cruder and rawer and all of that and the alcohol flowed, and it was real liquor, pure schnapps and mixed drinks with whiskey in other words; no homemade wine here, no sir. And erhm . . . well, let's just say whores quite simply, not in order to heighten the pleasure factor or the like . . . and the whores in other words, they did what they were there to do as much as they had time for, more and more, the later it got, so that everyone saw. The

clock was ticking in other words, it got later and later, but Sandra sometimes managed to stay a rather long time, as a gradually
more invisible presence, as invisible as she could possibly become . . . Little by little everything was one big wound-up chaos
and the party culminated.

Howling men—also in that respect the Islander who had the
ability to be the worst—and prostitutes who danced on the tables
sometimes completely naked except for their glittering shoes with
high silver heels . . . and then everything continued exactly in
that fashion toward the climax point whereupon it always quickly
disintegrated. And thereafter you could be witness to the most
bizarre scenes in different places in the house. Grown men who
suddenly cried like children, shrieked and wailed over all of their
shortcomings in life. Never, in a place like that, more than one
man, but often more than one whore. And women who cried
over all of their shortcomings, though in other places, alone or in
groups. Whores who spoke about their dreams, talked and talked
and talked, but to themselves as it were because no one, above all
the men, heard them. They were just whores and that they always
would be, that and nothing else, suddenly became important too,
for the men—like a last defense against a threat, something something, which you did not know what it was.

But at the same time, for the whores, whoring and having just
that job and no other in that situation took on a completely different meaning. It became a way of concealing and protecting all
of the other stuff that was also inside you . . . inside the whore
herself that is. A way of protecting what was fragile and wounded,
those places inside that are soft-hard and transparent. Those that
are inside every person, and that, according to one of Doris's terrible pop songs, are, to quote, "the best she has." Suddenly, pros-
titution as protection in other words. But zero communication
with each other, whether it be the men or the women, afterward.

The truly great loneliness, in other words, and it was terrible
but also interesting to see.

That no one was listening to each other, that no one was listening to anybody, but suddenly everyone still had such a need to find an outlet for their own personal woes. Of course it resulted in a rather intense and hot atmosphere in the entire house (except in Sandra's room of course; it was strictly forbidden to go in there, on that point the Islander was adamant; and Sandra had also been encouraged to lock the door to her room where she finally, despite all of the escapades that were going on around her, was lying and sleeping quite peacefully in the marital bed).

Of course there would have been a thousand women from the garden on the First Cape for example who, if you had told them about what happened at the hunting parties in the house in the darker part of the woods, would have had the opportunity to really feel sorry for the "poor men" who could not have any real fun. But there were also others. For example, Inget Herrman who during Sandra and Doris's study visits to the city by the sea asked Sandra about this and that at the fishermen's pub after the art exhibit or the good movie they had seen.

Inget Herrman listened to the description of the party and smiled in recognition. Then she said both learned and interested that these were actually the kind of parties that closely corresponded to the original definition of a party, as it came up in the time of the ancient Greeks. Where there had not really been a question about losing oneself in a bourgeois way, "to have fun" (which Inget Herrman pronounced with contempt while at the same time taking a big gulp from her beer glass), rather to leave your entire day-to-day life and all of the role playing there. Divorce it for a while, like during a carnival.

"You don't do it for relaxation or that sort of thing," Inget Herrman continued at the fishermen's pub where she loved to sit and talk and drink and talk and drink, more than, you suspected, go to a nice movie or an art exhibit, more than anything. "But to cleanse yourself," said Inget Herrman. "Those men, they've understood that. This is one of the original meanings of the ancient Greek's bacchanalia.

"In other words it's not the fun that is the main thing," said Inget Herrman. "It's the cleansing bath."

And the girls, Doris and Sandra, Sandra and Doris, their eyes had opened wide, but they had understood. They had truly understood.

Though the idea during the hunting parties themselves was that Sandra was not supposed to be part of them for so long.

"Ahem, ahem," someone usually started at the dinner table already, "isn't it the little girl's bedtime?" It might be, for example, one of erhm, the working girls, or perhaps Tobias Forsström the times he was there. Tobias Forsström was in some way visibly troubled over sitting at the same table as one of the students in the school where he worked, but still, he did not go home, he did not make a move, say thanks and leave, not at all.

But on the other hand he was careful in other words about getting Sandra to bed, sometimes even before dessert.

Then, when someone said that, it happened that the Islander came alive and as it were discovered his daughter over the candles on the other side of the table and said something along the lines of:

"Aren't you going to go to bed, my dear?"

Interestingly enough when he said this, his voice was not filled with a bad conscience. Yet in other words he had, somewhat earlier, not been able to do anything but agree with the cousin's mama when she had said to the Islander, speaking of Doris Flinkenberg's banishment and that it had to be kept, that the hunting parties really were not the environment where a child belonged. Furthermore he had sworn that he would make sure Doris's banishment was upheld.

But when it came to his own Sandra he made no connection to her. The Islander was, so to speak, the first one to forget about his daughter at the hunting dinner table, and it did not directly depend on nonchalance or bad parenting but something else, which Sandra had an understanding for deep down in her bones, though she did not think about it anymore. Just her and no one else. It was namely a reminiscence from the time they were living the jet-setter's life, when it had been the three of them, Lorelei Lindberg, the Islander, and herself. In the jet-setter's life, what it now had involved (honeymoon trips, nightclub scene, interesting people, famous movie stars, artists, and beauty queens, which had also floated together into one big soup in her memory), they had shared everything and for the most part been together. There had not been very many limits. And the little girl had always been *there*—and she would always be there (also according to her own opinion, as said, otherwise she would have burst into tears).

But all of this was, as said, something in the marrow. And difficult, almost impossible, to make someone else understand, in words.

"Of course, Dad." Sandra would not have wanted to make the Islander sad. She had gotten up without protest, said good night, and left the party to its fate. Almost to its fate, that is to say, just looked out now and then afterward, in certain places, if it was necessary.

But Pinky, at night, toward the morning, to become a woman, was that it? How the white legs would glow against the fire-colored chiffon and bright pink organza, Pinky's white white legs. It was edging on early morning after just such a party when Sandra had gone to bed right after dinner. She had woken up early, it was only four or five o'clock, but suddenly with an almost Doris-like hunger in her body. She had just quite simply been forced to get up and go get a midnight snack in the kitchen.

She wrapped herself in her bathrobe, stuck her feet in her morning slippers, carefully unlocked the door, opened it, and crept out into the corridor.

It was completely quiet in the house, all of the doors in the cramped upper floor were closed: the one to the Islander's bedroom, the one to the parlor, the one to the guest room, and the one to the library. You could only imagine what was going on behind these doors. But in reality it was not very interesting, in and of itself—as Doris had said once when Sandra had reported, "If you've seen a coitus like that then you've seen them all, can't you tell me about something more interesting?"

And she was right, Doris—but now, still, there was something that got Sandra to stay on her toes and that was when she discovered that the door to the Closet at the opposite side of the corridor, next to the entrance, was ajar. And, could sounds not be heard from in there?

Muffled, half-stifled shouts and louder groans. Small, small screams. And oh yes, somewhere Sandra certainly knew she should not have been so curious, but she still had not been able to stop herself. She just had to turn around and peer in through the gap, carefully.

And there, somewhere among all of the fabric, among Dupioni, habotai, crepe de chine, and silk georgette, among silk brocade and jacquard, there was, lying with her head in the beautiful fabrics, her head buried so to speak, the unforgettable head that belonged to no one other than Pinky Pink, the Bombshell, you could not see it but you did not need to see, you knew. Because it was enough with the following: backside in the air, the short pink skirt pulled up over her stomach, like skin on a grilled sausage, the white thighs glowing—and he was at it behind her, pants pulled down, on his knees but not on his stomach like her, it was Tobias Forsström. He had a hard grip on Pinky's neck, pushed her head down into the fabric as if he wanted to suffocate her, and just when it looked as if she was not getting any air he pulled her head up again by tearing at her hair and then down with it again, at the same time as he was fucking, fucking her for dear life, for everything he was worth.

Then, suddenly, as if he had felt the eyes on his own neck, he turned around.

And discovered Sandra in the door opening.

It was a few seconds, but it might as well have been an entire eternity.

But Pinky, her white thighs. A silver shoe was still lying in the corridor. Sandra took it with her to her room like a treasure.

Yuck, Pinky.

In the morning Pinky was clearly in a bad mood. She was sitting at the kitchen table completely dressed with her jacket on while drinking black coffee out of a mug when Sandra came into the kitchen for her breakfast.

"My God, what a disaster last night really was!" she exclaimed and maybe she was going to say something more but she did not have time because a car honked its horn out in the yard and a voice called from somewhere:

"Pinky! The taxi is here!" And Pinky got up at once and hurried off.

Sandra did not tell Doris Flinkenberg about what she had seen in the Closet. Not because she kept any secrets from Doris, but because it just was not right. And she did not want to make Pinky sad—more so than she already was. Because Sandra knew, and maybe Pinky herself had understood, that all of this marked the beginning of the end of Pinky's era of greatness in the house in the darker part of the woods.

The heart is a heartless hunter, as the American girl used to say, one of her lines.

Because where was the Islander when Pinky was lying with her rump in the air among the fabric in the Closet? Of course he was in the house, but in his bedroom behind a door locked from the inside. With Inget Herrman, who had shown up in the middle of the night; the phone had suddenly rung in the middle of the night and it had been Inget Herrman from the fishermen's pub in the city by the sea and she had just said, "I'm taking a taxi and I'm on my way!"

Later Inget Herrman told Sandra that she really respected the Islander.

"It's so interesting to discuss things with him. Has so many interesting stories. Has experienced so much. Interesting."

The heart is a heartless hunter, Pinky.

That had been the first time Inget Herrman showed up in the house in the darker part of the woods when there was a hunting party, but not the last. She would also continue coming to the house, arriving via taxi at odd times of the day, often quite late at night.

But still, on the morning after the night when Sandra had surprised Pinky and Tobias Forsström, Sandra went to the Closet in order to clean up there before Doris came. She discovered then that someone had certainly been in there and tried to put everything back in order again. Some of the fabrics had been helpfully folded and organized on the shelves.

But there was also a shoe lying there. Pinky's other shoe. The silver glittering one with the thousand-foot-high heel and platform. Sandra took it to her room as well and hid it—from everyone, so that not even Doris Flinkenberg was allowed to see.

And Doris, she had come later, walking up the stairs up to the house where they changed into their Four Mops and a Dustpan cleaning overalls and Doris sniffed the air, "Hmmmm, it smells like a brothel in this house," and then they took their buckets and rags and steel brushes and dug in, and everything, everything was actually good again.

And when the fall became winter Bombshell Pinky Pink was disposed of.

"How's your dad?" Inget Herrman asked at the fishermen's pub.
"Good."

"But now to the art exhibit," Inget Herrman said. "You must have a lot of questions."

"Nah," Doris and Sandra said at the same time but still tried to sound interested.

"Your dad, he certainly has a melancholic streak," Inget Herrman said at the fishermen's pub. "It must get lonely in the house sometimes. Right?"

"Maybe."

"Strong stuff," Inget Herrman said about the movie or the art they had just seen. "Is there a party every Saturday? Also tonight?"

It was later, that Saturday night or the following one. Sandra had left the dinner table and gone to bed and the party had, true to form, continued without her participation. A few hours later she was woken up by a noise out in the corridor. There were angry voices, and at the same time, in the background, the doorbell at the front door was ringing.

Nach Erwald und die Sonne. Die Sonne. Die Sonne.

"Over my dead body is she coming into this house!" Sandra heard that it was Pinky, who was standing in the corridor howling. And then there was the other voice, which you immediately understood was the Islander's, calming and appeasing.

"But Pinky. Calm down now."

"But Pinky. Of course I wouldn't do anything to make you sad."

The entire time, in the background and rather loudly to boot, that unbearable verse was playing, over and over again.

Nach Erwald und die Sonne. Die Sonne. Schnapps . . .

And of course you understood that there was someone out there on the steps whom Pinky did not want to let in.

Then it had been quieter for a short while again, something happening at the front door, and then, suddenly, there was a knock at Sandra's door.

"Sandra. Are you awake? She wants to talk to you."

Sandra got up and opened the door and outside, in the corridor, Bombshell Pinky Pink was standing and was as upset as Sandra had ever seen her, holding Sandra's jacket in her hand.

"Here," Pinky said and handed Sandra her jacket. "Sorry that I woke you. But this is an emergency. She's out there. On the steps. She wants . . ." Pinky's voice broke. "I said she's not setting a foot inside this house!"

Sandra put on her jacket and went out and it was of course Inget Herrman who had been outside the door and not been let in. Inget Herrman who had taken a taxi to the house in the darker part of the woods again but now the taxi had driven off. Pinky had not let her in, what was she going to do? All of this was hanging in the air when Sandra came out to her, but it was nothing she said, instead she cheered up, Inget—because she was, despite all unexpected obstacles, in a wonderful mood—and that it was actually for her sake, Sandra's, that she had taken a taxi all the way here from the city by the sea.

Because she had come up with something she wanted to say to Sandra, something important.

"Let's have a seat here." And they sat down on the steps, Inget Herrman and Sandra, and there they sat in the darkness and the cold but it was so beautiful anyway because there was a clear sky and thousands of stars were glittering in the sky above their heads. And suddenly Sandra did not regret it at all that she had gone out to Inget, suddenly she had no thought that it was stupid for the adults to wake her and more or less drag her out of bed in the middle of the night.

Just the opposite. This was suddenly a moment she did not want to miss. Not on her life.

Inget Herrman next to her, Inget, messy and drunk, whom you still could not help but like. You liked Pinky too, and that was what was also making everything so difficult.

Inget Herrman who had put her arm around her and started saying that she had come all the way from the city by the sea in

order to tell Sandra, but she had of course been a bit too dazed
to really remember what it was, the words in detail . . . but she
got out enough, by the way of the stars:

"You have to look at the stars, Sandra."

"Carefully, Sandra."

"And then, then, you just have to . . . follow them."

And it did not matter if what Inget Herrman said was not
the most shocking truth, it was nice anyway. And suddenly,
it was almost fantastic, they were interrupted by a movement
below at the corner of the house, and suddenly the Islander was
standing there in the flesh, with a tray of drinks in hand.

And sparkle sticks, or sparklers as they are also called, were
poking out of the drinks.

So burning, glittering so fantastically—

And the Islander came with a big, wide smile, balancing the
tray with the sparkling drinks in his hands, up the stairs up to
heaven, where they were sitting in the middle, up to them.

The heart is a heartless hunter, Pinky.

Love does not save on humiliation, Pinky.

That is the way it is.

In other words, Pinky alone in the house where the Islander had
snuck out via the basement, the "catering entrance," as it was
also called.

Yuck, Pinky, Pinky.

And later, much later that same night, Pinky in the corridor on
the floor outside the Islander's bedroom, in front of the closed,
locked door. Pinky sobbing in her short, pushed-up skirt, pink
underwear in the air, like a dog. Pinky, gradually sleeping a light
and unhappy sleep, in the cramped corridor in the house in the
darker part of the woods, on wall-to-wall carpet that was so ugly
so ugly, so beige.

. . .

The heart is a heartless hunter.

Love does not save on humiliation.

That is what you can say about it.

And so, in other words, Bombshell Pinky Pink was finally disposed of. "I'm no longer a free man," the Islander would rave the next day when he would explain to his daughter that in the future Inget Herrman would be spending more time in the house in the darker part than before. "At least not one hundred percent," he would add, which would in any case be interesting in that he would namely never have said something like that even during Lorelei Lindberg's time.

Without realizing it we are transformed into gray panthers, Islander. Was it like that?

Or something else.

Something with Inget?

It had namely never been part of the Islander's style to *not* be with someone a hundred percent.

In the morning when Doris came to the house in the darker part she did not utter her usual "it really smells like a brothel in this house" in her Doris-specific way as she had a habit of doing. She understood intuitively there was something with the mood in the house, that something had happened. Something happy, something sad—or whatever it was.

But something that made it so that all comments were superfluous.

And when she went out into the kitchen she got to see Bombshell Pinky Pink at the kitchen table with a mug of coffee that was so cold and almost all of it was left in the mug.

"Never become a who—striptease dancer," the Bombshell said to Doris Flinkenberg with quivering lips and did everything she could to act impartial, but her face was red from crying and her makeup was in streaks of dark green and dark brown and black everywhere, and in the next moment, when she had said that, her face wrinkled up and she started crying again.

"They just despise you . . . in the long run."

"They say everything, but they don't mean anything—"

And the sound of a car that had driven down to the house below.

"Pinky, the taxi's here," someone mumbled in the background.

And then later, Inget Herrman came strutting so energetically fresh out of the shower and stuck her head in the cubbyhole where the girls were changing for the day's work.

"Didn't I say that she would seduce him?" Doris Flinkenberg whispered.

Then the hunting season was over.

Shortly thereafter the women also left. The rental contract had run out, time to leave the house on the First Cape. The bus *Eldrid's Spiritual Sojourn* did not want to start, so the women had to take a group taxi to the bus stop on the main country road in two trips.

They could have asked Bengt also, but the day the women left Bengt was in his barn, drunk, and refused to come out.

Also Sandra started leaving. To Åland, in order to visit relatives now and then.

It was in some ways a period of breaking up. "Everything that was wide open becomes a closed world again," played on Doris's radio cassette player.

And gradually at the beginning of the new year a family moved into the house on the First Cape. A completely ordinary one, they were called Backmansson and were mom, dad, son, and as it turned out the lawful owners of the house, or how it now was, their descendants in any case.

And Sandra and Doris continued to be together, continued to play. The mystery with the American girl, that, but also other games. Sandra and Doris continued to become obsessed with the details surrounding the events at Bule Marsh, Eddie's death and all the rest. But they always came back to the same old thing. Besides, it was starting to become a bit tedious. They did not get anywhere.

The American girl, like a riptide.

But the little girl, Sandra, she sat on her windowsill in her room and hummed. She hummed the Eddie-song, which she knew pretty well now.

In Eddie-clothes, that was a secret. How she sometimes, in secret, away from Doris Flinkenberg in particular, put on those clothes, the American girl's clothes, and walked around in them in the house in the darker part when she was alone there.

The boy. Bengt. Was he there? Was he?

She stood and watched him through the big panorama window in the basement of the house.

Sometimes he was definitely there. Sometimes it was less certain. Sometimes you did not know at all.

But also, sometimes it was enough just to imagine his presence.

And she grew, not up but she became older, and hummed her song, Mom, Mom, my song!

And looked out at the boy, the eternal, at the beginning of the woods.

Eddie in the darkness: it was those nights when she was alone in the house in the darker part and she did not know what she was playing.

"I'm a strange bird," she whispered into the darkness. "Are you one too?"

Breathed on the windowpane, drew figures in the mist that came from her breath.

The end of the Mystery with the American girl

IT WAS AT THE END OF THE SUMMER ALMOST HALF A YEAR LATER.
"Doris! Where are you going?"
"Out."
This restlessness when Sandra Wärn was gone.
Doris Flinkenberg wandered through the woods in the direction of Bule Marsh.

The death of childhood/What Doris saw in the woods. Doris stood on Lore Cliff, on the farthest edge of the cliff's precipice, like so many times before. She looked down at the smooth surface of the water about nine feet below her. She tried to see the bottom. She could not. And it was not the first time either. She and Sandra had stood at the same spot several hundred times earlier and they had realized the same thing every time. *It was an impossibility*. Bencku had never seen anything, for real.

What was on the map, it was just an idea. A picture.

Not a lie directly, but just what it was, a picture. An expression of.

"An expression of feeling and as such completely true." Inget Herrman had said that to Doris Flinkenberg when Doris on her own—without Sandra—had gone to the Glass House and spoken with Inget and with Kenny, Inget's sister, about something in connection with the mystery of the American girl. Completely private. It was not that it was supposed to be a secret, but a thought that had come and gone, and when she and Sandra had been busy with the mystery for a while Doris was strongly convinced that what had once been said was true.

Good news. And she wanted, completely privately, to make Inget Herrman, whom she liked so much, happy—and Kenny, who was of course Eddie's sister also—with the news. And it was not unreasonable that the first people you told what you almost knew to be true were those who were directly affected by it. In other words the relatives. The closest.

Sandra had not been there, besides she was gone, on Åland, with her relatives. And besides, something strange started coming into the Eddie game too, something foreign, something that in some way made Sandra drift away from her, Doris, a bit. Though Doris Flinkenberg could not exactly put her finger on what it was, it was something with those clothes, and the mannerisms. Sometimes Sandra dressed up for herself too, when Doris was not there, when they were not playing. Went and hummed that song for herself in her own way, the American girl's song. The Eddie-song. *Look, Mom, what they've done to my song. It looks like they've destroyed it.*

In any case, Doris had gone to the Glass House when Inget Herrman was there. That was after the women had left the house on the First Cape, but Inget spent a lot of time in the District anyway, with the Islander in the house in the darker part of the woods, and sometimes she visited Kenny in the Glass House, just sometimes. Otherwise they did not seem to have much in common, Kenny and Inget Herrman.

"I suspect that she didn't die. The American girl, that is to say, Eddie."

That was what she had said to Inget Herrman and Kenny de Wire, in other words, she had gone to the Glass House expressly to say that.

But it had not gone the way she thought it would, not at all.

"What?" Kenny had said, as if to say she had not understood a bit of what Doris was talking about.

Inget Herrman, on the other hand, looked at her thoughtfully, really looked. And then she had almost burst out laughing, or not directly, but in some way had been, well, a bit amused. But when she had seen that Doris had been so happy and had wanted to surprise them, then she had become serious again, a bit motherly so to speak, like when you are talking to a two-year-old.

"But dear girl," Inget Herrman had said, accordingly, "who is it who has fed you those kind of whoppers?"

"No one in particular," Doris had mumbled and her spirits sank.

She had come to make them happy after all. Kenny and Inget. She liked Inget Herrman so much. The tea saucer eyes. The sexiest of the sexy.

But, "fed you those whoppers"? What were you supposed to say to that? And Doris had pulled back, wounded.

Not answered the question at all.

"Oh. It was just a thought. A game."

She had said and then quickly changed the subject. And nothing more about it. But she had certainly had a hard time swallowing Kenny and Inget's—well, what would you call it?—almost indifference. Lack of enthusiasm.

"Who?" Inget had asked in other words. And she would have been able to answer, for sure.

Rita. Rita Rat, one time ages ago. When they were younger.

It was because she, Doris, had thought she had seen something strange at Bule Marsh once, something that she really did not know what it had been. But it could have been—

And since Rita and Solveig had also been there at the marsh then, she had as it were tried to get closer to them, at first. In her own way. She had teased them a bit first, Solveig and Rita and Bengt, but for fun that is. Pretended to shoot them in the back when they were sitting by themselves on a pier on the Second

Cape, keeping to themselves, so secretive, and had not wanted her to join them.

They had been so terribly frightened by it. In, yes, an interesting way. Rita had also become very angry and threatened to drown her most prized possession, the wedding present she had received from the cousin's mama when she had come to the cousin's house the first time, the Poppy radio cassette player, if she did not disappear right away.

She had been so angry, Rita, and there was something interesting about Rita in general. She was, also when she was angry, so obvious. You could see that something else was going on.

But later, one time in the woods, Rita had come to her. Not so long after. She had been different then. Normal. Easier to deal with. The way she actually always was, Rita, when Solveig was not there. When they were, as Solveig always nagged, "the two of them."

And then Rita of her own accord had brought up the events at Bule Marsh. She had explained how she believed, or actually knew, she said that, how it was. She said she would tell Doris even though she really should not say anything, it was a big secret. Simply no one could be told.

They had promised her that. Her, the American girl.

Eddie de Wire. They had not known her of course, but they just happened to be in the right place at the right time, "or at the wrong place at the wrong time, depending on how you look at it," Rita had said, and they had, against their will, been dragged into something, something big. Which could be dangerous.

"We helped her," Rita said to Doris. "That's our secret. Now that you know can you promise to keep it to yourself?"

Of course Doris had not promised anything right away, like on the spot. She was admittedly young then, but very used to having the wool pulled over her eyes. So before she promised anything, she wanted to be sure about what she was promising and why. She had in other words kindly asked to know more.

Rita had hesitated, but later she nevertheless met Doris Flinkenberg halfway. She and Solveig happened to be on the beach that morning. The girl had come there, the American girl, something had happened, she had told them. There had been a big fight, not between the American girl and Solveig and Rita but something the American girl had been a part of just before . . . in any case she could say nothing more about it—and yes, admittedly, the American girl fell into the lake, but she came up again.

"As luck would have it," Rita said, relieved. "And guess who it was who saved her? It was Solveig." Solveig who could swim so well and was truly capable of saving lives in the water.

The American girl had been so moved and thankful. She had as a matter of fact not really known how she should express her gratitude.

Finally, as a thank-you, the American girl told them everything about the rather terrible story that she had been dragged into with some people, not Bengt and Björn and them, but some others. And because of that she had to get away. She had to disappear. Completely.

And she had in other words asked the girls to keep quiet about everything. That they had seen her that morning. She had to disappear.

Could she trust them? the American girl had wondered.

And Rita and Solveig gave their word.

And then, when Rita had told Doris Flinkenberg this, she asked Doris the same thing.

Could she trust Doris now? That she would keep the secret now that she knew everything? When Doris was still hesitating a bit, but mostly for the sake of show, she had probably already started thinking that it was quite nice just being entrusted with something so big and important and vital, that she could have thought about going along with almost anything, Rita had said again:

"Do you understand, Doris? This is a story involving many people and if it gets out it's possible that nothing will ever be the same again. Not even in the cousin's house . . ."

And that of course put the screws in Doris Flinkenberg. The most terrible thing Doris Flinkenberg could think of was that something in the cousin's house would change irrevocably, something that could result in her being without a real home, and she would be forced back to her marsh papa and her marsh mama—

So Doris had finally promised, truly sworn, too. No, she would never ever say anything.

"Not a word to the cousin's mama. Promise."

That had been the hardest thing of all.

"Remember, Doris. It will become very complicated if a lot of people know. And you know how terrible this has been for her already. With Björn . . .

"Because the worst thing about this story," Rita finally said. "Is. That it probably is the way it seems, that Björn went off and killed himself for Eddie's sake. He was so in love with her. And he didn't know her. He didn't know who she was. He took it very much to heart to discover that she had been someone other than who he thought she would be, the whole time. But remember something else, Doris. Björn had a violent temper. And he wasn't the first person in his family to off himself. Almost everybody there had snapped. For all sorts of reasons.

"The cousin's mama would find it so hard to go on."

And Doris Flinkenberg had been able to understand that, no problem. So she had promised. And finally, promised. And it was a promise she kept.

Doris Flinkenberg was not someone who let the cat out of the bag once she had given her word to someone.

The most difficult thing had been the cousin's mama. But on the other hand, there were so many other fun things happening in her life then.

And with Sandra. That had been something else. She had

thought, maybe in some way, they would be able to play their way to the truth.

And then you would not be breaking a promise if someone, so to speak, came across something by means of play.

At the same time she certainly saw that now, if she thought more carefully about everything, how many holes there were in Rita's story. How many questions to ask about relevant points, how many HOLES.

So turning to Inget and Kenny had been like a test. Well.

It had not gone well at all.

So. Okay. If someone told a lie, if the story had holes in it and you knew it, what did you do with that knowledge?

If the story, so to speak, had holes.

When none of those affected even wanted to know about them.

And then Sandra. First, she was gone. On Åland, damned Åland. Second, she was going to run around making a fool of herself in the Eddie-clothes and hum the song and be so damned silly and fateful the whole time—just when you thought we were going to start advancing methodically, collect facts and really get to know the American girl.

Walk in her moccasins. As the Indians say. Even if only for one day.

Pretend for the idiot. Bengt. Yes yes. Doris had certainly seen it. She had certainly noticed it, yes. Sandra, she was so obvious.

So, all right. What do you do with this information then? Obviously not so much.

Doris Flinkenberg stood and trod on Lore Cliff at Bule Marsh (because at the same time, this damned cursed restlessness when Sandra Wärn was away).

The Mystery with the American girl. Ha. Ha. Ha.

. . .

But such a quiet day, moreover. Quiet not only there by the marsh, where it was always quiet, but in the woods as well. No wind. No rain. No ripples on the water. Nothing.

It was abnormal. A highly abnormal silence in the abnormal weather forecast.

The latter, the abnormal weather forecast, was at least an objective fact, which had been talked about on the radio as well. In the local radio's morning special that same morning, rather a few hours earlier to be more precise, in the cousin's kitchen, when true to form Doris had been feeling the anxiety around her for a while.

Sister Night, Sister Day. The strange restlessness when Sandra Wärn was gone.

Though Doris Flinkenberg had not known what the day would bring.

"The ground is boiling," the weather expert on the radio had explained. "A highly local phenomenon. But very interesting. It really happens at these latitudes. A combination of the high humidity in the air and . . ."

Of course Doris had not listened to it very carefully, she had tuned to another station where one of her favorite songs was being played.

"*What snow conceals, the sun reveals.*"

What a good song, in other words. But she also had not interpreted it as a sign of what the day would bring.

Nope. Instead Doris Flinkenberg had true to form connected the words in the song to her own rich world of thought and feelings.

And sometimes to put it mildly in an extremely unbearably sentimental way. There was this mushy side to Doris Flinkenberg. And in Doris Flinkenberg's head it was accompanied above all by different melodies that she snapped up a bit here and a bit there.

"Everything that was wide open becomes a closed world again," for example, only this little bit from a song sung by Lill Lindfors hid oceans of meaning for Doris Flinkenberg.

A relic from the time of the women. She had gotten the record from Saskia Stiernhielm when the women left the house on the First Cape and Saskia Stiernhielm had traveled home to the Blue Being again. Like a memento.

And Doris remembered. Every time Doris listened to that record she remembered.

And *longed back* to the women, to when the women were there.

When the women were there. Not an eternity ago. A few months, maybe a little more. A little more than a half a year. The past summer. Most of the time. But still. It was the kind of thing you barely remembered anymore. How it had actually been. And Doris, who really wanted to remember, had already forgotten so much.

Second to the end, of course. You certainly remembered that. That sallow day when they had stood on the cousin's property, the cousin's mama, and Rita and Solveig and herself, and watched while the women stowed their belongings in the bus *Eldrid's Spiritual Sojourn*, which later of course did not want to start and you had to call Lindström's Berndt and Åke and ask them to come up with the group taxi and drive the women, in two loads, up to the bus stop by the side of the road, the side that led to the city by the sea.

Their light red bus, *Eldrid's Spiritual Sojourn*, would remain parked on the cousin's property many months afterward and would finally be towed away, not by the women but by the family who moved into the house on the First Cape after the women. The Backmansson family. Which would be a normal family, made up of a mother, father, child who, as said, for the thousandth time, on top of everything, were the direct heirs to the house's rightful owner.

An ordinary family. As it should be. And utterly terribly pleasant people, pleasant, as Liz Maalamaa would say somewhere in the future. So not because of that.

But there they had stood unaware of this continuation, the cousin's mama and the twins and Doris Flinkenberg, this, in other words, rare mute day in the history of the world when the women packed up their things and left the District for good, stood—and if you were Doris Flinkenberg in any case—and thought thoughts that were melancholy. Also the cousin's papa in the living room window somewhere in the back, you knew this without needing to check; the only one who was not there was Bengt who was beside himself with a heavy drunkenness, like superduperdrunk, which he was sometimes when he wanted to have nothing to do with the world outside, in his room in the barn. And when the women had left and it had become empty in the garden and Lill Lindfors had sung melancholically and fittingly in Doris's head "everything that was wide open becomes a closed world again," this delicate mood would not be allowed to remain in the air for any longer period in time because suddenly another melody would practically be echoing over the property:

"IT IS REALLY PEEEACE WE WANT TO HAVE . . . AT ANY PRICE?"

And that would be Bencku's music, from the barn.

But still, the very last minutes in which the women were there: the District people on one side of the cousin's papa's property and the women next to the bus *Eldrid's Spiritual Sojourn* on the other, road easement in between. Stupid, Doris Flinkenberg had thought, where did this boundary suddenly come from? During the women's time there had not been any division of this kind.

But clearly the cousin's mama had also been gripped by the terrible mood that prevailed because she suddenly turned toward the first best person who happened to be standing next to her and it had just come out:

"They come through like a circus in a small town. They rig up their tents and invite us into their colorful and reckless performances, but before you know it they've left and gone on their way. Then you're standing alone in the square in the bitter wind, with hard cotton candy in the corners of your mouth, shivering in the rain and in the bitter wind."

Unfortunately, the first best person who happened to be standing next to her was Rita, Rita Rat. She had wrinkled her nose and said with a voice filled with apathy as only Rita Rat could:

"What was that?" And added some illustrative swear words in the District dialect, "damn," like "fuck off." "Fuck off," Solveig had sighed along, a sigh that was not directed at anyone in particular, but a sigh of tiredness and boredom in general.

But Rita Rat had not let the cousin's mama go, rather repeated, "What?" almost bitterly when the cousin's mama had not answered. The cousin's mama had rushed to say "well, well, well, well" but it was certainly clear she was a bit afraid of Rita.

Rita Rat. She did not want to be in any small town—was it maybe the center of the world?—where circuses constantly came and went. Rita Rat, she wanted to go in the world (she did not say this out loud, you would not ask her either, but she was quite obvious, Rita, and you could read quite a lot based on her "nose position," which you said in the District dialect, quite simply). Think metropolis then, think London, Paris, and so on. *And why not*, Doris Flinkenberg had said to herself, where she was standing outside the cousin's house in the muddy yard under the low sky of late fall . . . why not? (or on Åland, where Sandra was, with near relations: why not, apart from the relatives?).

Doris had thought like this and afterward she tried to exchange looks with Rita, but Rita had not caught on. Rita had quite simply stuck her tongue out. Solveig had also noticed something was going on after Rita's tongue sticking, and she had, so to speak, seconded it by saying "damn" again and stared maliciously at Doris Flinkenberg.

To accompany Rita: it seemed to be Solveig's main task in life. There was another thing she went around saying: "It's the two of us. Us two." And one time when Doris Flinkenberg had, with the best of intentions and meant only as entertainment, shown Solveig an article in *True Crimes* about the two telepathic identical twins Judit and Juliette, who had murdered their respective lovers with fifteen hammer strikes to the head (at least one of them) at the same time without being aware of it and Solveig had not laughed. She had adopted a serious attitude. Solemn, so to speak.

"Others don't know what it's like to be a twin," she had said. "What it means to be two."

There was something, yes, not exactly frightening about it. But certainly sick.

The women were gone, in other words. The house's real owners moved in. Backmansson. A small family that had inherited the house. Mother, father, child.

Normal.

And the friendliest. Still Doris Flinkenberg came to miss the women so that it literally gutted her.

"Everything that was wide open becomes a closed world again." So damned normal.

But Doris Flinkenberg started to suspect that normalcy was her enemy.

In other words, when the Backmansson family appeared almost out of thin air and took possession of the house on the First Cape it had been a huge surprise in exactly a few minutes. Right about when the mother and the father and the boy, who was called Jan and was a few years older than Doris Flinkenberg, had knocked on the front door of the cousin's house and later when the cousin's mama had kindly opened the door for them and they had come all the way into the kitchen to say hello to all members of the cousin's family who were gathered there for dinner.

Well, in any case. A normal family in a nice normal turn-of-the-century house on the hill on the First Cape, so normal that normalcy endured being repeated many times over again. He was a journalist, she was a photographer, they also had a daughter, but she was not there, she was studying the art of dance (modern dance and artistic fusion dance with Eastern influences the mother, Tina Backmansson, clarified in the kitchen in the cousin's house, just as if it made anything clearer) in New York.

The boy, as said, who was with them was named Jan and had said good day; he was going to be a marine biologist when he grew up—but they found that out later. And the following had happened. Rita had looked at him across the bowl of sausage soup. And she, yes—you could not even say "seduces," "seduced," "had seduced" him.

It was so damned predictable all of it. So normal.

And Doris Flinkenberg, as said, seriously started suspecting that normalcy was her enemy.

So then she was standing there that strange late summer day in the strange weather on Lore Cliff at Bule Marsh feeling sorry for herself. Suddenly experiencing such an unbelievable feeling of abandonment.

It was like a desert.

". . . everything that was wide open becomes a closed world again."

Doris also suspected that growing up would also mean that you would not know where you should go. The damned abandonment.

If Sandra was not . . . in other words Sandra. On Åland again.

This damned restlessness when Sandra Wärn was away.

So, consequently, Doris Flinkenberg was standing there on Lore Cliff at Bule Marsh shivering. In the middle of late summer. That so quiet, warm, overcast, mushroomy.

Flash. Flash. Flash. Flash.

What was it? Was something not flashing shrilly and red in the corner of her eye, in the reeds, down below to the left? Something she had been aware of for quite some time already, but in the midst of her self-pity she had not taken it in?

Something strange in the corner of her eye. Red. A red color in the reeds.

Poor Doris.

She went closer. Really close, as close as she could get. And then—she heard her own scream.

And then she started running. Rushed blind and wailing like a bolting moose in the soft, calm, quiet woods.

Ran in the direction of the cousin's property, on the path, and wailed.

Straight into Rita and Jan Backmansson. Collided with them and fell to the ground like a reed.

"Is she dead?" Rita's voice could be heard from somewhere above.

But: pop in the head. It became dark and quiet. Doris had passed out. And when she became conscious again people were swarming around her.

That was how Doris found the corpse.

Eddie de Wire. Her remains.

The American girl. She had floated up in the swamp in the reeds in the marsh after so many years in there.

"A relatively unbelievable phenomenon," said the expert on the weather forecast who was being interviewed on the radio again. "But not at all impossible. Just the opposite. A totally logical natural phenomenon. As a result of the strange weather we've been having, at times very strange, locally speaking, this summer.

Drought and humid heat at the same time. Technically speaking it's called earthquake vibrations. What is under the surface bubbles up again . . . down in the earth . . ."

Plastic is an eternal material. This is what Doris saw in the woods. A hand (from the skeleton). The red raincoat. Plastic is an eternal material. Red and terrible. Cruelly visible. So because of that.

Rita Rat. It was a Saturday in the month of August, Rita and Jan Backmansson were walking in the woods. They were walking on their own paths as they had a habit of doing, Rita a few steps behind Jan Backmansson. Jan Backmansson was talking, Rita was listening. And carefully. She loved it when Jan Backmansson told stories, it was almost as if she had been there herself. And the best thing of all: they were no fantasies or made up in any way, it was for real, it was true.

It was the same day Jan Backmansson had come back from Norway where he had been traveling around with his parents. It had been a working vacation. Jan Backmansson's parents were journalists, they wrote and photographed as a team and their reports were published in well-reputed nature magazines, not *National Geographic*, but almost.

They had been traveling in a small rubber boat with an outboard motor over the dark water of the fjord that was lined with high mountains sloping straight down into the deep. They had driven far out over the cold water, mother, father, child, all three in yellow oilskins and red life vests. Exactly the day Jan Backmansson was talking about while he and Rita were walking in the woods in the District, and as it were, getting to know each other again after a few weeks apart (otherwise Rita more or less lived with Jan Backmansson in his room in the tower in the house on the First Cape). It had been an overcast afternoon with rain that just kept coming down. It had also been almost completely still when they

left the city on the coast to head off on their assignment, but now
the wind rose suddenly, a wind that was blowing inland, straight
into the narrow but certainly not very wide fjord that just continued inland and they were moving quickly as that was the direction
they were going.

Otherwise it was quiet, just the little ten-horsepower motor
growling, no people anywhere, not on the water, not along the
beaches. In the water near the beach there were mussel cultivations: large white balls that had been anchored in a field in neat
rows and would lie unspoiled for so many years. The occasional
house here and there, mountain goats in the crevices of the steep
mountains, birds in the air. Large blackbirds against a sky that was
gray and white.

At the beginning of the trip Jan Backmansson had been
lying in the bottom of the rubber boat just looking up toward
the white sky with the dark birds. It had been an amazing experience. But suddenly the motor had coughed once, twice,
and then stopped and they had not been able to get it started
again no matter how the three of them tried. The motor had
just been dead and they had not even had oars with them, just
a boat hook you could row around with in an emergency, but it
was rather useless in the wind and the currents. And they had
ended up like that, in the rubber boat, drifting in the fjord.
The same silence everywhere, not a human being anywhere,
not a boat, and the current, as said, was strong, the current was
running away with them. Then the rain had suddenly poured
over them and the darkness continued to fall and very quickly
it became like a bag around them. They had drifted on, helplessly, the radiotelephone connection was also broken. And it
was cold; the chill from the ice-cold water hundreds of feet
deep was forcing its way up to them.

The quilted jackets and padded pants that they had on under
the rain clothes and life vests had not been able to provide
enough protection against the bad weather in the long run; in

the end they curled up on the bottom of the rubber boat, all three, mother, father, boy, close together, in the darkness. At regular intervals the father lit the flashlight and shone it over the beaches in order to provide a sign of life in case someone happened to see them. But it was a matter of being thrifty with the light because the bulb was growing yellow, which was a sign the batteries were running out.

A solitary flickering spire sweeping over the water. Otherwise nothing. Empty.

They had waited for help. Just waited. Of course there had been nothing else to do while the boat was drifting farther and farther into the apparently endless and empty bay.

Minutes as long as hours, a minute like an eternity, but suddenly, where they lay tightly pressed against each other on the bottom of the rubber boat, wrapped in all of the outer clothing that was on hand, they had nevertheless been able to discern a new noise, a muffled hum slowly growing and becoming stronger and it stirred both hope and anxiety in them. What strange thing was it, not rapids, or a waterfall? They continued drawing closer to the sound, which was becoming louder and louder sounding like a giant heart beating, a heart as big as the entire world, but the current was also becoming stronger and it was quite threatening.

But suddenly everything became bright behind a bend in which a ship popped up, a brilliant, enormous passenger ferry—one, it would turn out, luxury cruise ship with a lot of foreign tourists on board. And their little boat had shown up on the large ship's radar.

Afterward when they had been rescued and been allowed to shower and change into dry, warm clothes, the captain had taken Jan Backmansson with him to the bridge and shown him all of the navigational instruments on the beautiful, new ship. He explained seriously that it really was not a sure thing that one would catch sight of a small rubber boat in the water in such foggy and rainy weather.

"So you were lucky," the captain said to Jan Backmansson and then they were invited to eat dinner as guests of honor at the captain's table. Jan Backmansson tried to explain to Rita how strange it was to come in almost directly from the cold and the darkness and the fear into the ship's beautiful, grand dining room filled with dressed-up cruise ship passengers, so discreet and cultivated.

But then, right then, in the middle of Jan Backmansson's story that Rita had become so absorbed in that she had almost lost track of space and time there where she was walking behind him, huge crashes and shrieks and the sound of twigs being broken and thuds could be heard in the woods in front of them and before either of them knew it Doris was there in front of them, Doris who came running straight toward them, Doris who saw and did not see them, so beside herself she did not even notice though she was calling for help and ran almost straight toward them. Just as you thought she was going to collide with Jan Backmansson she stopped as if she had seen two ghosts, opened her eyes wide, and sank slowly to the ground lifelessly where she came to lie as a dead person.

Jan Backmansson had fallen down on his knees next to Doris and taken her hand in order to check her pulse.

"What's wrong with her? Is she dead?" Rita had asked, certainly worried but not without a splash of her usual harshness in which there was probably a tone of *someone always has to come and destroy things when you're in the middle of doing something important.*

Eddie wonderful, on a stretcher in the woods—the remains of her. Inget Herrman threw up. Kenny was deathly pale. The sisters staggered away, leaning on each other. Bencku was not there then. He was drinking himself into a stupor in the barn. But he would certainly wake up later, in the night, when it started burning in the woods. Suddenly a significant part of the large woods

was ablaze, and the flames lapped up to the house on the First
Cape where the Backmansson family in any case had enough
time to get to safety before that.

Rita.
　　Doris looked at her.
　　Rita met her look.

Rita looked back. But it was later, at Bule Marsh, when the house
on the First Cape had burned up, the Backmansson family had
moved to the city by the sea again and they had not taken Rita
Rat with them like they promised. When it was fall again, and
everything was too late, too late.

Later. Not yet. Just that day, that day when Doris made the discovery, she was dazed and beside herself, Doris. People were
standing in groups, both known and not known, on the whole
half of the District (even some sea urchins) at the cousin's house.
Doris had straggled past all of them, in the arms of the cousin's
mama, and up the stairs to her room. There the cousin's mama
had helped Doris get in bed, given her both sleeping pills and
headache powder and closed the shades properly, which covered the whole room in darkness at once, because they were real
blackout shades used during the war, and Doris had put ear plugs
in her ears and then fallen asleep and slept for a thousand years.

One and a half days, to be more exact. An entirely satisfactory
amount of time so that everything would be changed when she
woke up. Just as dark of course, but when she crawled out of bed
and pulled up the shade the daylight flooded in. Doris opened
the window to air out the musty smell of sleep.
　　As soon as she had woken up everything that had happened
the day before—she still thought it was the day before—came
back. The marsh, the red plastic, the hand and the bracelets—

also of plastic, wretched white plastic. A wave of discomfort had traveled through her. But it still had not been unbearably horrific then; she was thoroughly rested and alert and could even think about it objectively, a little bit in any case.

Suddenly she longed for Sandra Wärn, why was she not here? Why was she always away, always somewhere else, when important things happened? Doris longed to tell her everything, go through it from beginning to end. "Just as I thought it had never happened. That someone had said, a long time ago. That the American girl hadn't drowned. She just disappeared because she wanted to disappear, or had to. She was like that. You know what Inget Herrman said. Someone who showed up and disappeared again but before she did she had time to cause a lot of unhappiness and devastation. Just like—"

"Rita told me that I was wrong. That's not what I saw—"

But now, in the morning in other words, renewed strength anyway, Doris had opened the window and breathed fresh air into her lungs, sensually and deep. But. There was something odd, something bizarre, but also something terribly familiar, in the air. A smell. Or, stink. She had never smelled such a smell and stink before. Or yes, she had. But in her former life, in her former existence, in the marsh Doris existence. And that was almost the worst because it made her not only afraid but literally rigid with fear again.

It smelled like someone had tried to burn down a house. Namely.

You have to remember that Doris was a child who all too well, of her own dearly bought experience, knew a lot about this smell in all its details. Not just once, but twice, Doris Flinkenberg as a small helpless child had with great difficulty and only because of her own alertness managed to get away from the flames both times (and both times helped someone else as well, tormentor number one, and marsh mama besides, to save herself).

You need to remember that in order to understand why Doris became completely cold with sweat and panic-stricken again. That damp and burnt smell, moreover it was almost unbearably strong, damp with extinguishing and stinging your nose. And Doris ran again, ran down the stairs and out onto the garden steps where she remained standing in the dawn—it was morning of course, but morning *two days* after Eddie, the American girl, had been found dead in the marsh, a skeleton in a red raincoat of the finest quality, the coat almost intact but the body almost decomposed. Doris had been sleeping for almost two days. They really must have been dynamite sleeping pills (they were) that the cousin's mama had fed her so she would get some sleep that terrible afternoon after the corpse of Eddie de Wire was found.

Doris on the steps of the cousin's house, stopped and looked around. At first glance everything looked so normal. The cousin's papa's blue Saab was parked in the yard, the old moped that was rusting away was by the corner of the barn, a few bicycles, a blue bucket, a gray spray can that was missing its sprayer, a garden rake carelessly thrown in the flowerbed at the side of the house among the everlasting flowers and sweet peas in violet and pink with delicate stems that were hesitantly forcing their way up the brown wall, trying to hang on to the nails hammered into the wall here and there. But they were sooty, the green leaves softly spotted with brown. And the stink, it did not disappear, it was everywhere. It was stronger than ever, and then Doris's gaze lifted and she looked toward the hill where the house that was the house on the First Cape was. It was crazy.

The house was still there, strangely enough. And still. It gaped black with holes on one side. It was completely open there. As if a piece of the entire house had fallen off. And the tower was crooked and several of the windowpanes were broken. *The house of luck* stood there and gaped so desolate and destroyed in the quiet, quiet morning. The woods off to the side later. There was a hole in it so to speak. It had burned down on one side, the ground smarting with pain and the emptiness ran like a wide furrow farther into the woods than what could be seen with the naked eye from where she was standing.

"Like a corridor of fire in the woods." That was how Doris would describe it later, when she would express it in words to Sandra, recently returned home from Åland, whom she would meet in the woods the same day. But still, morning at the cousin's house, and Doris stood on the steps and reflected on everything she saw without understanding anything while at the same time she tried, and this reflection was a means in this attempt, to overpower the panic growing inside her. Somewhere she also became, which was calming but at the same time an insult to everything, aware of how normal everything around her seemed.

What happened?

Why has no one told me about this?

If you listened carefully for specific sounds in the summer morning, in addition to the silence that was a result of no birds singing (but they did not do that anyway this late in the summer; and far away, by the sea and the Second Cape, which was like another world now, a world by itself, the cry of seagulls and the like could be heard), you could hear the usual noises from inside the house: the radio was giving the weather forecast for seafaring or playing a familiar piece of music at a low volume, the cousin's mama was clattering with cups and containers during the morning dishes, but always made sure to leave a clean bowl for oatmeal and a clean coffee cup on the table for the one who happened to sleep too late. The cousin's mama. *Mama*. Doris, so small again, heard from the cozy sounds that the cup and the bowl really were there and above all safe and all of that. She was so thankful but at the same time it made her furious, and suddenly, before she knew what was happening she had run back into the house, thrown open the door to the kitchen, almost steamed in, and screamed at the top of her lungs in the cousin's mama's face:

"WHAT HAPPENED? WHY HASN'T ANYONE WOKEN ME UP?"

In other words right in the face of the person she loved the most and who loved her the very most, with moreover a practical love that was expressed in action and not in these incessant puns and words. The cousin's mama, at the sink, had looked overwrought, for a moment quite simply wounded. But then she had become herself again.

"But calm down, Doris," the cousin's mama said so calm and motherly. "Calm down." Put her arm around Doris's shoulders and looked at her with all the tenderness left in the world, and that, Doris determined, who so often saw that when she looked at the cousin's mama, that tenderness, it existed. "You needed to rest. You were sleeping so soundly. After all of that terrible . . . you should thank your creator that you have the gift of sleep. Otherwise there have been more than enough horrors and dreadful things. As if the other thing had not been enough . . . The alarm sounded, Doris Flinkenberg. There was even talk that the cousin's house would be evacuated."

And then Doris's eyes had grown to tablespoon size again because you never forget the terrible experiences of your childhood.

And suddenly, again, Doris had forgotten all her indignation, all her anger, and just peeped, perplexed like a small, small child:

"But THEN you would have woken me?"

And inside the cousin's mama all the love that existed in her overwhelmed her in just that moment.

"My goodness," said the cousin's mama, so to herself that she barely got the words out. "That's clear. Doris, small beloved child. Doris, little little child."

And the cousin's mama wrapped Doris in her arms again, so overwhelmed by this extraordinary person, Doris Flinkenberg.

Sometimes the cousin's mama had that feeling with Doris: that Doris was a like a world, her own planet.

A planet in and of herself, and not even she, the cousin's mama, had access to it.

"Have a seat here and we'll warm the oatmeal and I'll pour some coffee and I'll tell you everything. And look. We've gotten our very own hero."

And the cousin's mama had gotten the morning paper and shown Doris Flinkenberg. There was a large picture of Bengt on the front page with a switch in one hand, with which he was hitting the burning ground, and a stick with a hot dog on the end in the other. "Two birds with one stone," the caption under the photo read.

But then Doris would not say much more. Strange maybe, and also not. The fire would not become the object of more specula- tion from her side; it was as it was, a forest fire that had started during the strange weather pattern, or maybe quite simply a result of someone having carelessly handled fire. Thrown a burning match away in the dry moss, or a burning cigarette, by mistake. And there had been so many people moving about in the woods at just that moment. Doris's discovery before she fell into her long sleep, the rumor of that terrible discovery at Bule Marsh, had put people into action then.

There were many who had made a pilgrimage to the marsh to see with their own eyes how the last question marks in the mystery surrounding the American girl could be deleted. What happened with her? Did she really drown? The correct answer was yes, in other words. She drowned. What a terrible tragedy of love. Based on the stage of decomposition in which the body was in, it was also clear that it had been lying in the marsh all these years. "The last question mark dispelled," it clearly read in an article in the local paper the following day. Under the caption

"Schoolgirl's macabre discovery brings an end to things." And a rather fuzzy picture of reeds and the like, which were then old pieces of a corpse.

Maybe there were questions also when it came to the fire for example. But there are things you do not understand. Some things do not become better by trying to understand them. And remember that Doris was a mistreated child and somewhere inside her, that fire was still burning. The real fire, the one from the match that had been struck against the striking strip and thrown into something you had moistened with gasoline and *swoosh*, it catches fire, the house, where you are if you happen to be the unhappy victim.

Doris had alleged reasons to respect fire.

"If you stick your finger in a candle flame it will get burned. Ow. But you don't always get off so easily. With just burns I mean. And now I don't know if I—"

That was how Doris would say it to Sandra, that it might be time for other games now. Of course not the only reason, but still.

"Besides, I'm tired of this now. In the long run it gets boring with these fateful looks and these hot, uncomfortable shirts," Doris would really clown about on the scorched ground out in the woods where Sandra and Doris would meet again that same day, in the afternoon.

"Life is waiting. Come on. Let's get out the map now. The real one. Because now we're going to travel."

And Sandra would also be gripped by Doris's eagerness in the face of something new. And so it became that the fire in the woods marked the end of Doris and Sandra's game the Mystery with the American girl.

Sandra was not there when the corpse of the American girl was found. She came home the same morning Doris Flinkenberg woke up after a day and a half of beneficial sleep after the terrible events at Bule Marsh.

Sandra was on Åland. She loathed these relatives, the uncles and "the aunt" who stood behind her when she looked out over the ocean that was so close it almost smashed against the veranda window when the waves were high. "The aunt," who before you even had a chance to experience it yourself, talked about how nice it was, with the sea, when it came toward you. How "wild nature's forces could be."

"The aunt" also stood there behind her and asked a bunch of questions that Sandra did not answer, partly because she was not listening properly; she had enough going on trying to concentrate on experiencing something herself for once. Without a middleman or an instruction manual.

But when she did not answer, "the aunt" just said:

"Yes, to lose yourself in the sea and open spaces, that's an Ålandic trait. The big dreams—" and she did not finish the sentence, not because she would have lost her train of thought but because the continuation was so obvious. That is the way it sounded anyway.

"The aunt," in other words, there behind Sandra, at the window, otherwise nothing happened. No telephone rang, no one called to tell her that something had happened in the District, that the corpse of the American girl had been found.

Loneliness&Fear. "The aunt" had poked at Sandra's shirt when she had arrived.

"Don't touch it," Sandra had said.

"What kind of thing is that?"

And when she had not stopped nagging her, Sandra finally forced out:

"A game."

And behind her again, so close.

"What strange games you play."

Sandra said nothing. Well, she thought. She was no islander. Definitely not.

She was no islander. She was from the District, the marsh, from where Sister Night was, Sister Day.

"I'm going to become Queen of the Marsh when I grow up," she had said to "the aunt" at another time. "A really slimy one."

"The aunt," to whom all of this was abracadabra, rolled her eyes but said nothing.

Queen of the Marsh. So lovely. She thought she had come up with something herself there. A new thing. A seed. A seed for a new game to play with Doris Flinkenberg. The Return of the Marsh Queen. When she came home from Åland that is.

And it struck her again how she longed for home, for Doris Flinkenberg. Longed so terribly for Doris, the American girl, the boy in the woods, Inget Herrman (yes, even Inget Herrman), the Islander, and the house in the darker part.

But despite all interruptions, all outside interference, Sandra would be able to swear to one thing afterward. That at the moment, exactly at the exact point in time when Doris Flinkenberg was standing on Lore Cliff at Bule Marsh in the District and suddenly and unexpectedly caught sight of something red in the reeds off to the side, then Sandra herself had been standing at the window on the veranda on Åland staring at the sea that was swelling toward her, humming a certain song, the Eddie-song.

And that, this simultaneousness, was something she would never be able to explain to anyone but Doris Flinkenberg.

"I heard everything, though later. When I came home. Just now. I was on Åland."

"Eddie then? What do we do now?"

Doris had shrugged her shoulders. Sometimes you are just wrong.

"You don't know everything in this world. And besides, it was just a game."

"Come on," said Doris Flinkenberg. "I'm hungry. Dorishungry. I have a hole in my stomach."

And laughed. And then they went from the woods to the house in the darker part of the woods and Sandra set the table with a little of this and a little of that and they ate and ate.

But then Doris had become serious again.

"Now it's about time we do something real. That we stop playing. I want to meet her. Now we're going to travel.

"Get out the map now. The real one."

And then they went to Sandra's room and spread out the enormous map of the world between them on the bed.

"Now I'm going to get to run in the Alps like in *The Sound of Music*," said Doris Flinkenberg.

"Now I'm finally going to get to meet her. Lorelei Lindberg.

"G-O-D. How I've been looking forward to it."

The boy in the pool. But the boy was lying on the bottom of the pool, with his eyes closed. The music was playing. *Here comes the night. So cold, so roaring, so wonderful.* She went to him. That was what it had been like.

The girl had been woken by the sound and immediately got out of bed. Put on her silk kimono and stuck her feet in the high-heeled morning slippers with muffs. Not Eddie-clothes, they were no longer needed, not now.

The door to the basement stairs was open. She walked down.

Sandra Harelip. She saw him in the pool. He lay motionless, his eyes were closed, maybe he was sleeping. She climbed down the ladder and went to him.

"Now I'm going to tell you about love," Inget Herrman had said to the girls at the beginning of one summer a long time ago, at Eddie's boathouse, on the Second Cape. "You don't fall in love with someone because that person is nice or good-looking or even because of that person's thousand good qualities. You fall in love with someone who brings something inside you to life.

"And what that is"—Inget Herrman paused before she continued—"you'll never know."

And she, Sandra, understood now, down there in the pool, what Inget Herrman meant. She understood it when she climbed down the ladder, those four steps, mile-long steps, like a sleepwalker.

Until she came to him. He opened his eyes and yes, he welcomed her.

Was it a dream?

And the whole house was sleeping, sleeping after yet another heavy hunting party of the kind that was still being organized in the house, sometimes, once in a while. Slightly different parties now that Inget Herrman had come into the picture, no "catering"—or in any case less—but with more room for—how should it be said?—the unexpected. Sometimes very strange people showed up during the night. Inget Herrman's friends, also some from the fishermen's pub. Magnus von B. and Bencku sometimes. Sandra could not believe her eyes. Though they were always drunk then.

And there was that thought already, that all which was beautiful was being transformed into one large wet party.

Still, the boy. Bengt.

It happened. And that, the boy in the pool, how do you convey that? Should you communicate that? Could you communicate that? To anyone? Even to Doris, the one who meant the most to you, who was more like you that anyone else in the whole wide world? The way you were yourself.

When you did not know what it was. Or exactly that: you knew. But still, it was so absurd. Where did it fit?

So she could not. Could not say anything.

"Bencku likes small chicks," Doris said to the cousin's mama in the cousin's kitchen one late morning in the month of October while she was eating sweet dough out of the bowl, "those small frozen ones." A glance at the garden, a Saturday morning and Doris looked out the window at the cousin's property covered by a delicate blanket of frost that would thaw in the sunshine as had been promised in the weather forecast; the sun would come out and make the day clear and bright and colorful just as a crisp fall day in the District should be. Empty bowl in hand now, Doris looked out over the property.

She saw Bencku come walking, from the woods. He really looked like what he had presumably been doing, partying all night. And—

"What are you saying, Doris?"

"Nothing."

"Where are you going?"

"Out."

And here she came later, walking over the cliffs on the Second Cape. Fall, fall, the summer guests gone, the rats dancing on the tables, all over the Second Cape wherever they wanted. And later in the day that had ended, just as it had been promised: the day sparkled. The glass of the Glass House played in the sun and the water. The sea, the house, everything was on fire. Not for real, but as the result of a sophisticated effect thought out by the architects.

But here she came now, Doris Night, in her pale skin. Her dark clothes. Sandra Night, in her pale skin, dressed in something pink. Princess Stigmata of the Thousand Rooms; those types of lips now, like such a princess, red and swollen.

Heavy with the caresses of the previous night. Doris probably saw them but said nothing.

And Sandra Wärn said nothing.

It was still the two of them, of course.

And without further ado both girls accompanied each other.

"IS IT REALLY PEACE WE WANT, AT ANY CONCEIVABLE COST?"

Echoed over the cousin's property. So loudly that it quivered all the way into Rita and Solveig's cottage.

"If Bencku's revolution would come tomorrow I would take the revolver and shoot myself out of pure boredom," Rita said to Solveig.

They had a revolver in the cottage. It was on a shelf on the wall. Papa's revolver. Not the cousin's papa's, but their own.

"*Pang*," Solveig replied with a laugh. "*Pang pang pang pang*." And pretended that she was holding a revolver to her temple.

Rita laughed.

At the same time, in the barn. Anxiety in his body again. Bencku washed up and changed clothes, packed and left.

"Bencku," Doris tittered when she and Sandra were making their way through all of the levels of the house with the cleaning tools. "He's crazy. Crazier than the two of us put together." The cleaning was the girls' own idea again, but with new motivation. Some reports were not important, there was not very much to report about. The work was being carried out as paid work at Four Mops and a Dustpan. Doris and Sandra were saving up for the trip the following year, the big trip, the one that would go somewhere that was *The Sound of Music* mountains. Austria. They were going to visit Lorelei Lindberg and Heintz-Gurt, the adventurous pilot. For that reason the trip was a secret until further notice.

"The Islander would lose it if he knew," Sandra said to Doris. "I've received strict instructions from Lorelei Lindberg to keep quiet about everything."

"They'll probably find out later," Doris said importantly. "Everybody. Time enough. We're going to surprise them."

"Bencku." Doris giggled again. "There's definitely nothing heroic about such a Bencku-silliness."

. . .

The Four Mops and a Dustpan overalls were too uncomfortable.
Doris and Sandra had put on other clothes. The old, discarded
Loneliness&Fear shirts. "Games of childhood," Doris Flinkenberg said contemptuously and stuck the arm of her shirt in the
floor wax and rubbed the pool tiles with it.

WHEN THE SUMMER THROWS YOU AWAY

(Sandra and Doris's story 2)

———————

PANG, DORIS SHOT HERSELF ON LORE CLIFF AT BULE MARSH on the eighth of November 1975. It was a Saturday, early evening, the shot echoed in the woods. Calm and cold, one of those numb days like the last days usually are before the snow falls and stays on the ground. A day for the lifeless, a day for death.

A day for death. There was only one shot but when Rita and Solveig heard it in the cottage on the other side of the cousin's papa's field, Rita immediately went to the cabinet where the pistol was stored in order to check—the pistol was inherited, the only thing of value that Rita and Solveig had ever inherited from anyone, a Colt pistol, purchased at the department store in the city by the sea in 1907. It was as she thought. It was not there.

All of a sudden Rita started moving. She snatched her coat and rushed out, Solveig after, but Solveig had a hard time keeping up because she had sprained her foot the evening before in Hästhagen (the dancing hall) and had a hard time moving around.

And to be honest. At first Solveig did not understand at all why Rita was in such a hurry. The hunting season was not over yet and it was not exactly unusual to hear shots in the woods. But on the other hand, Solveig certainly knew that a pistol and a rifle make different sounds. And this had been a slightly different bang: it had sounded like a large paper bag had been filled with air and then placed in the hands of a giant. Like when something "that is filled with nothing" pops, which Doris Flinkenberg sometimes had a habit of saying about her head. *Bang.* Then it was no more.

But Rita had known exactly how and where she should go and that it was urgent, perhaps too late. It was too late. When she came to Bule Marsh, Doris's body was on its stomach on Lore Cliff, her shattered head and clumps of hair were hanging over the dark, quiet water that would freeze to ice just a few days later.

Rita rushed forward and started pulling on Doris. At least that is what it looked like from a distance.

Solveig screamed and screamed. When Solveig reached them, Rita was sitting on her knees by Doris's dead body and shaking and pulling at it, moaning and sniffling and whimpering. For a brief, absurd moment Solveig thought Rita had attacked the already dead Doris Flinkenberg with her own blows and slaps. "Stoopp!" Solveig roared, but Rita, who was already entirely smeared with blood, had turned her face toward her, and in that face there was an expression that Solveig would never forget, she had bellowed:

"Help me! Don't stand there staring like an idiot!"

Then Solveig understood that Rita was trying to lift the dead Doris there where she was lying on the cliff and carry her in some way.

"Rita! Stop! She's dead!"

But Rita did not hear anything then.

"Help, I said! We can do it with the two of us!"

"Rita, come on! Doris isn't alive! We have to get help! She's deaaa—"

And Solveig had tried to pull Rita away from Doris, but Rita had not wanted to let go and in the end they had both become filthy and the smell of baked coffee rested heavily everywhere. That is how blood smells, but you could not sense that smell right then, but you would have it in your nose for a long time afterward.

Carry Doris over dark waters.

But it did not work. You were helpless. You could not. You could not do anything.

Suddenly, some time must have passed but they were not aware of it, they were not alone at the marsh any longer. Suddenly the cousin's mama, paramedics, and the police were by the marsh. And Bencku, so drunk he could barely stand. Bencku walked around at the scene and coughed and snuffled and stumbled and fell over and over again among all of the police officers and the paramedics and curious spectators who were there, thank goodness not many because it was already late in the fall, dark and winterlike.

"Bencku! Go home now!" the cousin's mama yelled at Bencku. She was hysterical, as if it was the most important thing of all that Bencku should go home and not be there and embarrass himself.

Rita remained, sitting a little way away from Lore Cliff and sobbed and cried. Solveig tried to put her arm around her, *it was despite everything the two of them*. But Rita pulled away from her sister's grasp.

And all of this, everything everything and more, while Doris Flinkenberg was being carried away on a stretcher and a heavy snowfall started. Large, heavy flakes that would drown everything in snow, even if it was the type of snow that thawed overnight and became rain again.

And yet. Nothing could change the fact that Doris Flinkenberg had killed herself on Lore Cliff at Bule Marsh and that at her death by her own hand she was only sixteen years old.

Sandra was on Åland the day Doris died, by the sea. The cursed sea. She was standing looking at it through the window on the porch in a large house where she otherwise shuffled around in a heavy, terry cloth bathrobe, homemade knitted rag socks, and a

woolen scarf wound in layers around her sensitive throat. She had
the mumps, the last children's disease. But . . . *this restlessness when
Doris Flinkenberg was not there* . . . even with a fever of 102 it was
difficult to keep Sandra in bed as she should, which "the aunt"
and the house doctor were both very much in agreement about.
And especially just at the exact point in time when Doris died.
Memento mori, by the cursed sea, and the waves that washed over you.

But she would find that out later when she counted back in
time and thought about what had happened. That in exactly the
moment when Doris shot herself she, Sandra, Sister Night, Sister Day, had been standing at the window on Åland humming
the Eddie-song. For dear life. For all she was worth.

Look, Mom, what they've done to my song. They've destroyed it.

Just as if this furtive, inaudible humming could have saved
anything at all.

Later, when Sandra received the news that Doris was dead,
it was already the next day and it was storming. The Sunday after the Saturday and Sandra at the window let the sea
crash over her. Not for real of course, *gooberhead*, but in her
imagination. A windowpane separated her from reality. Like
alwaysalwaysalwaysalways. The sea was gray, foamy, and the
waves were several feet high. They were like houses. Right at
the moment when you had the sea in front of you like a wall
and you thought it would fall over you and drown you or suck
you out into the terrible dark currents, it pulled itself back an
itty-bitty bit so that the wave crashed down on the cliff below
the bay window instead, just foaming and spraying against the
glass. Piquant. This for the image of nature and the simile:
interesting. She had, she determined again, zero emotions in
her befitting an islander, for the person who should have been
inside her, which all of these relatives whom she did not understand nagged about here in the house and on the whole island.
"The aunt" who stood behind her and wanted to put her arms

around her, who stood there the whole time as if fully prepared to embrace her. And wanted to whisper, what? Blood is thicker than water? *When it was not like that at all.* Sandra took a step to the side.

Somewhere in another room in the big house the phone rang. At first "the aunt's" voice could be heard distantly, then, in the moment that followed, behind her again. "Sandra. It's for you. Some Inget Herrman. What kind of name is that?" What in the world were you supposed to say to that? She had already said it herself, "the aunt," in her tone of voice. It was quite simply not a real name.

But still, when all is said and done, when Sandra turned around and looked at "the aunt," who looked genuinely troubled, Sandra understood that she was too congested, too sick in general, to be able to work up any real indignation over anything at all. And furthermore, everything changed the following moment and that which at one time had been important lost all meaning in one fell swoop. Because it really was Inget Herrman on the telephone. She explained everything, her voice thin and horridly foreign even before she had carried out her errand.

Sandra had wanted to go home immediately, but the home doctor on Åland had strictly forbidden her to do so. He said her swollen glands and feverish body would endure neither a flight nor a trip by boat, and she had not protested. Or insisted. She had not said anything at all, not really. Except yes and no as if she had been replying to ordinary questions, the kind of questions that should have answers. Like a robot. Open and take your medicine. Turn on your stomach so we can take your temperature. Shouldn't we change pajamas? To comfortable and clean ones? How you're sweating. Sit up now, stretch out your arms so we can get your top off. There. Nice and cool, isn't it? Head on the pillow now. Now we're going to rest. Now we're going to get better. Now we're going to sleep.

She let herself be cared for. And she was a robot. Or actually, there was a very definite image she had of herself in her head: the girl in the moon boots, on a snowy field in the Alps, in the middle of a painting that was so beautiful it could have been the motif for a puzzle of several thousand pieces.

But there was no satisfaction, either abnormal or ordinary, in these fantasies now, nothing to wallow in.

Therefore, strictly speaking, there were no real fantasies either, or even thoughts, just dizziness and sentences and words that hung in the air or showed up in her memory like billboards on a high-rise building where it was dark in all of the windows, nighttime.

And she was a doll, a harelipped one. Not a reserved, mainland girl, which you had a habit of saying about her when she was there on Åland, when she came to visit what, "the aunt," the relatives. If you stayed here a while you'd become normal again. That undertone. She had not bothered about it then, but then there was Doris Flinkenberg. But also now, it hit her with such force where she was lying bedridden and crying (though the crying, it showed even less on her; it could not be seen at all), she did not bother about it now either, maybe even more, now when Doris was . . . no longer alive.

She was the Michelin girl, the one in the moon boots, who was so precious and fragile that she stumbled about, fumbled about like a drunk Bengt at the scene of the death. Was missing all feeling for the ground or what it was now called in her absolutely photo-friendly footwear, her absolutely impossible-to-walk-in boots. This was the planet without Doris, namely. And it might as well have been the moon.

Voices in her surroundings.

"It's a pity about her. Her good friend—"

"These melodramatic kids. If they could just understand that there is a tomorrow."

A cool hand on her forehead, "little, little silk dog."

But the clock was ticking, time was passing, the swelling in her cheeks and in her throat lessened, though too slowly. And then it finally turned out that Doris Flinkenberg's funeral and the memorial afterward in the fellowship hall up in the town center, during which the pop version of "Around the Beggar from Luossa," one of Doris Flinkenberg's favorite songs, played on Doris Flinkenberg's Poppy radio cassette player one last time so that everyone heard, took place without Sandra Wärn, her only friend, her best friend, being present.

Click, Solveig turned it on and off, and there was not a dry eye anywhere.

> *What I love is gone, hidden in the distant darkness*
> *And my true road is high and wonderful*
> *I am driven in the middle of my turmoil to pray to the Lord*
> *Take away the earth, then I want, what no one else has*

But that, that was in the month of November when all hope was gone. Now it was still July half a year before, while all possibilities still remained. And there came Doris Flinkenberg now. Walking through the woods in the direction of the house in the darker part. Doris with her small, light blue bag, with her traveling purse, also in light blue with a picture of a bunny's head with long front teeth, Doris with her passport and part of her traveling money in the beige-colored bag with a string around her neck (the rest of the money she had sewn into different places in the hem of her pants and under her right sock), also with a light blue bunny on it. It was, she later stood and explained to Sandra filled with excitement, the first thing she did when she came inside the door, a *set*, and that she purchased with the money she had earned by raking the cemetery in the town center as a summer job up until now.

Doris pulled out the neck pouch also and started demonstrating it and its different compartments and everything that fit into them, all of the zippers and so on, and she did this with an enthusiasm that absorbed her to the point that quite some time had passed before she realized Sandra still had her pajamas on.

"Aren't you going to put on YOUR traveling clothes?" Doris Flinkenberg stopped what she was doing, not abruptly, more like taking a pause.

"Doris," Sandra started seriously. She was forced to begin with the same seriousness a few times before Doris was properly paying attention, which made the whole thing even more awkwardly drawn out. "There isn't going to be any trip. Heintz-Gurt called. Lorelei Lindberg. She's gone to New York."

"And then," Doris objected impatiently as if what Sandra had said was only a few words standing in the way, an almost technical obstruction to the dream still living inside her, which she was living on, floating around in like hanging in a wonderful blue helium balloon, so delightful, that she had butterflies in her stomach—in an instant, and it was gone. "She'll come later," Doris added. "And if she isn't there when we get there then someone else in the family can meet us at the airport!"

"But don't you understand? She's not there. She's never ever going to come back. She's left him. Taken her stuff and left. Early yesterday morning. Didn't even leave a note behind for him. There won't—"

Sandra had to stop herself here and prepare herself again in order to finish her last sentence.

"—be a trip, Doris Flinkenberg."

Doris remained standing a few seconds, unmoving as if she had been struck by lightning.

The balloon filled with gas burst. That is what happened with that mystery: to fly and float freely. It still ended in one and the same way. Crashing to the ground.

"And you're saying that just now!" Doris yelled then, at first more angry than disappointed, but it was still as though her body already understood what her head did not. Her hands fell to her sides, the traveling purse that had obtrusively been hanging in the crook of Doris's arm during the demonstration of the neck pouch fell to the floor with a tumble.

"I only found out last night. Heintz-Gurt couldn't know either that she had been thinking about leaving him right now. He was completely crushed—"

But Doris was for the moment not in the mood for any Heintz-Gurt stories.

"I'm not starting!" Doris yelled shrilly like a child or a wounded animal. It was disgusting to hear her like that, utterly heart-wrenching. Her face became red, her bottom lip quivered. Doris crumpled down onto the beige wall-to-wall carpet in the narrow hall, legs spread out in each direction, head hanging.

"I never get to," Doris whispered while she fought against the tears and the anger slowly growing inside her. Quite simply Damn! Damn all of it! "I neverneverever get to!" And then, it could not be stopped, the tears came. They gushed forth, in floods. Not ordinary teenager tears either because now they were gushing like springs from Doris Flinkenberg.

Sandra did not know what she should do. She had never seen Doris Flinkenberg like this before. So pitiful, so helpless, so heartbreaking. A real crybaby, and it affected her badly, it did. It embarrassed her as well, and for a brief moment Sandra did not have any trouble at all holding back the big and happy smile that had been growing inside her in the silence of the previous hours and minutes, the entire morning all the way up till now. Ever since the Islander and Inget Herrman early that same morning had stowed their things in the Islander's jeep and *finally* driven off. "Toward unknown adventures!" Inget Herrman had intended and in that moment Sandra had in her own mind truly been able to agree with her. And hopefully prolonged ones, had been her own ill-bred addition in the silence. *Don't talk to me anymore now.* She really was not interested in where they were going (they were going to go over *the seven seas*, as Inget

Herrman termed the voyage that would last for weeks, down to Gotland, Öland, and so on. And, one could hope, even farther, Sandra had thought in the cheeky and expectant moment that preceded the Islander and Inget Herrman's departure that never seemed to happen. *Leave now already*).

Because now she would get to be alone in the house in the darker part. Alone with Doris Flinkenberg, for an almost infinite period of time. Two whole weeks, fourteen d-a-y-s. That with Heintz-Gurt and Lorelei Lindberg, the Alps, all of that, it was so peripheral in comparison with this, it had been cast into the back of her head and hidden there long ago.

So why was Doris carrying on like that now?

When Sandra witnessed Doris's outbreak, which did not look like it had an end in sight, she finally could not hold back an indignant yell, "But my God, Doris!" And while she yelled the energy came back, the joy burst in her like a flower blooming. "It's not that bad! Stop sulking! I've had my hands full trying to get rid of the Islander and Inget Herrman anyway! I've had to do everything in order to get them and the whole world to understand that we can take care of ourselves! Just the two of us! Here in the house! We aren't kids anymore!"

But Doris still was not listening; instead she remained sitting on the floor with both legs spread out, moaning slowly as if she had pain in her body. Or, perhaps, a schizophrenic like Sybil who had seventeen different personalities living side by side in the same body which, to say the least, made life unmanageable; Sandra and Doris had read a really good book about it once. A schizophrenic named Sybil on the border between personalities, different lives; in one of her more incommunicable states in that dark area bordering on insanity and unconsciousness.

"God damn it!" Sandra clarified, who was starting to grow tired of watching Doris's fit. "Don't you get it? We have the house to ourselves for two weeks! We have your traveling money and we have my traveling money and we have the food account at the store and we have color television and a stereo system with speakers in every room except the bathroom and we have all the comforts! Bar! Swimming pool! Marital bed! And NO ONE who's looking for us because they think we're in the Alps!"

Then, finally, Doris Flinkenberg lifted her head, her fingers still fumbling absentmindedly with her neck pouch, pulled thoughtfully at its strings, and for the last time, maybe for the very last time in Doris's entire life, scenes where the two girls Sussilull and Sussilo, as they were called in the song, were running over mountains and green valleys, Middle European valleys, and behind them a cheery nun in civilian clothing, with the guitar, had fluttered through Doris's head.

The hills are alive with the sound of music. That kind of picture. Which was slowly, slowly growing still now. It froze in the imaginary television screen in her head. Became smaller. And even smaller. Became smaller and smaller and smaller until only a small spot remained. An itty-bitty spot that later, little by little, procreated and became several spots. Spots, spots, spots. Black, gray, marbled. And all of these spots received a life and started moving, dancing eagerly around each other and making noise—one of those irritating noises that you usually heard when the television program was over, after the national anthem. It was a sound you could not be bothered to listen to, it was so irritating. And SNAP you had turned off the set and everything was calm, quiet, and empty again.

The end of that show. That dream—

"In shambles," mumbled Doris Flinkenberg. "That dream in shambles," she continued a little louder, maybe mostly only for herself. But still, even in her inimitable Dorisway, in her very own Dorislanguage, a language that Sandra recognized also as her own because it had also become hers during the long, remarkable time it had just been the two of them and no one else. A language that they had already been in the process of outgrowing for a long time now in this puberty that had just started and that would never lead them back to a fun childhood where there were their own worlds, many lives, many games and personalities. But just the opposite, out into the real world to become grown-ups like the Islander, the cousin's mama, Lorelei Lindberg, and the Bombshell. And yes, they all had their good sides, but in the grand scheme of things you still had to say, yuck.

The language had mostly become something used in a game. But now, in this situation, it was a good sign in any case. Because one thing was certain: Doris never used that language nowadays unless she was a little bit in the mood.

"But," she later said, sure enough, brightened up and peered cunningly as only Doris Flinkenberg and no one else could peer, "there are others."

And in that next moment she got up terribly quickly, with a new energy in her body, her head high again and smiling at Sandra with the smile that had once been so practiced but that now had become an integrated part of her remarkable person, very genuine: *our crafty fiendishness*, while you could almost see how her mind was filled with everything she suddenly realized lay ahead of them now.

All the possibilities.

And it was the beginning of two weeks with just the two of them in the house in the darker part of the woods. It was a summer when great things happened out in the world. Presidents and regents from all over the world gathered in the city by the sea to sign a historic peace treaty. Now all countries were going to support and help each other instead of fighting with each other and spreading hate and discord among their enemies. Even Anneka Munveg, who was a television news reporter, had a splash of emotion in her otherwise so crass and businesslike voice. But there was something in the mood itself and that it was summer too and quite decent weather. Both presidents from the superpowers shook hands for the first time in an eternity and then grand closing speeches followed and the historic document was signed. At the very end the carts with the white glasses and the strawberries were rolled in. It was a late, sunny summer day, the day when Liz Maalamaa crushed the windowpane in the outside door of the basement and stepped in and stood there among the shards of glass and, she had in a way surprised the girls in the pool, in a dance. In a strange dance of hate/love, of union/discord, and of very real distress and evident despair. *The dream was over because true love had ceased to exist.* But Liz Maalamaa did not understand that. She stood there and quoted the Bible by heart.

Then she sighed and said that "it was so hot there in Florida you had to take your inner Turk away."

She pronounced Florida as if there were two *i*'s in it.

But up until then it did not matter what was going on in other places in the world. Because it was in only one place that everything was taking place, everything of importance, in any case. The ordinary was put out of action. The most important things that happened, and it was of decisive importance, they happened in a rectangle. At the bottom of a swimming pool without water, a pool in a basement with panorama windows facing an almost impenetrable jungle of ferns on the outside, toward the marsh. And of course it was that time of year when all the plants in nature were at their tallest and greenest. It was a jungle that blocked all views while also providing protection from the world outside. From the summer and all of the people in it. All other people. And it was effective. In the beginning no one knew what the girls were doing, or where they were. In the beginning no one knew that the girls had not left on their trip.

The only thing they were not able to hold their own against were all the insects: bullymosquitoes, supersized rainbow flies, fern ticks. Both green fern ticks that did not tick and ticking ticks. These and other marsh insects forced their way into the house and toward the end of the fourteen days you could see them crawling out of the unused ventilation holes in the pool, also forcing their way through the cracks in the mortar, all the more noticeable cracks. During this time there was a period when it rained a great deal; this period occurred just before the sunshine finally came and lasted a few days during which everything had time to become so porous, so porous.

But at the same time, it was also the case that both of the girls in the house, Sandra Wärn and Doris Flinkenberg, actually had so many other things to think about than rigging up mosquito nets, swatting with flyswatters made of plastic in every room and floor, and bug spraying.

These days were, in other words, the world in a rectangle, the world in a small rectangle.

The pool in the basement in the house in the darker part of the woods: zoom in on that now, for the last time. Because when the Islander and Inget Herrman come home from their cruise which, without either of them needing to say anything at all, you would understand it had not gone like either of them had planned, one of the Islander's first measures will be to have new, better tiles laid in the pool and allow it to be filled, this for the first time during all the time they had lived in the house in the darker part of the woods. With Inget Herrman, whom she personally had nothing against, pointing out in between gulps of wine, as the "instigating factor." "Can be done," said the Islander. "Your word is my command," he said, with all of the feigned enthusiasm he could muster. So fake that not even he, the Islander, who was no thinker, understood that he was standing on the big glitter scene and performing a terrible number.

The wear and tear started showing on the Islander. It was clear it had been a long, long time since he was a man in his prime, for example in the snow in Central Europe, on the one side of a white field with a certain house on the other side. That was one thing. But another thing, which might even be creepier, was that it really was not all that long ago, almost eons since that night at the end of the hunting season when Inget Herrman had come to the house in the middle of the night and the Bombshell was disposed of. "Over my dead body is she coming into this house!": Pinky had stood in the hall while Inget Herrman, recently arrived via a taxi, rang the doorbell without being let in. And Sandra, who had gone out in the night because Inget Herrman had wanted to talk with her, and then they had sat in the middle of the stairs up to nothing and talked about the importance of following your own star and realizing your dreams. And while they were talking the Islander had suddenly appeared out of thin air with a tray in his hands; there were drinks on the tray and in the drink glasses there were sparklers or *falling stars* or whatever they are called. And the sticks had sparkled in the night and in some way, though it was not pretty, though nothing was pretty, it had become just that, the Islander with the tray, the sparklers in the night.

We're transformed into gray panthers without us knowing it, Islander. It was rather creepy, if you thought about it. And if it was in other words you and your father who needed a lot of . . . protection . . . because there would, starting now, come so many difficult things. How crazy he was, the Islander, he still had his strange, persistent inimitable power.

What snow conceals, the sun reveals.

But was it like that, there were things that had happened you could not shake off? That just continued to come back? And about not being able to hold your ground, had he really not considered that?

But the summer before everything, the world in a small rectangle, maybe there was a storm when they sailed by certain "cliffs of home," the Islander and Inget Herrman. He did not look to the side. He still looked straight ahead. Straight, straight ahead.

. . .

Well. Everything the girls needed was in the house in the darker part of the woods. In the beginning they did not even need to go to the store to buy food. They ate what was in the refrigerator and they found an entire moose steak in the freezer from the previous year. A large forgotten clump of ice all the way at the bottom. It lasted quite a while, until they could no longer eat the moose steak, and they lived for a while on hard candy, chips, and chocolate.

They went into their own world, with their own games, their own talk and allowed themselves to be devoured by them. Maybe it started as a farewell to childhood. During the year that had passed, especially since the Mystery with the American Girl had been solved and left to its destiny, so many of the old games and stories had not had any meaning for a long time.

But childhood revisited for a few days: you cannot step down into the same river twice as a Greek philosopher and Inget Herrman used to say. It was not the same thing. It did not become the same thing. It started burning. "If you put your finger in the flame, it burns," Doris once said to Sandra, as a statement. Now she would get to experience it herself. For real.

At some point during this time with Sandra in the house in the darker part, in the small rectangle, the swimming pool without water ("Little Bombay?" she started saying, bitterly questioning when they had carried as many silk fabrics as possible down in the basement and built Maharajah's Palace, moreover one of the last things they did before *the sexual awakening*, and Sandra had jumped, "no," she had resisted, then tried to laugh it off, do everything like normal, by saying, "no, still not that now, but almost"), it happened that Doris would remember something she had left at home in the cousin's house, which she had not taken with her, because when she left the cousin's house she was on her way out into the world, and which she missed a little bit and got the idea that she needed. Certain music cassettes. Not "Our Love Is a Continental Affair" because even Doris Flinkenberg had finally grown tired of that hit (and it was not a day too soon, thought everyone, even the cousin's mama, who were tired of hearing her play it over and over again on the Poppy tape player), her book for worship of an idol, her little memory book. All those things she had a habit of dragging around with her. But *you can't return home*. That is the price you pay. Everything has a price. You have to pay something.

But: pay for what? That was what would be cocked and loaded, that was what would no longer be clear, after almost fourteen days with Sandra Wärn and just the two of them in the house in the darker part of the woods.

The world in a rectangle, small.

When Doris came back to the cousin's house she would on the one hand probably be thankful for still having all of these things, which she had not taken with her, up there in her room. But they would have lost their meaning, all the meaning they had ever had in their own contexts. The stories about them would be, if not worthless, then shattered to bits. In shards from the crushed window on the floor in the pool section next to the television that was on but the screen snowed and snowed.

A red raincoat in a photograph.

"He came in a white Jaguar—"

"One thing, Sandra. That telephone number. It doesn't exist."

"Let me tell you something, dear, blessed child. That the mercy God has measured out for just you, it is so great that not a single human being can grasp it with their intellect."

The old connections did not exist, the ones that together had formed a world you moved in as a matter of course. Now it was a matter of building new worlds.

But with whom? Sandra. For alleged reasons they would not be able to be together anymore, though it must be seen.

Sandra and Doris. They had danced on "the wicked ground," barefoot (in the pool). The dream had ended because true love had ceased to exist, Nat King Cole was playing on the record player, and it was true even though it was only a song.

But in other words, in the cousin's house: Doris would be grateful to have her things anyway. They would be needed to the highest degree, as navigation points. Concrete grounds for recognition that would help her find her way back to the best number of them all on the glitter scene. Doris Flinkenberg, everything is like it always is, everything is normal.

Robot practice. Walk around the planet without a name.

Look in control, happy. Bring out the best mood you have.

Pull up the blackout curtain. Discover Bencku and Magnus and Micke Friberg in the yard.

Say to the cousin's mama:

"I'm going out."

"Where?"

"Out."

Drink beer with the boys. It was always a solution. If only temporary.

The world in a small rectangle, 1. This was how it started. First: they were still themselves. They made the house theirs and took up their old games. For fun, on a small scale. Doris Flinkenberg was Lorelei Lindberg who met Heintz-Gurt at the nightclub the Running Kangaroo, and Sandra played the American girl, to the hilt. "Nobody knew my rose of the world but me." "I'm a strange bird." "The heart is a heartless hunter." She recited this until the words had lost almost all meaning. And Sandra crowed, "Look, Mom, they've destroyed . . ." at the top of her lungs and made crazy erhm-movements, exaggerated and obscene, with her body, and Doris could not help but try and crawl in the same way . . . though just for a while. Then they stopped. Grew quiet. Felt ill at ease over the sacrilege.

Because it was too real, in any case.

Eddie, she had not lost her magical power over them. And Doris could still playfully, easily in her memory call to mind a certain summer day when she had found the body—or what was left of it—wrapped in a red plastic raincoat that was so whole so whole, completely intact. And there was still so much that was dreadful and unclear about that memory.

So they let the games be for a while and were just like two ordinary teenage girls: got drunk on what was in the bar, smoked the Islander's cigarillos, taking deep drags that made both of them throw up. That night both of them fell asleep in the pool among the soft pillows from the rec room's sofa, which had ended up in the pool again, which they always did when the Islander was not there, when only Doris and Sandra were in the house. And wrapped themselves in fabrics from Maharajah's Palace. "Little Bombay," Doris Flinkenberg tried again, but Sandra flinched, she did not catch on. "No, not that." "Why not?" "Stop pestering."

And Doris stopped pestering. Willingly. Since there was something else in the air, had been the whole time. A fragile mood, like a rubber band being stretched, stretched between them. That was the strange thing but also what was in some way most delightful.

And suddenly Doris seemed to understand that was why they were actually there. That was why there had not been a trip. She thought that Sandra looked at her sometimes, carefully, in hiding. With a new look, or an old one, whatever you wanted to call it. But a look that wanted something from her. That wanted her so much it became shy, looked down or away or just gave way.

And Doris. She enjoyed it. A memory from one midsummer evening a long time ago floated up more and more often in Doris's head, but also in Sandra's, the evening they had started solving the Mystery of the American Girl. Something in the moss, something, which was then aborted. And it was okay like that. But now.

That was what was lying in between.

And suddenly, in the middle of a game, Sandra kissed Doris. Or was it Doris who kissed Sandra first? It did not matter. It was beautiful. It was the way it was supposed to be. And they both had the moss inside them, the memory of the moss . . . and when they started kissing nothing—lightning nor thunder—could stop them.

"No one can kiss like us," Doris Flinkenberg whispered. Though then it was already after the First Time, with cigarillos and gin and tonics.

It happened in the middle of a new game, a cat-and-mouse game, their own version of it (it had in other words nothing to do with Rita and Solveig and the others, who broke into the houses on the Second Cape during the fall when the summer guests had left and did what they wanted to there). This was much more innocent, mostly a pastime. A whim, an idea that maybe came about because Sandra and Doris in any case, despite the fact that they enjoyed each other's company and were probably still themselves, started thinking it was sometimes a bit boring just staying indoors.

"'The primal scream freed me,'" Doris Flinkenberg read out loud from a magazine, an ordinary women's magazine, which might have originated from Pinky's time in the house in the darker part.

"What is it?" Sandra asked listlessly and Doris explained it was the scream you screamed when you came out of your mother's belly and many people would feel good by screaming that scream again as adults. It sounded rather vague, so Sandra asked apathetically:

"When then?"

"Well, for example," said Doris, who thought it was important to be able to provide answers to questions in all situations, "if you're terribly afraid of something it can help you to release it with the primal scream. Face the fear with a scream so to speak."

She added that last part with a tone Sandra had learned meant that she really did not have a clue what she was talking about.

"That is just . . . crap," Sandra determined and Doris admittedly agreed with her too, but shortly thereafter Doris Flinkenberg tossed the magazine aside anyway and suggested:

"Should we do it, then?"

"I wasn't thinking about standing on the steps and yelling if that's what you were thinking. Besides it's important . . ."

". . . that no one sees and hears us so we can be left alone," Doris filled in.

"Yes, yes, I know. You've said that. We have. But I'm talking about something else. A game. How does that sound?"

Interesting. It certainly sounded interesting.

A strange tension already existed between the two of them. There were looks and touching, or fear of touching. The wrong kind of touch. Those who had earlier rolled around all over like two young rabbits now kept themselves at a proper distance from each other, even down in the pool.

Sandra with her business at one end. Doris at the other.

"What are you making?"

"I'm sewing," Sandra explained, then completely calmly, "glitter clothes for the American girl's funeral. And the Marsh Queen's resurrection. It's almost the same thing."

Or did Sandra say that, was it a dream?

Whatever. All of this was in some way devoted to increasing the tension between them even more.

"The cat-and-mouse game," Doris Flinkenberg explained. "But in our own way.

"The game is called Assignment: Master Fear," she explained further. "Do you follow? I give you an assignment and you give me an assignment, I decide for you and you decide for me. Since it's like this, that sometimes, when two people are close, then one sees the other more clearly than she sees herself.

"So now it's a matter of us learning how to overcome our greatest fears. And we help each other with that. You give me an assignment and I give you an assignment."

"Now I'm telling you," Doris Flinkenberg started, "you should go straight to Bencku's barn and get the American girl's bag with all her things in it and bring it to me. Or to us. Here to the house. As you know, you said it yourself, it's important that no one sees you.

"I know you're afraid of going in there. Now go there and do it. Understand?"

Sandra nodded. Yes. She understood. And the game itself. And suddenly, cold shivers ran down her spine, she not only understood but was also even very interested.

"And now I'm saying to you that you go to Solveig and Rita's cottage and get their pistol. The one you are always talking about, that inheritance. It's not the fact that you talk about the pistol, but always when you talk about Rita and Solveig in the cottage you become so very strange. Or not always. But pretty often."

And the strange thing was it had an effect on Doris.

"How do you know that?" Doris asked quickly, as if she had been unmasked.

"Well. The game starts now. How much time do we have? Half a day?"

And Sandra and Doris carried out their assignments. Sandra shot through the woods to the cousin's property, she took the long way, which went past the moss where she and Doris had kissed each other for the first time a long time ago. She had butterflies in her stomach, and no, she was not at all scared, not nervous. Not to go into Bencku's barn anyway. She knew he was gone. He was gone the whole summer. He had said that to her when she came to him the last time, late in the spring, in May. He was going to live with Magnus von B. in an apartment in the city by the sea.

Sandra out of habit, and without thinking, took the key from its hiding place and opened the trapdoor in the floor and took what she needed, and then shot back through the woods, carefully so no one would see or hear.

And Doris came back with the pistol.

"It was so easy. No one was there."

"Did anyone see you?"

"No."

"Did anyone see you?"

"No. At least I don't think so."

"Are we less afraid, then?"

"Maybe."

"Maybe."

They were down in the pool and both started laughing at the same time.

And Doris, on all fours, had crawled over to Sandra who was sitting at the other end of the pool.

The world in a small rectangle, 2. The first time. Doris, in the swimming pool. "Be quiet, be quiet," because Sandra was still laughing.

"And now I'm not the American girl. Now I'm myself."

And then Doris kissed Sandra. And it was NOT factor X or anyone else who was doing the kissing. It was Doris Flinkenberg who kissed Sandra Wärn and Sandra Wärn who kissed back. And Doris remembered the moss, the soft green moss, and Sandra remembered the moss and . . .

No one can kiss like us. Definitely not. But it was serious. And one thing led to another. And then they traveled inside each other in Maharajah's Palace, which they had built for themselves out of the fabrics and pillows on the bottom of the swimming pool. And moved, two bodies tightly wound around and over each other, on the soft, beautiful ground.

And lightning and thunder could be seen in the television at the edge of the pool, and it was storming.

The soft, beautiful ground.

Follow-up discussion. ". . . as if I've had dykes in the family going back generation after generation." Doris Flinkenberg sighed happily.

It was afterward, when Sandra had gotten a tray on which she laid out cigarillos and gin and tonics. And they sat naked and smoked, inhaled so their eyes watered and it swirled in their heads, their naked bodies in silhouette in the half darkness, glowing cigarettes, glasses steamy with damp in which the ice clinked.

"You know what?" Sandra held out her glass in order to clink glasses with Doris's glass, *clink*. "I've never seduced anyone before."

Sandra, playful.

Doris herself: she had no desire to talk or investigate anything at all. She said nothing. She curled up like a happy good-for-nothing as close to Sandra's body as she could come.

And someone turned on the television. That night, the night after they had been together the first time, they watched television down in the pool without water, where they had dragged mattresses and covers and so on. "A LOVE NEST," Doris Flinkenberg said maybe a few too many times, for once, thought Sandra. "Don't talk so much."

Words. Too many words. That night there was a strange film on television. The film was about a spaceship or something similar, whatever something like that could be called, that was traveling around in a human being's body. As if the body were space, or a foreign solar system. Traveling through veins, these yes, could you call them astronauts?

Doris did not know. She did not follow the plot. She would not remember a bit of the story afterward. But she would remember the red, the violet, and all the warmth, the warmth of the images, which were emphasized by the fact that the color television was set on too much red and poor contrast so everything fused together in some way. Doris would also remember the pounding heart . . . which the astronauts, or whatever they were called, were afraid of being sucked up into . . . or however it actually was . . . she would not know . . . she would not have A CLUE because she would lie there like a happy fool, a blessed fifteen-hundred-caliber lover.

Tightly pressed against her loved one's chest.

Against Sandra's body, which was warm, almost hot, and smelled keenly of sweat.

AND what was it that the fabrics smelled like? "Maharajah's Palace," Sandra had said. "No, Little Bombay," Doris had said, but she would not repeat it now because Sandra would become upset. Little Bombay, now. Now, thought Doris, which you do when you are stupid and in love and think you are invincible, now I'm starting to understand what it's about.

The astronauts in the Blood Woods.

In the aorta, the planet's pulsating guts.

Allowed herself to go to sleep. A hand on Sandra's stomach.

"When you told me we weren't going to answer the telephone because you didn't want the cousin's mama or anyone else to come and take me away from you, then I understood," Doris Flinkenberg squeaked.

"Shh," Sandra whispered absently from where she was in the middle of the film.

And with this *shh* Doris understood that the time for pillow talk was over. But it did not matter. Talk. All this talk. In reality she was tired of it as well. She was tired too, happily tired and exhausted.

The sexual awakening.

From the Blood Woods the astronauts traveled in toward a heart that was very dark and red.

The world in a small rectangle 3. Rain. Days passed. The moose steak had been finished. The girls ate hard candy and chocolate and chips. It started raining. The rain made everything damp. At first it was a pleasant dampness because the period behind them had undeniably been too warm and dry. But the damp started forcing its way into the pool too, and it was not as pleasant. And with the chill and the damp came the hunger, the real one, the Dorishunger.

"I'm hungry. Warm food," Doris Flinkenberg squeaked on Sandra's chest. "The flesh is weak. Real food."

"Oh God," Sandra said, bored, "can you really not control yourself?"

"No."

"I know," said Sandra. "We'll call the store and ask them to drive out a bunch of food under strict orders not to tell anyone. We have money. We'll bribe the lady in the store."

"Good idea," said Doris. "I'll call."

Doris called the country store in the town center and was laughed at.

"He who does not work shall not eat," said the lady in the store.

"Doris Flinkenberg will have to get here on the apostle's horses then."

They had in other words been found out.

"And stop being pretentious now. Incidentally, what does Mom think about it?"

"That's great," Sandra Wärn said when Doris presented the conversation to her lover. "NOW all hell is going to break loose. Thanks a lot."

"It wasn't my idea."

"Well, we can go to the store then. Now it doesn't matter anymore."

Nach Erwald und die Sonne. They were in the Closet, shortly thereafter, a day or so later, when the doorbell started ringing. And sure enough, they looked out through the porthole, it was the cousin's mama there outside at the top of the tall stairway up into nothing.

"Open up! I know you're in there!" The cousin's mama rang and rang the bell. The bell played and played and played. Nothing happened. The cousin's mama changed to knocking, gradually banging on the solid door.

"Doris! Sandra! I know you're there!"

Inside the house the girls remained frozen. Inside the Closet they pinched their mouths shut and made faces at each other. They saw the cousin's mama through the porthole. They saw her, but she did not see them.

It was in the rain. The cousin's mama gave up. She started walking back down the stairs with slow steps. Her back, a blue rain poncho with the hood drawn up, black rubber boots. It was moving. To see the cousin's mama this way made both of them speechless for real. The cousin's mama turned around a few times in order to make sure the door had not opened anyway . . .

"Ooh no," said Doris Flinkenberg and had tears in her eyes.

But in the Closet, Sandra lay her hand on Doris's chest. And so they started again. Wild kisses, caresses.

And then the first kiss, the second kiss, the third followed . . .

And in the midst of the kisses and the caresses Doris led Sandra out of the Closet and into the bedroom. The Islander's bedroom. They had never been there, in other words, never been together in that way before.

Lightning and thunder. The soft warm ground. Toward the Blood Woods . . .

. . .

"That bell," Sandra stated in the bed afterward. "We have to do something about it. Now I'm going to get the pistol."

When Sandra left, Doris remained in bed. It took quite a while before Sandra was back. Doris became restless while she was waiting. She looked around in a new way, or an old one, the old one. With great attentiveness, in order to obtain information.

Her hands fingered this and that in the vicinity of the night-stand, in the drawer of the nightstand. And there, under a lot of papers and sailboat brochures, she found a photograph. She picked it up and studied it carefully.

The image represented Lorelei Lindberg and the little girl, they were standing in the rain outside a shop. It was a store, a fabric store, you could see that if you looked carefully, which Doris would do at a later stage, but not now.

Sandra with her ugly, fractured lip; cold shivers of tender and loving recognition raced through Doris Flinkenberg. And Lorelei Lindberg. It was easy to see, it could not be anyone else. But at the same time, she looked so different in the picture in some way, not more as a stranger, but it was creepy, more familiar.

Doris's heart was pounding, and it was a horrid feeling that crept up inside her and with that came the sick feeling, she had to swallow, swallow in order to stop the nausea. While she saw. Because suddenly she understood what it was she saw, and what was familiar.

Lorelei Lindberg in a red raincoat.

Plastic is an eternal material.

The red raincoat was, there was no doubt about it, or was confusingly similar to, the same damned coat that she had seen at Bule Marsh.

Not that long ago. The one that had been on Eddie de Wire. On her in other words. The corpse of the American girl.

. . .

When Sandra came back she had the pistol with her.

Doris had quickly shoved the photo back into the drawer and said nothing to Sandra about her discovery.

"Well, should we see who has better aim, then?

"Hey. What's going on with you? You look as though you've seen . . . a ghost? Or what was it now: a phantom? Come on. Nothing's going to happen here. Now we're going out to shoot."

And out in the yard they competed to see who would be the first to shoot and destroy the doorbell.

Doris won.

They put on makeup. They were preparing themselves for the moment when the ugly duckling would become a swan, or like this: the moment when the marsh child would become Marsh Queen, also a pun that meant nothing then, yet. That moment did not seem so far away. In any case, not if you looked at one of them.

In other words at Doris. And it was only Doris, not Sandra, who was also a surprise. You had thought it would be the other way around.

Because what was actually happening was that Doris was growing up. Sandra also, but Doris more strikingly. So very striking it could not be ignored. So that you had to, in order to maintain the balance between the two of them, do something about it.

If nothing else than to reinforce, clarify.

The baby fat was falling off Doris Flinkenberg. Doris grew thin. She did not become skinny, but her body developed curves like a Coca-Cola bottle. Doris's dust-colored hair, which bleached by the sun had shone over the cemetery where she had raked and planted plants, it showed no signs of returning to its normal color.

Despite the fact that the girls kept themselves inside for the most part, except for the very end.

After the sexual awakening it seemed as though the blondness would be Doris-as-a-woman color. Long and soft too, the light hair fell over her shoulders and down when it grew and grew. Impossible to ignore. Sandra, at the bottom of the pool, combed and brushed and played with it.

The telephone rang. Sandra did not answer.

"It could be Lorelei Lindberg," said Doris. "Aren't you going to answer?"

"Not now," Sandra replied stiffly from the middle of the game. "Now I want to play."

"Oh," said Doris Flinkenberg, gradually growing impatient at the bottom of the pool. "This is boring. Can't we DO something instead?"

"Activities of the night belong to the night," Sandra whispered, full of secrecy.

"I mean actually DO," said Doris Flinkenberg. "Even if we love each other I'm not some rabbit who wants to copulate all the time. GO OUT. Why don't we go out?"

"Well, we can go out, then. To the store. But wait. We'll make you the Marsh Queen first. The Marsh Queen goes to the store."

The Marsh Queen goes to the store. Doris was allowed to put on the glitter clothes that Sandra had actually sewn for another occasion, that which would soon take place, the American girl's funeral in other words. And Pinky's shoes, the forgotten silver shoes with the foot-high heels that glittered too.

It was a game. They went to another store this time. Not to the store located most centrally, up in the town center, rather a country store Doris knew, toward the north above the marsh where the marsh people had carried on earlier (the area that would now in other words become the recreational area for the town's inhabitants).

The return of the Marsh Queen, Sandra Wärn said to Doris Flinkenberg and they marched away.

"What kind of movie star is that?" asked the lady in the store when they came in—she was alone there.

"It's the Marsh Queen," Sandra said softly. And Doris smiled and the lady smiled. She understood games, so far so good.

"And what do you girls want?"

And Sandra started calling out everything on her list and Doris, the Marsh Queen in the glitter clothes that Sandra had sewn for her, filled in when needed.

That was when the door opened and she stepped into the store, Liz Maalamaa.

Grunting and groaning in the summer heat.

"It was so hot there in Florida you had to take your inner Turk away."

"We have guests from far away," said the lady in the store. "A real lottery winner."

The world in a small rectangle, 4. The trespasser/the Marsh Queen in the pool. Another time, when Doris was the expectant Marsh Queen, Sandra climbed out of the pool and pulled the ladder up after her so Doris did not have a chance of getting out on her own.

"Stop it now," Doris suddenly complained in the pool. "Throw down the ladder. I don't have the energy to play anymore. I want to come out now."

But Sandra pretended not to hear. She disappeared up onto the top floor and when she came back she had the pistol with her.

Sandra was standing at the edge of the pool like once a long time ago, with her hand raised, aiming the pistol at Doris. "*Pang pang*, you're dead."

It was after all not the first time so Doris had not become very frightened. Besides, even at this stage she would never have thought she should be afraid of Sandra who was a part of herself.

But it was the last minutes of innocence,

Because at the same time something odd happened. The game became serious, and for both of them—

"I said stop."

And Sandra, there was a strange simultaneousness in everything, she suddenly remembered something from a long time ago, eons back in time, when Lorelei Lindberg was still there.

Lorelei Lindberg in the pool. Looking for a ruby the size of a tablespoon. The Islander somewhere else, but not for long. Could come at any time. He had taken the ladder away in order to keep her there, for safekeeping. It had been a game, the kind where you made up after, but now it was not like that anymore. "Sandra! Get the ladder!" Lorelei Lindberg hissed. "The ladder, Sandra! Please! Hurry!" and Sandra Slowly, sleepwalker . . .

Walked past. Heard nothing. Though she did hear.
And the Islander was back. He had the rifle with him then.
Shots, I think I hear shots.
But no.

Sandra walked in her sleep, as said, at that time.

It was strange, in other words, what happened. Sandra had never, never been so close to telling Doris Flinkenberg everything everything. So close . . .

And yet she had raised her hand, still aimed at Doris in the pool. Or the Marsh Queen. Then. Or whatever she should be called.

"Help. Don't shoot. Mercy. Have pity."
Who was it? Certainly not Doris. No. It was Lorelei Lindberg in the pool. And there was no question she was afraid of the Islander. For her life. Scared to death.

It's a game with high stakes, the Black Sheep had said in Little
Bombay. And we haven't seen the end yet.
MMMMMMMMMMMMouse.

"WHAT ARE YOU GIRLS DOING?"

Suddenly the cousin's mama was standing there, inside the door.

Because while everything was happening in the pool section the cousin's mama had shown up on the other side of the outside door down there, "the catering entrance," the door with the glass mirror on top. She had pounded on the door and yelled.

"Open up right now! Right now!"

And when no one had opened she had taken out her key and opened the door and now she was standing there on the inside, for a moment a bit speechless in the face of everything.

"What?" Sandra said with an indifferent, provoked expression, so to speak completely unsympathetic.

"YOU DON'T AIM A PISTOL AT ANOTHER LIVING HUMAN BEING!"

The cousin's mama screamed again, almost hysterically.

But then she caught sight of Doris in the pool. So to speak anew.

Doris, very much alive and so pretty, so beautiful . . . so princesslike among all the things. One moment, two: the cousin's mama's look rested a bit too long on Doris Flinkenberg because in the meantime Sandra was able to put the pistol away.

"What pistol?" Sandra said as calm as could be.

"I SAW!" the cousin's mama continued, but now more viciously as if to convince herself.

"What?" Sandra asked again, calm and nonchalant. And turned toward Doris and asked, as if the cousin's mama was not there, in the third-person singular, "What is she talking about?"

. . .

Doris between two fires. Sandra. The cousin's mama. She realized, on the one hand, it would be difficult to love Sandra. But on the other hand: WHAT THE HELL WAS LOVE FOR? If not for: belonging. *You love something in someone that brings you to life*, Inget Herrman had said. You and me against the world.

And there were not always fun things (and my God how many songs Doris had in her cassette collection on that topic).

So it was an easy choice, but not without difficulty.

The cousin's mama's presence had also given everything a splash of reality again. Reality. *That Sandra would* . . . My God, Doris Flinkenberg, Doris said to herself, now it's running away with you.

The cousin's mama then asked a highly normal question. "Incidentally, what are you doing here? Weren't you going to . . . leave?"

A completely and totally normal question that it really was about time someone asked. Doris Flinkenberg had also really wondered, and actually, she had not gotten a proper and exhaustive answer to that question. Not an answer you could believe in any case.

Lorelei Lindberg was in New York. Really. When a working number in Austria, in the old home, was also missing.

It was another part of her that had crept around in the house, when Sandra had been somewhere else or busy or been sleeping, and been checking and finding out about a few things. It was that part which could be called the twin detective, which had been in operation earlier, during the solving of the Mystery with the American Girl, but without a twin now.

She had called Heintz-Gurt's telephone number in Austria. She had gotten nowhere.

In fact the number did not exist. That was the laconic message that had been stated on the line over and over again.

. . .

And, the red raincoat. On Lorelei Lindberg in the photograph in front of Little Bombay on a rainy day. That was almost the worst thing of all. So terrible she did not even want to think about it and did everything she could in order to force it out of her consciousness.

But . . . on the other hand . . . Sandra, beloved.

So actually, the cousin's mama's question had not sat well in the situation in which it was now being asked, a situation which, considering Sandra's presence, required taking sides convincingly.

And Doris said, heard herself say, more precisely:

"We're here, don't you see? Leave us alone once and for all. Go away," and when she had gotten started she worked herself up even more. "I said leave. Nothing's going on here."

The cousin's mama remained standing a while, uncertain. But later, she actually turned around and straggled away.

And that time it had been final. She had not, during the entire rest of the time in the house in the darker part of the woods, the world in a small rectangle, come back.

. . . But still at night, they slept together, in the marital bed. They slept among paper, a book on shopping malls, *the future of consumption is consumption*, among all of the fabric. Satin silk, rough silk chiffon, thin habotai, a few old thumbed issues of *True Crimes, Teach Yourself Classical Greek*, . . . and so on.

Bread crumbs, crackers, and marmalade.

And when there was nothing else to talk about anymore, they came back to the American girl, again.

"Maybe she loved him and couldn't stand the thought that he was in love with someone else," Sandra whispered to Doris Flinkenberg in the darkness.

"But my God," Doris Flinkenberg objected, though quite eager, barely daring to breathe because now she felt it and very clearly so, Sandra's hands on her body. On her naked skin.

"And besides," Sandra continued and crept closer. Doris felt the breath in her ear and it tickled and those fingers which were playing over her stomach and in her navel, *play with me like you play your guitar* . . . "Maybe Eddie didn't have to do anything wicked at all. I mean, toward her. It was enough that she was there. As a motive. Just by existing in comparison to . . . you saw how strange, how faded, abnormal the cousin's mama was with her will, with what she felt. Desire. She felt unmasked. Undressed. Naked. What does that mean?"

My God, whom was Sandra talking about anyway?

"She was an old lady after all," Sandra continued. "She had two boys. Half grown . . ." The palm of Sandra's hand, soft and definite and so familiar over Doris's chest and legs and there was no doubt over where she was going. Sliding up the blouse. Doris helped, imperceptibly. Suddenly she felt ashamed of her desire. How strong it was, how definite.

And furthermore *had always been.* And to avoid thinking about it, in order to avoid thinking at all, she pressed herself against Sandra and took in the scent, the strange one that was a bit musty and far too spicy, but still fleeting. The one called Little Bombay.

What was it? A fabric store?

Doris in the bed realized there was so much she did not know about Sandra, so much she had not asked.

". . . not even her own children . . ."

Who was she talking about anyway?

But at the same time the desire came over Doris Flinkenberg again. And the love.

No one can love like us.

No, really.

Afterward:

"Have you thought," Sandra asked as if bewitched by herself, by her boldness plus the thought she was about to express, "about everything you don't know about her? Do you really know her? Really?"

They were talking about the cousin's mama again, always coming back to it. Then Doris said, she had to admit it:

"Well."

That is how it was. Both yes and no.

And suddenly it made her desperate.

Everything, all of it. Both what Sandra had said, and it was of course true, what did she really know about the cousin's mama? What did she know about anything or anyone?

What did she know about Sandra, her best friend, her most beloved?

And she had so wanted to ask, but it got caught in her throat. About the red raincoat in the photograph, about the telephone number that was out of service, about everything . . . but she could not bring herself to. She was afraid.

Afraid of knowing, but also afraid of.

Afraid of Sandra. Was that possible?

But it was in and of itself a thought so impossible, so upsetting, so tremendous, she did not have the energy to be someone who was thinking it. She could not go on! She wanted to forget about! Everything!

"But can't we forget about the American now? Can't we leave her to her fate?"

Silence.

"Yes," Sandra said later, "we can. But we have to bury her first."

The world in a small rectangle, 5. The American girl's funeral. Sandra was lying in the pool, at the bottom, on the green tile, she was lying on the fabric, on dull green silk Dupioni and she was wearing the glitter clothes, the ones she had sewn for Doris as the Marsh Queen's outfit, but they would also have to suffice now. The scarf, it was Eddie's real one, and the blouse, the one that had once belonged to Sister Night: the Loneliness&Fear shirt.

And Sandra lay there and closed her eyes because she was dead, and Doris spread flower petals—they were supposed to represent rose petals but they were just ordinary field flowers, but the theme was: nobody knew my rose of the world but me—over Sandra's body on the bottom.

Nobody knew my rose of the world but me, Doris mumbled. "The heart is a heartless hunter," she mumbled. And said, "It was a strange bird, now it's dead."

And Doris wrapped Sandra in fabric, in more fabric, fabric so she was covered. White and bordeaux red rasgulla crepe, which fell so softly, like snow. "Like snow," Doris Flinkenberg also repeated. "Buried in snow."

And Doris went out to the rec room and put on the music so that it flooded on maximum volume into all of the rooms in the house where there was a speaker. And the music, it was beautiful, it was Nat King Cole.

"The dream has ended, for true love died."

Those were the words in the song and when you listened, it was suddenly true.

Sandra lay in the pool and closed her eyes and was carried away and suddenly one moment she was the woman at the bottom of the pool, she was the one on Bencku's map. Who was she really?

One moment, just one moment, she brushed against the knowledge, and it was terrible, so horrible. What had Bencku actually seen?

Because she got up again of course. And the Islander had crumpled together on the edge of the pool and let her go, and a car came, and she left. Not even toward unknown fates, if it had only been so easy . . .

But now, fantasizing finished now, because Doris's dull voice somewhere, "I now pronounce you dead AND resurrected. And therefore we will dance, the very last dance."

Because the dream has ended now. True love died. And suddenly it was real.

And Sandra stood up, and the music played, and Doris was there and took her in her arms, not in a hug, but like in a dance. A slow slow, slow dance.

To the swaying song and they both, almost, cried.

Somewhere a telephone rang, suddenly Doris was in a hurry, she rushed to answer it.

"Now we're answering!"

And Doris rushed to the telephone and answered and Sandra was left at the bottom of the pool waiting.

And the one who had been on the telephone was Liz Maalamaa who said she was now going to come with all of the food they had ordered from the store.

"We haven't ordered any food," said Sandra.

"Who cares?" said Doris. "We're going to dance now. Let's start the song again."

And they did, they danced.

And suddenly in the middle of everything, a deafening *CRASH* could be heard and glass scattered: it was Liz Maalamaa who had come in, when no one opened she had shattered the window in the door. And where she was standing, Liz Maalamaa, at the lower entrance, standing among shards of glass and with ticks, bullymosquitoes, and insects crawling on her, said solemnly:

"Girls, girls, what are you two really doing here? Girls, Girls, you aren't hurting each other, are you?"

And then when she had gotten the girls' attention:

"Jesus loves you. My goodness how Jesus loves you. And he shall have his Damocles sword with which he will cut through the fog."

And Liz Maalamaa, she had a small whimpering dog in her arms.

Rita Rat. The summer vacation was in progress on the Second Cape. Sea urchins were sea urchins as usual, true to themselves and their task: to be sea urchins on summer vacation. Dressed in white, supreme, preferably associating with others in select company, that is to say, only with each other. For the most part Kenny lived alone in the Glass House this year. It was rumored the baroness was sick, but she came out a few times that summer. She was driven out in a taxi and sat in a wheelchair wrapped in blankets, wearing dark sunglasses on the cliff next to the Glass House. If the weather was bad she stayed in her Winter Garden. Then if you really tried you could see her as a dark shadow on the inside. And you saw. Sometimes. Rita saw. She had gone to the house on the First Cape, stood in the unsteady, perilous half-burned-down tower, and looked around.

Then, when the baroness came to the Glass House, there were no sea urchins there. It would be properly cleaned before the baroness was driven out for her visit. Four Mops and a Dustpan was summoned. Solveig and Rita. Earlier she had refused to set foot in that house. That had been a limit. It was not anymore.

"The barbarians must be summoned," Bengt had said once earlier in the spring, with the "class perspective" he pretended to be imbued with. So tired of everything that had half-choked dejection in it. Her siblings, they seemed to be so good at it. Where was it located? In the genes?

And "pretended" was the right word. Regarding Bengt in other words. Altogether. This summer Bengt WAS NOT taking a Nordic course on Marxist theory at the union center's central summer course center, he was not on peace training in Moscow or at work camp in the German Democratic Republic or in Poland. He made no effort whatsoever, not a one, for the peace-loving people in the world.

But he was not "dustpan" either for that matter.

No. Bencku was adrift. And it was programmatical (he had read a book). Bencku was adrift with Magnus von B. in the city by the sea. Where they were living in an apartment owned by Magnus von B.'s father and working in the harbor when they needed money. Otherwise they were partying; quite simply loafing about.

Adrift. It was in and of itself loads of fun. But just about the right amount of fun for someone who was left behind and had all his work to carry out.

But actually Rita was mostly, above all and most of all, angry because he was not there. And it was, in principle, something Rita had a hard time demanding at this point in time.

Everyone who was not there but in other places instead. For example, Jan Backmansson and his family: they were on Fiji. Some particularly interesting reptile spot that existed only at those latitudes needed to be studied and it was persevering. Furthermore, Jan Backmansson wrote in his letters, it is so wonderfully clear in the water here. These damned letters. "Shimmering azure."

And people who did not keep their promises. She so clearly remembered Tina Backmansson's: "And of course it's clear Rita is going to move in with us in the city by the sea. We have a large and spacious apartment and Susanna's room is empty."

That had been after the house on the First Cape was damaged in the fire and the family moved back to the city.

"We'll go over the practical details later," Tina Backmansson had said. "It's just a bit messy right now when we're in the middle of moving."

"Later, Rita," Jan Backmansson had said over the phone in the spring. After the summer. "Later."

"Though you wouldn't like it here. There are strict Muslims where we're living. The women have to wear clothes in the shower (or when swimming). Mother has a hard time with it. Greetings. Your J."

The Second Cape, the Glass House, the sea urchins. Rita found she was fascinated by them too, against her will. Especially Kenny.

. . .

Kenny was often with a girl from another house on the Second Cape this summer. Her name was Anna Sjölund or something similar and she had gotten a Nissan Cherry, bordeaux red of course, as a graduation present from her parents and now she was celebrating her "last summer vacation" or whatever it was called before she started studying interior design in the fall, a program she had been accepted into even though it was incredibly hard to get in. Anna Sjölund had some sort of job, she sold records in a store in the city by the sea, but it still seemed she was going to stay away from it enthusiastically because what she was mostly occupied with was driving around at breakneck speeds in her Nissan Cherry on the small roads around the District with Kenny, that is to say when they were not busy being sea urchins who were messing around with their surfboards and sailboats and et cetera on the beaches on the Second Cape.

But this had happened: one time when Rita was walking on the little road that led from the country road down to the cousin's property she was almost run down by that wretched Nissan Cherry with Anna Sjölund and Kenny in it. They braked on the road several feet in front of her so that the dust swirled, in order to, as they said (but they were laughing loudly, though not a mean laugh, Rita who had the reputation of not being so nice herself understood the difference), apologize.

They waited in the car until she caught up with them.

"That wasn't our intention," said Kenny.

"We're coming face-to-face with death," said Anna Sjölund.

"No you're not," said Rita. She heard herself say it in other words. It was not planned. It just came out. And she found a strange satisfaction in it. And it made an impression, her entire laconic attitude, she saw it. Then of course she did not know how to continue. *That's nothing.* It was the final line, but you did not say that sort of thing. So she did not say anything. And it became a bit awkward. But it was in any case Anna Sjölund and Kenny who hesitated more than she did.

But then of course, almost immediately afterward, the effect of the triumph had become properly disrupted. She had still been working in the two-window ice cream stand then, at the very beginning of the summer. Kenny and Anna had driven up to the two windows at the square and parked a little way away. Then she remained sitting there, on her place on the stool among the ice cream cones and the different ice cream flavors that no one wanted to buy because it was still quite chilly in the air then, in her light green ice cream blouse and with her light green J.L. kerchief on her head, in the ice cream stand and stared like an idiot at Kenny and Anna in the bordeaux red car parked in the evening sun. They were using snuff and had the music turned on high.

"Shit this is so pedestrian," Kenny yelled with her special accent and stuffed a pinch under her lip and then, *vroom*, they had driven off.

Up in the two windows, in other words. That was how the summer had started. Rita had already decided early in the spring that she did not plan on spending her summer trudging around for Five Hundred Mops and ONE Dustpan—who in other words had not even, after many ifs and buts, chosen to be present, but adrift in the city by the sea. Her intention had been to make an escape, perhaps insignificant, but still. *I'm not planning on walking on your leash anymore.* Something like that.

She had in other words organized a job for herself in two windows up at the square in the town center. Two windows was the ice cream stand owned by Jeanette Lindström, Businesswoman of the Year, who had a monopoly on the ice cream stand business at the square in the town center, not a particularly lucrative business in the beginning of the summer but certainly later, with the summer guests and, above all, with the traffic passing through on their way farther west.

A window to the left, a window to the right. In other words it looked like a proportionately large stand from the outside, but inside you sat on stools when there were no customers to serve, when the square lay empty and deserted before you, and only the seagulls were flying around and around, next to each other. Almost in each other's arms, if it was meant to happen, the one employee and the other.

It was a sought-after job because there were not many summer places in the municipality for young adults Rita's age and Rita had taken it on herself to arrange it. This had been done through the persistent persuasion of Jeanette Lindström, the mother of Daniel Danielsson (notice the last name: Daniel's father had been "even more unbearable," this according to Jeanette Lindström herself, they had a rather tough jargon with each other, mother and son), her crazy classmate. And he was in other words crazy, Daniel, there was no doubt about it.

To top it all off, which Jeanette Lindström would really emphasize later, in light of what happened, Daniel was in some way fond of her. Of Rita that is. That was in itself something tremendous. At school you were not fond of Rita, you were afraid of Rita. She had knocked Synnöve Lindbäck's teeth out a few months earlier, and it had not been an innocent girls' game but for real.

When Rita informed Solveig she had arranged a job for herself it had taken some time for her to convince herself it was really just jealousy that made Solveig claim that Rita had gotten the job only because Jeanette Lindström had been blackmailed by her son. In the beginning. At first, it had looked good. Susette Packlén was the other employee in the stand that first week, and she was quite all right. She had a lot of stories about her impossible boyfriends you could listen to.

And it had also been very satisfying that it was so obviously clear to Jeanette Lindström that of the two of them Rita was the one you turned to, the one who carried the main responsibility for the work at the stand when the boss was not there.

"You might become a full-fledged businesswoman one day," she had said in the spring already when Rita had sought her out and asked for this job because she was so very motivated and had a thousand and one ideas about how they could get zoom on the ice cream sales at the square during the summer months. "I'm looking forward to realizing them." And etc. she had piled it on.

She did not really have any ambitions whatsoever. There were actually more important things to waste your time and your energy and your mental activity on. She had planned on reading, there in the stand. She had planned—to the extent it was possible, when Susette Packlén kept her mouth shut (slept and kept her mouth shut: she had a phenomenal way of sleeping sitting upright, Susette)—to be alone and think.

"We women need to support each other in sisterhood and entrepreneurial activities," Jeanette Lindström had raved. Phewt, Rita had thought. All of that chatter had blown away like pollen off a dandelion, away from the house on the First Cape anyway. *Eldrid's Spiritual Sojourn*. My God. And fallen like "tears on rocky ground," as it was called in one of the songs that played on Doris Flinkenberg's radio cassette player.

But with these words Jeanette Lindström had hired Rita as a seller of ice cream in the two windows at the square in the town center.

It had gone to hell as much as it possibly could have. And Rita had already understood that it would on the Monday morning of the second week after a few promising first days. But that Monday of the second week Susette Packlén, who had been her "stand buddy" as Jeanette Lindström said (she was careful so that this summer job that she did not pay very high wages for would not sound like too much work), had not shown up at ten o'clock when the workday started and the stand was going to open. Exactly two hours later, when the church bells at the square rang twelve muffled times, Jeanette Lindström showed up together with her son Daniel Danielsson and laconically informed Rita that Susette Packlén had been sent to pick strawberries and other berries in the inner parts of the country where Jeanette Lindström had her own strawberry field on rented land, and that Rita's "stand buddy" from here on out would be her son Daniel Danielsson who needed to get practical experience from the practical working life, as well. She said this seriously to Rita in Daniel Danielsson's presence, but when her son was out of hearing distance she whispered to Rita:

"Between us women I'm going to tell you that there isn't going to be anything of my vacation with him in the house. HE needs to get out and learn what life is all about. Make sure you don't give in to his whims. Be firm!" And then she tousled Rita's hair in a friendly way, as luck would have it before the time of hugging and cheek kissing. "You have guts, Rita. I like that. You'll be fine."

Daniel Danielsson already ran amok on the third day. It was no surprise. You had expected it. There were no reasons or explanations either. Except for Solveig's irritating and highly malicious (since Rita also shortly thereafter would be back among the mops and the absent dustpan):

"Bad genes. I told you so."

The story about Daniel Danielsson in that light was the following: Daniel Danielsson's grandfather on his father's side had been a veterinarian who hated cats, but he was an enterprising devil who came up with the idea that God had blessed him with a higher mission than puncturing cows' swollen stomachs. And that was to free his veterinary district from the cat's yoke. The wild cat, the farm cat, the house cat—even the neighbor's angora little Frasse's—yoke. He had in other words started snatching the cats and cremating them. All cats he came upon. He got hold of them in more or less sophisticated and ingenious ways, but preferably in the traditional way, with the net. And thereupon he drugged them.

And transported them still asleep in bags to Jörgen Bäckström, one of his lackeys. In smaller communities, then like now, a large deal of the day rolls by on the power of a similar lackeying. In more elegant language it is called quid pro quo, but in reality it is a misleading name because in that system there is always one side that is stronger, the one who has the power to decide which favors should be exchanged, for what, and how. There is almost always one side at a disadvantage in relation to the other, and that part is for the most part people like Jörgen Bäckström who is not chairman of the city council, parish clergyman, bank director, or in this case a city veterinarian like Daniel Danielsson's grandfather.

Those sorts of people who have order and the power of interpretation on their side.

Jörgen Bäckström lived in a house that veterinarian Danielsson rented out to him at a truly favorable price, and in that house there happened to be a hot and spacious furnace. And it was here, and expressly to Jörgen Bäckström, who did not have anything against cats for example, quite the opposite, that veterinarian Danielsson in his assiduousness transported the sleeping cats for cremation alive. And it was Jörgen Bäckström who would throw the cats in the fire. The city veterinarian personally was not really very hands-on in the handling of the actual animals but he happily remained and ENJOYED as the smell of fried cat filled the cottage.

Jörgen Bäckström had no choice. He was a nobody—it is also a psychological mechanism, you see yourself like that from the beginning, you see your disadvantage and are chained to it—in comparison to veterinarian Danielsson.

When Jörgen Bäckström finally got to the police it was too late for his part. He had already become crazy for good. Besides they did not believe him.

It was not until the police commissioner was called by the parish clergyman that the whole thing came to an end.

In other words the whole story unraveled when Danielsson the veterinarian went after the neighbor's cat, the clergyman's spoiled angora—a gift from the missionary station on Formosa. Danielsson the veterinarian was caught red-handed. A Saturday afternoon when the clergyman was sitting in his study writing the Sunday sermon and just happened to cast a glance out his window and was met with a scene that to begin with was quite amusing. Danielsson the veterinarian, the clergyman's neighbor and brother in the lion's club or whatever the corresponding organization was called at that time, was on all fours in the garden with a net creeping along after him, like a jungle luma (which was the name of a wild species of cat one had tried to tame for domestic use in certain missionary stations where Frasse in the clergyman's garden originated) after his thirty-pound treasure, *little Frasse*. But when the clergyman realized what was going on in his own yard it was not amusing anymore and he grabbed the receiver of the telephone and called the police.

"I said bad genes." As if that was an explanation. As if it REALLY was. It started taking hold of Solveig as well, the way people thought in the District. Rita noted it, surprised and with disgust. This thinking did not agree with everything that existed outside in other places, with all possibilities. But Solveig seemed to have set her boundaries. Solveig from the District. Rita from the District. As if there was nothing else, for real. As if that were it.

Descendant Daniel Danielsson had a mouth from which he exuded some kind of solitary rap millions of eternities before the multinational music companies or the remaining music companies noticed it. Gangsta rap, in other words, but this was Daniel

Danielsson without a gang, totally alone, socrazysocrazy that he kept everyoneeveryone at a distance. But Rita, Rita Rat, in his fantasies, most beloved.

Rita Rat locked in two windows with Daniel Danielsson, which, as said, seen from the inside in any case was a rather limited space. The world, here as well, though in another way, in a small rectangle.

What was she going to do about it then? Complain to the boss?

Jeanette Lindström, who had a license to practice stand business as a monopoly at the square in the town center during the summer months, was Daniel Danielsson's mother, as said, it deserves to be repeated.

"I have an obscure familial relationship with her," as Daniel Danielsson himself expressed it.

I don't particularly like Wednesdays. There is a dramaturgical rule that there is reason to regard with skepticism. The rule says that if a rifle is hanging on the wall in the first act then it should be fired at the latest in the last act. Nothing unnecessary is allowed in a play. It is a matter of upholding the dramaturgical tension. Yes, it sounds logical. But that is just what it is, logical. And then there is a risk that the play—if you do not happen to be Chekhov and have written it—just becomes tedious and stylistic. And does not provide room for the loose threads of life. When we weave we choose colors and patterns: they do not arise of themselves. And some threads ARE and remain loose. For example just such a thing.

Everything is as it is, in other words, rather clumsy, really.

Well, accordingly. In life on the other hand everything is, as said, another matter. And regarding Daniel Danielsson it is written so, not in any books on dramaturgy but rather in "the stars from which I read from life's true book," which it was also called in one of the songs on Doris's insufferable *Lasting Love Songs for*

Moonstruck Lovers cassette, that an idiot like Daniel Danielsson brings an air rifle to two windows (where his mother, whom he in other words, among other things, suspects for homosexual tendencies, which he has to point out over and over again, at the same time drawing his tedious evidence on the ice cream in the containers, has placed him to have him out of the way and get a little peace and quiet and summer in the summer house—"she wanted to be alone and make out with the dykes"—during the vacation) and already after the breakfast break on the morning of the third day it follows that then the same rifle will not only have been fired but also have caused a massacre before the church bells at the square had time to strike their three muffled chimes (as a sign that Daniel Danielsson's workday was over and Jeanette Lindström, "the Dyke of Dykes," according to her son, would drive up to two windows in order to give her son a ride back to the summer home, that is to say "the sea queen" on the Second Cape).

When Daniel Danielsson showed up after the breakfast break that day in two windows he had his rifle with him. He came on foot. The idea had been to take the bus just that day since the Dyke of Dykes was busy and did not have the opportunity to drive him to work, but it had not worked out. Partly because of political reasons: to turn to public transportation was in agreement with how Daniel Danielsson saw the world as the apex of proletarian. But most of all because Daniel Danielsson, certainly with good reason, had suspected it would have been difficult to transport the rifle all the way to the town center. A few hours later he definitely had enough of the afternoon silence on the square, this stillness that in a book he would write a number of years later would take on metaphysical features. *The silence in the world, in the universe.* In that book, which Rita would not read, she would be the cute shop assistant, short and sweet, who screamed Help! Help! and had tried to talk some sense into him in a motherly way. She did none of this in reality. But fiction is wonderful and in it they would have gotten married as well and she would become mother to his many children for which he would tell just this story about his childhood in "small-town hell."

A silence that was broken only by the screams of the seagulls, the seagulls that flew around and around in the square as if bewitched, screamed and shed filth, screamed and screamed.

Screams that accompanied and further reinforced the peculiar throbbing that was going on in Daniel Danielsson's head, nonstop, twenty-four hours a day. And he was suddenly gripped by such an utterly irresistible desire to give expression to it.

First by pounding the rifle against different surfaces in the stand, then by aiming the rifle a bit wherever it would fit. To one side, to the other, toward Rita Rat, his "stand buddy."

"Hands in the air or I'll shoot you, my dear!"

Rita, she almost obeyed. She probably became completely terrified, there was no question about that. Furthermore, she did not doubt for a second that Daniel Danielsson could shoot her out of love. "He just wanted to make an impression on you," Jeanette Lindström, the Dykes' Dyke, would say later, and by this mean the entire episode from beginning to end, including the massacre, and get it to sound a bit like all of it was Rita's fault.

But still. There was something in Rita that in spite of the fear said: Stop. This is enough. And managed to ward off her own reflex to obey. *Stare into the face of death.* Maybe this was it, then. And instead she said as calmly as possible while staring at him hard:

"Well, shoot, then. What are you waiting for?"

Daniel Danielsson had paused for exactly a fraction of a second. Then he said, also as calmly as possible:

"You mean it. Thank you, my dear!"

And Daniel Danielsson's face had twisted into an almost satanic smiling grimace, maybe something snapped in his head right then, as if to confirm that he had now come up with something unusually sick. And the madness triumphed.

. . .

"Boys will be boys," Jeanette Lindström would say afterward. "They have such a hard time showing their feelings.

"You're undeniably a cute girl, Rita."

The gulls, in other words, who were making a terrible racket. *Skwaak.* They were the only ones who had managed to drown out Daniel Danielsson and his loud thoughts and his desire to make an infringement on the world, an action that would definitely be seen and felt in some way, which became especially obvious in just those long seconds when Rita with the muzzle of the rifle pressed against her chest—it really was cramped in two windows, as said—sat absolutely frozen and did not obey. It was just the seagulls, the damned seagulls, that did not care about anything.

NOW Daniel Danielsson knew, exactly the second Rita said, "Well, shoot, then," what he was going to do about it. Slowly, slowly he turned the rifle away from the "stand buddy" toward the birds, raised it and aimed and fired. And fired and fired and fired and fired. Daniel Danielsson was an excellent marksman, a real hunter when he was in the mood.

So he managed to hit quite a few seagulls, which fell to the ground, damp damp, and injured many and evoked a blasted chaos of seagull intestines, blood and feathers. Birds that lost their ability to orientate and flew into the window of the stand, damp damp, against the glass and blood and feathers and guts in the ice cream, especially in the vanilla ice cream because the lid of just that one happened to be standing open when the seagull massacre started.

Seagull feathers, guts in ice cream. Blood in chocolate. Pistachio and nuts, feathers, and sinews and small bird bones, terribly stringy. In the streusel.

I don't particularly like Wednesdays was how Daniel Danielsson officially explained himself afterward. Of course the event aroused attention and Daniel Danielsson was given fines to pay, but above all he was interviewed and so on. *My notorious fame originates from* . . . would be the first words in the book *The Seagull Massacre* that would be written a few years later and translated into a thousand languages and become a real classic, an excellent, pulsating, and anarchic portrayal of a childhood in a small-town hell. The rats from the boomtown orchestra might read it and be impressed because later they would want a "punk hit" or whatever it was called that would climb the charts with the song "I Don't Particularly like Mondays," which would be about a girl in a small town in England who starts shooting wildly around her on the playground on a completely ordinary Monday morning just because she is so bored, and of course it becomes an awful massacre.

But this is where Rita got off. She did not care about any continuation, either this one or Daniel Danielsson's own.

In the middle of the massacre she got up, not to mention appropriately calm, opened the door to the stand, and left the two windows that way.

Freedom. It was that simple. Just open the back door and walk out.

A moment of freedom, in other words. Because for Rita's part the whole thing meant a return to the mops and that dustpan who was always absent anyway when it suited him.

"Back to your roots," as Solveig would have said, and maybe she said it too. But Rita did not listen to her anymore. She had stopped listening.

She started, sometimes in certain moments, it actually felt, becoming desperate.

That year she and Solveig cleaned the Glass House on the Second Cape alone.

"We are such a good team," Rita and Solveig said to the cousin's mama.

The memory of Jan Backmansson. It faded.

. . .

And the baroness in the Glass House, later, when she came out and you could see her from a distance from the First Cape. During rain and hard winds you could see her inside the house, in the same way wearing sunglasses in a wheelchair turned toward the sea, in the bay window, the veranda, "my fantastic Winter Garden" or "my lovely garden," which she also said, but that was such a long time ago. Like a pilot in an airplane who was going to take off. Like the captain of a spaceship. Miss Andrews. The windowpanes so clear clear. Rita knew. She and Solveig had been the ones who had washed, washed these windows, rubbed them.

"One should get a pistol."

It came from somewhere.

The memory of Jan Backmansson. It faded.

One time, a bit earlier, in the middle of a workday in the Glass House Rita had suddenly become nauseous and just dropped everything and gone home to the cottage to rest.

She had caught Doris Flinkenberg red-handed: rummaging in the pistol cabinet where the pistol she and Solveig had inherited was kept, like a priceless object.

"What the hell? Aren't you supposed to be in the Alps?"

"No," said Doris Flinkenberg, who had an ability to appear in a lot of places when you least expected it. "As you can see. No."

"What are you doing here?"

"Looking for the pistol. Can't you see? I need it."

"Well, you can't have it. It's not yours. You have no right to be here."

Then Doris said slowly, almost drawling:

"Erhm. Weren't you the one who said that about the American girl. That a certain person saw wrong. That was me. That she was alive anyway."

Rita stiffened.

Then she stated as calmly as she possibly could:

"Well. Maybe it wasn't really true. But, on the other hand, Doris . . . there are things you don't know. There are things that . . . it is in any case . . . well, we'll talk about it later."

"We'll have to do that, then," said Doris Flinkenberg on the glitter scene. "We'll do that. Can I have the pistol, then? Just for a little while, to borrow?"

"Take it, then," Rita hissed. "But you're coming back with it later."

"Oh. Not a word to anyone."

"I said go away."

"Shhh . . ."

"Go away."

The world in a small rectangle, 7. When the summer throws you away. And they are driving a hundred miles an hour with Liz Maalamaa on the highway in a sports car that Liz Maalamaa has rented for the day. It is open, the girls in the backseat, Liz Maalamaa turns around sometimes and looks at them and laughs, an encouraging laugh, now we're going to have fun. And the dog next to Liz Maalamaa, it is whining too, it has curled up next to Liz Maalamaa on the driver's seat, it seems to like riding in a car, it seems like it is used to speed.

Liz Maalamaa, in sport gloves, scratches behind her ear sometimes, on the go.

And the girls, they say nothing, but they are so joyfully expectant. This trip with Liz Maalamaa, it surpasses everything already, even before anything has happened.

They are on their way to the Eagle's Nest, a restaurant on the outskirts of the city.

"I'm so hungry, girls," Liz Maalamaa said there where she was standing among the shards of glass in the basement of the house in the darker part, "and my dog is so thirsty. Yes, his name is Jack. And you may pet him."

And the girls, still so at a loss, had pet the dog. But now, when Liz Maalamaa had gotten started, then they had instantly caught on.

"You like to dance?" Liz Maalamaa asked because she had of course seen them and heard the music, down in the pool. "Should we kill two birds with one stone, then?" and Liz Maalamaa clapped her hands, "I'm hungry, my dog is thirsty, and you—you actually look like you need to get out a bit, you're so pale. Get out and look around in the world. And take a dance with the presidents. You need, quite simply," said Liz Maalamaa, "to get out and dance a little."

And they arrive at the Eagle's Nest, it is located up in a tower and what a view: a round restaurant with a round dance floor in the middle. And they take a table by the window, the dog Jack on the table, he drinks water out of a mug on a tray. And Liz Maalamaa eats beefsteak and the girls also want some.

Though later the music starts playing and at the same time the presidents come. And the regents. The peace treaty is signed, now there will be BEEF and DANCING. And so they dance. Sandra in the glitter clothes, and Doris as she is, but she is so beautiful— like a day, so she gets asked anyway, most of the time. And they dance with America's president, they dance with the fat Leonid Brezhnev from the Soviet Union, they dance with Kekkonen and quite a few from the Bernadotte family . . . but suddenly in the middle of the dancing, Doris falls to the ground unconscious.

Liz Maalamaa calls from somewhere, "But I'm going to tell you girls that grace is so large so large. Little Doris, did you trip, is there something wrong with you?" But no, there is nothing wrong with Doris. She has just heard another song:

"Yet every wave burns like blood and gold, but the night soon will claim what is owed."

And it comes from considerably closer and farther away. From a certain tape player, from a certain cassette collection. And suddenly she longs to be there.

"Home," says Doris. "Now I want to go home."

And Doris says, "I'm going now and no one follows me."

And Liz Maalamaa and the dog and Sandra and the presidents, they just stare.

"I'm going by myself. Now."

And Doris leaves the Eagle's Nest and walks away.

Home. The whole long way home.

And that is how it is, when the summer throws you away.

This was how it was when the summer had had enough of you and you went home.

Doris Flinkenberg was red like a lobster, beyond sunburned, when she returned to the cousin's house.

Home.

At home.

What to do?

Lock yourself in?

Lock yourself into the cousin's mama's kitchen with the crosswords and all of the magazines. *Ladies' Home Journal* and the others. *True Crimes*. That is what my life has become. The dictionaries. Learn to spell new beautiful words. Like for example "apotheose," "anomaly," and "monkey business."

Should you actually do that? Was it possible?

"Doris, you should know that I came down too hard," said the cousin's mama when Doris came home. "I want to ask you for forgiveness. May I?"

"You can ask for whatever you want," said Doris Flinkenberg.

And the cousin's mama had, with a lump in her throat, nodded.

"Here, take this salve and rub it over your skin. Sweet child, how you've burned yourself."

"Thanks."

"Here. Take the sleeping pills as well. Lie down now and rest. Get enough sleep."

"But we have to go to the house in the darker part . . . we have to clean."

"Shh, Doris. We'll have time. Sleep now."

And the cousin's mama pulled down the blackout curtain. And *ritsch*. When the cousin's mama had left Doris pulled it up again. Sleep. Sleep did not help.

Look through the window. And who was there then, in the yard, as if on cue? Normalcy.

Bencku and Micke Friberg and Magnus von B.

With their bags of beer. Go out there, to the barn, to the boys, drink beer with them. It was something to do in any case. Something that was normal.

". . . manufactured," said Magnus von B. In the barn. And counted all the ingredients needed to manufacture dynamite. There really were not many and could, said Magnus von B. expertly, be gotten almost anywhere. And Bencku nodded. And opened a new bottle. And Magnus von B. talked.

That is how it was in Bencku's barn. As usual.

But Doris did not look at them. She looked, yes she also looked at the map, but only quickly because then she looked down. Below the map. Where Micke Friberg was sitting, on Bencku's bed. And plucking at his guitar.

Dazed and Confused. On the one hand, and the other. Forward and backward, just about. He was that skillful with the guitar. But he also looked up.

And then, suddenly, he discovered Doris-lull in the barn opening, against the light.

"Is anything going to happen here?" she asked with a drawling, inimitable Dorisvoice.

"And I was a sold man," Micke Friberg said to himself in that moment and a thousand times later to Doris Flinkenberg during the fall, before Doris died.

"No one can love like us," Micke Friberg whispered in Doris Flinkenberg's ear already shortly thereafter.

And Doris paid attention. He was so beautiful. And it was a solution. For a time.

"Where have you been all my life?" Micke Friberg whispered in her ear just a few hours later, during one of their first hugs.

"What do you mean?" Doris whispered back, tenderly and devoutly.

And so, after that, it was the two of them together.

The day after Doris hooked up with Micke Friberg she and the cousin's mama cleaned the house in the darker part of the woods. After the summer. Which had now gotten rid of you so it did not really matter what happened with everything, or most of it, later.

Sandra was on Åland. Wherever the hell she was. New York?

Couldn't care less, Doris thought with a lump in her throat.

She was surprised about the lump. What was it now? The voice of the blood? Oh, damnation.

And traces could be seen and not be seen in the house. But everything she could sweep away, she swept away.

And the strange thing: the window in the door that had broken when Liz Maalamaa came in, it was whole. It had never broken either. The same dirty window as always.

She was going to search for a lot of things, when Sandra was not there. Evidence. But she did not. She did nothing.

She did not bother about anything and went to Micke Friberg afterward.

Though she found the pistol and she took it home with her.

"I don't like it when you're like that," said Micke. "Swearing and like a teenage girl. When there's so much else inside you. Style.

"Besides you have a good voice.

"We're going to sing together," said Micke Friberg. "We're going to have a band. Micke's Folk Band."

The pistol. Liz Maalamaa. The love that died. The red plastic raincoat on Lorelei Lindberg and on the American girl.

And the telephone numbers that did not exist in reality.

Sandra, what was it?

Sandra. Where is Lorelei Lindberg, really?

And the image on Bencku's map. The woman in the pool. She forgot it now. On purpose.

Because it *belonged to the hard things in the soul from which nothing could be woven.*

"Do you think so, Micke?"

"What did you say, Doris?"

"That I can sing?"

"Of course."

"Well. Are we going to sing, then?"

They were the Rats. They went from house to house, from villa to villa, over the empty Second Cape. It was late in the fall in the middle of the week, for the most part, those times just before the snow was going to fall, everything was theirs. The rats, they went into the houses: sometimes it was easy, no effort (a window was open, a door was not properly locked), sometimes it was harder (you had to break a window, or so, but not worse than that), never impractical. They went from room to room in the houses, from floor to floor, through all of the floors from floor to ceiling: opening cabinets and drawers, reviewing the contents of them. In the kitchen, ate their crackers, crumbled them over the floor, stuck their fingers in their old marmalade jars and smeared on the sandwiches and on each other and sometimes on the furniture. Bombarded each other with old hard corn kernels, macaroni, rice.

Sat on the sofa groups in their living rooms, parlors, on all of their verandas. Sofa groups, what a word. Solveig, for example, she was quite good at imitating it. "Come and sit here in the sofa group, Järpe." And Järpe came and opened his never-ending beer and frothed over the fabric the sofa and recliners were upholstered in. In their dens, lit long matches, pushed them still burning against the white tiles over the fireplaces. There were marks of course, but not worse than that, it could be washed away. It was not THAT bad.

They were the Rats. Järpe, Torpe, Solveig, and a few more, and Rita, Rita Rat above all. She was the one who was, so to speak, the essence of it all. And it was strange because all of it everything was for her completely totally immoderate plus minus zero, indifferent, did not mean a DAMN thing. A way to pass the time, just as meaningless as all other pastimes.

Skimmed through their left-behind magazines, tore out a page, made paper airplanes out of others, filled in the WRONG LETTERS in different places in their crosswords if such lay unsolved on the tables. Relics from summer delights gone by, they would be sabotaged now. But it was not THAT bad. Nothing more than that.

Looked out their windows.

Admired their views. So exquisite.

It was an unusually rainy and windy fall. Pouring rain, storms, and for the most part it was dark when the Rats were moving around the Second Cape. Pitch-black. Saw nothing in front of you. Not even as much as a finger.

One could then so to speak in other words just as well have been anywhere. *Damn nice here like this.* And pfft. Blew on the windowpane and drew figures on the glass. No obscene words or shapes, that was just childish. Stupid words. Meaningless.

"Look at this," Järpe Rat said and drew a smiley face in the damn steam.

"Whatever," said Solveig Rat and blew on the windowpane and drew a smiley face in the damned steam next to his. "And the two of us are here." The latter meant what Solveig loved to say in the language of the District: "Now we're two. It's the two of us."

"Go to hell!" One time when Rita Rat was too drunk she crashed her hand through a windowpane. But it was later and she was wasted. And it was in the Glass House. The special thing with the Glass House and the Rats was that it was accessible to only a few of the Rats. Solveig and Rita, and so. So it was not the Rats exactly who made a lot of noise in the Glass House, who for example demolished what had once been the baroness's Winter Garden.

It was only a few.

When Solveig got started she was hard to stop. She imitated the summer guests from the Second Cape, their speech.

And of course, it was easy to laugh at them: the summer guests, who strained to have what they called a "free and equal" relationship to "the local people," were almost the best thing to make fun of when they were not there and were going to get involved in everything. The ones who "understood the barren conditions out at sea" and so on, though in actuality there was almost no real archipelago outside the Second Cape, just a few occasional fisherman who still lived in the municipality and they lived farther inland and got to have their fishing boats moored at the rented jetty next to the county's new public beach because the beach by the sea was private.

Spoke about *these conditions* loud and clear, as if they knew exactly what it was all about. Rita would get to hear it with her own ears a few years later when she came to the city by the sea and lived with the Backmansson family. Not the Backmanssons, they did not talk that way (and that further strengthened Rita's solidarity with the Backmanssons, they were from the same planet as her).

When she would hear that talk in the city by the sea then she would think what did they really know anyway. And it could make her feel so downhearted that she actually for a moment— but only for a moment—thought about leaving everything and going home.

But immediately, on the other hand. Home. What was home? Not the cousin's house, not Solveig's (when she was living in the city by the sea with the Backmanssons, she would no longer think "Rita and Solveig's cottage," she would just think "Solveig's") cottage.

But still at the same time, Solveig who was going on like that with the Rats. It was so petty.

For her the Rats were almost a dead period during the fall. A pointless, and thus lacking in meaning, pastime.

Rita with Torpe in the boathouse. She was lying there with her bra up by her neck and Torpe Torpeson had just come inside her in his insistent way that was rather arousing anyway. But still, she could not let herself go, not even then. She was lying on her back with her legs spread on the same bunk where the American girl had once lain. Though she did not think about that, she stared at the guitar on the wall, it was still hanging there and was cracking in the cold, the strings that had broken were curling like locks, and while Torpe was busy she thought maybe, "Everything is so necrophilic." It sounded terrible and it was but she was also cold inside at the thought of it. And then tenderness welled up inside her because Torpe Torpeson, he was here after all, and he warmed you.

It happened to be one of the unusual clear nights that fall, and when she was lying there with Torpe she suddenly saw just the sky and the stars—it was still so beautiful, so wonderful.

But suddenly, almost simultaneously, it became so strangely dark. A dark figure covered the window. It was the shadow of a person. And it WAS NOT Bengt because Bengt was holding house in other places for a change.

"Who the hell was that?"

Torpe jumped up and tore open the door and called out into the darkness. But the Shadow was gone.

"For Christ's sake . . ." Torpe started.

"Oh. Don't worry about it. Come here."

The Shadow, Rita knew it, was Doris Flinkenberg.

. . .

Doris was following Rita. No one noticed, not even Solveig.

"You're the one who's seeing things. Has a screw loose. What would Doris . . ." but Solveig stopped herself.

"She's following me no matter what you say," Rita said almost in a long and tired sigh as if she did not care about Solveig's opinions one way or the other. That made Solveig uncertain. When Rita did not even have the energy to fight her.

"It's the two of us," a sentence that was so infinitely important to Solveig. And now Solveig suspected there was a part of Rita that was not in the District anymore, that might not stay regardless of whether or not the Backmanssons had taken her with them. Rita was going away.

And Solveig would not be going with her. That seemed like the whole point of it. Solveig was not going to go with her.

Solveig herself worked at Four Mops and a Dustpan.

And when Doris was dead in about a month, Solveig would take over everything herself. The cousin's mama would not be able to work for a long time, Rita would have run away, and "the dustpan" would, true to habit, come and go, gradually more and more go. And Solveig would be equal to the task: only a few years later Four Mops and a Dustpan would have its own office in the town center with four employees. Solveig would sit in her own office and decide over everything.

And Rita, she would go away. *She would really go away* and not come back for many years.

Rita attended the high school up in the town center; some days when she went home from school on the school bus she got off a few stops early in order to have some peace and quiet, think, be alone.

Then, if Doris Flinkenberg was on the bus, it happened that Doris noticed and got off as well, at the same stop, and followed at an adequate distance, dawdling after Rita. And if someone

low, idling steps it was Doris Flinkenberg. That
she was alone; in the company of other people,
stuck in them. Imitated. If anyone was an imperson-
it was Doris Flinkenberg.

The new Doris. Ha-ha. Micke's Folk Band. Doris and her miserable boyfriend . . . or was it ex-boyfriend? There were rumors that Doris Flinkenberg had given Micke Friberg himself the boot. In favor of . . . whom, you had to wonder, then? For what? To, maybe, ramble around alone in the leafy woods and pursue other people. *I walked out one evening, out into a grove so green.*

Though. Doris, anguished, walked around at school as well, alone. The other girl, Sandra, could not be seen. "Ha-ha," thought Rita in the woods, "maybe the dykes are having a lovers' quarrel."

And something there behind her in the woods. Yes, there she was. Doris. At the same time: another seed of, not panic, but certainly anxiety, was growing inside Rita.

What did Doris Flinkenberg want with her anyway?

And Rita continued walking. She walked and walked. Until she came to Bule Marsh. That was not where she had been headed. Though it would be wrong to say that it was Doris behind her who had driven her there. It was something between part compulsion and own will.

One day in the middle of October: Bule Marsh lay there so deep and solitary, so special, also on an otherwise sunny fall day like this one, where in other places it could still be warm and with a lot of color. But the warmth, the colors, it was as if they did not extend all the way to Bule Marsh.

And it was as if they had never really done so.

Now Rita walked up onto the highest cliff. Looked around. Could not help but be gripped by the strange beyond-time feeling and *the great loneliness* that ruled there at the marsh.

Otherwise Rita was not like Doris and Sandra or her brother Bengt who roamed around in the woods just because, roamed and roamed so to speak and still always ended up at Bule Marsh in the end.

For Rita there was for the most part a purpose and a goal.

With Torpe and Järpe and Solveig, a place where you could drink your beer in peace and quiet.

Or, with Solveig a long time ago, in order to swim. When they were little and the public beach had been there at Bule Marsh for a short time. Of course the opening in the reeds was still as public as you could get, but nowadays there were real public beaches in several places in the municipality. It had just been those years following the housing exhibition when the public beach had to be moved quickly from the Second Cape when that area became private. And it was as if no one in the midst of all the bustle had thought about somewhere other than Bule Marsh.

But what happened here, the American girl, all of that, had brought an end to everyone's desire to swim in the marsh water, as if *swimming with a corpse*. Already that following year a new public beach with piers and diving platforms and all sorts of things had been opened by one of the larger lakes in the west. Rita and Solveig had also gone there in the beginning, continued with the swimming training they had devoted themselves to earlier, together, a while anyway. Because they had a plan, that they would become swimmers or world-famous divers like Ulrika Knape for example. Private plans, highly private. Something like that. With quite a bit left open in the details of the plans themselves. Something in that area anyway. Amaze the world in some way so to speak, both twins.

Stupid dreams. When the new beach by the lake in the west had been inaugurated the following year Solveig had made quite a nice leap from the thirty-foot landing, and it had been rather unforgettable. Rita herself had a cold and could not participate. She

sat in the audience on the newly built stands on wheels that could
be pulled out when needed and caught her sister's whirling jump
in the palm of her hand; in a certain perspective she had, her
sister Solveig looked so small. And been quite proud. But then
the swim camp, which for the time being was being arranged in
the neighboring municipality with participants from swim clubs
from around the whole country, had its show. And really, you
could see the difference. Rita anyway, and Solveig. So they had,
little by little, actually that season already stopped with training
and all of that. Not based on any verbal agreement, it just happened that way.

And, yes, at the marsh, in the end, she had also been there with
Jan Backmansson sometimes. When they had strolled around a
little bit everywhere and examined the flora and the fauna and
all the natural phenomena in the woods. Jan Backmansson who
had known so much about this and that, for example, regarding
the hole in the bottom of the marsh that produced such strong
whirling currents that could in no time carry a grown person to
the brink and a certain death by drowning, which had happened
with the American girl, Jan Backmansson also had a scientific
explanation handy.

"For example. Let's say," said Jan Backmansson. For example.
That was how he always started: pour water in a coffee cup with
a hole in the bottom. What happens with the water? It runs out.
But put your finger in the cup while it's running. Do you feel
anything? Doesn't it pull? Doesn't it flow? The hole sucks the
water in.

"*The hole sucks you to it and you're helpless*. You can also say it
that way, but you don't because it isn't scientifically valid. But the
effect is the same. The water is sucked into the hole, there where
it's filled with nothing."

In some way Rita had liked hearing it. That is to say as an
explanation. It was so plausible. And so calming.

. . .

Jan Backmansson. She visited him yet again in his home in the
apartment in the city by the sea. Every time she was together
with Jan Backmansson in his beautiful home that was so large
and filled with rooms with roughly thirty-foot ceilings, it struck
her that there was no place else. There was no place else in the
world to be. It was another world.

Yet: she was there less and less frequently.

And something else had started to gnaw on her lately. That
also: how some parts of life were connected and how others
hung loosely and that all of it was really rather arbitrary. How
certain parts could be linked with each other at all.

More and more it had become so that on the one hand there
were the Backmanssons in the apartment in the city by the sea, her
with Jan Backmansson there. And there was also Susanna's room,
where Rita sometimes sat and read at the antique desk. A room
that was so high that from its windows you could see out over the
rooftops in the city by the sea, toward the city. *The wonderful room*,
that was what she called it, in secret. A secret for Jan Backmansson also.

On the other hand there was the District. The Rats and Solveig.
Solveig, Järpe, Torpe, and so on. There was Four Mops and a
Dustpan, and the latter, the dustpan, who was absent for the most
part. Bencku with his projects of which nothing ever came of any
of them. He just talked. He was going to become an architect; he
was going to become a cartographer, for real; he would also start a
world revolution, though there had been less talk about that lately.
He had also starting talking about "getting himself together," because there had been a lot of beer lately. And about "the women";
to Rita's and Solveig's surprise he did not have a lack of them. He
moved from woman to woman and played the lottery. Won unnecessary things. The latest: a water bed. It arrived at the cousin's
property on the bed of a truck and you thought it was some kind
of joke.

And the cousin's mama with the cousin's papa in his room, where he had been for almost all of Rita's conscious life, since childhood. *Something inside him has broken*, said the cousin's mama, and yes, for lack of other explanations, you had to make do with that. But on the other hand, "damn it," as you swore in the District. Damn it.

It was another world.

"You might have to decide WHO you're actually with," Solveig had said. "And not carry on with this double-dealing."

But Solveig did not understand.

Torpe in the District, Jan Backmansson in the city by the sea. It was not double-dealing. It was just two sides of life that had nothing to do with each other. At some point in time she had been able to talk to Solveig. Not anymore. Not now.

Sometimes it was also as if she was afraid of Solveig. She did not know why. There was something so uncontrollable about her. The same uncontrollability she had inside herself. But could nothing change? Must it be this way for all time and for all eternity?

Jan Backmansson. Again that was something she barely wanted to admit herself, that uncertainty.

"I knew it," she had said to Jan Backmansson quite a few times lately, in other words regarding the agreement made a long time ago, after the house on the First Cape had burned and the Backmanssons returned to their apartment in the city by the sea. That she would be allowed to move with them. "It's clear that you'll also be coming, Rita. It would be good for you to come out in the world a bit, and go to high school somewhere else." That is what Jan Backmansson's mother Tina Backmansson had said calmly and decidedly. They were just going to "take care of the practicalities" first, but later—there was no later.

"They hadn't even seriously thought about it," she had started saying to Jan Backmansson lately. "It was just an idea. One that you throw out when you want to have a good conscience."

The creepy thing was that Jan Backmansson had stopped asking her to be patient. He was also no longer talking about everything being arranged, that it would probably happen later. He had become angry and said, very irritated, "Oh. You're impossible. Talk to them yourself."

And Rita had been quiet. She quite simply did not dare say any more. It had also been very humiliating.

Now Rita walked up onto Lore Cliff. She stood there and looked down in the water, which inspired discomfort, like always. She did not see Doris Flinkenberg, but she knew she was there somewhere in the vicinity. In the silence. In the calm. No clouds; the sun that was shining from a clear blue sky. But it was still so dark, like always, around Bule Marsh.

Suddenly she had an impulse. Tit for tat.

"Come out now, Doris Flinkenberg," she said loud and clear.

And strangely, strangely: Doris came. Showed up, true to form, from just the direction you least expected, that is to say from a few bushes directly behind Rita. If Rita became a bit frightened by it she did her best not to show it.

Doris came up beside her, there, on Lore Cliff.

Doris, inside her old usual show with Rita, the one she had been busy with ever since the corpse of the American girl had been found. Not that it was noticeable of course, not to others, but when it was the two of them, alone. She always had to come to the part about Rita not having told the truth. That time a long time ago. That Rita had tricked her.

"And they were going to come and get her," Doris Flinkenberg mumbled slowly, in her evasive and soft way, true to habit. Threatening and mildly irritating and insinuating: and then she enjoyed the fact that Rita was at a loss for words. That she, Doris, as it were, had the upper hand.

It was like a game, that too.

But there was something else with Doris now. Something new—and not only that that way of being, threatening and silly, so poorly matched her new so elegant looks, the big faintly red shimmering blond hair that you could become so crazy about!

And so on, with Doris's looks.

Though it could not be heard in what she said. But there was something else now. A real anxiety, a real hesitation.

"But they didn't come," Doris Flinkenberg continued. "It doesn't look like they're going to come. And she's . . . alone."

"Who?" Rita interposed as calmly as possible even though she knew exactly whom and what it was that Doris was referring to.

"She got the boot," Doris continued. "Was forgotten. Poor Rita."

And suddenly, thought Rita, it is do or die. She could not go on anymore. Not one second.

"Oh! You mean the Backmanssons? And me? That they didn't end up keeping their promise? That I didn't get to go live with them, even though they promised. That it was shit for manners, so to speak. Well," Rita continued, more self-confident, also fired up in some way over finally getting to say everything, a clean slate, "it's true. Shit for manners. A damn shame. Are you satisfied now then? When you get to go around and remind me about it all the time?"

Doris did not answer. She stood and looked at Rita, with the same insidious facial expression that she had the whole time, but she did not say anything. And her face twitched a bit, it did.

"And what it is you want, anyway?" Rita asked. "Say it, then. Once and for all and then it's over."

And then the strange thing happened: Doris sort of collapsed. She did not start crying or anything, did not lose her head either so that it was obvious. You just saw the energy ebb out of her, that she sank together as it were, her face grew slack, there was nothing Doris-like about her at all in those seconds; and it was in some way nasty as well.

"I don't know," Doris said suddenly, completely perplexed, "when I don't know."

And it came out so desperately so to speak. And then in the middle of it all Rita saw all of the sadness in Doris, the great and terrible and bottomless sadness—and it was among other things that would lead Rita, one and a half weeks later when Doris shot herself, to immediately understand that Doris had shot herself. That damned pistol! She should have at least made sure she got it back!

"When I don't know!"

And Doris had sat down on the cliff and not said anything. And in that fraction of a second Rita thought about sitting down next to her, but nevertheless did not.

Doris just sat there and ached and Rita, slowly, groping, she started, it was do or die.

"Now Doris it's just as well you should know everything. The cousin's mama, she was the one who said you should be protected. You had been through so many terrible things. And we . . . I. It was such a hell then, Doris. You don't understand. We were so young.

"Solveig and I, we were completely shocked—a long time afterward.

"But Doris. I haven't forgotten. I'm not going to forget. The American girl, you don't know, that face—it's like it was in you. The cousin's mama, she—"

"Don't you understand I don't care about how it was!" Doris suddenly shouted.

"I don't care. I don't want to hear it! That doesn't mean anything!"

"I don't know anything about anything!"

And Doris stood up and rushed away through the woods—later, yes later. Rita had not seen her again. At all.

That was how it had been. She *should* have looked for Doris, she would think afterward. She *should*.

But she did not. One thing after another happened. Everything went on.

Shortly thereafter it became fall for real. You know how it is: someone suddenly just turns off the light regardless of whether or not the snow has come. Suddenly everything is just gray and hopeless. But weather here and weather there, actually you did not bother about any sort of weather, but now, just this fall, the days before Doris shot herself, everything harmonized in such a strange way.

Crapweather. Craprats. Crap. Crap. Crap. Crap.

Shortly thereafter, a few days before Doris's death, the Rats demolished the Glass House. Or, it was an exaggeration to say that. Demolished and demolished. There was actually only one spot where the Rats went crazy and that was the Winter Garden, the veranda extension where the baroness had once cultivated her fantastic flowers and been unreachable. Now there were only a bunch of half-dead potted plants because Kenny, who was actually the one who had been living in the house most, had not had the same thoughts and ideas as the baroness, you could see that. Behind her flower cultivations. *My lovely, lovely garden . . .*

On the other hand she had tried. And later maybe given up or not followed through either or new things had come along to interest her or the summer had been over and it was time to pack things up, yourself and the sea urchins, and go away, away, to the city by the sea and there, another life. Another life there.

You saw that: the attempt in other words.

So Rita went after all of it, she was drunk of course. And she was surprised with what energy she had; she broke quite a few windowpanes before anyone was able to stop her. And she was rather pissed off, rather ill-tempered as well.

Solveig really had to do her best to calm Rita down.

And—here, another thing. Which was also false information. It was not the Rats who did all of that. It was Rita, and a bit Solveig, and Järpe and Torpe were present, but they were mostly watching. With surprise. Understanding nothing.

No, it was not the Rats, it was not that kind of game (it was not a game, that was probably in some way the worst part). It was just Rita, Solveig and Rita, but mainly Rita. Because she, for a moment, could not stand it any longer. Any of it.

And it was actually, and it was not constructed in hindsight because she had already thought that before Doris's death, when everything happened, something with Doris and all of this too. Somewhere in the back of her mind the image of Doris desperate at the marsh, also somewhere in the back of her head the pounding knowledge that you really should go looking for her and once and for all explain everything, and the frustration over not having done so. And it was in earnest. You had, in some way, understood that Doris was desperate, that she could have done anything.

But such a strange thought that you had not dared think it through to the end.

But what Rita had seen when it went amiss for her in the Glass House on the glass veranda that at one point in time was Miss Andrews's beautiful Winter Garden, was an image in her mind. An image of a rat running in a wheel, around around around around, and it was her. And an image of another rat, in another wheel, which was also turning. And it was little Doris Flinkenberg. And why why must it be this way? There was no opportunity in that moment.

That is how it tends to be in certain situations when you are drunk.

Of course Rita became normal later, and calmed herself down before she had time to demolish everything.

And of course, ha-ha, besides, they were the ones who

cleaned up afterward. Four Mops and a Dustpan. "On behalf of my work."

Though of course no one knew it was Rita—and Solveig, a little—who had gone crazy in the Glass House like that. Run amok.

A few days later Doris Flinkenberg shot herself at Bule Marsh. When Rita heard the shot she knew immediately what had happened.

That is how it was, in light of all this. In light of all this is how it was.

Four Mops and a Dustpan. And a few days after Doris's death Solveig came home after a day working in the city by the sea, among other things in the baroness's bright apartment (where Rita never set foot).

"She's dead now," Solveig said calmly. "She died. I'm afraid it wasn't very peaceful. But"—and Solveig had shrugged her shoulders—"you can't always choose how you're going to die."

It was the baroness she was speaking about. Who had given up the ghost after being sick so many, many years.

Doris's death

I walked out one evening, out into a grove so green
There I met a girl, so fair and so beautiful
There I met a girl, so fair and so beautiful beautiful beautiful
There I met a girl, so fair and so beautiful

"It's over now," the cousin's mama said to Doris Flinkenberg on her return home after fourteen days in the house in the darker part. "Now you're home again. None of that has happened. Sleep now."

Or maybe she did not say it in those words exactly, but that was the essence.

Everything was over, forgiven. Doris had come home again, now everything would go on.

None of what happened in the house in the darker part was a subject of discussion.

And you could SEE it on her.

"We have to clean there," Doris Flinkenberg said to the cousin's mama. "Sandra . . . she's going to Åland. Or what do I know about where she's going, maybe New York. And change windows . . . anybody can get in . . ."

"Later," said the cousin's mama calmly. "Later. Go up to your room now and sleep. I'll come up with the pills."

But Doris did not want to have the bottle with pills. She could not sleep. She did not want to sleep. And Doris red in the face like a summer crayfish.

"My goodness, child, it looks like a third-degree burn."

The cousin's mama gave her a cream to smear on the red places. Doris smeared.

. . .

Ritsch she pulled up the blackout curtain that the cousin's mama had pulled down when she left.

Movement in the yard. She looked out and discovered the boys with bags of beer in the barn. She changed and went out to the barn and there she met Micke Friberg. The guys' guy, or whatever it is called.

"Where have you been all of my life?" Micke Friberg whispered in her ear just a few hours later.

"What do you mean?" Doris had whispered back, tenderly and devoutly.

And that was of course the story that was now starting, which should have been the main one. *The summer I met Micke.* And she had enough time. It was actually still summer. A few days still until school started.

And still she had already experienced everything.

And she was an older Doris now, another Doris, but most of all, sadder. A Doris who was alone and afraid, for real. Scared of life, scared of death. Could you see it?

KNOTS in her stomach.

"Come on, let's get out of here," Micke had whispered, and they had left the barn. They walked over the Second Cape to the boathouse and sat on the veranda in front of the open summer sea that was suddenly so calm.

Earlier in the day . . . was it really the same day?

Liz Maalamaa and the presidents.

Sandra the-dead-American-girl Wärn.

Someone has destroyed my song, Mom.

Had it actually been the same day? When the world could be so beautiful also, so calm, like now. So right, Doris had thought, on the veranda of the boathouse, with Micke.

"I think I'm also a bit in love with you too," she then whispered to Micke.

He laughed and they had kissed again. Or what was it that it was called again: making out?

You became happy with him, thought Doris. And it was true. Micke Friberg made you happy.

And in the eyes of others. Micke Friberg. Who would not want to be together with someone who could play Dazed and Confused back and forth and backward if you pestered him enough?

In other words, what had happened in the house in the darker part of the woods during the summer was confirmed when the fall term started. The ugly duckling became a swan, marsh kid marsh queen. The baby fat was gone. She was not skinny, but she was luxuriant, had so to speak become *proportioned* and her blond, shoulder-length hair shimmered a light red.

An apple that had fallen from the tree. Not a sea apple tree exactly.

A woman. Fully mature.

Sometimes when she saw herself in the mirror she burst out laughing.

Was that her?

> *She promised me her heart, she promised me her hand.*
> *She promised me her heart, she promised me her hand.*

The first time with Sandra in the schoolyard after the summer vacation.

"Look who wants something," Sandra said apathetically. They were standing and hanging around the exit. "The idiot." For this name, *the idiot*, had been what they called Micke Friberg in private, just the two them, the previous semester, before the summer.

It was Sandra who had come to Doris where she was waiting for Micke Friberg outside the school building at the end of the school day. It was in other words Micke Friberg she had agreed to meet, not Sandra, but Sandra had been gone—on Åland or whatever it was, New York?—so as usual she did not know what had happened.

Doris had just opened her mouth to say something in response but she did not get any farther before Micke Friberg quickly skidded up to her and covered her half-open mouth with his own mouth and absorbed Doris Flinkenberg in a hug that left no room for doubt for any outsider as to what it was all about.

"This is Sandra," Doris said to Micke Friberg. And to Sandra, "This is Micke Friberg. We're together now."

"Nice," Micke Friberg said, uninterested. "Doris has told me so much about you. I'm really looking forward to getting to know you. But so long for now. We're going to go and sing and play a bit."

Sing and play a bit? That was news for sure, you could see it in Sandra's expression.

"Doris has a good singing voice," Micke Friberg advertised. "I have a band she sings in. It's called Micke's Folk Band."

And somewhat later, during morning assembly.

"Hi. I'm Doris and this is Micke and we have a band together, Micke's Folk Band. And now we're going to sing some old well-known folk songs in new arrangements, they're our own arrangements, they're Micke's arrangements. So, first *I walked out one evening, out into a grove so green.*"

And Doris Flinkenberg started singing.

But sometimes, when Doris was singing, she still thought about everything, about Sandra, everything with Sandra, everything, and the tears started streaming down her cheeks. But it happened less and less now. And sometimes, rather often, though it was so, her tears could not be seen. She "cried inside" as it was called in one of the stupid pop songs that had once played on her radio cassette player but that she no longer listened to so much anymore because if there was something Doris Flinkenberg had to herself in the whole world, it was her intolerable taste in music, *Lasting Love Songs for Moonstruck Lovers*, "Our Love Is a Continental Affair," Lill Lindfors, and all of that.

Not even Micke Friberg could put up with it.

As said, Doris's tears ran "inside." Also while she was singing. But it was, as said, increasingly seldom now.

Micke's Folk Band. It was the music. But there were also many other sides to Micke Friberg. For example, what is called "the world of literature." In other words Micke Friberg read books. Real novels. By Fyodor Dostoyevsky and the like. He had plowed through *Crime and Punishment* over the summer.

"You can divide your life between before and after Dostoyevsky," Micke Friberg said to Doris Flinkenberg. "You have to read *Crime and Punishment*. I want to share it with you."

"What's it about, then?" Doris Flinkenberg asked.

"It's about guilt and reconciliation. About the possibility of reconciliation. There is always a path and a possibility to reconciliation. That is what Dostoyevsky wants to tell us. It's just a matter of the human being choosing it."

"What?" Doris Flinkenberg said and for a moment she looked like one Doris question mark.

"I mean," said Micke Friberg searching for words. "Suppose I killed someone, then you would get to be a Sonya who would save me and at the same time the whole world . . . You would be a good Sonya, Doris."

"Who's Sonya?" Doris asked. "Sonya who?" and Micke started explaining to Doris Flinkenberg that Sonya in Dostoyevsky's novel was an erhm, working girl, or prostitute, "or quite simply a whore," a woman "from the street," Micke Friberg continued to add, "who was the only one who believed there was light in Raskolnikov's dark soul, and it was Sonya's belief, this Sonya's love that was a love of action, not words, that saved Raskolnikov . . ."

And then Doris started laughing. Laughing and laughing so that tears sprayed from her eyes.

Ahem . . .

Laughed also because everything fit and at the same time nothing did.

"Hey, now I don't recognize you," Micke Friberg whispered nervously. And he put his arms around her and so Doris Flinkenberg and Micke Friberg hugged and kissed some more.

"No one can love like us," Micke Friberg had whispered reassuringly to Doris Flinkenberg after her crying spell.

And. Oh no. Micke, he was not stupid. He was so sympathetic and kind. Stupid. It would have been so much easier if he had been.

He made you happy. It really was so.

"GIVE ME THAT BOOK, THEN," Doris Flinkenberg said in the middle of the embrace.

And they started reading Dostoyevsky together.

The idiot Micke Friberg started with *The Idiot*.

"It's about goodness," said Micke Friberg. "That there is a possibility of being good."

"Doris," said Micke Friberg, "you are so . . . good."

But what was happening?

The bonds we tied, no one can undo.

"Hi. I'm Doris, this is Micke, we have a band, it's Micke's Folk Band. And now we're going to sing some old folk songs in our own arrangements, Micke's arrangements."

Micke Friberg, the first time, after talk.

Doris said to Micke, suddenly, afterward, "There are a lot of ideas in my head, from here and from there."

"What kind?"

"Bits. From songs, magazines, what people have said. This and that. Can't get hold of it. Like a melody. It falls short all the time. A song that someone wants to sabotage."

And she had ALMOST started humming the Eddie-song, the American girl's song. She almost thought about telling—everything. It was the first and only time she had thought about it and been close to doing it with Micke Friberg. If only she had done so!

"You with your sabotages," Micke said lovingly and enveloped Doris in his arms. They had in other words been lying in his parents' bed in his parents' bedroom after the first time—it was the weekend and Micke's parents were at the summer cottage. *The first time.*

"I can't explain it any better," Doris Flinkenberg mumbled.

"You don't need to," Micke whispered. "I like you the way you are. Idiot. You don't seem to understand what a fantastic and sweet and sexy young woman you are. Though that's part of your charm. Your unawareness. Child of nature." And then he whispered, "My woman." And, "I'm so happy that I was the one who discovered you first."

"Woman." Doris Flinkenberg, christened child of nature, tasted the word in Micke's parents' bedroom.

"And this," she explained loudly, as if it was news, which it was not, they had planned ahead of time, she and Micke, to be sure the first time would be unforgettable, "was the first time."

And continued:

"Now I'm not a VIRGIN anymore."

"Was it good?"

"Yes." Doris answered that question yet again, though maybe a bit too impatiently already then. "Yes. Yes. Yes." Micke Friberg was so eager about being a good lover with a woman whom he loved and who loved him. And it was fun but could they for goodness' sake talk about something e-l-s-e now?

"Do you want to hear something funny?" Doris whispered to Micke. "One time Bencku was going to order books from a mail-order firm that sold the kind of weird books he's interested in. He found a book he really wanted to have. It was called *Architecture and Crime*. He was terribly disappointed though he tried not to show it when he got the book because it wasn't crime like in criminal cases but crime as in spaces. Spaces between the ornaments. Do you get it?"

"No." Micke Friberg shook his head in the dark and impatiently fingered the coral necklace he had gotten from Doris a few days ago when they had celebrated their being together for a month and a half.

"Bencku, he sure is crazy . . ."

But Doris had not gotten any farther before her open mouth was covered by Micke's mouth, Micke's teeth, Micke's tongue . . . and one thing led to another, whereupon—lightning and thunder—they did *it* for the second time.

It was later, at home in her own bed, that Doris Flinkenberg had the chance to think clearly again.

What was happening? Was she starting to go crazy?

"You're filled with surprises," Micke Friberg had said. "With you it's never boring."

Micke. Micke's voice. Just thinking about it helped. Imagining Micke and nothing else. Making him so big in her head in her heart in her body that everything else drifted into the background.

"Can we agree on something?" Micke had asked. "That we keep Bencku and Sandra et cetera outside of this? Our relationship is something separate."

"You're jealous," Doris had clucked.

"Of course," Micke had replied. "Is that strange? I want to have all of you. I love you! Do you love me?"

"Yes," Doris had replied frankly. A large calm had welled up inside her. They embraced each other again and in that embrace

Doris had been one hundred percent present. That was how she explained it to herself afterward. But I did like it. I was "one hundred percent" present.

So what, may you ask, was happening then?

"What do you see in him?" Sandra asked jealously on the school-yard one of the few times they spoke to each other during that time.

Stupid question, they both knew. Anyone would be overjoyed to be together with Micke Friberg. Half of the school's girls thought so anyway.

Still Doris Flinkenberg stood there in the schoolyard and hawked in the presence of Sandra Wärn and did not know what to say.

"You sing so beautifully," Sandra had said with something in her voice that got Doris Flinkenberg to just leave, leave the schoolyard and run away.

Sometimes Doris Flinkenberg went out in the woods on her own.

Also before things ended with Micke Friberg.

Must be alone. But a lot of songs and words and rhymes and everything from here and there starting popping up now and multiplying in her head.

> *The bonds that we tied, no one can undo*
> *The bonds that we tied, no one can undo*
> *Only death, only death can loosen these bonds bonds bonds*
> *Only death, only death, can loosen these bonds.*

Doris, during the morning assembly.

"Hi. I'm Micke, this is Doris, we have a band, Micke's Folk Band. We sing old folk songs . . . Oh!" Doris stopped abruptly, everyone laughed, she started again. "Hi. I'm Doris, this is Micke, we have a band . . . oh God, now we're going to sing, it's an old folk song and it goes like this."

Toward the middle of the month of October, around the time when Doris Flinkenberg started understanding for the first time in earnest the impossibility of everything about her relationship with Micke Friberg, she and Micke Friberg were reading Dostoyevsky together. She was reading *Crime and Punishment*, he was reading *The Idiot*.

"I should kill someone so that you could be Sonya. You would be a good Sonya. One who saves the world with her goodness. You are so good."

He could not get away from it, Micke. He just could not leave it. And suddenly it was not funny at all.

Doris felt ill. Doris became seasick. Doris had to vomit.

She ran to the toilet, and vomited, vomited.

"It's that boating accident—it's just terrible."

"*No one can love like us*," said Micke Friberg, but suddenly he did not sound very convinced anymore either.

"I think that you make everything difficult," Micke Friberg philosophized when Doris Flinkenberg was feeling better. "It's a sign that you aren't like other people. You are unique and strange.

"And I," Micke continued, "love you. Just because you're you and no one else."

"Oh shut up now." Doris realized that she had been lying and thinking. Why does he have to carry on like that. And disturb? Does he have to carry on gluing the word "love" on everything before he has properly checked what it is he has in front of him?

And what was it he had in front of him, then, Doris?

That was the question.

Only death, only death can loosen these bonds bonds bonds.
But in other words, what was it that really happened?

. . .

"Should we keep reading?" Doris said to Micke instead. "I'm already on page 234. And I have to say that it's really starting to get interesting."

Micke laughed, his well-read laugh that belonged to someone who had a certain lead and knew how to carry a conversation about a major novel and a major writer, a real classic.

"You're certainly special, aren't you?" he said again. "That's why I lo—"

"Be quiet now," Doris Flinkenberg whispered devoutly. "Let's read now."

Micke and Doris. On Lore Cliff, she and Micke stood there and felt cold above Bule Marsh, Doris shivered and said, "She's standing there spying on us. In the bushes. Sister Night. Can't let go."

Micke let go of Doris and looked around.

"What, who?"

"Oh," said Doris. "I was just kidding. It was a joke."

What was happening? What was she talking about? Why was she carrying on saying those things when she should have said, "Sometimes it goes around in my head. Sometimes I'm frightened. Maybe the cousin's mama was right. You shouldn't root around in old things."

Don't play with fire, Doris Flinkenberg, the cousin's mama had said once a long time ago when she understood what Doris and Sandra were doing, the Mystery with the American Girl, all of that.

"There aren't many who have the ability to crush my heart," the cousin's mama had also said, "but you, Doris, are one . . ."

And it was then, exactly right there at the marsh, that Doris Flinkenberg finally understood what she had been suspecting for a long time. And she finally got it out of her as well: "I shouldn't . . . But it's like this. I can't love you. There is something wrong between my ears."

"It's damned helpless," she said while Micke Friberg just stood there next to her struck dumb. "I won't become happier because of it. Namely."

Because of the shock Micke Friberg had not been listening so carefully, but he certainly caught the important bits in any case.

"Is it over?" Micke Friberg said loudly and clearly, in an utmost sober tone of voice.

Sister Night. And she was standing there. Sure enough. In the bushes, spying.

Or, was she?

"You mean it's over?" Micke Friberg repeated when Doris did not answer.

Doris nodded and whined, "Yes."

Then Micke understood everything. He left Doris Flinkenberg on Lore Cliff and went on his way.

"Sandra!" Doris yelled, weakly. But she was not there. Just silence. Nothing.

Doris searched for Sandra in the woods. She made her way to different places where Sandra might be. Sandra was nowhere. But she did not go to the house in the darker part of the woods. She did not want to set foot there anymore for alleged reasons. But she came pretty close.

And it did not really surprise her when from where she was standing in the reeds by the marsh she could see into the basement through the panorama window and saw that the pool was filled with water now, a completely ordinary swimming pool. And for a moment it rushed through her that it had always been like this, nothing terrible, nothing had ever happened.

But it was just a flash through her head as said.

Back to reality. Otherwise it was empty and dark in the basement. Only a few lamps shining in the water, cold and blue.

And the next time she saw Sandra it was in the schoolyard. Sandra came out during the break in one of those girl gangs that consisted of Birgitta Blumenthal and other silly and rather meaningless girls—this in other words according to Sandra's AND Doris's highly subjective opinion, during the time they were still together, Sister Night and Sister Day.

Doris was off to the side now, alone in the schoolyard. Micke Friberg, with his broken heart, was allowed to stay inside during the breaks and play guitar in the music room. He had an exemption and avoided being forced outside because he was seen as being so musically talented—and musically talented he was of course. Micke's Folk Band was disbanded for the time being. It was taking a break because of current circumstances. Micke Friberg made no secret of the fact that Doris had hurt him deeply, crushed his heart. He wanted to be left alone now. But he was also careful about pointing out that they had separated as very good friends, in any case.

That Micke made no secret of the fact that it was Doris who had left him and not the other way around made Doris more exciting in everyone's eyes of course. But she shook off everyone who came near her.

Doris off to the side, the girls with Sandra Wärn, Sandra Wärn as a girl among others, and all of them glanced furtively and rather interested in Doris's direction. Sandra did not stand out in that group in any way, she was just there.

But so, it happened once that Sandra broke away from the group and came up to Doris Flinkenberg. They talked to each other for a while, a rather short moment because then it was time to separate, they were going to different classes, but also for other reasons.

And very concrete ones. Sandra was going away, she said, to Åland again, to visit her relatives again.

Doris did not say anything. Now she had a hard time carrying on. No one but she knew how hard. On the one hand she understood, as soon as she started talking with Sandra whom she had not properly spoken to since . . . the summer (and she was the one who had gone on her way, "home," to Micke Friberg, all of that), that she would not be able to continue . . . with anything . . . before everything would be finished. Before all of the questions inside her got answers. And it was a pop song that for once was so true it did not tug at the corners of your mouth, whether you liked that kind of music or not.

And that she, if Sandra did not take the initiative, needed to start asking these questions. Herself. And how would that go?

Because it was obvious Sandra would not be taking any initiative.

On the other hand she understood, and it chilled her inside when she realized it, just like it did on that day in the schoolyard when she and Sandra carried out their last conversation with each other while Doris Flinkenberg was still alive, that it was impossible quite simply impossible not to continue with Sandra.

SandraPandraHarelipSisterNight&Day and all of it, highly beloved.

Such terrible things. Such an insight. What was happening? Whom do you ask? Whom should you turn to?

The boat. The same fall Doris died, a boat with five youths on board sank sixty miles to the west, in the middle of the sea. All on board drowned. The accident and the circumstances surrounding it bewitched Doris Flinkenberg the last weeks she was alive.

The accident happened on a Saturday night at the beginning of October. The youths had the intention of celebrating the weekend on board a rather large motor boat, a Nauticat.

Witnesses who saw the boat at a gas station in a sound in the inner archipelago would later explain that the mood on board had been merry but in no way exaggerated.

The wind had already been hard during the day. Toward evening it reached storm force. The boat went aground at eleven o'clock and started taking in water. At two thirty, almost four hours later, it went to the bottom.

It had in other words been a rather slow course of events. The youths had plenty of time to fire off flares, all that were on board. When no help came and the boat slowly, slowly started filling with the water, they moved on deck and lit a fire.

When the fire had been put out by the water that started washing over the deck they understood that all hope was gone.

Why did no one come? Where was the coast guard?

The boat sank, and the youths died, one after the other. All of the people on board drowned or froze to death in the ice-cold water.

When all was said and done it was this event that Doris Flinkenberg had spoken to Sandra Wärn about in the schoolyard, that last time—which neither of them knew—they were in conversation with each other.

"I'm always going to remember what I was doing in that moment," Doris said to Sandra there in the schoolyard, for some reason one of the first things they had spoken about, properly, in a long time.

"I slept with Micke it was the first time it's over."

She glanced at Sandra quickly and in secret, who registered and registered, but still, it was not as though she was really listening.

And yet she was.

"I was at Blumenthal's," Sandra said dully. "A pajama party. Me and all the girls."

And then Sandra started talking in detail about the party and what had happened. There had been a party at Birgitta

Blumenthal's. Just for the girls. A pajama party, an idea someone had gotten from a foreign magazine, the kind of thing you
did in other places, for example in America. But what you were
supposed to do, actually, at a party like that was more unclear.
So they put on their pajamas and "romped" in pajamas in different ways, among other things EVERYONE nipped at the
bottles in the Blumenthals' well-filled bar—the parents were
teetotalers but they needed all of this liquor for appearances,
Sandra explained as if she were reading from an instruction
manual for the normal life for her friend—a sip or two.

And they voted Birgitta Blumenthal the most beautiful
woman in the universe in a game that Birgitta Blumenthal herself had initiated, a beauty contest where the result was known
ahead of time, "like it happens in reality too of course, you
agree ahead of time who is going to win." Birgitta Blumenthal
had shed tears of joy where she was sitting on the edge of the
bed with a red towel over her and a paper tiara, and then they
danced in the dark, all of them, and told each other secrets.

"You know what their secrets are like," Sandra stated, dully.
"Tobias Forsström pinched my butt, but I didn't tell anyone.
That kind of stuff."

Sandra laughed and Doris laughed and Doris thought again
about how much she appreciated Sandra's stories, not what she
was telling, but her manner.

And then they had played Truth or Dare. Sandra was dared to
French-kiss Birgitta Blumenthal. A lasting memory: how it felt to
have Birgitta Blumenthal the bookworm's learned tongue in your
mouth.

"Damn," Sandra said in the schoolyard, and she was angry.
"Damn. Like some freakin' dyke."

And Doris got a chill inside because—did Sandra mean her?

And then they had, Sandra said just as dully and lightheartedly, played cops and robbers.

And Doris got a chill inside, again.

And the school bell rang.

"I have to . . ." Doris had immediately started moving toward the entrance, almost half running.

"Hey, Doris! What happened?" Sandra squeezed out, calling after Doris. Doris turned around quickly, or was it her imagination, in Sandra's eyes there was suddenly all pain, like an injured animal.

Dearest, dearest. Everything is coming to nothing. We were going to be together. What's happening, now?

She should have asked a lot of questions, then, in the schoolyard. She did not. Sandra went to Åland. Doris was left with everything she now had to find out for herself. And she would. She did.

At the end of the same month, October, the Rats vandalized the Glass House.

A few weeks later the baroness died. But then Doris was already dead.

And the second Saturday in November Doris took the pistol that she had never returned to Rita and Solveig's cottage after the summer and went up to Lore Cliff at Bule Marsh and shot herself there.

Things were happening pell-mell in Doris that last period.

It was these questions which should be answered and that she, lacking anyone to ask, tried to find the answers to herself.

Why was there no water in the pool?

All normal people have water in their pools, right?

You could start like that. And so, further. Like the twin detective you had also once been:

"Sandra, that telephone number to Heintz-Gurt in Austria, it doesn't go anywhere.

"I mean. It doesn't exist. I know because I've tried."

Then the one question, the one about the pool, automatically leads over to the other questions:

"Lorelei Lindberg. Where is she really?"

"That story about the helicopter, what was it actually? Was it true?"

And then you came to think about certain other stories that had actually been told. The one about the ring with the table-spoon-sized ruby that fell down into the pool and that Lorelei Lindberg called to Sandra to look for.

But she did not.

So Lorelei Lindberg went down into the pool herself. And where was the Islander then, who was so angry at Lorelei Lindberg? The Islander with his rifle?

But: there was Bencku's map. Doris Flinkenberg started suspecting something about the map on the whole. That it was not as innocent as it looked. That it hung there in Bencku's barn like a shield: "I know this," like a message.

Not images of how it actually was, as Inget Herrman had characterized Bencku's maps. "But images as expression of." That meant what was on the maps was not necessarily true, had not necessarily happened.

Well. Now Doris Flinkenberg had reason to doubt it worked that way. After the American girl's death . . . there had not been any image. She had been there, on the bottom. Doris had found her.

Not to mention wearing the plastic coat. That terrible coat.

And now there was something else on Bencku's map. Doris was there and checked it just before she shot herself. A woman in the pool. And she was dead. So dead.

Was it Lorelei Lindberg?

Where was she?

And then there was all of that which would later be in the farewell letter.

". . . it was the game with Heintz-Gurt. What a name. The happy pilot. I found that too. In one of her scrapbooks. Almost word for word. I found, when I started reading other stories properly too. There is one, I have it in front of me now. *Father and daughter hid the mother in a brick wall. This macabre crime united them for many years.*

"I don't know what's happening. I can't live with it anymore. And then there's so much else. The red raincoat the American girl was found in. It's in a photograph in the Islander's bedside table. Of the girl and her mother. And she, the mother, has the coat on."

And Doris wrote so much more in her last letter. But it was not a letter to Sandra.

She did not write a letter to Sandra.

But she went to the house in the darker part one last time.

It was empty, it looked like. She got in using the spare key as she had always done, already the first time, a long time ago when she came to the house in the darker part of the woods. It was only a matter of knowing where it was. And Doris knew. It was just that simple.

She had gone to the house in the darker part of the woods. She had gotten in there, in secret. She had her boots with her, she was going to leave them by the edge of the pool.

And suddenly a voice could be heard behind her:

"It's always like there's a stranger in this house."

And she walked with Inget Herrman over the cliffs on the Second Cape, one last time.

"What do you do if you're carrying a terrible secret?" she asked Inget Herrman. They stood by the sea, on the veranda of the boathouse, laughing.

"Throw yourself in the sea with it. Then you sink. A terrible secret tends to be heavy to carry."

"Seriously," Doris said impatiently.

"Sorry," said Inget Herrman, suddenly serious because she also saw Doris's need. "But I can't give any abstract advice. I need to know more essentially. Otherwise I'll just say like somebody said: *Poor people who must suffer so terribly*."

Feel akin to Inget Herrman. But they had walked out on one of the longest jetties on the Second Cape, in the wild wind of fall.

"Here everyone thinks that it's just sea and horizon," Inget Herrman said. "That there isn't any land on the other side. That nothing happens on the other side. But there are: places, locations, other countries. And when the weather is clear then you can almost see it from here."

"Walk on the water, then," Doris said abrasively.

"Now the young lady was clever clever." Inget Herrman laughed.

But Doris had not laughed.

She turned around and started walking back.

"Oh! I'm sorry, Doris," Inget Herrman said. "Sometimes— well, it's so hopeless." And her thoughts had gotten stuck on the Islander who left the house in the darker part of the woods in anger during a fight they had a few hours earlier. "I'm going to tell you, Doris Flinkenberg, never grow up. Be as you are NOW, and always. When you grow up . . . then you have to have relationships and *scenes from a marriage* and things like that."

"Hmm," said Doris Flinkenberg. She melted because of those words, she liked Inget Herrman so much, of course, also when Inget Herrman talked like that. Inget Herrman who said the kinds of things no other grown-up said.

And of course all of it was not Inget Herrman's fault. And she had thought that maybe, maybe she would be able to tell Inget Herrman now, how it was, ask her if she knew.

But she did not. And they went their separate ways. Everything was strange. She decided then already.

Never be a grown-up, Doris Flinkenberg.

. . .

Dearest dearest, what is happening? We were supposed to be together!

"Where are you going, Doris Flinkenberg?"
  "Out," Doris Flinkenberg replied. "I'm going out."

And the fall had advanced to the month of November when Doris Flinkenberg took Rita's pistol and set out in the darkness on an early Saturday evening. Went to Bule Marsh and shot herself there.

"The devil take you Sandra Wärn," Doris Flinkenberg stood and screamed in the pool without water, when Sandra had pulled up the ladder once so that Doris could not get out. That had been during the summer, during a game.
  And when she came back she had the pistol with her.

Sandra, in the middle of the summer, stood and pointed at her with the pistol.
  "Are you scared?"
  "Of course not."

Going away

SOMEONE ELSE WHO LEFT EVERYTHING AND THE ENTIRE DIS-
trict was Rita. The evening after Doris's funeral Rita left under
sensational circumstances—even if the attention itself came later.
First Rita crashed Solveig's car, the red Mini Cooper that Järpe
had fixed up. She rammed it against a tree in Bäckström's field
north of the town center. Possibly on purpose. Highly likely, but
there would be no opportunity to talk about these possible opinions, not for Solveig's part anyway, not for a long time. Thereafter Rita had, muddy and furious, wandered up to the main
country road where she positioned herself to catch a lift in the
direction of the city by the sea. Anders Bäckström and Sabrita-
Lill Lindholm from the neighboring county (Sabrita-Lill, that is,
Anders was the son in the house on Bäckström's farm, the soon
to be only farmers who farmed the earth in the District out of
tradition and custom) who happened to come driving in Anders
Bäckström's father's rather new BMW had stopped and driven
Rita into the city by the sea. It was their statements you had to
turn to if you were Solveig and you wanted to know where your
sister had gone. And at that point, just after Doris's death, there
was chaos in the cousin's house, the cousin's mama was out of
her mind with grief and powerlessness, there was no one other
than Solveig who even had the energy to worry about where
Rita had gone. "Don't you care about any of this?" Solveig asked
Torpe Torpeson, her own boyfriend Järpe's brother, whom Rita
had been together with, but Torpe had truly shaken his head and
shrugged his shoulders; he was mostly relieved after everything.
Rita had a screw loose and it was best when Rita was so far away
that farther away did not exist.

"Oh hell," Torpe swore in the District language, "she's not really really right in the head," and had in other words spoken about Rita but shrewdly smiled at her sister Solveig who looked pretty much the same of course, was just a little plumper, a bit softer in the face, which was actually also an advantage, and little by little nature would take its course and it would "become" Torpe and Solveig, and Järpe would have to look around for a new "chick" and he would find one of those and many more. But that Mini Cooper, Järpe would grieve it deeply. He would be furious for a while, kick rocks in every direction so that they scattered in every direction at just the thought.

What a pity it would also be for Solveig. So much life to maintain, all on her own. Everything that fell to bits. The cousin's mama who after she was released from the mental hospital in any case would never return to the cousin's house.

Solveig who would try and take care of all of that. But she had a child in her stomach. For a long time it was her own knowledge. A secret. And her only hope.

But the evening when Rita left. She had been drunk but not at all impaired when she got into Anders's father's car, Sabrita-Lill in other words explained to Solveig on the telephone. Dirty, as if she had waded through a few hundred feet of swamp at least, in other words no on-the-side-of-the-road spray on her clothes. You could certainly see something had happened in the fields there. You had not been able to ask about it then because she had not exactly been in the mood to answer any questions. This, in other words, according to Sabrita-Lill Lindholm on the telephone. And she had been absolutely determined. She was going to go to the city by the sea. And there had not, for either Sabrita-Lill or Anders Bäckström, been any reason to doubt the seriousness of it.

They had not seen any other option than to do as she wanted and drive her all the way. That is to say they could not just leave

her like that, to fend for herself. Certainly not in the shape she
was in, not very drunk, in other words, but certainly out of it.
And both Anders and Sabrita-Lill were known as youths with a
sense of responsibility, no hooligans like Rita and the Rats and
those, a little bit better than the marsh pack at some point in
time, but not in any considerable way—

You could trust them, in other words. They drove Rita into
the city by the sea where they left her on the street by the beach
in the exclusive part of the city where the Backmansson family's
residence was. The houses on that stretch of beach were beautiful and calmly inspired respect, substantial stone houses that
radiated constancy and an obvious peace that can be purchased
only with money. That kind of self-evident money, quiet money.
So self-evident it was not something you spread the word about.
You lived at the sea in other words because you "couldn't" live
anywhere else; you had high ceilings in your apartments because
you got headaches in other ones. You were now once and for all
normal in that way.

It had been around two–three o'clock in the morning and
otherwise quiet in that part of the city. But people were standing
on a balcony farther down the street and it looked like there was
a party going on in that apartment. Not a youth party, but a more
dignified and adult—though certainly merry—gathering: The
balcony doors were thrown open in the dark night and the clear
sky twinkled with stars the whole fantastic fall night; those were
the very last days before winter would start.

And that was where Rita was headed. Toward just that balcony, that party. Toward just that bright light, whether she was
invited or not. She had gotten out of the car without so much
as a thank-you to the remaining occupants, in muddy clothes, in
an easing intoxication, with only a red-and-blue plastic bag in
her hand.

That was how Rita Rat finally arrived at the Backmansson family
in the city by the sea.

"Get out of here!" she yelled to Anders Bäckström and Sabrita-Lill Lindholm in the BMW so they would drive off immediately after she got out. They had not been thinking about staying to spy on her either, Sabrita-Lill Lindholm explained to Solveig. They were just thinking about waiting to see how everything turned out: maybe Rita would not be let in, maybe she would stand there all alone afterward and need help. And when it looked like her command would not work, Rita finally kicked the side of the car rather hard.

That was the last straw for the couple in the car. Then they left Rita to her fate and drove off. You do not kick someone else's BMW.

Solveig, who was listening to Sabrita-Lill Lindholm, had not had a hard time imagining Rita at all, her anger, her mood, the drunkenness, the dirty clothes, all of it, the muddiness. And it had affected her badly, of course, like a spot on a terribly visible place, a *stain* as it were, or something. But polite as she was she ended the conversation with Sabrita-Lill Lindholm by offering to clean the interior of the BMW at the cost of the company.

But as soon as she had said it out loud, she had heard herself, how stupid it sounded, how silly.

But at the same time, something in her had not been able to hold back a cold, quiet, and tired smile: Rita. Rat. Her sister. You always had to pick up after her, Rita. You always had to clean up and sweep up the tracks after her. That is how she, Solveig, had been thinking then, but that was before she realized Rita had actually left now. And she would not be coming back either.

(. . . *but from the werewolf, one last greeting*). Brushed dark red nail polish on her nails. Saw herself in the mirror, a bathroom mirror without a frame, which she had placed on the long table in the room, leaned against the cottage window because that was the cottage's only mirror. Saw herself in the mirror, the book *Were-wolf*, thumb marks on the surface of the mirror, they were sharp and clearly visible, greasy and revealing in the sharp light from the desk lamp that she had aimed toward the table.

"Take that picture now."

"Monkey business," said Solveig who took the picture because Rita wanted—it was the last night in the cottage together, but Solveig did not know that yet. Solveig took the picture because she was a nice person even if she otherwise thought you should photograph real things, things like nature in its "splendid display of colors" and different kinds of lighting depending on the seasons, like a postcard; or a birthday party, a name day's party and Christmas party, Ärpe Torpeson as Santa Claus for the unplanned child Allison Torpeson, who believed in Santa Claus even though she had turned twelve and oh my goodness how fun it was to still be "a child at heart." Real things were also ordinary people. Ärpe Torpeson was in more than one picture in Solveig's diligently used camera, Ärpe at the cement foundry in the town center, Ärpe next to his wife Viola who loved to drive too fast on the roads in the District in her old Skoda so that the rocks whirled up against other cars' mudguards and sometimes cracked their windows. If you said anything about it, if you, for example, called Viola Torpeson in order to work things out, she would say "kiss my ass" or something along those lines if she was the one answering the phone and then hang up.

"There is one thing about you, Rita," Solveig had said the last day when Rita was still in the cottage. "You pretend to be something you're not."

"Well," Rita answered calmly but ice-cold. "tell me then. Since you know. Who am I?"

But Solveig sure enough had not answered. They had drunk wine, it was the last evening, the evening after Doris Flinkenberg's funeral, and they were going to go to Hästhagen—a dance place—for lack of other places to go, and you could not be at home, certainly not after the funeral, you had to get out.

Long, slender, attractive. Black hair cut in a page. The were-wolf who was laughing at the mirror. Looked down at the one taking the picture as if from above. *Snap*. And maybe it was, thought Solveig, due to the mood, due to the fact there were so many pictures that needed to be exorcised from her head: Rita's face next to Doris's dead body, Rita's face, the look, the blood, the expression.

"Take the picture then," said Rita.

"*I am the seducer*," said Rita. "*The happy one*."

And then they had sat a while longer and talked and it was during that conversation which had been short and almost natural in its shortness that Rita had understood it was impossible. Everything. Now she had to.

And she had gone to the shower and showered until the warm water was used up and even a few more minutes after that. When she finished she was even colder, almost ice-cold, and clean.

She changed clothes. Put on her black pants, red shirt, brushed her dark hair, pulled it away from her forehead with a black hair tie, and put on her makeup at the dinner table in front of the mirror. "Hurry up now!" she said to Solveig. "Go and get ready now, go and shower, we're leaving then, I'm waiting." And Solveig had gone to the bathroom and to the toilet and in the shower and during that time Rita took Solveig's leather jacket, her car keys, the wine bottle (the unopened one), and the camera and left. A classic scene: a car starts in the yard. Solveig, who heard it from the toilet, knew exactly what had happened. Rita had not kept her word, Solveig had been tricked. And now, now Rita was gone, and the car too—forever.

A few weeks later the picture came in a letter.

". . . a last greeting from the werewolf. The seducer. The happy one."

Rita had driven out on a small entrance road north of the town center. There she drank the wine from the bottle she had with her. When she had enough of that she started the car and drove back on the long stretch of road where there were fields on both sides. She sped up and floored it and turned off and traveled out over the fields. Her firm intention had been to drive the car into a swamp, but the ground had been dry and hard, an all too good surface. Instead she had taken aim at the tree on the other side. Slowed the speed, just right, just right, then pushed down on the gas pedal again. *Vroom.* The car's short little nose had been mashed against the tree.

When that was done she took her things out of the car, a plastic bag full, not more than that. Locked it and threw the keys away far, far into the field.

Then she walked back to the bus stop, a few miles. A little snow had fallen but it transformed into rain before it reached the ground. No bus had come, but a car. And she immediately recognized it, it was Anders Bäckström and Sabrita-Lill Lindholm in Anders Bäckström's father's BMW.

It was the middle of the night when Rita arrived at the Backmanssons'. A party was going on in the apartment. People were standing on the balcony facing the sea and the street when Rita came wandering up the sidewalk. The balcony doors were standing wide open, music and laughter and party noises could be heard from inside. Someone on the balcony caught site of Rita down on the street. They called and waved to her. Maybe they thought she was one of those lonely nightwalkers in the night who needed to be cheered up.

No one on the balcony was familiar to Rita, except Tina Backmansson, Jan Backmansson's mother. She was also one of the ones who waved: obviously she did not recognize Rita in Solveig's leather jacket and the dirty jeans, with plastic bag in hand and the makeup running down her face.

Rita stopped below the balcony, which was located on the third floor in a substantial stone house on one of the nicest streets in the city by the sea, and called hello. A moment of confusion arose on the balcony but shortly thereafter Tina Backmansson had recovered from the surprise.

"Oh! Here we have you now!" she called down to the street. "Welcome! One moment!" She disappeared into the house and while she was gone the balcony emptied so that when she came back and threw down the bunch of keys she was alone. "Take this! It's for the street door and the other entrance! You know!"

And in the darkness of the stairwell on the third floor, in the door leading to the main entrance of the apartment, Tina Backmansson had already been waiting for her so that Rita did not need to use the keys. It was that entrance which was the "kitchen entrance" in the apartment and naturally Rita understood she would be smuggled in away from the party itself. But on the other hand, it was also the door leading to what in the Backmansson family's vast apartment was called "the children's corridor." Jan Backmansson's room and the guest room were located there, the room that had originally been Susanna Backmansson's—Jan Backmansson's sister who was studying dance in New York. And really, the party, it meant nothing. If she was a disgrace there or not, all of that was gone and not important now. Everything that belonged to the District, that way of thinking.

And Rita, she was the strongest and the weakest in the world in that moment when she thought like that.

Jan Backmansson was not at home. "He told you didn't he? That he would be at camp?" Tina Backmansson asked in a voice that hinted that she understood maybe Jan Backmansson had not said anything at all to Rita. Not out of meanness or the desire to mislead Rita—Jan Backmansson was completely incapable of that sort of thing—rather, quite simply because it had started happening lately as expected, which the adults more than the children had known would happen. Step by step Rita and the District and the life with Rita, the girlfriend, had become increasingly out of date, due to the distance, due to all sorts of things, you were young, you had your own interests, different interests, other things happened.

And no one, not anyone in the Backmansson family anyway, had thought about moving a finger to change it. All promises that had been made, for example the previous year, in the fall, for example after the fire on the First Cape when the family had to leave their house not to return—"It's clear that you'll come, later." "You're coming along, of course." "To go to high school in a good school in the city is not a bad alternative"—yes, they had stopped mattering, they had been transformed into words, talk and a lot of water had flowed under the bridges since then. They were young people after all, Jan and Rita. Yes ALSO Rita. It happened of course, you could suspect, things in her life that made it so that what you planned one year appeared in another light already the following year, that of childishness, sudden eagerness. And Rita was a cute and intelligent girl. She certainly had so many other possibilities.

Tina Backmansson showed Rita into Susanna's room and said she could sleep there that night. At a loss and suddenly powerless Rita had come to be standing in the middle of a rather empty room that she had always thought was so pretty (and it was) and that she had always dreamed about staying in . . . The kind of room where someone becomes different, not better or worse, just different.

And childish, yes, but it struck her in that moment, after everything that happened, though she was tired, confused, and dazed and actually void of all thoughts and feelings, how much she had longed for this room.

She would hold on to this with hands and teeth if needed. A strong thought, saucy. But as said, right now Rita was the weakest and the strongest in the whole world. And she looked at Tina Backmansson, who had offered her a place for the night, with all the confusion that existed in her, but also with all the will, strength, and determination.

"I'm here now," she whined with an indescribable babyish voice. "I've come to stay."

And then it was as if Tina Backmansson had taken in what she had in front of her. Not just the filth and the terrible things she tried to keep away, what was intruding, but the other, the heartwrenching. A wreck. Rita Rat—she had a hard time even taking that name in her mouth and it was difficult with Jan Backmansson because she honestly wanted to be a good and liberal parent—was a wreck who was falling apart in front of her eyes.

"My goodness, child. What have you done?"

And then a dam burst inside Rita. She started crying, tears sprayed out of her and continued and when it had once gotten started it just remained. She lost her balance and fell on the edge of the bed while the tears just gushed. Tina Backmansson, smelling like a party, sat down next to her and she took Rita's hand. Neither Rita nor Tina was much for hugs. It would not have occurred to either of them to throw herself into the other's arms. It was okay.

Rita cried. Tina Backmansson sat next to her and held her hand. It was a moment of devout nearness though they did not understand a thing about each other.

And Rita cried and cried, from exhaustion and joy over being in this room, over her embarrassment when she understood how intensely she had longed to come to the Backmanssonian apartment. But she also cried over everything else. Everything. Doris Flinkenberg, the cousin's mama, Solveig—

And over herself. Her loneliness. Poor Rita.

And not immediately, but while she was crying, she also gradually understood that her tears had an effect on Tina Backmansson.

"Poor child," Tina Backmansson whispered, "poor child." Tina Backmansson who smelled the difference between them both—expensive perfume, expensive party clothes, expensive— all that is easy to disregard if you are the one who smells better. Which for Tina Backmansson was so self-evident she had never reflected on it; the comfort of being able to live how you wanted, the security in having things.

But then Tina Backmansson got up and got some blankets, and when Rita had calmed down she fell asleep with her clothes on, on Susanna Backmansson's bed in the wonderful room in the Backmanssonian apartment.

She slept for maybe twelve hours: when she woke up it was completely quiet in the apartment again and the middle of the day. She got up and went out into the apartment, through "the children's corridor" through the kitchen to the living room and the library and the workrooms and through, quite simply, the vast rooms. No traces of the party anywhere. It was empty, completely cleaned, and if anything it smelled of disinfectant cleaning solutions.

She waited for Tina Backmansson in the middle of one of the large rooms. And she showed up, sure enough, in jeans and a shirt now, weekday clothes. Just as fresh and clean, no trace of the party left on her.

And they spoke to each other from a distance of about nine feet in the beautiful, white living room. Rita listened, paid attention, on her guard as always, Tina Backmansson just as abrasive and cold as always.

"Since you're here now it's best that we agree on the rules of the game," said Tina Backmansson.

Whatever, Tina, thought Rita. I'm here now. Everything else is negotiable.

And they carried that conversation to its end; then Rita went to shower and washed herself really clean. She went to Jan Backmansson's room and dressed in his shirts and pants, which she already had a habit of doing in the house on the First Cape, when they had had, and still had, almost the same size.

Later, in Jan Backmansson's room, she became tired again and crawled down under the quilt on Jan Backmansson's bed.

And fell asleep. And later on Sunday evening when Jan Backmansson returned from camp or the trip or wherever he had
been she was lying there under the quilt ready and waiting for
him like a present.

Jan Backmansson became happy over seeing her and immediately crawled down to her.

. "You stay here now," he whispered. "It was good that you
came. I've waited . . ." Jan Backmansson burrowed his face into
Rita's neck, Rita's hair.

Rita had come to the wonderful room. She would stay there.

And what she left behind in the District was: a few photographs (above all that of Rita Rat, the last evening, *time of the
werewolf*), the taste of decomposing leaves and damp earth and
bitter wine the night before you crash a Mini Cooper against a
tree, the smell there in the woods, the smell at Lore Cliff. The
smell there in the woods, the smell of gunpowder, the smell of
baked coffee, blood, the smell of Doris Flinkenberg's blood.
And it could not be changed. All of that which could not be
changed.

And the smell of fire . . . but suddenly another symbol, a con-
trasting picture, the sea urchins, here they came walking, the
white, white in the strange night when everyone was moving
around, was it the night after the American girl had been found?

But no, it was only one. Kenny. Kenny with a glowing cigarette in her hand, Kenny who looked completely wild and came
toward her—then it started burning in the woods. Kenny in
white, white clothes.

And she left the fire the blaze behind her, a corridor of fire
in the woods. It was a strange dream that was no dream, she
was standing at one end of the corridor, her sister Solveig at the
other. Solveig in the corridor of fire.

"You did it. You set fire to the woods."

"You did it. You burned it up. Are you cra—"

. . .

And that last evening, after Doris Flinkenberg's funeral, before Rita went into the shower, Rita had said to her:

"Apparently there's nothing you aren't capable of Solveig."

Then she had left everything, fled. Gotten into Solveig's car and driven off.

II.

Let me tell you something dear, blessed child. That the mercy God has measured out for just you, it is so great that not a single human being can grasp it with their intellect.

— LIZ MAALAMAA

THE MUSIC
(Sandra's Story 2)

———————

FROM THE RETURN OF THE MARSH QUEEN, CHAPTER 1. WHERE did the music start?

The Marsh Queen: I don't know about music, if what I mean with music, is music.

From The Return of the Marsh Queen, Chapter 1. Where did the music start?

Richard had a T-shirt he tore up and made holes in. He took an ink pen and wrote "Kill me" in big letters on the stomach. Malcolm aka "the Worm" McLaren saw the T-shirt and thought: awesome. I'll take it with me to my trendsetting boutique Sex in London. Then I'll pick up the boys who hang around the boutique and dress them alike and it's a band and we'll call them the Sex Pistols.

From The Return of the Marsh Queen, Chapter 1. Where did the music start?

The American West should have been conquered with red body-hugging rubber overalls and platform shoes and the Soviet flag in 1974. Money was scant and times were hard. You—that was Malcolm aka "the Worm" McLaren and "the boys": Arthur "Killer" Kane, Johnny "Thunderstorm" Thunders, Sylvain "Clothing Monster" Sylvain, David "Hot Lips" Johansen, and Jerry Nolan—lived in a trailer park outside Los Angeles for what felt like several weeks. At Jerry Nolan's *mother's*. They ate her sticky spaghetti night after night. After night. Malcolm aka the Worm encouraged "the boys" to think about the big picture in order to deal with the present. It was doomed. In fact, the very hardest was to score. Downright a near impossibility. And for someone who has to score but cannot, every hour, every minute, every second is as long as an entire lifetime, an eternity.

There are, in other words, those who maintain that if there had been access to heroin in the American West at this point in time and in this place in history then *punk music* would never have been born. Because the following is history. It was just that night, at the dinner table at Mama Nolan's, that the legendary glitter rock band the New York Dolls broke up.

A few segments from the dinner table discussion that followed (and that deteriorated):

"Now we've had enough of you, Malcolm, you old worm," Johnny Thunderstorm and Jerry Nolan said at the same time— they were the ones who were the band's junkies and had to score for their lives. "Now we're going to stop with this pandering with the Soviet flag here in this wilderness and go back to New York."

"What the hell," said Arthur Killer Kane, he wanted to ease some of the tension. He did not have the desire or the means to stop and he did NOT want to go back to New York. *In any case not right now.* He had a more or less successful alcohol withdrawal behind him and his girlfriend Connie who had stabbed Killer with a knife before the departure was in New York; and the combination of these two was less tempting.

And he did NOT want to disband the band.

He did not have a plan B. The glitter rock band the New York Dolls was his salvation.

"Go to hell," Johnny Thunderstorm and Jerry Nolan replied at the same time and that was the end of that discussion, the end of the New York Dolls, the whole story, the whole *glitter scene*. In a flash they found themselves on the main country road, on their way to the airport and New York where Richard Hell would so conveniently be waiting for them (though that was something they did not know yet: "What flight will you be on, boys?").

Maybe Malcolm aka the Worm had made a miscalculation. You don't start a revolution in the American Midwest. But could he admit that? Admit to himself, in front of the collected world press, that you are wrong?

"Go to hell," said the Worm. "I'm going back to London now, will cure my venereal disease, but in the reverse order . . . first cure my venereal disease and then . . ." and yada yada yada followed . . . which some Englishmen with a certain accent never understood, aka the Worm, when it was time to quite simply shut up. "FIRST, that is, I'll cure my venereal disease so my wife, the daring fashion designer Vivienne Westwood, won't get mad at me, then I'll borrow Richard Hell's T-shirt, figuratively speaking, and start a new band, we can call it the Sex Pistols based on the ambiguity of the name. It will, unlike you small vermin" (ALSO aimed at Mama Nolan and the sticky spaghetti because Malcolm was angry now, quite simply furious), "be a truly successful project also in regards to the public and sales. WE are going to make songs with nice punk messages, unlike everything we've been able to do with you, losers.

"With you we've only been able to lose, losers."

"Oh, hell, what am I going to do now," thought Arthur Killer Kane. Good question. Especially since he would not have much more to do in the history of music. His time on the glitter scene was over.

From The Return of the Marsh Queen, Chapter 1. Where did the music start?

Malcolm aka the Worm McLaren came home from London (healthy and fit again) and ran straight up to the boys who were standing and hanging outside his and his wife's trendy clothing shop.

"Now boys," the Worm said to the boys, "we're going to start a band that mixes politics and music and we'll give it a *subversive* name. I have a good idea for a name, how about the Sex Pistols? There's a lot to be angry about too. Lots of inequalities. It's not far-fetched to liken the English monarchy to a fascist regime. Write a song about it."

"Uh," said Snotty, who would gradually replace Glen Matlock on bass in the band and who according to legend was exceptionally stupid and crazy when it came to big words because he certainly had not attended any school for upper-class boys rather an ordinary one, whatever it's called in the complicated English school system, "what does far-fetched mean?"

"Go to hell, Snotty," aka the Worm replied. "You have the right attitude."

And shortly thereafter Malcolm aka the Worm McLaren locked Rotten Johnny aka Johnny Rotten and the remaining "boys" in a room with refreshments.

"I'm going to lock you in this room now," the Worm said before he turned the key in the lock on the outside. "And I'm not letting you out until you've written a song that is like Television's 'Tom Generation.'"

X hours later the boys came out with a draft of a song finished, "Sweet Tom."

And a record was made and the boys made history with it.

"Oh, but what the hell," Richard Hell said when he heard "Sweet Tom" there where he was on the other side of the Atlantic with Thunder and Jerry Nolan united in yet another, it looked like, loser project, however subversive it may be. "McLaren. What a worm.

"That was my song," Richard Hell swore. "That was my everything."

From The Return of the Marsh Queen, Chapter 1. Where did the music start? And who was Richard Hell?

He was a singer in the trendsetting punk orchestra Television, which is legendary because, among other things, not a single film recording has been preserved in which the original band members play. But those who were present and saw it understood that this was something new and tremendous.

The end of a scene, *the* glitter scene. So far from the New York Dolls, so raw, like Iggy Pop, so cool.

The music started here: a deserted field. Richard Hell and Tom Verlaine were members in the original band. They were best friends. They had met at a boarding school in the Midwest and both had other names then. They had a habit of running away from school. Bumming rides and reading poetry. *French* poetry. Rimbaud, Baudelaire, Verlaine. In redneck country: it was like asking for a beating. Being chased along the country roads.

One time they stayed out in the wilderness, at the edge of a very deserted field. They made a fire to warm themselves or maybe just because they had the desire to see something beautiful and different and tremendous on this field. So they set fire to the whole field.

And ran, ran away from police officers, authorities, rednecks, others.

Then it's the information. It comes at night. It doesn't mean anything.

— MARTIN AMIS

The planet without Doris

. . . WHEN SANDRA RETURNED TO THE DISTRICT AND THE HOUSE in the darker part everything was the same as before but yet it was not. It was like coming to a new planet. The planet without Doris Flinkenberg. She would live the rest of her life on it. How would that go, anyway?

Someone's arms around you from behind, like an octopus.
   "I'm here, Sandra. I'm not going anywhere. I promise."

It was Inget Herrman and a violent nauseous feeling welled up inside Sandra and she threw up over Inget Herrman's hands, which still had not let go.

"Dear child, I'm here."

The planet without Doris. This is what it looked like on it.

Then she went to bed.
   Then she slept for a thousand years.
   ZZZZZZZZZZZZZZZZZZZZZZZZZZZZZ
   And then she went out in the Blood Woods.

The road out into the Blood Woods

SHE WAS THE GIRL IN THE GREEN SPORT CLOTHES, THE SKATING girl. The skates tied together by the laces, hanging around her neck, one skate on each breast. In the sunshine. The skates were also green. Painted with old paint, she had done it herself. The leather had become hard and dry because the paint was not expensive leather paint rather the first best thing that had been at hand. An old can with green paint inside, ancient. She had been surprised that it was still possible to dissolve with turpentine.

But. To paint her white skates to match the green outdoor suit she had sewn for herself was the first thing Sandra had done when she got out of the marital bed where she had been lying, not for a few months or a year, but certainly for several weeks.

Other concepts of time had ruled inside the room. Time had been different, quite simply. Both long and short and no time, standing still, unmoving.

But now it was March, clear and beautiful, the first Monday after spring break during which Birgitta Blumenthal had, time after time, inquired with the Islander about how she was doing. "She can't even come out and skate on the ice? Dad has plowed it!" the Islander conveyed Birgitta Blumenthal's case to his sick daughter in the bed who refused to have any personal visits during the break when there was not any homework to do and, in other words, no external reason for being together.

The daughter reported that no, she was not up to it. And turned her face toward the wall, and for a moment in the door opening the Islander might have been about to speak his mind once and for all, that there was now going to be an end to this nonsense. But he said nothing. The seriousness of the situation prevented him.

It was, despite everything, not that long since Doris had died by her own hand. And despite the fact that he did not understand the entire story he decided to leave his daughter alone.

"A sick animal also leaves the herd for a while when it's hurt itself," the Islander said downstairs, which Sandra heard through the house when she lay in bed with the door open. "A hunter knows that better than anything."

"Do you see a herd of animals anywhere?" Inget Herrman asked, certainly in a friendly way, even straining to be friendly (maybe somewhere she still suspected that she was in the house on borrowed time; "I'm not mature enough yet to live under the same roof with a woman," the Islander had said and continued saying to her).

Inget Herrman's question only confused the Islander. He did not answer. Sandra understood him. She, and Doris too, *she would have understood*. The reason why they had promised each other in the swimming pool never never to grow up was in order to avoid carrying on those ambiguous scenes-from-a-marriage conversations.

"Should we . . . go and shoot?"

"No," said Inget Herrman.

Inget Herrman did not shoot. She was a pacifist.

Inget Herrman really did not want to shoot. She wanted, but she almost did not dare say it out loud, to go to a restaurant. For a long time after Doris's death that was the only thing Inget Herrman wanted to do when the idea of leaving the house in the darker part and doing something else sometimes came up. She did not say it of course, but it could be heard in her voice. Sandra recognized it.

"Shoot," Inget Herrman snorted. "It's always about shooting."

"Daaaaaamn fun," the Islander could be heard saying down in the basement where he and Inget Herrman were hanging out on the weekends with their drinks at the edge of the pool. It echoed throughout the entire house: daaaaamn fun! Sandra wondered if Inget Herrman detected his irritation.

"Maybe we should try to get her out of bed gradually," Inget Herrman suggested kindly. "Out of the *marital bed* or whatever it is you two usually call that thing?" That is how it was. She could not talk without everything becoming poisonous and ambiguous.

But with a laugh too. The Islander laughed too. And then he put on a gramophone record. He played *The Jungle Book*, a children's record that he liked a lot. It was one of the numbers he used to charm people, also, when together with someone. He liked playing songs from children's records.

He put on the monkey song from *The Jungle Book*.

Louis Armstrong, the black jazz musician, was singing on the record, in English.

"Oobee doo. I wanna be like you. I wanna walk like you. Talk like you."

And the Islander sang and danced along:

"You see, it's possible; an ape like me can learn to be someone like you."

"Imperialistic shit," Inget Herrman declared and turned down the volume.

"Then you know," the Islander said after a quiet pause, "the art of killing the joy another person feels."

They were scenes from a marriage, before it had even started, the film version.

Though it was a pity about them both. The nicest people ever when they were not together, the nicest otherwise. But together—why did it turn out like that? It seemed like they had no idea either.

It was a pity about Inget Herrman. It was so obvious. The Islander would never . . . whatever she was thinking, with her.

But it was a pity about the Islander too. Inget Herrman would never . . . whatever he was thinking, with him.

And both of them were sitting here and trying their best and still nothing came of it.

But now, in other words, it was the Monday after spring break, the middle of the day, students back at school, the Islander at work, Inget Herrman in her apartment in the city by the sea where she was during the week (the Islander was consequently very definite about the fact that they should live apart) writing her thesis, collecting material half of the day, writing during the other half. She had changed topics again, or if anything, narrowed it a bit more.

"To a more manageable format," she explained to the Islander. "This topic is a more realistic goal, so to speak."

"I see," the Islander said, and tried to make it sound as though he found it interesting.

But now, in other words, away from that. Sandra had come out into the world again, outside. And now she was walking through the woods to Bule Marsh where there was a newly plowed ice-skating rink on the ice. While she was walking she was, almost from the beginning, aware she was being observed. The boy was standing in the bushes watching her. And he was no boy anymore.

He was Bengt and he had turned twenty in December.

Now it would happen. The meeting. After water that had washed under bridges, had grown still. After winter, darkness, ice. After death. Now, in the light of spring.

But at the same time Doris-in-Sandra said to Sandra: dance on my grave.

How did that go together?

And sitting in a drift of hard snow Sandra laced up her skates and then she glided out onto the ice. The ice princess on the big glitter scene, in front of an invisible audience.

Doris Day said DANCE.

Show what you can do.

. . .

And bam. Landed on her butt on the ice. Not to mention it was uncomfortable. Sandra's feet were too big for the miserable skates and her joints were searing, like fire. Sandra hated skating. Now she remembered it too. Plus her passionate loathing for having ice skates on at all.

I can't dance for you, Doris. My shoes are too small. My feet have grown. And my toes, they've become so long and so chubby. Quite simply supersuperhuge.

And legs like jelly too after so many years in bed. And trembling, like Bambi's thin legs. Trembles that at a distance might have looked like movements but they felt like ordinary cramps . . . there in the sunshine she understood, quite simply, accordingly that she could not dance, she would just topple over again. So she had to hurry this up and she turned toward where the eye was and shouted, "But come on then. What are you waiting for?"

In other words she was the one who started the game, she was the one who made herself known. Shortly thereafter, not more than half an hour later, they found themselves in Bencku's barn.

Longing. Skin. Body. Longing. Skin. Body. What was it other than words that poorly rendered the experience that followed in the moment when, after fumbling to get each other's clothes off, they could finally be united as man and woman. Fumblingly, yes—

Now I'm definitely kissed black and blue, Sandra would think in front of the mirror in Bencku's small bathroom. Still in the middle of that bright day and she would be fascinated by her pale face and the almost blue, swollen lips and she would almost be happy.

But first: she was carried away by his hands everywhere, all of her body's cavities were trembling inside and butterflies whirled in her stomach. She wanted this, it had not been like this before. Not with him, not with Doris. Because it was new now, she had decided that; it would be new and wonderful.

He came inside her, he lifted her pelvis toward him, her legs spread wide were ridiculous when they sprawled out in the air, but she wrapped them around his legs and it went very quickly and very slowly.

Now it's happening, now it's happening, it pounded inside Sandra.

And he bent his back like a spring, his chest thrust forward naked and exposed like on Saint Sebastian with the arrows, he breathed heavily and the wave of warmth welled over her too.

Back to the room.

Seemed foreign. Words. Most things were foreign to her after Doris's death. Most of the words that described different kinds of feelings. How were these words applicable to the feelings and the mental state that they bore reference to? Was there any connection at all? It was not clear.

"I accept everything, Doris. I'm an anomaly." She had lain there in the bed in her room and spoken to Doris, that had been her lifeline. But a Doris who was not the Doris who had been there alive not such a long time ago, but another, half imagined and constructed by her. A Doris-construction that did not exist any more than Doris's flesh and blood existed in life, but that was needed so she would not fall apart completely. A Doris to talk to. So that was what she did in bed when she did not masturbate or sleep. Spoke with a Doris whom she knew did not exist, whom she knew she had made up.

The masturbation was less sexual than a means of creating a room for herself away from what was outside. Away from the world and the unpleasant facts in it. Among others the fact that Doris Flinkenberg was dead.

It was like sleep. It carried her away.

But gave a kind of awareness of her body.

"I'm probably a bad dyke," she had said with regret in the bed where she was lying alone in the room behind closed curtains without knowing whether it was day or night. "You'll have to forgive me."

But does it matter, Doris Flinkenberg replied very clearly, and she could not answer that, so her fingers found their way down over her body to between her legs and so on.

"Sexuality is communication and creativity," it said in red letters in a brochure that had been handed out in school once. She remembered that right when she got her threehundredmillionfourth self-inflicted orgasm there in the marital bed in the dark little room in the darker part of the woods, and could not resist smiling.

Communication and creativity.

"My God," she said to Doris Flinkenberg inside her and Doris laughed. Pulled her spit-filled mouth into a smile, showed her gleaming teeth. "You're supposed to learn all kinds of shit and then find out later that it isn't even true."

It was during the breakdown, or just after it. But the breakdown itself, this was how it started. It was six weeks after Doris's death, the last week before Christmas, a Saturday evening at the Blumenthals' where Sandra had been visiting. A completely ordinary Saturday evening when the parents were home. Mom and Dad Blumenthal were at that moment in the sauna on the floor below the cozy living room where Sandra and the daughter Birgitta were sitting and watching television while they discreetly and unbeknownst to the parents were nipping at the bottles in the well-filled bar that the Blumenthal parents used only for show. He was a pediatrician, she a nurse—but was sitting on the city council—they were complete teetotalers. The breakdown started in the just aforementioned living room, while the

Blumenthal parents were getting changed in the dressing room after bathing. A *bonk* could be heard, a great thud, when Sandra tumbled to the ground in a half-conscious state. Mrs. Blumenthal who, having time to think "the war is coming," had traumatic childhood memories from the bombings of the city by the sea where she had lived, she screamed, an open, childish scream. But the second thereafter she knew enough to get herself together and run upstairs to the girls. And when she saw the girl on the floor, not their own daughter, thank goodness, she rolled up her sleeves to provide first aid—but of course it was not needed, said her husband, the pediatrician, who had already made it to the patient's side. It was not that life threatening. Sandra Wärn had quite simply passed out, it was probably a result of overexertion and certainly understandable after everything that had happened. He did not bother about what her guilty friend, their own daughter, tipsy and excusing herself, had to say right then. He was a doctor after all and understood immediately that this had nothing to do with alcohol regardless of how Birgitta Blumenthal, in a half-hysterical and drunken state, was standing and clinging to him with her childish confession. "We were just tasting."

So that is how the breakdown started, and it did not come unexpectedly though it looked that way. Sandra had actually gone and waited, though it sounds a bit bizarre to say that. But it was also just as bizarre to carry on like nothing had happened. Which she had done to begin with. She understood the whole time that it was not the way it was supposed to be, that it was not normal either. But normal, what was that now anyway? When Doris was gone the words paled as well, the worlds they hid, all the nuances and associations, their own meanings. Normal was normal again, in a normal sense. Of course it facilitated communication with the outside world and the possibility of establishing an understanding, but it also took something away, something essential, a taste.

And the big question that should have been answered was quite simply the one that had been pushed forward the whole time before the breakdown: was it possible to exist at all without this taste? If you said yes right away then you were lying just as much as if you said no and took action accordingly—found new friends, for example, just as if it had been a question about having a friend. This is the dilemma Sandra found herself in after Doris's death. She did not want to die, but she did not understand how she would go on living.

It was real as real could be. And if she started thinking about it, no that was it, it could not be thought, for entirely logical reasons. There was only one solution, death die, but in other words she did not want to so it was a matter of pushing the thoughts aside as best she could and, what, NOW Doris spoke in her, "trot along?"

Right after Doris's death, when Sandra, recently recovered from the last disease of childhood, which was the mumps, had returned from Åland and was stubborn about immediately returning to school, she had the feeling that everyone was watching her. First because of what had happened. A bunch of students she barely knew had been polite, even held open doors for her, at the same time as they had been careful about maintaining a proper distance. Later, especially, when the days passed and you still could not see anything noteworthy about her, not a trace of unusual emotion for example, there were those she thought looked at her crookedly, and whispered things about her and whispered behind her back.

Then there were of course those, both teachers and students, who came up and gave their condolences. The grief. "The grief," said the adults. It sounded strange and big and heavy and Sandra became even more depressed by hearing it.

"She didn't have an easy time of it, that girl," said Tobias Forsström, who taught English and history and came from the

District, in the same way Doris's biological relatives had. "All odds against her," Tobias Forsström stated with a tone of voice as if he was holding a lesson even though it was during a break and it was centuries since Tobias Forsström had been her teacher in any subject at all. "There are many here who come from such poor circumstances, almost destitution, that others, outsiders, have a hard time imagining. Therefore you think it's truly unnecessary when things turn out like this for a girl who had been given every opportunity to get out. Break the cycle so to speak." And then he smiled resolutely and patted Sandra on the shoulder. Sandra had certainly taken the resoluteness and the somewhat forced pat on the shoulder to interpret to her own disadvantage. She certainly understood. There were those in the District who looked down on residents like the Islander and herself.

Who built impossible houses for a fortune, and settled there, otherwise lacking all ties to the District. It was easier to relate to the summer guests: they did not claim to belong in the same way, and furthermore they were, in any case when seen from a certain perspective, a bit moving in their goal of separating, in their eyes the "genuine" (sea-) and the "false" (upstarts like the Islander who thought they could buy everything with money); so careful about always being on the right side.

"Now we've gotten a proper young lady in our class," Tobias Forsström said with a crooked smile a long time ago already when Sandra had started in the school in the town center. "A proper young lady from the French School in a completely or-dinary English class, then we'll have to see how this is going to go." The class on the other hand had not laughed, at her or at Tobias Forsström's attempt at light humor. Tobias Forrström was not a well-liked teacher. The aggression that oozed around him under the oily smile and the so-called ambiguous jokes with which he tried to entertain a highly uninterested world around him were repulsive in and of themselves, you pulled away out of instinct. And furthermore, on the other hand, who wants to be reminded that you belong here and nowhere else, once and for all and no matter what happens, whatever you undertake in the world? When you were still young, a child and looking ahead at the big picture? On the surface the world was also filled with lots of messages from here and from there saying it was open to everyone to become and to do anything.

Sandra had not bothered about Tobias Forsström, either then or later.

"But was a fantastic young person." He was actually the one who had said that too.

Him. Tobias Forsström, of all people.

And yes. You could agree with that. Her way of talking, being. DO YOU UNDERSTAND HOW UNTHINKABLE IT IS TO LIVE WITHOUT HER? Sandra had the desire to shout in Tobias Forsström's face, but of course she had not, she had just walked off, politely and kindly, just like a "young lady from the French School," where she would incidentally return and quite soon, would be expected to do.

Pain was a mild expression for what it was like even to brush against the memory of the first time in the house in the darker part of the woods, the first period, then before everything became complicated.

Doris who had come to you like a gift. So wonderful, so unexpected—had changed everything.

No one like Doris. No one who talked like her.

I didn't abandon her. Sandra Wärn said solemnly, as if she were in a church and was going to confess her sins out loud. This happened at school again, suddenly and without reason, and the one who happened to be standing in front of her turned around. It was yet another schoolteacher: Ann Notlund, the music teacher, who took a step closer because she certainly also wanted to hug Sandra.

"Sometimes you wish you could get the young to understand that there is a life after this one," said Ann Notlund. "I mean," she corrected herself when she heard how it sounded, "in life. There is something other than a large and fateful NOW."

Then, sure enough, she opened her arms and came closer so that Sandra ended up right in between them.

Sandra stood there stiff as a stick and thought, still a bit unaware of everything around her, out loud:

"It wasn't me. Wasn't wasn't me."

"But dear child, what are you saying?" Ann Notlund said devoutly but absentmindedly as if she still was not really listening.

Maybe, thought Sandra while she slowly returned to reality, Ann Notlund was quite simply no woman of words. Had a hard time hearing, speaking, and understanding.

Maybe, thought Sandra, the only weapon she had in that case was just this hug.

The only weapon she had was her hug.

"What a funny saying, Sandra," Doris said to Sandra a bit later and in the middle of the school day. Loud and clear, but so that no one other than Sandra heard it.

Hugs. How Sandra hated hugs, especially in school right after Doris's death when she appeared to be the only one who seemed to be careful about carrying on as if nothing had happened. Well aware that it was an impossibility and that out of necessity the breakdown must be lurking just around the corner if she continued (which she did, there were no alternatives) living in something so unreal.

"But how are you, really?"

"How are you doing?"

The talkative ones who carried on like that.

But my God, what are you supposed to say? Isn't it obvious? Not so great. And what are you going to do about it? How are you going to make it go away? Should we hug?

Then it was definitely better with people like Tobias Forsström who just pressed out a sympathy because he so to speak had to (with her that is), or those who said nothing at all, who just looked at her a bit sadly but were visibly relieved when they noticed that she did not look sadly back. Relieved over being allowed to be like before. Like always.

In Doris's own classroom they put a photograph with flowers and a candle on Doris's desk at the very front of the center row. In the beginning the candle was lit all the time and the roses stood in warm water in a glass jar; the water was changed regularly, the jar was refilled with new roses. The photograph showed Doris with big red, shimmering hair, the Doris who had actually existed for only a short period of time, the very last months. Doris in a photograph her boyfriend Micke Friberg had taken. The new Doris. Her from Micke's Folk Band. "Hi. I'm Doris, this is Micke, and we're Micke's Folk Band. Now I'm going to sing a happy folk song in our own arrangement—'I walked out one evening.'" Micke Friberg left school shortly after Doris's death. He had to think. He could not stand it.

From The Return of the Marsh Queen, Chapter 1. Where did the music start?

Micke Friberg: I don't have a clear memory of her. She used to stand in the schoolyard sometimes, pale in the face. They had identical blouses on. Her and her friend. They said Loneliness&Fear on them.

I mean, a hundred years BEFORE the punk music began.

But her that is, maybe it's stupid to put it this way, but I don't have any memory of her. She was my first love. And you know how that can be. She committed suicide later. And if it hadn't been for the music I probably never would have gotten over it.

From The Return of the Marsh Queen, Chapter 1. Where did the music start?

Ametiste: the rise and rise and rise Ametiste, that was me, before anything at all had started happening. Before I met her who became the Marsh Queen on Coney Island, in one of the record recording stands, there are still some of them left over there.

Debbie had a '67 Camaro, she inherited it from her mother. To have a car in New York was both luxury and insanity, but it was probably, and Debbie had also said that, what kept us in our right minds, making short, fun trips to Coney Island and the beaches around it.

But the parking in New York was a full-time job. Three mornings a week you had to get up in time to move the car before seven o'clock because if the parking police got there first you would have the car nicely chained until it was transported to the burial site for abandoned cars far outside the city, wherever it was.

That was my job. To park Debbie's car. To get up early in the morning and then sit in the car on one side of the street and wait for the parking on the other side of the street to go into effect. I used to sleep in the car sometimes. And later when Sandra, the Marsh Queen, came, we were two. We wrote some songs there.

Debbie was busy then. She had broken through and was busy being famous over the entire world. Almost. But then they took her to France and got her to lip-sync dirty words in French and it was "punk" according to the ones selling the records.

Though also for her, earlier: Debbie also said she wrote most of her earlier songs while she was sitting in the car waiting—with the engine on when it was winter—to be able to park the car on the other side of the street.

In other words it was there, among other things, that the music was born. In Debbie's '67 Camaro a few blocks from the Bowery where we all lived back then.

A lot of other legendary types were also living there then. For example William Burroughs. I remember him like a ghost. A white ghost.

We lived at the Bowery and William Burroughs haunted the place: it's fun to remember it like that. It was a fun time.

We hung around Debbie: she was big, the biggest in the world, almost. She became famous in a short period of time, a few years, there were those who were surprised that it was precisely her.

That there was a time, a few months, maybe half a year, when she was the biggest in the world.

Biggest in the world. There's something in music called a "peak." That's when everything culminates.

But I didn't see much of Debbie later. Almost nothing. She was always on tour.

And when she was at the Bowery she was surrounded. By everyone who suddenly wanted to come into contact with her.

And we left later, me and the Marsh Queen.

Incidentally, I picked her up on Coney Island, in a record recording stand. And she was a crazy girl, you better believe it.

But she could write songs.

The punk music started there in other words.

At the very beginning. In New York. When we waited to park Debbie's Camaro, in the mornings.

And it snowed.

Heavy flakes fell.

Write like this, I said to the Marsh Queen.

That heavy flakes were falling.

Write like this, I said. And the Marsh Queen, she wrote.

Gradually the candles stopped being lit as the first thing you did when you came to school. The flowers withered and no new flowers appeared. The flowers had dried and they were beautiful that way too, so they were allowed to remain. Then someone knocked over the glass jar by mistake and it fell to the floor and went to pieces. Not large, normal shards, but grainy damp splinters that were a pain to sweep up.

In that moment the roses went into the trash can.

"Maybe we should have thought about you," said Ann Not-lund, the music teacher who was also the homeroom teacher for Doris's class. "Would you have wanted them?"

Before Sandra had time to answer this or that (but these flow-ers, what would she do with them?), Ann Notlund continued: "Then there is another thing. Her desk. Her things. I've under-stood that her mo . . . her foster mother is not well and can't be bothered right now."

"I can," Sandra said, calm and businesslike. "Of course."

And she emptied the contents of Doris's desk into a plastic bag. She took everything Doris had in it home with her, threw nothing away. Did not go through it either. The full plastic bag stayed there in her room in the darker part, under the bed. She thought about taking it to the cousin's house, but before the breakdown when it was of immediate importance, the cousin's mama was in the hospital, and after the breakdown, yes, after the breakdown, nothing was of immediate importance anymore. And, to be honest: there was no one else who made a claim on these things either. Schoolbooks, booklets, paper. Paper, paper, paper. And then a scarf that smelled of young-fresh-woman per-fume, the new Doris, Micke's Folk Band Doris.

Sandra had in other words emptied the contents into a plas-tic bag that she had carried home and taken to her room in the house in the darker part.

The desk had been carried out of the classroom. The spell was broken, life went on.

Out with Doris and in . . .

. . . in with Santa Claus!

Said Doris-in-Sandra and Sandra could not hold back a big smile. Because it was Christmastime, undeniably.

Ann Notlund and some other students from Doris's class who happened to see her smile looked at her strangely. What was there to laugh about?

No. No one understood. It was incomprehensible.

"Nobody knew my rose of the world but me."

Said Doris-in-Sandra AND Sandra at the same time, together (though of course no one could hear it).

AND Eddie, the dead girl. Eddie's raspy voice, on that record. Another voice from the dead.

And anyone could understand from this that the breakdown was close now.

The connections of thought-feeling words were looser in Sandra. What existed instead was, for example, this: music. Strange melodies that played inside her, melodies that sometimes had a counterpart in reality, sometimes not. Melodies that were recognizable, that existed. Sometimes those that were unrecognizable, those that obviously did not exist.

The Marsh Queen: I don't know if the music is music.

Sandra hung out with Birgitta Blumenthal, in a normal way. They did their homework together. Birgitta Blumenthal was good in school. Sandra needed quite a lot of help in many subjects, especially math because she had been gone so much earlier in the fall semester.

Birgitta Blumenthal helped her. She was good at explaining things so you understood. Sandra appreciated that. She also appreciated that there was quite a large amount of seriousness at Birgitta Blumenthal's, that is to say, she did not diverge from the topic more than necessary. If homework was going to be done, homework was done. If it was math, then they would do math.

No monkey business. No "games." Like with Doris Flinkenberg.

Later there was time for relaxation. What was called *spare time* when you were in school. Sandra understood now, maybe for the first time, relaxing things. You watched television, read, played games, made puzzles, spoke about "everything between heaven and earth." Ordinary things, most of all, as if it was the most remarkable thing of all: boys whom you were in some way or another interested in. Birgitta Blumenthal was also completely hypersuperextranormal in that respect. Her secrets on that front were completely ordinary secrets but she still acted as though they were anything but. She admitted under solemn circumstances that she was in love with her riding instructor whose name was Hasse and she could not stand that Tobias Forsström looked at her in "an unhealthy way." "But you know old men." Birgitta Blumenthal laughed. And yes, yes. Sandra laughed along, she knew about older men even if she did not have a clue about the details here but that was not important; the important thing was she acknowledged normal behavior when she saw it and acted properly accordingly.

There were things that never arose, which they had done with Doris Flinkenberg, in their world. Things that never swelled over the borders, that never ever became larger than, larger than life, everything. That never burst. Burst. Exploded.

Even if you then, that is, afterward, paid the price for it.

The dream had ended. Real love died. If it could be said like that.

They talked about what they were going to be when they grew up. That is what they were talking about when the breakdown occurred. Birgitta Blumenthal loved animals and dreamed about becoming a doctor for animals. "Not a doctor like Dad though everybody says so," Birgitta Blumenthal assured her. "This is my very own idea."

"I don't know," Sandra said when it was her turn and the gin and tonic they had found in the bar had started taking effect. "Clothing designer, maybe."

It rolled out of her, over her tongue, and then it had been said.

A highly normal wish, a totally normal answer to a totally normal question. That was how it was.

"So exciting," Birgitta Blumenthal said taking part and took a big gulp from her glass and made a face. "Wow. This is strong." She whispered the latter, so that her parents who were taking their Saturday sauna on the floor below for sure would not hear them.

"You think so?" Sandra said urbanely though she started feeling strange right after she had said it. "In the beginning maybe. But you get used to it."

"And it doesn't taste good at all."

"It's not supposed to taste good either." Sandra said this with emphasis because now it was just as well to keep nagging about this one thing until the other—clothing designer—went away. This was normal, now it should be normal. Not like with Doris Flinkenberg in the end, and suddenly she remembered the terrible time too, when everything had flown away beyond rhyme or reason, into their own meanings. *Yet every wave burns like blood and gold*, as it had once played in Doris's cassette player. *But the night soon will claim what is owed.*

And the summer threw you away.

In truth, it had been, with Doris, the best time. AND the worst.

"Cheers." Birgitta Blumenthal giggled. "It's rocking, rocking."

But also for Sandra the floor was rocking properly despite the fact she had only tasted her drink. Rocked, rocked. The breakdown was an assumption anyway, alas alas, it could not be stopped, and it was not dependent on the alcohol rather on two words that had been said: clothing designer. It sang in her head quite cruelly. It was Doris-in-her, Eddie, and all order of other voices.

A cacophony of the unbearable, of everything. Try now to be calm as though nothing had happened and celebrate a totally normal and relaxed Saturday evening.

And this was the last thought that was somewhat normal inside Sandra.

"Oh, now I'm starting to get drunk," Birgitta Blumenthal whispered. And then she raised her voice, made a face in agreement at Sandra who tried not to look back. Everything was dangerous now, she stared at a seal pup who, with its flippers flapping desperately, was trying to get away from the poachers who were after it on the blue ice on the television screen, a hopeless undertaking. *Living Nature*, was the name of the program and it was on every Saturday evening at the same time.

"So exciting. Wanting to be a clothing designer I mean. Tell me more." And continued whispering, "It actually feels quite funny! I wonder if I'll have time to sober up before Mom and Dad come up and it's time for shrimp sandwiches?"

At the Blumenthals' they ate shrimp sandwiches every Saturday evening after the sauna; it was a pleasant ritual.

Pang, the seal pup was shot.

And the little silk dog wagged her tail.

With Birgitta Blumenthal for example . . . one would certainly be able to solve a mystery and it would be the game it was intended to be, neither more nor less. Nothing else.

But Doris, also the most lovely: would one be able to live without it? That which spilled over all banks?

And PANG, unexpectedly it all came together. And it was there. The obvious answer to the question that it was impossible plus a lot of other things about guilt and secrecy and the most terrible of all, which they had come to, both of them together, more than brushed past, touched.

And the consequence of it: Doris's death.

In light of everything there was no possibility. It was not possible to live without Doris. There was no life after. No other possibility.

Carry me, Doris, over troubled water.

Oh! Who then? You then? Doris-in-her chuckled, full of scorn and derision. And with that it happened. There was no longer any security. PANG the breakdown crashed inside her.

Like a stone in the well and the well that was her, Sandra, dark and bottomless. She quite simply passed out, falling to the floor with a thud. On the bottom floor Birgitta Blumenthal's mother screamed, a short and suddenly childish cry, she remembered, or her body and head remembered, the bombs falling in the city by the sea and the bomb shelter. "The war is coming," she thought but in the next moment she realized that this, it was absurd, but her husband was already paying attention to another cry, the kind that only their daughter Birgitta could produce when she was really upset or afraid. And now she was calling for HELP upstairs. And both parents had run up, barely had time to put on their identical light blue, terry cloth robes, and shortly thereafter they found the passed-out girl on the floor of the living room.

"I don't know what happened," Birgitta Blumenthal said. "She just passed out. Maybe it's . . . alcohol poisoning." And she started confessing to what had been going on up in the living room without any of the adults really listening to her. The parents understood immediately that the alcohol was not the problem. This was something else, maybe something more serious than that.

"She's warm," said Mr. Blumenthal who was a pediatrician and was kneeling on the floor next to Sandra Wärn. "Fever. Maybe it's meningitis."

So besides: Sandra had in other words been farsighted enough to collapse in good hands.

You could also look at it that way.

Unlike Doris. Doris who had not had any safety nets. Doris who had to look death in the eye for real, absolutely defenseless and on her own.

You could also look at it that way.

. . .

CLOTHING DESIGNER.

Sandra did not know what happened. When she woke up the next time she was in her own bed, and the Islander and two unfamiliar young pucks of the female sex, rather made up and with teased hair and in some way exaggeratedly elflike, were standing next to the bed. At first she thought these strange women's faces at the Islander's side were part of an ongoing hallucination and that she, since she certainly recognized the Islander and understood she was lying in her own bed, thus found herself in a state between consciousness, insanity, and illness. But in the next second she understood that everything was for real. There was a realism about all of it and that was the Islander standing there with a Santa Claus hat on. Sandra had happened to collapse at exactly the point in time when a small, playful Christmas party, which the Islander had been looking forward to, had gotten started and these two unfamiliar female faces belonged to two, this you could say first after pediatrician Blumenthal had left the house in the darker part of the woods, erhm.

Two unfamiliar female faces and a pale papa Islander face in the middle. Sandra smiled a faint smile at the whole situation, which was so amusing and in order to assure the Islander she was certainly still alive. Then she drifted off into confusion again. The fever rose to 102 degrees.

Clothing designer. The thought itself became even crazier.

She took one whore elf's hand and squeezed it for all she was worth.

Because it was Saturday evening and the party had, as said, almost started when the doorbell rang—a shrill buzzer signal (that doorbell was newly installed AFTER Doris's death)—and Blumenthal the pediatrician almost scared the life out of a groggy Islander with guilty conscience at the ready, if nothing else just because in the capacity of his profession Blumenthal the pediatrician could inspire in any parent in a giddy party mood, when there were finally no children in the house, a bad conscience.

"I have your passed-out daughter in the backseat. I could use some help." Blumenthal the pediatrician's first line had not exactly made the situation any better. And he, Blumenthal, was also known for his rather special, sometimes rather sadistic humor. And his predilection for drama. For example, once a long time ago during the time when Lorelei Lindberg was still there and everything was still different (that is to say, you could venture to be a bit drastic—later on sympathy for the Islander, who was carrying the load himself, so to speak, got the upper hand), in passing he pointed out to Lorelei Lindberg in the food store in the town center that a harelipped child who had been operated on would not always be able to count on a normal life without a division after. Admittedly physiologically, he had said, but maybe not mentally.

Blumenthal the pediatrician was standing on the steps to the house in the darker part of the woods and during a fraction of a second he enjoyed the effect of his words, and then, when it slowly started taking effect, donned his objective doctor's role again:

"Presumably a fever. Nothing worse. Possibly as a result of mental exhaustion. The girl has been through a lot lately. And she has shown great bravery. Maybe too great. Now she has to rest and become well again at her very own pace."

With these words Sandra had been handed over to her own home, in her own bed, the great marital one, and in the middle of the party besides.

The sudden interruption caused the party to stop abruptly. It did not end because of a command, but ebbed out. In any case right there, in the house in the darker part of the woods, maybe to continue somewhere else. Just before midnight a long line of taxis left the house in the darker part. Those were all the guests, with the exception of two women who stayed.

She sat on the edge of the bed and held Sandra's hand, with tears in her eyes. Who dried Sandra's hot forehead with cool tissues that the other woman brought to the room. She also boiled tea, made sandwiches, lined up gingersnaps on a small plate, and brought everything in on a tray.

Sandra did not eat or drink anything, she just squeezed a hand. A hand. She longed so terribly. Missed. And in that dazed state she found herself in, the longing was shaped into a name that just came out of her time and time and time again.

"Bombshell. Pinky. Pink."

The women, who unfortunately did not know the Bombshell, of course did not even understand what she was talking about but did their best to calm her down.

The Islander had locked himself in the rec room. He was in a bad mood. The party would have to continue and culminate without him. Not just the party. Everything else too.

The next day, however, early on Sunday morning, he got up and started cleaning. He sent the women home of course because when Sandra woke up in the middle of the day the house was clean and empty. He also called Inget Herrman and asked her to come. As an exception Inget Herrman stayed in the house the following days also, even though it was the middle of the week.

Sandra went through the house and searched—yes, for what? The party? It was melancholic in a way. Then she went to bed again. Lay there. Lost herself in lethargy. Did not get up for ages. Slept, slept, slept. For a thousand years.

The fever came back, it rose and fell. Then suddenly, a few days later, it was gone. Days passed. Sandra had recovered physically but she stayed in bed regardless.

No one said anything.

"Rest," pediatrician Blumenthal had said. "Become well. At your own pace."

.   .   .

Sandra had personally made a decision. She would get up when there was a point to getting up. She had not thought about taking her own life. She thought about just remaining in bed and in the worst case dying, just by itself. But as long as she did not find a reason to get up she would not get up.

All the voices in her were gone.

But what looked like extreme passivity and monotony still were not. In any case not directly. Thoughts floated in and out of her head. A transistor played at night at the slightest disturbance in the air and the radio waves could reproduce themselves freely all the way to Luxembourg or wherever that radio station was where the kind of music that was like pouring rain rushing in and through her head played.

"I'm not in love. It's just a crazy phase I'm going through now."

Longing, Pinky, it had been one word. A formula, a memory, an association. Now others came. "Just because I'm looking you up, don't misunderstand me, don't think it's sorted now. I'm not in love, it's only because—"

It was the Boy. The longing that ran in that direction, again. Because he was there. The boy who was not a boy any longer. He was Bengt.

She was not surprised to discover him outside the house. Not really. For the most part he stood on or near the jetty, which you could see well through the tree trunks now when the leaves had fallen and there was snow on the ground. He looked up at her room. She understood he wanted something from her.

And she—

She sat at the end of the large marital bed in the darkness in her room and stared out into the darkness. Looked straight at him, whom she discerned as a shadow there.

Sometimes he stood unmoving and she had the idea they were looking at each other without seeing, but for the most part he moved nervously, like someone who is waiting and waiting and soon has been waiting too long usually does.

"Who is that?" One day right before spring break when Birgitta Blumenthal had forced her way into Sandra's sickroom she happened to catch sight of him, a shadow that was moving at the edge of the ice in the twilight.

"Someone." Sandra had shrugged her shoulders.

"He's staring this way. He doesn't look . . . completely well."

"Mmm. And so?"

"Are you scared?"

Sandra sat up in bed and said:

"Man. Why would I be afraid?"

There had also been a distance, almost a threat, in her reply. She did not want Birgitta Blumenthal to be there. Did not want her pathetic everyday depictions, her pathetic homework assignments, her pathetic dreams (Hasse Horseman!), her pathetic dreams for the future and future prospects. Remember a saying from so long ago: *a matchstick house with matchstick people who live a matchstick life.*

The Black Sheep, in Little Bombay: I wanted to show you what your dream looked like.

Is this what your dream looked like?

Maybe Birgitta Blumenthal was harmless, but not stupid, either. She certainly understood—everything in her own clever way. She said, right before she left and it was very soon thereafter— Sandra had turned on the television, which was showing skiing competitions that were taking place in the Alps somewhere and Franz Klammer was going downhill precipice by precipice at sixty miles an hour in a fantastically clear, snowy, white Central

European landscape drenched in sunshine, but it did not give her any associations and it would in the future not give her any either; figuratively speaking it would never mean anything else, it would, like skiing, just be a winter sport—that she had actually started believing a little bit that they were right, the ones who said Sandra was not normal. That there was something about her. Something really twisted.

"I've started doubting you in some way," Birgitta Blumenthal said before she left, but certainly so calm and kind.

"What?" said Sandra and could not tear herself away from the TV screen. "I'm not God anyway."

"That's not what I meant," Birgitta Blumenthal answered calmly and patiently. "I mean . . . that I don't really . . . believe you."

It came a bit carefully, a bit vaguely. But when it had been said, she added quickly, as if to reassure herself that it was right to say it (ethically right that is—was she allowed to do this, was she allowed to say this to a . . . friend . . . who had gone through so much, had a breakdown after her best friend's death . . . and everything?):

"That's how it is. Quite simply."

"Maybe the others are right."

She had—Sandra that is, somewhat later, when it was dark and Birgitta Blumenthal dismissed herself and left her hesitant anxiety hanging in the air—sat on her knees by the bed with all of the lights on. Given a sign. Two. Waved.

Then, when she was certain that he had seen it, she started painting her ice skates.

"The ones who say that . . .

"In other words, Sandra, I don't know if you're telling the truth." That was the last thing Birgitta Blumenthal said before she left the room and the house in the darker part that time which would be the last time she would be accepted into the house.

Sandra decided then that, yes, she would go out and skate. Sewed a green sports suit for herself, suitable for practicing such an outdoor activity in. Took out the paint, the one she had once painted certain nylon T-shirts with, the viscous green. There was still some of it left in the can, and so she took her ice skates and painted them with it.

And later: out into the bright, bright day.
She had gone to him out of real longing.
Game start. And not as Eddie, or anyone else, but as herself.
Princess Stigmata . . . the ice princess, her in the green clothes.

She had gone to him out of real longing, real desire. She wanted to have. Him. Her body had bellowed. And she had been impatient waiting for the right moment. The Monday after spring break when she knew no one else would be there.

"You fall in love with someone who brings something inside you to life."
Yes, Inget.
And now she was finally ready to meet it.

In Bencku's barn (where she was lying on a massive water bed and thinking). Later, in the future, they would talk about the day she followed him to the barn without saying one word, without either of them saying one word, he would tell her that he had waited for her for such a long time, but that it had taken time for her to discover him. But that he had taken that into consideration. He had been prepared for that, he would say.

He would also say, Sandra fantasized further where she lay rocking on the water bed while he left her alone to go to the bathroom or something for a while, that he had not forgotten her as she had been two years before, that fall night in the house in the darker part of the woods. When she had come to him in the pool. He would ask her if she remembered it. Did she remember?

She nodded. She smiled.

It was namely like this now, so clear and obvious. A new, entirely different story was starting now, here in the barn, after the unrestrained union. The first time of first times, that erased the memory of all first times which had ever been before. She would tell him.

What she would say was—she had already decided, and she would do it as soon as possible—about Little Bombay, everything, from beginning to end. Once and for all. Clean slate. If it was possible. But it was worth a try.

Love heals. Love saves lives.

She also thought she understood now, that was so fantastically simple too, that side by side with all of the other things that were happening and had happened, side by side with Doris's death even, he had been there the whole time. Like in a pop song, really. She closed her eyes in Bencku's bed one second, and for a moment no voices could be heard in her head, except for one of those normal and simple melodies: the sea was never so shimmering, or similar.

And what would happen then? Sandra, undressed and sticky in the bed, was lying and staring at the green clothes on the floor in the barn and looking at them like the clothes of a stranger. New things would happen now. News.

They would get married and have children together. Several children. Maybe not right away. They had schooling and studies and that sort of thing to finish first.

But like a picture. She and he. Who found their way to each other through loss—and found.

"Two castaways," as the cousin's mama once said in another situation that they both were, her and Doris Flinkenberg.

. . .

But Bencku? Have you become crazy? Doris-in-her in her head interrupted now. It was a voice that was not really welcome here. Besides she had completely forgotten it, for a while. But now it was back.

And Bencku came from the bathroom. Tripping over the floor in his socks. Had not gotten his socks off, they had been in a hurry. And the socks were also green like Sandra's clothes in a pile on the floor, and he turned up the music.

And he came back to the bed and he looked straight at her while he was walking, into her eyes, and she was embarrassed and closed her eyes and in other words waited for him, that he would come to her again, with eyes closed.

The expected embrace failed to come. In the following, when she opened her eyes again, he was sitting on the edge of the bed with the music blaring.

He was sitting on the edge of the bed with his back toward her. He had hidden his face in his hands. What was coming out of him sounded like a whimpering. His shoulders were shaking. And she was just about to stretch out her hand in order to clumsily touch and caress when she realized he was not crying, he was laughing.

And then Bengt started speaking, softly and quickly, as if he was angry. In fact it was not really laughter, it was a kind of bitter laugh that in some way, it did not need to be said, was directed at her. Not many words, but they came out of him like a waterfall, and at first she understood nothing.

"Anna Magnani," Bencku started, "had incredibly huge breasts. She was curvy in the way working women are on film, you know, Anna Magnani, the real one. That the breasts swell like clumps of earth in their clothes. She was like that. And she was on her way all the time. Not away, but a little everywhere, she got her fits of rage when she was going here or there, things flew around her, she was in other words temperamental. And the cousin's papa's and the Dancer's tongues hung to their knees when they saw her. And she liked to be looked at, not for that. She willingly gave them a show. And others. She was like a walking cliché but they didn't understand it, and she, she didn't understand very much, she wasn't all that clever either, and that showing, there wasn't anything wrong with it. It was what it was. It was okay. Then there was still someone, he had a white Jaguar, an old one that is, 1930s model, and it was really stylish and for a while it was like he just had to drive it on the roads here. She had probably caught his eye. He flirted with her. But he had a way with her that you don't forget. It was so descriptive for everything. It was one time, she was going to be off again. From here. From the District. She had something going on with the Dancer, some tiff again. The Dancer, that was Dad. And she's already on the road running away. And then this guy happens to come in his car. He stops next to her as if he was thinking about picking her up. But not next to her, thirty feet in front. She thinks she's going to get a lift and not because she's thought something like that, but suddenly she thinks it's a really good idea. So she turns around and gives the Dancer the finger and catches up with the car. But just as she's about to get in the guy accelerates. She stumbles, doesn't understand what has happened. And he stops maybe thirty feet in front of her, he thinks this is a hell of a lot of fun. And she runs again, and it's as though she doesn't really get that it's a game. He even backs up, waves to her to come, and she gives it all she's worth again; the dark hair whirling, sand and dust and sunshine like in a movie or in the rearview mirror and he watches with great interest. She's at the car. She's taken hold of the door. And then he floors it. She falls and hits herself pretty hard. Then maybe she understands something because she doesn't do it again. But it's enough. She's fallen hard, and everyone has seen it too. That was Mom." And Bengt paused and later added. "You don't understand that. Ones like you.

"And it's not the event itself. It's a damn image too. Of how it is. And there's always going to be a difference between—nah, I don't need to say it."

No. She did not want to be a part of this, now she was freezing for real. Freezing. But she understood this was not the right moment to get a quilt, blanket, to get, even ask for, something. What would you say? She was speechless.

And maybe it was good she did not say anything because then he came to where he was going, to the extraordinary part. She could not believe her ears. Everything cracked again. But despite that, she had to hear this, there was no other option.

"And," Bencku continued, when a moment as long as an eternity had passed, she lay there and understood and understood nothing, the water bed quietly lapping beneath her, like an irony, "I KNOW about you. Everything about YOU. I know what you were doing."

"But Doris . . ." Sandra started because at first she thought he was thinking about her and Doris, all of their games, also the one that was about the American girl.

"I'm not talking about Doris now," Bengt hissed. "I'm talking about your . . . father. The Islander. And—" Suddenly he did not seem to know how he would continue, he just said, "You've seen there on the map. All of it is there. I know what's there under that wretched house, under the pool.

"I just haven't understood how far you could go."

"Me and the Islander then?" Sandra asked in as sober and innocent a tone as possible.

Bencku did not answer.

But Sandra understood.

And now she was small again. Sandra vulnerable Wärn. She wanted to get up and get dressed, she wanted to leave, but at the same time, she was as though frozen. In order to counteract the petrification she got up and started gathering her clothes. But then she stopped herself, it was too overwhelming.

"But Bengt," she then heard herself peep. "My God. Where have you gotten that from?"

And suddenly she understood so many things. First that on the map, on Bencku's map, the woman who was lying on her back in the pool and was dead, it was not an expression of some-thing as Inget Herrman had once said about Bencku's maps.

It was too unbelievable. But then also another insight, and it shot through her head like lightning and it made everything stop for a second. Because why now? Why did he say it first now?

"You didn't say this to Doris did you?" She heard herself ask, clear and loud and obvious.

"You didn't need to say anything to her either," said Bencku. "She already knew everything."

The boy in the woods, the one who saw, the girl in the house, the woman in the pool, the Islander with the rifle. Once a long time ago. And he aimed it at the woman in the pool—

That was what Bencku had drawn, what Bencku had seen.

"No," whined Sandra. "Don't you understand anything? You saw wrong. It wasn't true."

The following days and nights she avoided looking out the window toward the place where he had a habit of being. Later, it was maybe a week later, when she did, he was gone.

"Bencku is at it again. That is the only thing that is normal."

It was Solveig who was talking. Solveig who came and cleaned in the house in the darker part of the woods, without a uniform, but otherwise like always. She brought news from the outside world. That was how she said it.

"Here I come with news from the outside world." Just as if nothing had happened. But typical Solveig. You would not think she had been the one to see the dead Doris, Doris with her skull blown into a thousand pieces just a few weeks earlier.

Life goes on.

That was also what she said. She talked about the cousin's mama that "she'll probably never be really well again. She was very attached to Doris."

And about Rita: Rita was in the city by the sea. Solveig knew that much. Not much more.

"So now I'm a twin without a twin. A half. Though that's not possible in the long run.

"But life goes on." Solveig repeated that many times, patting her stomach.

"And I'm pregnant. That's my secret. YOU are not allowed to tell anyone. Not Järpe Torpeson . . . since he isn't the father. Rather Torpe Torpeson, his brother. But we're going to get married soon, so it's not a secret."

Solveig went around in the house in the darker part, where she had never been before with her mops and her dustpan—

From the Closet could be heard:

"She certainly left a lot of fine clothes behind. Just THINK that she didn't want to have any of this. To Austria. Or wherever it was she went?"

"To New York," Sandra said weakly, though it was actually completely pointless to carry on with that story any longer. She could just as well have said it like it was, but she did not in any case. She was silent.

"And it's not clothes, it's fabric. *Material*."

Bencku's barn. She went back later anyway, as if to check, not what Solveig had said, if he had left or not. But what had been. A yesterday. The warm light. The music. The map. It was like a dream. Did it exist?

"It's probably best you stay away from me. I'm not . . . I can't . . ." That is what he had said later, finally.

"I'm sorry." He had also said that. "Sorry."

And she also understood something else: the Eddie game, all of it. He had never understood a bit of it. It was not the American girl he had been enticed by, it was by . . . her.

"Sorry. How everything is still such a load of crap."

And she left him then and thought that she would not any-more. But now—

Had it existed? She turned on the ceiling lamp. A naked bulb shone sharply and implacably over the emptiness.

Cleaned, clean. Everything put away. The records that had lain spread over the floor with and without covers. Books that had been torn out of bookshelves, clothing, the empty bottles and cigarette butts in the ashtrays, bottles, over the floor. The smell, sweet and musty.

Gone.

The whole smell of yesterday gone.

The map. He had taken it down from the wall.

And while she was there a noise could be heard behind her, a voice.

It was the cousin's mama, who appeared from the darkness.

"Murderer! If you take him from me as well I'll kill you!"

It should not have been like that. Somewhere in a corner of her mind she had still seen something completely normal in front of her. How it should have been between her and the cousin's mama. How they should have sat in the cousin's kitchen and talked about Doris, remembered Doris. How the memory of Doris would have built a bridge of understanding between them. Not an intense closeness, but still.

"No," Sandra whined, "no."

But then Solveig was there again and pulled the cousin's mama away.

"It's just Sandra . . ."

And led her back out into the yard.

The cousin's property. Swampy, dead. The cousin's papa in his eternal room, a yellow light burned in there. Dead. Nothing.

What I love is gone, hidden in the distant darkness and my true road is high and wonderful.

What? On Doris's cassette player, such a winding tune.

The shoes in the Closet.

Sandra had been left standing on the cousin's property, for a moment at a loss. Then she had gone home and strapped her backpack on her back and started walking toward the main country road. She emptied the Islander's wallet in secret before she left the house in the darker part. Had over a thousand marks in her pocket, a decent capital to start with. And where?

She was the lifter, she was the nameless, she was the one to whom the woods whispered its secrets, secrets of words, secrets of blood, swishing secrets from the District . . . she was Patricia in the Blood Woods, the unusually lively shop assistant who had finally gotten her messy life in order when she went out for a walk and a strange wild man came and strangled her.

NO, that was not her! Sandra turned around and went home again.

This restlessness when Doris Flinkenberg was gone.

And later when she did not come up with anything she took the bus into the city and enrolled herself as a student at the French School again.

So it was not as a result of Birgitta Blumenthal who went around and spread strange rumors about Sandra that she changed schools. Said that Sandra was not completely *normal*, that there was something odd about her and the whole house in the darker part of the woods. Who knew what secrets the house hid, really.

No. It was also quite simply so that in relation to the District, the school, and the municipality, everything: that when Doris Flinkenberg was no longer there, there were no reasons not to go to the French School anymore.

The Lover

ALMOST NO ONE AT THE FRENCH SCHOOL—EXCEPT FOR A FEW occasional people, more about that below—remembered her. The school had effectively obliterated the little harelipped girl from its collective memory. Most of her new classmates who had been in the same grade as her a long time ago had to think in order to form any kind of memory of Sandra from the lower grades.

The school nurse was also a different one now. She was one who spoke sex talk fluently, wife of a retired ambassador and like a fish in water at the French School. More like a fish in water than the so-called student body that still proved to be a hodgepodge in all respects. The superb children of diplomats expected to populate the school were, in the past as there were now, so few they could be counted on the fingers of both hands.

It was safe. Sandra had not changed in that respect either. She still did not belong to any group. She was still neither good nor bad in school.

There was a new arrogance about her. New, so far in that it could sometimes be seen. Definitely not all of the time. But sometimes it flared, often unexpectedly. She could say strange things in the middle of class. The kind of thing that got people to raise their eyebrows. Was she really sane? No clever, hilarious, or interesting things, but inappropriate and stupid comments. Like for example, suddenly during that discussion about Kitty G., more about that later. You really did not understand what she said and why.

She also had a lot of absences, which she could not justify. She forged the Islander's signature on the absentee list where her absences had been recorded in order to be seen and explained in writing by a parent or guardian and be signed by the latter. But this did not happen all the time either. Just sometimes.

Not nearly often enough that it in some way would have affected the image you had of her at school. Sandra who? Sandra *qui*?

She continued to be a shapeless person, someone who blended in. One, as it said in the psychology book, blind follower. One of those who witnessed the murder of Kitty G. from the windows of their homes: saw and saw without doing anything. Did not even call the police while there was still time. Just thought: someone *should* call. Somebody surely already called. This is just so terrible.

Kitty G. was a young woman stabbed to death in a parking lot outside her home in an apartment building in an American suburb. There had been many witnesses to the murder. These witnesses were made up of several of the other inhabitants of the apartments in Kitty G.'s building who had windows facing the parking lot. They had stood and watched while the murder was happening before their eyes. Just stood there behind their curtains and stared, quite appalled. But no one moved a muscle to help her. Even to lift a telephone one single time.

And what made the crime exceptionally cruel was that it was very, very drawn out. The man with the knife chased Kitty G. around the parking lot for minutes. She even managed to get away a few times and managed to run a ways away before the man caught up with her again in order to continue stabbing her.

While all of the others watched. The blind followers. Behind their curtains. *But was there nothing you could do about it, afterward?*

Kitty G. Sandra picked her out for her scrapbook. The first material in a long time. She had already stopped collecting new material during Doris Flinkenberg's time.

Partly because she had been occupied with other things, but also because she had come up with other ideas. New ideas.

The Mystery with the American Girl. That had been her task then, to be Eddie de Wire. Walk in her shoes. Dress like her, be her, talk like.

"I'm a strange bird. Are you one too?"

"Nobody knew my rose of the world but me."

"I have a feeling," Doris Flinkenberg had said then, ages ago in Bencku's barn, and she would never forget it, they were words that had already become legendary, "that she is the mystery. That through her all of the unanswered questions will get their answers. We need to get to know her. We have to . . . find out everything we possibly can about her. We have to walk in her moccasins. We have to be her."

She quickly stopped with her mediocre material collection again. The scrapbooks were nothing other than something obsolete, ritualistic, which she had lost touch with. Dead stories.

An interesting document. But about what?

"Long live passion," her teacher at the French School suddenly whispered in her ear.

What would you have done if you were one of Kitty G.'s neighbors in the apartment block who, from the comfort of their own homes, watched as Kitty G. was murdered? That was a question asked aloud during psychology class. Most of Sandra Wärn's helpful classmates were certain they would have called the police immediately, another that he would have gotten the pistol in the drawer of the nightstand (of course all Americans have a pistol in the nightstand drawers, *les américaines*, well, well!) and opened the window and fired into the air in order to frighten him, a third would have killed the murderer, and so on. Many of the reserved and uncertain diplomat children suddenly came alive. They were not any stupid middle-class Americans made passive by all kinds of hamburger culture and a-dime-a-dozen entertainment.

They could separate fact from fiction even when it was a matter of life or death.

But the anxiety could not be eased.

"I suspect that I wouldn't have done anything at all."

That was Sandra.

"Guilt must be borne," the teacher said and naturally had no idea he was saying about the same thing as a certain Micke Friberg had said to Doris Flinkenberg a few weeks before Doris had preferred to blow her head off, but this talking about Raskolnikov and Sonya in *Crime and Punishment*, which he had read (and, yes, he had gladly seen that Doris had been more Sonya-like). "You couldn't run away from it. Of course, it's possible. For a while. But you won't get away. But there is a pardon."

Sandra also did not know Micke Friberg had said that to Doris. But those words touched her anyway in a way that made it so that she just had to stay behind after class when all of the other students had gone home, with him, whom she had asked to stay, and he was a friendly teacher so he did.

"I suspect I wouldn't have done anything."

And made a pause. So that, so to speak, what should have come after remained hanging in the air between them like a great abnormal emptiness.

He looked at her with great sympathy. "I can't live with that thought. I can't live with that guilt. It's a guilt in and of itself, isn't it?" It was something like that, words in that style, which they both had expected she would add.

But consequently she did not. Instead she said, "Not out of cold-bloodedness. But because I'm so slow. So extremely stiff in my joints."

He was staring. On the one hand, she shocked him, repelled, with her coldness and her arrogance. On the other hand. The invitation could not be misinterpreted. And he recognized her, from years back. *La passion, c'est un emmerdent*. Passion is only devilry.

But she got to it first.

She went and bought herself a really warm winter coat, a muff to stick her hands in, and a briefcase of an expensive brand to keep her schoolbooks in, and then, finally, she went to the bookstore and bought a French classic for him in the original, one of those small hardbound volumes that were both elegant and expensive.

In front of the class he had a habit of complaining he was poor, that he earned so little with his teacher's salary he did not even have enough money to buy the French classics in the original, which he loved so much. For example André Gide and François Mauriac. Great writers, who wrote about real things, like guilt, reconciliation, and mercy.

She bought him a novel by François Mauriac, *Vipers' Triangle*. That silenced him.

And then he took her somewhere and then they walked in the city and suddenly they were at a third place and they slept together there.

I'm NOT in love. It's just a crazy phase I'm going through right now.

It became like that. Though neither of them wanted it, not really. Desire, that was another thing.

But they were like Doctor Pavlov's dogs, both of them.

But what was the clock that triggered the drool in the dog's doglike jaws?

Memento mori.

"You fall in love with someone who brings something inside you to life."

Prr. Remember that you are going to die as well.

It was the same teacher she had written a certain essay for a thousand years ago, shortly before the adventure of her life, Doris Flinkenberg, started and she was fearless and audacious enough to leave the French school altogether. Lupe Velez's head in a toilet or Passion's death was the sunny name on the essay and he had eagerly used his red pen in the margins and in between the lines because Sandra was quite horrible when it came to writing proper French.

He had not known if he should laugh or cry, but on the other hand, if there was something he was used to from the French School in particular then it was young, stigmatized, spoiled girls with an exaggerated inner self and a lot of strange fantasies in their small and empty heads.

He was the first one Sandra recognized from before when she returned to the French School. But not immediately because he had recognized her first.

"Long live passion," he had half whispered to her as a first greeting in the middle of the auditorium, in the middle of the school day. And asked politely, with a certain adult and kindly amused glint in his eye:

"To what do I owe this pleasure?" In French of course, above all because it was the only language in which such an indiscreet and ambiguous politeness could be expressed without becoming coarse, so that the humor and innocence were retained.

He, of course, did not know anything about Doris Flinkenberg and later, in some of Sandra's most advanced fantasies, she told him about Doris after one of the two to three sexual encounters they carried out with each other at odd times of the day. Fantasies as said: in the situation itself she always stopped, she never even got started, it was never possible to tell him anything at all. It was shyness and a strange role-playing game the whole time, and neither of them enjoyed the game, which was a part of the game, which naturally stopped being a game before it had even really gotten started.

She remembered Lupe Velez who drowned in the toilet bowl, and in light of everything that had happened, life at the marsh,

Doris Flinkenberg, she could not keep from laughing. It had been so different. She had been such a different person then. The laughter just poured out of her and it surprised her teacher who was expecting another reaction. In some way he had the idea that it was his light irony that would be mild and kindly shocking. He had thought she would become shy. Not this fool. He stood there and became embarrassed. And even though they were just the two of them, it felt as if the entire school's teachers and students and remaining personnel were standing there watching them.

He was one of the teachers at the French School who also commanded respect because they showed their light disdain for the well-mannered and wealthy students—above all the female portion of the student body. Name something that stirs more latent aggression in an ordinary, friendly boy or a highly normal poor man on a single income who is trying to muddle along on only an hourly wage from his teaching job than a spoiled female student with all the outer signs of conventionality: pleated skirt, blouse with lace, briefcase, the right last name, and so on. One who lives on Daddy's money, as it is called.

He had been used to being received as expected by such a conventional and predictable young lady. That she would blush out of indignation when he came with his well-balanced truths and bits torn from real life, which he knew something about but she did not.

The boring thing about those youths who, as it were, take for granted that they are the only ones capable of seeing conventions and thereby break against them, the only ones with surprises at the ready, or just new, other thoughts, is that when you get down to it, when someone makes them speechless, they pull away, back up, as if indignant instead of advancing curiously, nosing about, and taking the invitation.

But the short relationship or whatever it should be called that began shortly after the conversation about Kitty G. and the guilt was like a means of coercion. He did not know what to do with her. She did not leave him alone, neither literally nor above all figuratively speaking, with her strange reactions—that laugh which echoed in the auditorium—and the strange things she said. Sometimes he also had a feeling she was pursuing him.

Yet, she did not "take" him anywhere mentally in other words, barely even physically.

She was the one who took the initiative with everything: the short relationship that consisted of only two brief sexual encounters on the sofa in sole breadwinner's apartment while the kids were with their mother.

Neither of them particularly enjoyed it.

She did not like the apartment imbued with children, the realism in it, which made no room for her fantasies. Obviously he did not think she was impressionable in the right female way since she displayed an almost total disinterest in his children and his role as sole breadwinner and family father as well as all of the everyday hardships, a subject that he had otherwise noticed hit home with women, old and young women alike, and further increased his charm and attraction.

Blah blah blah blah. She put on music, noisy music. He had a good record collection with, for example the Rolling Stones' "Satisfaction" and the like, and that, my God, had to drown him out.

When they were finished on the sofa and the music had played for a while she got up and got dressed and asked if he wanted to go out with her to the shops and provide advice since she was going to buy winter clothes.

"I'm pretty crazy about clothes," she said again with the same arrogance—and it made him crazy!—as when she had spoken about her slowness, the stiffness in her limbs in connection with the murder of Kitty G. She was standing on the glitter scene, acting.

"My mother had a fabric store that was called Little Bombay. Little Bombay in an ordinary suburb! Of course it was a disaster.

The business went bankrupt. She never recovered. She took it very hard. I mean my real mother that is. Not the woman my dad is thinking about marrying NOW."

He understood she was playing a part and my God my God how he regretted seducing her. This girl was deeply unhappy, she was desperate, she needed help.

"You miss her?" he asked, more as a teacher, a fatherly protector than as a half-naked lover who had slept with Lolita on the sofa in his own sole breadwinner's home (among all the toys).

"She grafted a love of clothes and fabric of high quality into me."

Grafted. It was a word worthy of a crossword solver and in the moment she had spoken it she understood from exactly which direction in her head it had flown. From the Doris direction, and now it was dangerous.

She stepped on a child's ball on the floor and it released a shriek that in no way crushed the mood but did stir additional stupidities in her head. She had to get away.

"Come on. Do you want that book or not? But first you have to come along and give advice."

That was it: he asked the right questions. And that was what was wrong. That he was some kind of human. Not even some kind. But she could not stand it. And he could not either; he was too aware of the situation, which was fundamentally wrong. Oh, if only they had started talking about the children and the ball and the loss and how it is not the easiest thing to replace a biological parent, that would have been a normal conversation. And from there they could have moved on to her parents' divorce (because that was what they had done, gotten divorced? Had she not said that? He could not say, he was ashamed to say he had a poor memory of what she had told him) and so on and so forth. But it was not like that, now they were going to the bookstore to buy a book as a present for him, which was called *Thérèse*.

He followed her to the store like a dog. Not because of the book, but because the whole thing needed to be rounded off in some dignified way. As luck would have it they skipped the clothing store. She seemed to forget all of that when they came out into the fresh air and he got started with his story.

They went straight to the bookstore. He hated her. His head was filling with half-formulated discomfort in the presence of her upper-class manners, her arrogance, her depraved childhood in contrast to . . . him. All of that which had been the subject of a thousand million classics but which still had its attractive force.

Ein Mann who wants.

Ein poor *Mann* in the big world.

On the glitter scene: she was an unscrupulous Lolita who pulled the clean young man into the dirt despite the fact that on the outside it looked like just the opposite.

And it would be the "secret" with the story. Yawn. Very exciting.

But in order to have something to talk about while they were walking to the bookstore he told her about the plot in the novel she was going to buy him. It was called *Thérèse* in other words and it was a French classic of the best sort. It was about a woman who tried to poison her nasty husband—and he was nasty, that was also clear beyond a shadow of a doubt. He caught her red-handed and carried out a punishment for her. He left her alone in the estate where they had lived together, in the woods—she hated living in the woods—starving, alone, no one was allowed to speak with her or touch her. When she had made amends, just before she faded away, died, he came back to the estate, held out his hand to her, and took her back to the big city where she always wanted to go, gave her her freedom, which she always wanted, and a reliable income. They went their separate ways at a café in the big city, in a peculiar mood that was characterized by if not direct friendship, then by a new, mutual respect for one another.

"You can't run away from guilt," said the lover. "It must be atoned for.

"Atoning is not talking," he continued. "Atoning is doing. Action."

"But how, Doris?" Sandra asked inside.

A sticky white snow was falling. The wind was cold, almost icy. And such a pain inside her, you could almost touch it.

They had walked past the clothing store and were standing outside the bookstore.

She turned toward him, on the great glitter scene, but now it was private, and fastened her eyes on him and said, "May I ask you something? Why are you telling me all of that ahead of time? If you tell the plot before then there isn't any excitement left. Why should I read it then? Why should I?"

But he did not answer. He ignored her. And then they were inside the bookstore. Just there, when she and everything were at their worst, she had understood that she would not be able to carry out the play or the game or whatever it should be called, to the end.

She was in the process of stopping. And a few minutes later, by the shelf with miserable classics. In the extremely well-sorted bookstore, which happened to be the only one in the big city by the sea at this time, she stopped altogether.

In other words, it would be wrong to say she had grown tired of her role. In reality, it would have been most flattering to say so, for all parties. But the truth was, and it was what she had properly been reminded of on the street when he was walking and carrying on about the plot of that book, that she could not pull it off. She could not play the role until the end. She absolutely loved the role itself. My God, how easy it would have been to walk on the street and through life with her overage lover, play out the whole Lolita role, or what it was now called.

But that is not what she was. She was just a little girl. A small child in the world.

She could not. Her legs turned to jelly on the glitter scene.

Poor poor Sandra.

And in the bookstore, by the French classics, she was suddenly standing and stammering like a child.

"Go away! I don't want to see you anymore!"

And it had not been the slightest bit erotic. Or any game. Just nasty, the awkwardness.

"Stop pursuing me! Stop harassing me!"

It was not a child acting, but a real one. A child with all her faults and shortcomings, with her egoism, her altruism, her lovability, her weakness, and her strength. Her confidence and her vulnerability.

A child whom no normal adult would ever dream of relating erotically to.

And he was no abnormal adult. It was not actually the child in her who had brought something in him to life.

He stood there in the crowd and understood everything. Pushed his way through the people toward the register, away from her. Paid for the book himself and left. Quickly, quickly, away from there. She was left standing by the French classics. And she cried.

A young girl's tears. Big tears rolled silently down her cheeks.

He stopped working as a teacher at the French School. He wrote a letter to her in which he asked her for forgiveness.

Sorry. Sorry. Sorry. Sorry.

She wrote an essay that she thought about giving to him as a farewell present. It was never finished. It was about a game called the American Girl.

It was *La fille américaine*, in French.

But at the same time she wanted to forget all of it instantly. She obliterated it from her memory, everything—

But otherwise it could not be seen on her. Otherwise she carried on like before. Stayed at the French School where she took her final exams the following year.

It was exactly that letter, the sorry-sorry-sorry-sorry letter from her second lover, which she was standing and tearing into small, small pieces at the edge of the pool when the Islander and his young, new wife Kenny returned to the house in the darker part after weeks at sea and a hasty wedding in the Panama Canal.

Inget Herrman's cigarette butts were still floating on the surface of the pool.

Tearing the paper to bits, after having made airplanes out of them.

And Kenny, Dad's new wife, a few days later: pulled in cigarette butts and pieces of paper with the pool rake . . .

In a shapeless clump of all sorts of crap.

"What's this? Love letters?"

And smiled her bright smile, not exactly innocent, but open, bright.

And then you could not say it like it was.

"I wish her all the happiness in the world, she hasn't had an easy time of it," said Inget Herrman, Kenny's sister.

The Islander had during the previous years sat in the rec room and been bored. And while he had been bored he had been thinking. And thinking. While he was thinking something started growing inside his head. It was a boat. Over time he began seeing it more clearly in his head. It was a sailboat. Little by little other details also appeared: length, width, height over the waterline, the like. A sea dog, truly.

And on the stern was its name. The boat was called, not surprisingly, *Freedom*.

Only then did the Islander understand that it was just a day-dream. *Freedom*. Who would want a boat called Freedom? The Islander had enough humor left when it came to himself that he knew to laugh when everything became all too clear.

And the Islander had laughed. "Ho ho ho." Laughed so that the ice clinked in the almost empty mixed drink glass that he stretched toward Inget Herrman or, when Inget was not there, toward his little daughter who finally grew up during these years. She had taken the glass and refilled it.

Handed him the glass again and taken the opportunity to turn down the volume on the stereo system; it sometimes happened that the Islander turned the volume up so loud during lonely moments that it crackled from inside the speakers. He had taken the glass and turned the music up again; he needed it to accompany his dreams. The dreams were, of course, despite the fact that they were for the time being only dreams, rather pleasant to find yourself in, and the music also served the purpose of acting as a solid wall against all the trespassing from the outside. From everything, enough, outside. From Inget Herrman, from everything with the girl, from everything!

Sometimes Sandra sat down there in the rec room with him, in the same extreme inactivity. Sipping at a glass, and she really had not had anything against the music but this happened to be the theme from *Spartacus*, a melody that in the Islander's world was the equivalent of the signature tune of *The Onedin Line*, the only series he watched on television. It was about, surprise surprise, a family of shipowners and an unmarried captain who travels around on the seven seas.

And no, Sandra really had not had the energy to follow along on all of these developments and the music, it was really the b-o-t-t-o-m.

But the Islander had closed his eyes again. Of course. It was still there. The sailboat. "Interesting," he thought, "fascinating." And turned the music up like a wall around it.

During that time the girl had left, gone up the stairs, up to the first floor. Up to her room, to kill time, do her own things. A car had driven up on the drive. Inget Herrman had run up the steps and come in from the rain outside.

"I think I'm going to start sailing again," the Islander had carefully said to Inget Herrman while she poured her first drink.

"Weren't we just on the water?" Inget Herrman asked and had a hard time concealing her irritation, but had still done her best because this was sensitive territory, this she knew.

At sea. The Islander had not favored Inget Herrman with an answer, just muttered something barely audible. "You're a lovely woman, Inget, but . . ." he had said to her once. It was just like that. She was a lovely woman, as wonderful as could be (the Islander had thought in a sudden moment of generosity), but she was not a suitable partner. Not for him anyway.

And so one day he had just been gone. Out on the seven seas again. And when he returned home he had his young, new girl-wife with him. The one who was Inget Herrman's sister: Kenny, born de Wire.

They had met sometime over the summer. On the Aegean Sea. Kenny had had a position as crew on one of the two sailboats that the Islander's little business rented out to people who wanted to travel on private sailboats among the islands. The Islander himself was the captain on one of the boats. To begin with not on the one where Kenny was crew, but on the other.

It was in a harbor. The Islander saved Kenny from drowning. She fell in the sea next to the jetty where the boat she was working on was moored next to the boat the Islander was the captain on, and was seized with panic in the water. She could certainly swim, but not very well, and the Islander, realizing the severity of the situation, jumped in after her and got her up on his boat. This according to legend, as it was told when the newlywed couple came home to the house in the darker part of the woods. The legend was important, would be important, so that there would be something real between the Islander and Kenny.

Without any further ado they had gotten married a few weeks after the event. The Islander sent a message home about everything after the wedding was over, just before the pair returned to the house in the darker part of the woods.

"This is, uh, Kenny," the Islander said, introducing "the young ladies," or whatever they were called, to each other and adding, rather pricelessly, "You might know each other."

"We've seen each other," Kenny said brightly and untroubled. She was sunburned and had long, light hair and white clothes. You, Sandra determined, truly had a desire to be in her company.

It was the charisma that Kenny had always had. Also back then, ages ago, the summers while Doris was still alive and Sandra and she had hung around her sister Inget Herrman in the Women's House while Kenny held court for the sea urchins in the Glass House on the Second Cape.

With Inget Herrman, who would continue to be a "good friend," especially to Sandra, the Islander more or less swore he had not known they were siblings. "Not until it was too late. After all she's . . . It went so quickly. Bam. And I was a captured man. Try and understand, Inget Herrman. You're a lovely woman, Inget Herrman, but . . ."

That was almost the worst, thought Sandra, who was eavesdropping on the telephone line. You're a lovely woman, Inget Herrman, but . . .

"I understand you," Inget Herrman said in a definitely sober tone of voice. "Kenny is special. Kenny is a *man's woman*. Take good care of her. She hasn't had it easy."

And added, after a well-considered and extremely sober pause:

"If I were a man I would definitely fall head over heels for her too. The only thing that surprises me," she had ended with a less sober dyke laugh, in which all of her wounded pride finally appeared, "is what in the whole wide world does she see in you?"

And, by way of conclusion, she hissed:

"And now Sandra is going to hang up immediately!"

The first time Kenny came to the house in the darker part of the woods and carried out an inspection she said "pretty" and "special" about almost everything she saw around her and even though you knew she could not possibly mean it, it sounded like she meant it. She did not dwell fatefully on her words like Lorelei Lindberg had done when she had walked around and stated "interesting" and "fascinating," did not wander restlessly from room to room with a wineglass and a burning cigarette, constantly searching for a place where she could settle in with her books and her papers, the material from her thesis that could benefit from being collected into a meaningful whole, like Inget Herrman.

Kenny was none of that. She was honest and untroubled. Which in and of itself could have depended on the fact that the house in the darker part meant nothing to her, it had nothing to do with her dreams and expectations as it had for Lorelei Lindberg (*"I was going to show you what your dream looked like"*), nor was it a place that she in some way needed to try and conquer from the Islander as it had been for Inget Herrman, which the Islander had always explained because he could not imagine living together with her in the house in the darker part of the woods. The Islander and Kenny were already married of course: that Kenny was going to live there, that it was also her territory now, that was a matter of course.

"Nice, pleasant," Kenny said and it sounded in other words as if she thought so. Maybe she would continue to think so, in the same cool way. Maybe that was how the house should be treated because it was a very calm and in some ways harmonic time, the time that Kenny lived there with the Islander and Sandra Wärn.

After a while they would move to an apartment in the city by the sea anyway. Not give up the house in the darker part of the woods, but certainly leave it, for the winter—which would turn out to be for good, but for different reasons for all three of them. But that would also happen imperceptibly, without any fuss. It would, quite simply, happen. And would have nothing to do with the house in the darker part.

Moreover Kenny was not someone who had a habit of expressing discontent, she was not like that, quite simply. She was truly an agreeable person to be around, Sandra could state that over and over again. Just like her sister, the one Inget Herrman rejected by the Islander, had said.

"If it wasn't Kenny. Then maybe I would . . . I don't know. Claw his eyes out?" She had laughed as if the thought were so absurd, so ridiculous. "No. Never in my life. Kenny is worth all of it. She hasn't had it easy."

It was deserving and generous.

But. But what were you supposed to do with such a bright and uncomplicated person around you?

"I'm going to live here," Kenny said the first time she came into the narrow hallway. "I hope I'm going to enjoy it here."

"I'm not the decorating type," she would also say, a bit apologetically, but not very, that was also not her style. She did not create problems where there were none, in that way she and the Islander were alike—time passed and it was the way it was in the house in the darker part of the woods, with the exception of the basement. "But I like plants. And that pool is horrible."

The Islander looked at Sandra, suddenly exposed, in order to get some support. He was not interested in any revolutions.

Sandra looked away. Suddenly she refused to have any sympathy for him. Any at all. She was so tired of everything, so tired. HE was the one who had gotten them into this, he was the one who had brought Kenny to the house in the darker part of the woods.

· · ·

"They buried her in the pool."

Damn overaged sex addict. She stood there on the other side of the pool's edge over the water where paper, cigarette butts, and other such disgusting items were floating around and thought about the Islander with Doris's words inside her. Suddenly so invisibly upset (not angry, especially not at Kenny, it was not actually Kenny's fault) that she forgot the hickeys on her own throat, forgot altogether to conceal herself.

"What a mud puddle." Kenny laughed happily and turned to Sandra. "Do you grow water lilies?"

The Islander left the two of them alone. She did not know what she was going to say. She just continued to be embarrassed and blush and finally she had to leave rather abruptly because there really was nothing else to say. The Islander was taking a long time. On purpose of course. He was an expert at disappearing during precarious situations and he rationalized this in the style that the young women, of almost the same age, needed to work things out once and for all. From the beginning. But maybe Kenny had even suggested it to the Islander before they arrived at the house just in time to see Inget Herrman standing in the rain among her bags, waiting for a taxi that she had naturally ordered a long time ago but that, of course, was taking so long that the humiliation became complete for her and all three of them had to stand there in the rain and talk to each other.

She was a "man's woman."

Kenny swept past Sandra on the stairs and said softly to her so that the Islander would not hear:

"And what have you been up to? Kissing disease. Here. Take this."

And she had taken off her scarf and held it out to Sandra who had not taken it but had taken the hint well.

The band of dark hickeys on her throat. She had forgotten about it then. Even on the morning before the Islander and Kenny arrived the sight of the marks alone had evoked a sensual pull in her stomach.

Nymphomaniac.

And it did not exactly get any better because of it either. That she thought Kenny was okay. So damned okay.

"Thanks," she replied. "For the reminder."

"Don't play with fire, Sandra," Inget Herrman had said about the same marks on Sandra's neck, the evening before, the last evening with Inget Herrman in the house in the darker part. "I ALSO mean to clarify it, that I would like to encourage you not to start acting like a psychopathological case study. You're playing with things you don't believe in, which aren't you. But suddenly they are you."

"Don't get any of it," Sandra replied nonchalantly.

Inget Herrman had impatiently thrown one of her countless half-smoked cigarettes into the pool and taken a deep gulp from her champagne glass and then tried to fix Sandra in a stare with a spine-chilling look. This, she had actually, despite the fact that she already had quite a bit to drink, partly succeeded in.

"Don't forget that if you do something long enough then you become it. Your hickeys and bruises—small fetishes that evoke feeling in you. Something that is reminiscent of lust. You want to feel alive. Life. Certainly there are a lot of people who would be tickled at being able to have a closer look at your so-called double life. It's something one would gladly like to write about. Read about. Preferably make a movie about. Without many drawn-out naked scenes out of that other life."

The girl in the blouse with lace and the pleated skirt and briefcase who is completely naked underneath. "My God." Inget Herrman sighed and lit a new cigarette. "You ARE a walking and standing dime-a-dozen sexual fantasy. You don't need to pretend at that at all."

"But the question is," Inget Herrman had finally said, "if it has anything at all to do with that which burns. The question is if everything isn't . . . the entire arrangement isn't just a camouflage in order to conceal something else."

And then they swam in the pool, she and Inget Herrman, together for the last time in the house in the darker part of the woods.

In the water that was also slowly, slowly trickling out in cracks, down in the earth beneath. Or was it a dream? Swimming among the cigarette butts. Rather disgusting, is it not?

"He shot her. By mistake. She died. In the pool. They buried her there. Under the tiles."

Sandra. She had liked the marks on her body. These marks on her neck had actually evoked a feeling in her stomach. Up until now. Kenny's eyes on them got her, more than Inget Herrman's words ever could, to understand that they were silly, childish, and laughable.

Kissing disease. Kenny's wide smile.

"A way of being with yourself."

Sorry. Sorry. Sorry. Sorry.

In the pool now.

And Kenny, "Do you grow water lilies?"

"If you think I'm going to clean up after you then you're wrong," Inget Herrman had said the morning before she left. "I'm not planning on cleaning up after you.

"Then we'll have to warm the sauna and wash off the old life," she had suggested the night before when it was clear that the Islander and Kenny would be coming home as newlyweds, together. It had been the last time with Inget Herrman in the house in the darker part of the woods.

"And discharge me," Inget Herrman had added, and then they had opened a bunch of champagne bottles and cheers, cheers.

The sauna had become warm and they had bathed. Washed themselves, dipped in the pool, drunk some more. Inget Herrman had sat on the edge of the pool and held expositions, which she had a very special predilection of devoting herself to when she was drunk.

About the weight of purposefulness and planning. Not just as a student, but otherwise. In life. "In life, perceived as a whole," she was always saying.

"Life perceived as a whole," Inget Herrman stated, "is rather short. It's wise to live consciously, as Thoreau says, and with concrete goals in front of you. How did that poem by Nils Ferlin go? 'Think now—before we push you away / You barefoot child in life.'" Inget Herrman lit a cigarette and continued. "The essence of that poem as I see it is that you're given a certain amount of opportunities and chances, but not an infinite amount. If you don't take care of your opportunities then there isn't anyone who comes and gives out new ones. And furthermore. Finally all of us are alone. There isn't anyone who gives us anything. We need to be prepared for that. To become an adult is to understand this. A cursed damned enormous loneliness."

And, after a pause, with an entirely different voice, a tormented one, like a small animal's:

"I don't know if I've grown up. I don't know anything."

And Inget Herrman had burst into tears. She sobbed, with her mouth open, without covering her face with her hands, for a minute maybe and it had been unpleasant to see, but at the same time, a wave of tenderness had welled up inside Sandra and she cursed the Islander and his awkwardness, to exchange this for . . . yes, for a sister besides. "Kenny is a man's woman," Inget had said. "It's not her fault, and she deserves all the happiness in the world, she hasn't had it easy. Someone he could go around and introduce, virile in the prime of life himself, as 'my young, beautiful wife.'"

And for a moment, exactly then—or had it just been the intoxication that had made Sandra think like that? She did not know, but one thing was certain: she would never be closer to complete surrender, to telling everything, as in just this moment, which was so tormented but yet suddenly so open, filled with possibility—the fantastic had traveled through her. What if . . . what if she were to tell Inget Herrman everything? From beginning to end? Without leaving anything out. Everything, honest, direct, and without detours.

Like a confession.

"Guilt is an action," the lover had said. He had bitten her neck blue during the second—and last—intercourse a few days ago.

"It cannot be evaded. But sometimes there is . . . mercy."

It had been a colossal feeling, a relief, freedom, conviction. But a second that was gone just as quickly as it had come. Inget Herrman had stopped crying. Stopped just like that. Laughed, lit a new cigarette, filled her glass, and acted like nothing. Nothing nothing.

And later, very quickly, she drifted off into further thoughts, into her endless monologues. Farther into words into words into words.

Her name was Lassie (Marsh-Lassie). A strange scene. There, at the pool's edge, in a wet bathing suit. She, wrapped in a terry cloth towel, with the dog Lassie on it.

An entirely different dog from the silk dog, the one who had existed earlier.

Later, in the final part of Sandra's life inside these borders, this doggishness would render her one last humiliating nickname.

Wrong kind of dog.

But still. Inget Herrman on her back in a wet bathing suit with a cigarette, the eternal cigarette, like a dead person, so drunk, so gone. Furthermore it was rather cold in the pool section and you could, for example, easily get cystitis if you did not take off your wet bathing suit after swimming, Inget Herrman did not seem to even be thinking about that.

The moment was over.

Inget Herrman had fallen asleep.

But she had been on her feet again the next morning.

And it was Sandra of course, not Inget Herrman, who caught a cold again and was forced to see the doctor and was prescribed a sulfur treatment against acute cystitis.

"Finally," Inget Herrman had said, "we're quite helpless."

And they never swam in the pool again.

The pool filled with slime, until Kenny had it emptied and furnished her subtropical winter garden in it.

Sandra was sleeping in the marital bed. She was sleeping alone, under the sky, the white, tulle-covered one (a mosquito net, newly obtained), between the light red sheets. Kenny did not want the bed. Kenny had laughed when she saw it.

In front of Kenny's eyes.

"Sandra!" Kenny called. "Time to wake up. Are you still sleeping?"

Not reproachful exactly, but still. Sandra pressed her nose deeper, deeper into the soft cushion. She was frozen, quiet, pretending to sleep even though she was awake.

"A dreamer in an alert state," "the aunt" on Åland had said. "That's what you are. Just like the other islanders."

"Up and at 'em now," said Kenny. "I need help."

And it was with this that Kenny needed help: she had emptied the swimming pool, cleaned it on her own. With Sandra's help she polished the tiles and admired the result. Later she bought many expensive plants, some tropical, unusual species. It was not for nothing that she had lived together with the baroness in the Glass House (which after the baroness's death was rented out under the care of the baroness's relatives, Kenny said that she had nothing more to do with it). She planted flowers in large, beautiful pots.

They were plants that needed a lot of light. She carried the pots down into the pool, rigged up lines with searchlights along the edges, a pearl necklace of strong lights that made the rectangular pool glow.

When the plants bloomed, which they did in due order—there was never a flower that did not bloom down there, bloomed audaciously and big and strong in different colors, obscene and white, very yellow and with large stamens—she carried down a small garden furniture set: a small table and three old-fashioned chairs with ornamental backs and slender legs.

"Here it is now," she said. "Our subtropical underwater garden."

It looked insane, but it was undeniably beautiful.

"It's not underwater at all," Sandra objected.

But Kenny was not listening. She had her eyes on her husband.

"Phenomenal," he said. "Great." With a new voice, one that came from somewhere in between passion and artificiality and nostalgia (the attempt at catching an old tone of voice and reproducing it with credibility). It was a voice that had come into being after Kenny. A voice expressly for Kenny. It related to the voice that the Islander once used with Lorelei Lindberg like really nice polyester fabric compared to clean silk. Just the experts, the very clever, can tell the genuine from the fake.

To Sandra he said:

"It will be fine." But he also had a new voice for her. A strange papa-voice.

Which made him like a stranger.

"Should we go out and shoot?" That time was over. The dad lay his hand on his daughter's shoulder and they stood there at the edge of the pool while Kenny filled it with plants so it looked like some kind of specially designed grave.

Sandra thought: I want to go away.

"The miserable garden," Kenny would say to Rita later in the big, bright apartment in the city by the sea that Sandra and Kenny lived in shortly before Sandra left the picture, went on her way.

"I think it was some kind of sublimation," Kenny continued, and Sandra was on the other side of the wall listening, eavesdropping. "I so wanted to have children."

The flowers would gradually wither in the pool. The light would not be enough, despite everything. No light in the world could brighten up the pool section, and yet it was the brightest place in the entire house in the darker part.

"I'm like a cow," she would say to Rita Rat in the city by the sea. "A barren cow."

Kenny so bright, so lovable.

Rita over the rooftops. She had come walking over the rooftops, knocked on the window in the apartment. Personally she lived in the Backmanssons' apartment on the same block, so the roofs between the two buildings were connected, she had worked that out. And she had looked at Kenny as though it was the most natural thing in the world that she showed up just like this, via the roof, and then she explained that walking over the rooftops was something that she just had to try.

Sure enough. Kenny was enchanted by it. Like all pretty, lovable women Kenny had a streak inside where she saw herself as if in a movie in several immortal scenes. How Rita came to her and they became best friends: this was one of them.

How one day Rita could suddenly be heard like a voice through the open window in the apartment, Sandra and Kenny. Rita from the District. They had looked out and there she was, swinging on the roof of the building next door, and she called out, "Come!" Kenny had of course immediately responded to the call. Just as naturally, Sandra made a face and stayed indoors.

And then Kenny and Rita continued to be enchanted by each other up on the roof. Two of them under a chimney, and the city below. What a scene, what a story. A story that received wings, and it flew. And Rita and Kenny shone, which they did otherwise as well. In each other's company, glittering.

Rita had succeeded. She made no secret of the fact that it should be seen just that way. She lived with the Backmanssons in the wonderful room, Jan Backmansson's sister's (the one who was studying dance in New York) former room, and Jan Backmansson was her boyfriend.

You did not connect her with the District, the nickname Rat had disappeared. There was, so to speak, nothing in her creature that alluded to it. She was tall and handsome and in all ways, yes, you had to admit it, one of those young women whom you rarely saw even on the streets of the city by the sea.

Sandra, on the other hand, she did not forget.

For example Solveig, Solveig who had stood there in the darkness with the crazy cousin's mama at Bencku's barn then not such a long time ago, taken long drags on the cigarette and been very upset.

"The last thing she did was steal my jacket and wreck my car. Drove it into junk metal on Torpeson's field. She left it there and hitchhiked to the city. Forced herself on the Backmanssons. In the middle of the night."

Rita, however, did not make her former life in the District a secret, all of that. It was so to speak not pertinent anymore. And when she saw Sandra the first time, she certainly looked at her with something that could be likened to triumph, however furtive. Now I'm here. But that was also mixed with a kind of calm indifference in the presence of everything that had been. Because it did not matter, everything with her and in her seemed to say. It is so different now.

And Sandra remembered Solveig who had puffed with such a nosiness and smoldering indignation that it surrounded her like a veil that you could almost cut through.

"She's half," Solveig had said. "We're twins. And then you're whole only when you are two."

But Sandra, when she came to the city by the sea later, she became defenseless. Without skin. But there was no one who was interested in her skinlessness. She lived with Dad and his new wife in a house in the older part of the city by the sea. Dad's new wife was, as said, Kenny.

She was the one who had picked out the apartment. An exquisite one with many rooms. Rooms rooms rooms and high ceilings, windows facing every direction. Toward the sea, up in the sky, toward the back gardens. But little Sandra. She could not find herself there.

She stamped her way forward on the sidewalk, in heavy hiking boots, stubbornly and without a goal.

She detested the city by the sea. It was not big and it was not small, there was exactly one boulevard in it and a few avenues and a whole lot of people who walked around in shabby clothes, leering at each other.

Sandra went home. She did not want to go home. But there was nowhere else to go.

She came into the apartment, went to her room and closed the door. LOCKED it after her. Still the voices from the next room could be heard.

"Mascot." They giggled. "The wrong kind of dog."

And they whispered about her.

Was there one or more? Or was it just her?

Rita Rat, here again. Over the roof. And the worst thing about that story was it was true.

It was Kenny and it was Rita, now Kenny's best friend, in a big, bright apartment in the city by the sea. And it was Sandra, the wrong kind of dog. The Islander, her father, had set out to sea. Again. Only about a year after the new marriage had begun. "Maybe he couldn't stand coming face-to-face with mortality." That was Inget Herrman's analysis, Inget, whom Sandra visited quite often in her small studio apartment on the outskirts of the city. There were long afternoons when they drank wine, red earth-colored such that glowed warmly and filled with promise when the sunlight reflected in the glasses. It was beautiful, the only thing beautiful in the city by the sea during this time. "That tends to be one of the negative effects of an intimate relationship between an older man and a younger woman," Inget Herrman continued. "You rarely talk about those kinds of negative effects, especially not when it's a question of an older man and a younger woman."

And Inget Herrman took a deep breath and laughed her distinctive, rattling laugh that Sandra and Doris had once fallen in love with so much that they had spent days trying to imitate it, but without success. Though it was like that with people you liked, you do not remember what they looked like, and the same goes for voices, Sandra and Doris had been able to determine a long time ago. "And a woman like Kenny, that's even worse. There are only four years between us but she has an ability to make me feel dejected and slightly demented. Like an older person who can get into a bad mood because of her own slowness and sudden difficulties in managing to do even the very simplest of everyday functions. We're all going to die. But it really isn't fun to be made aware of it. Remember I'm saying this with good intentions. The young woman we're talking about is my sister."

"Or breed it's called," someone on the other side of the wall in the big, bright apartment continued. And raised her voice, so Sandra would hear. Yes, it was Rita, Rita Rat. She had an exceptional ability to carry on like that.

"And, can we ask ourselves, which breed?"

Kenny laughed, but happily. Rita was coarser. Kenny was not coarse. She could not be, she was so bright, so excellent, so lovable.

Little Sandra. Poor Sandra. Poor poor Sandra. Her mouth so dry besides. Wetting her lips with her own wet tongue. Let the tip of her tongue get stuck in the top lip's imagined furrow. And it was deep.

The process by means of which Sandra was transformed into a mute and a harelip had started again.

It must immediately be said that this and what followed, a description of Sandra's last time in the city by the sea before she left, originated in an extreme subjectivity.

Sandra's *own* perspective.

Because there were no others. The world diminished.

It is in other words possible that Kenny and Rita were talking about entirely different things. That Sandra just imagined all of that on the other side of the door. In reality it was highly likely. They probably had more interesting things to spend their time on in conversation than on Sandra, who only in her own grandiose fantasies was the interesting center of everything (negative or positive, the harelip's contemplation of her navel, so it had started again). For example, when Kenny said something friendly to Sandra, asked Sandra if she wanted to come along somewhere (and she actually asked sometimes, in the apartment in the city by the sea, in the beginning anyway), Sandra had the ability to discern undertones and dissonance in what was said.

Says one thing but means another.

"It's important to her to be everyone's friend," said Inget Herrman. "Maybe she is. I don't know. If you only knew how little I know about my sisters. Should I tell you about Eddie?"

"You HAVE told me about Eddie," said Sandra who had left all of that behind.

"Yes. But not everything. Not anything at all about how little I understood her. I think she was capable of almost anything. Even murder."

And you're saying that now, thought Sandra. But she did not say anything. She finished her wine and reached for the bottle on the desk between them in order to refill it. She drank. Inget Herrman drank.

Both of them were quiet for a while and changed conversation topics. The sun sank behind the rooftops, it became dark, and when the wine was gone it was evening, early evening, unpleasantly early. Inget Herrman was going somewhere, meeting someone, and she started getting ready. Sandra, on the other hand, what would she do on such a night like this when it was too early to go to bed and impossible due to the wine in her body to do anything else? The mere thought of going home—yes, it was unthinkable.

It was in a mood like that, in such a state, that she headed out on the prowl for the first time.

"Eddie," said Inget Herrman. "We don't know what happened. But we have good reason to believe that it happened exactly the way people thought. Personally I don't doubt for a second Eddie was in a position to drive the people close to her insane. That boy, Björn, for example. Or Bengt. Poor little Bengt.

"And I said that to Doris as well," Inget Herrman continued, "the last time we met. It was in the house in the darker part, incidentally. She was there when I came. And cleaning she said. But she was very upset, completely beside herself, poor thing. If only I had understood . . . But you know what she was like . . . you couldn't believe, think.

"Because she seemed so desperate about everything I told Doris she should stop thinking about the American girl, all of that. That it was over and forgotten now. Life had to go on. I actually said so too.

"Doris"—and Inget Herrman's voice caught in her throat—"she . . . yes. And that cleaning. I wondered about that also. Its effectiveness, I mean. Because it was certainly nice and clean everywhere in the house but when I came down to the basement after our short walk together I saw someone had dragged out a pair of big, muddy hiking boots in the pool section. They stood there a bit fateful at the edge of the pool. And of course I understood it was a joke. They were her boots. You know which ones I mean. No one had boots like her. So later, I took and cleaned them up."

And Sandra, on the street, on her way to the underground disco Alibi, thought about her, the American girl. How she was, so to speak, surrounded by her now, for real. Her sisters. And she should have gotten to know her better, gotten to know much more about her.

But now when that was not the case. You could say something about a person using her family as a reference point. But the person herself still remained something else, what she was—or had been. *The American girl.*

Walk in her moccasins. That is the only way.

"Sometimes I wonder, Sandra," Inget Herrman had finally said, "what were you really up to? You two, you and Doris, when you were together?"

The shoes at the edge of the pool.

I see, it was like that.

Your last message, Doris. Thanks for that.

But so: a not unimportant part of the short time she was living in the apartment in the city by the sea she spent deciphering and decoding all of the messages the surroundings gave her. Above all Kenny's and Rita's messages, since they were almost always close by.

Though Rita did not need to be decoded. She was unusually, shockingly direct. Sometimes, though, it was not unpleasant, it was a relief. You knew who she was (a bitch). You knew where you had her. You knew what you could expect from her (nothing, nothing, nothing).

But otherwise. If Kenny said yes, Sandra was convinced that she meant no. Little by little everything Kenny said had secondary meanings. Also, maybe particularly, when she was at her nicest.

"She's hopeless," Kenny sighed in Rita's company on the other side of the wall. "There's no life in her. She's like a dead person."

"She's obsessed," Rita stated, "with herself. With that little split-lip pathetic face that she can see in the mirror when she looks in it, which she is occupied with at all times of day."

"What split lip?"

"A little harelipped girl. Haven't you heard?"

"No, tell me."

From The Return of the Marsh Queen, Chapter 1. Where did the music start?

A: . . . the Marsh Queen and I: then we went out into the world in order to earn money. We stripped in Tokyo, in Yokohama and in Alaska. It was there, in Alaska, we started becoming a little desperate anyway. A pitch-black New Year's Eve in a caravan, beyond everything. Would nothing ever become of our plans, our music? So we sat down and focused. And then made our New Year's resolutions. I wrote in my notebook for the month of August that same new year: Wembley Arena. It didn't come true. But almost.

A significant portion of the remaining months in the city by the sea, before Sandra disappeared, she devoted herself to wandering around in the city and selling herself. She was invited to many small, small rooms where young students of the male sex from the whole country lived. She met these boys at the disco in the basement of one of the biggest student boarding schools in the city center of the city by the sea. Only it cannot be called by its real name, the real one is too descriptive; the place was called Alibi.

Sex. She got herpes and scabies and an insight into a new shade of loneliness. She could not take it anymore. Either with the boys or the loneliness. She could not take it anymore with the student hovels that smelled of loneliness and unwashed clothes, or just overgrown boys, uncertainty, and bad sex. Most of the boys had too much to drink and/or came from small hovels where sexuality was something shameful and vulgar in a way that Sandra did not understand even if she was the last to maintain that sex was something beautiful and natural—it was not at all, not at all. She used sex to evoke something in herself—and was it even sex, in that case?

She could not take it anymore, but that was, so to speak, the whole point. Maybe she met something of herself in those rooms. Something worse than shame and promiscuity.

And even if it was good—it was in any case NORMAL— then it was in no way comforting. She suddenly realized just that, without Doris-in-her she could not live. It was like cutting something vital off of herself (could she say that? "There isn't any life in her," of course, "she's like a dead person").

It was not possible. She had to live with Doris. There was no other way.

When she could not stand the students any longer she changed location. HUNTING GROUNDS, which some idiot would say (Pinky?). She started dressing more conspicuously, doing her makeup in such a way that for the initiated it left no room for misinterpretations of what she was after. She wanted to be "the initiated." She was looking for "the initiated."

It was a game in a way.

She visited hotel bars and certain cafés at strategically chosen times. There were many hotels, but particularly one whose name also cannot be given, it is so significant, it was called President. For example at lunchtime, which as a jet-setter had been called cocktail hour (she had no idea if it had been called that, but she noticed it amused certain men—and these were men, the real thing, not overgrown bullies and that she was grateful for—when she sat and said stupid things about Mom and Dad and herself in Central European ski resorts in the interesting jet-setter lifestyle and how difficult it was to adjust to a normal day in a different place after that. After such a life).

Sometimes she accompanied them to hotel rooms, sometimes just to the restroom, sometimes to cars parked in garages under the city's tall buildings, sometimes she said no right when it started burning. Sometimes she pretended to become morally indignant.

"But why are you sitting here then?"

"I'm waiting for Dad," she whined.

Sometimes she said something long and incomprehensible in French.

She put the money she earned in an envelope she kept in the lining of her backpack (the only real one, which she still carried with her). Just about the most obvious hiding place there is, and sure enough, when one day just before she left the big apartment in the city by the sea the money was gone she was not at all surprised.

At first she saved the money in other words.

Not for anything in particular. Just saved it.

She had everything you could have.

And she had also started classes at the university. She enrolled in a degree program in a department that had been easy to get into. She had participated in the admissions interview but had not needed to do much more than answer a few questions competently and in detail. Competently, in that way, it was not an art form. It was just a matter of reading—or making up.

Inget Herrman might have wrung her hands in despair if she had known how poorly Sandra's studies were going. It happened that Sandra remembered: Inget Herrman at the edge of the pool in the house in the darker part, those days when the Islander was gone and no one really knew what he was doing. But soon they would find out. He would come home. Newly married.

With Inget Herrman's sister, Kenny.

"I can't be your mother," Inget Herrman had said. "But look at me like a kind of a godmother. Your guardian angel."

Inget who lectured to her about the importance of planning and purposefulness, the importance of having thoughts concentrated on the task at hand and nothing else, the importance of having goals, intermediate goals as well as big ones, overarching, neatly written down on a piece of paper or in a notebook.

"Time doesn't wait for you," Inget Herrman had continued, later, in her workroom in the city, at the beginning of the fall. She had lit a cigarette and raised her glass with the sparkling earth-red wine inside. "Cheers, Sandra. That's the way it is. There are small and decisive moments. Before you know it you've experienced them. They're gone before you know it. If you don't hold on to them. That's the way it is, Sandra. Before you know it . . . You shouldn't waste your time."

And Inget Herrman had passed out on her bed, a mattress in a corner of the room in the small apartment which lay on the outskirts of the city. Though by then it was quite late in the fall.

Women in a state of emergency. It had started so differently. Early in the fall, she had sought out Inget Herrman in her workroom and Inget Herrman offered her a job, she had been filled with determination, plans, and energy. ("Otherwise I'm training for a marathon. It's a difficult and intensive program.")

"I'm going to write my thesis," Inget Herrman had informed her at the end of the summer already when it had become clear that Sandra and Kenny would move, and the Islander also, but Inget Herrman had not exactly wrinkled her nose when it came to light just as quickly that the Islander would be heading out on the seven seas again.

Inget Herrman thought it was good Sandra was going to move to the city by the sea where she had her combined living quarters and work den because then Sandra would be close at hand.

"I'm offering you a job in other words. Before I deal with my doctoral thesis I have to write my licentiate thesis but above all I have to finish my master's thesis. I have a lot of material. I need help sorting it.

"I'm giving you an offer that won't take your breath away.

"But what I can offer in return," Inget Herrman continued generously, "is good company."

Inget Herrman's material. That was a lot of paper. You had no reason to be disappointed on that point.

Everything from neatly written archive cards, big and small, small notes with more or less legible handwriting that Sandra learned to recognize and even decipher, notes on napkins, on advertisements, on the backs of envelopes. "You can get an idea wherever and whenever," Inget Herrman explained.

It was decided that Sandra would work at Inget Herrman's three days a week in the morning, when Inget Herrman had "the day's first shift" at the library.

This first shift lasted from nine thirty when the library opened until twelve thirty, whereafter Inget Herrman had a short break for lunch before it was time for the second shift of the day.

Inget Herrman often came home at the beginning of the second shift or at the end or even in the middle of the first shift. In any case, while Sandra was still there, and she often had one or more bottles of heavy red wine with her, which they chugged while they talked. And talked.

It was almost always Inget Herrman who was talking.

But it was different from that other talk, the tittle-tattle in the apartment, the big, bright one, the voices from outside and inside your head that threatened to slit open your lip so that it could be seen, it was not a game—if the world was a divide then the world was a divide but you could not be in that divide if you did not want to be obliterated and die.

And Sandra did not want to be obliterated and die.

Doris-in-her, who should have been a friend and an ally, just laughed and asked strange things.

. . .

Inget Herrman's talk, a talk you could find yourself in. The afternoons in Inget Herrman's research lair. A bright memory. Inget Herrman who raised her red-wine glass so that all of the afternoon's clear sunrays that seeped in through the window gathered in the glass and reflected in glitter, glitter.

Cheers. Endurance.

And what they talked about. All sorts. Nothing. About Kenny and the Islander and their crumbling marriage. Not much, but a little.

And Inget Herrman's life, which in the beginning sounded so exciting and eventful, with the marathon training and the thesis and the film criticism and the essay book and all the rest.

They talked about "old times." And the Women and the house on the First Cape.

"What are they doing now?" Sandra asked and thought about the women in the house on the First Cape, *Eldrid's Spiritual Sojourn*.

"Planning the first menstruation rituals. For their daughters.

"Well, joking aside. Managing to get along somehow. Trying to finish their studies.

"And well," said Inget Herrman because it really was not true. "There are those who are DOING something." Laura B-H, who recently finished and had success with her big romance novel that was set over four centuries and on sixteen continents. Or Anneka Munveg, who could still be seen on television. That is to say if you had the energy to turn it on.

Have the energy to turn it on.

But Inget Herrman, she did not have a television. "There are far too many good books to read," she also had a habit of saying. But all the more hesitating.

"I don't know," Inget Herrman said and just looked more tired and the book fell out of her hand and it was as if Inget Herrman, during a brief moment, actually saw her own narcissistic pettiness in contrast to the big worlds, ideas, and perspectives. All of the real. Everything that had been.

Eldrid's Spiritual Sojourn.

The travels, revolutionary in the world and the senses, not necessarily geographical, but in space and time.

Because that was what it was about, in the end: not about how you did or did not want to march in line, rather how you wanted to believe in a change.

"I don't know," said Inget Herrman.

During this time Inget Herrman was still a "highly attractive woman," as the Islander also had a habit of characterizing her, next to "lovely" and all of that.

Sometimes she pretended to stop drinking. Put on her outdoor clothes at the same time as Sandra and said she needed to take a walk in the fresh air before she started the evening shift. Any idiot could see on her that she was on her way to the bar. And sometimes she did not even bother trying to hide it.

"And in certain states I drink. I DRINK."

They also talked, in the vaguest terms, about Sandra's future. Inget Herrman continued to give Sandra good advice. In her usual, general terms. *And there wasn't anything wrong with that advice, Inget, there was something wrong with me.*

Purposeful, according to plan.

But that was before Sandra, among Inget's things when Inget was not there, made the discovery of a certain letter. Doris's last letter.

Which Inget had not even opened. It was just lying there, forgotten, among yet another bag of collected material for Inget Herrman's thesis.

Dear Inget,
When you read this I will have shot a bullet through my head . . .

She, Inget, had not even opened it. It was Sandra who did, in the end. Alone in Inget Herrman's work den. And then she fled.

But when she regretted it a few weeks later and tried to get in touch with Inget Herrman again, find her, in order to tell her everything, it was too late.

Inget Herrman was not in her work den. In the beginning Inget Herrman could not be found at all.

So later when Sandra, one of the very last days before she took her belongings and got on the ferry to Germany, would look for Inget Herrman in her apartment there was a person who opened the door whom she had never seen before. One of those boys, a youth, whom she recognized anyway, in some way. He was one of those boys she had a habit of, as it was called, picking up at the disco she sometimes visited, it was underground and was called, in real life, Alibi.

Inget Herrman did not live there, he said. He also could not say where she was either. No idea.

He had rented the apartment via an ad on the university's bulletin board. He came from another city and was mostly happy about having come across an apartment so easily.

She, Sandra, had been left standing on the landing. Then, suddenly, in some way for her unexpectedly also (she actually did not know why she said it), it had slipped out of her:

"Can I come in anyway?"

With a tone of voice that left no room for any doubt.

For a moment he had a questioning look, then with permitted disgust so to speak—she suddenly remembered Pinky, a long time ago, one morning in the kitchen in the house in the darker part, "never become one of those whores, they just despise you in the long run"—mumbled, very quickly:

"We aren't buying any." And pulled the door shut with a slam that had gotten the narrow, dark stairwell to whirl.

A few minutes afterward.

Sandra had sat down there, namely, confused, without any orientation points whatsoever.

Then she had gotten herself together and carried on.

Snob. She strolled down the steps and out onto the street.

She would run into the same boy a few more times. One more time at the underground disco Alibi, which she went to exactly one more time before she disappeared, just a few days before: not well, you could think, to say good-bye?

She would stand at the bar and suddenly feel arms around her, octopuslike everywhere, breath stinking of beer in her ear. She turned around quickly and did not recognize him at first. He would slur about some girlfriend who had come to visit that time in the apartment. But now, he would say and take hold of her again, and she would have to tear herself free and try to escape to the restroom but he would also be waiting for her there outside. For a while she would think it would be impossible to get rid of him. He would not be "nice" either. He would be aroused and wild as if he knew WHAT he was dealing with.

An erhm. Like Bombshell Pinky Pink.

Also later, at the university, she would run into him. So many times those last days when she was still there in the city by the sea, she would start wondering if he was real or some kind of crazy mentally disturbed hallucination in line with the one the French movie star Catherine Deneuve experienced in the movie *Repulsion*, which depicted a young and unusually beautiful woman's gradual sinking into insanity.

(But if he wasn't a hallucination, what was he then? An omen? Doris-in-Sandra was having fun, or was she? Sometimes Sandra could no longer tell Doris-in-her's laugh from Doris-in-her's crying. They were so alike.)

She had seen the movie *Repulsion* in Rita's and Kenny's company a few weeks earlier, at the Film Archive. Rita and Kenny liked the kind of movies where tall, picture-perfect women who were similar to them became crazy or showed their emotions intensely in various subtle ways—for the most part that they needed to start tearing off their clothes during the main scenes was a part of the description of the illness or the intensity of the range of emotions.

Sandra remembered Inget Herrman again: "Kenny hasn't had any childhood. She has so much to make up for."

Though most of all they loved going to the Film Archive, where everyone who was anyone in their circles, who counted, would go back then. And Sandra, Sandra tagged along. Sometimes it was actually like that. She did not want to. But she had nothing else to do, the loneliness became too great. She tagged along.

But the youth. The insecure, shy, skinny, unpleasant student. Sometimes she thought he was following her; it was possible of course, but she would never get clarity in the situation while she was still there. If they met, for example at the university, she would look past him, pretend not to see him. The strange thing was he would do the same. He would definitely not give any hints that it was him, the same person who had chased after her in an intoxicated state on the city's streets the same night she had tried to shake him off in the underground disco Alibi.

But he would be there. Everywhere.

Maybe she was crazy. Not in the Catherine Deneuve way.

But in her very own, invisible, unsubtle way.

The harelip way, Doris-in-her filled in.

Yes, yes, Sandra surrendered. And then, when you have surrendered, it was just a matter of carrying on.

Then it became as she said. The harelip is here again. But completely without power or energy. Just crazy. Shut up in her own craziness.

For example that time, the very last time she met Inget Herrman before she left (when she had already given up all hope of meeting Inget Herrman again: Kenny maintained she was wandering around on the streets in a bad state, she had friends who had seen Inget Herrman, and Kenny said troubled, that she so wished she could do something for her. But nothing became of that either. To do or not to do. You could do nothing for someone you could not find), then it might as well have been a part of Sandra's inner landscape that was in the process of drifting away without any foundation, without reason, Sandra realized that herself. But that it was real made the whole thing even more confusing and crazy.

IS it like this, has everything tilted? For real, in reality, she would have liked to have asked someone, but there was no one to talk to now when also Inget Herrman was sitting there in the stairwell in the university's other main building, bleating. And it was Inget Herrman she had turned to then, earlier. Inget Herrman who had said to her, "See me as a bit of a mother. I can help. Try . . . provide protection."

She had looked at Sandra as she usually did when she meant what she said. Sandra had not doubted. Not then. Not later.

It was just that—looking it in the eye—she did not need a mother right now. It was quite simply a letter she needed to show. A letter to you. Doris's last letter.

"I took it from you. I was going to give it to you. But. Here it is now."

But it was not like that, not such a loaded meeting. These weeks when she tried to find Inget Herrman, without success, but just seemed to end up in the arms of overgrown boys all the time, she had reconciled with the idea of telling everything. About the game, the games.

But what would Doris have said if she had known about the letter, that it was unopened? She had to show it to Inget Herrman, talk about it. She had to. Was it not all a bit ironic?

And the height of irony. Because suddenly, one day, Inget Herrman had been there.

On the stairs. It was in other words a staircase, another staircase, an ordinary one, but one of the very longest in the university's new main building. It was a staircase that went around,

around through the building up until the highest floor right under the roof where the department of drawing was located and where Kenny sometimes went to sketch.

Sandra had a lecture on the fourth floor this semester and she did not know if she was on her way to that class when she suddenly found herself on the stairs that afternoon. She did not know: it should be said just that artificially. She had wandered around in that way the last few days. From the streets where she walked around, walked and walked in her heavy hiking boots, to the hotels' lunch cafés, to the university, but less and less in any systematic or logical order. It would actually happen that she found herself in the wrong type of clothes—clothes worthy of a striptease dancer in courses for oral proficiency, in boots in hotel bars. And what you did not get then was a "bite" (or how it should now be said), you barely got let in.

Just this afternoon when she almost tripped over Inget Herrman and one whom she knew was called the Birdman, she was dressed in hotel clothes, a striptease dancer on wobbly high heels on her way to oral proficiency on the fourth floor. But she did not get any farther than that in other words. Because Inget Herrman and the Birdman were sitting on the stairs drinking wine and being in the way. And it was no hallucination brought on by insanity, that she could swear to, it was for real.

"Shhh Sandra," said Inget Herrman who immediately recognized Sandra despite the clothes, despite everything.

"We're sitting here waiting for our professor. We're going to have a serious word with him," Inget Herrman whispered but certainly loud enough so it more or less echoed everywhere. "Namely we have a definite feeling he's been hoodwinking us in his review of our thesis."

And while she said that, that subjective feeling inside Sandra, all hope was lost.

Maybe Inget Herrman saw Sandra's openly unhappy, desperate expression because then she changed her tone of voice and, as it were, pretended to speak normally, as if she had complete control over a bizarre situation that in reality you could have no control over at all.

"I'm having my bohemian period," Inget Herrman whispered. "Don't say anything to the Islander. Do you have money? I'm broke. Can I borrow some?"

And it had echoed everywhere and Sandra fumbled in her pockets after bills, coins, but Inget Herrman had grabbed her entire bag.

"Let me!"

And Sandra tried to pull her bag back.

But Inget started singing, or humming a bizarre little melody while she dug in Sandra's bag for bills, coins.

And while Inget Herrman sang and picked coins out of Sandra's bag, roughly, so that pens and things, for example paper, for example the letter, flew around, the boy came. On the stairs. They were in the way, a moment, all three (Sandra, Inget, the Birdman). He looked at her, Sandra, and recognized only her and then managed to squeeze past. Said nothing, but then, at that stage, no words were needed.

And then the guards were there and were going to throw all of them out. Inget Herrman was not in the mood to accept any orders from anyone and was not thinking about giving in without a fight. Then Sandra saw her chance and ran away, out. Collided with people in the swinging doors and almost rushed into the arms of two tall, beautiful, superb women. Rita, on her way to one of her lectures, and, yes, of course, Kenny.

"Aha. Where are you off to in such a hurry?" Kenny asked nicely when Sandra had practically landed in her arms, but it was too much, it was enough.

Now it was enough with all of it!

Sandra tore herself free and ran away, raced through the city, which you do when you race. Was on her way forward at a high speed, but without knowing where.

And Doris-in-Sandra laughed.

She was really having fun now.
You're really going bananas.
The bonds we tied, no one can undo.

Then it had already happened. Inget Herrman had thrown the letter away herself, among many many other papers. Scattered around her in the tall stairs in the new university building without any of them being able to stop it.

Doris, Doris—if you only knew—

"When you read this I will have . . ."

To the sea, yes, she had run. It had glittered so. And she remembered another time, many years ago, on another planet in another life.

A midsummer's day with Doris Flinkenberg and Inget Herrman. How they had walked over the Second Cape down to the beachhouse and how the sea suddenly opened itself up in front of them, so new and glittering. And Inget who told them about the American girl.

Light blue glitter, the water reflected in the monstrous façade of the Glass House.

"Walk on the water for me, idiot," Doris-in-her whispered in her overstrung way.

"You are just," said Sandra to Doris-in-her, "not really right."

And now it sailed up, finally. The image of the two of them, Sandra Night and Doris Day (and vice versa) who knew everything and could. The girls in the game with Loneliness&Fear in green paint over the stomachs of the shirts that Sandra had sewn for them.

How they had thought there was something invincible in it in any case.

Everything's weary pettiness, instead. Stand face-to-face with it. Seeps through the fingers.

Pang. Doris shot herself.

Doris wrote a letter to Inget Herrman.

A letter that Inget Herrman never read. Never opened, it remained there among her material for her thesis.

Everything's weary pettiness.

It was a pity about Doris.

It was a pity about Sandra too.

The mother by the sea. Come, come to me. The attractive, attractive Lorelei, like her in the poem. On Åland. "The aunt." Standing at a window.

"Come to me."

The most secret story

AS RITA TOLD IT TO KENNY IN A ROOM IN AN APARTMENT IN the city by the sea, in the middle of the night, while Sandra was eavesdropping in the hall, in her pajamas, on the shoe rack, among the shoes.

. . . To some children who are alone or just in need of excitement, attention, a splash of eccentricity, if even self-made or imagined, a Pippi Longstocking in a frock and red pigtails, or Mary Poppins with an umbrella and a fiancé with a fedora and striped suits comes along. To us, Solveig and me, came, maybe a little too late in life, we had already turned ten, a Miss Andrews.

Our godmother. That's what she said about herself anyway, that was what she wanted to be for us. We named her. We loved that name. She liked it too. She said "Misss Andrews."

Solveig and I, we had a habit of hanging out in the garden outside the empty house on the First Cape, in the tumbledown garden, the one in English style. That means everything in it is measured exactly to a T and planned ahead of time, even though it can't be seen because it should give the impression that it's overgrown. She, Miss Andrews, taught us that among other things.

She spoke a lot about her interest in gardens, "not necessarily the practical work, it can certainly be monotonous sometimes and there are gardeners for that," but for the ideas behind everything, the thoughts themselves. She spoke about her own Winter Garden that she had put so much time and effort into. We were, well, fascinated. Miss Andrews stirred a lot of things in us.

Longing, want, and desire. All of that before we knew who she really was, where she came from.

We didn't talk about those sorts of things those mornings at Bule Marsh when Miss Andrews taught us English and in return we taught her how to swim; it was a trade. We never asked any questions either. In some way we learned early on that it was important we not ask any questions. That it was a matter of waiting until she told us. Sometimes we waited in vain; then we just had to satisfy ourselves with that.

But this was before everything. Before Eddie, the American girl as she was called in the District, all of that. It was before Doris Flinkenberg also, in the beginning's beginning. In the evenings, in the dark, we found ourselves on a fixed place in the garden on the First Cape where there was a crystal ball. From that place you had a view over the entire District. You could see the cousin's house, where a light in the cousin's mama's kitchen was shining as always. She was in the kitchen, with newspapers, crosswords, and her baking, it was comforting to know that. Later in the evening, always at the same time, she called us in. All her "boys," which included the girls, that was just the way you talked in the District, for evening tea in the cousin's house. Bengt, Björn, Solveig, Rita. When the cousin's mama came out on the steps and called out into the twilight, "Boys, time to come home now," everyone started moving toward the dull light in the kitchen window of the cousin's house from their own directions. It shone warmly like a lantern in a valley.

Later, when Björn was dead, that changed too of course. Bengt didn't come in anymore. The cousin's mama took tea in a thermos and a sandwich in a basket out to him in the barn. Solveig and I, we stayed in the cottage by ourselves. In the beginning anyway because we were scared senseless. And yes, when Doris came, everything became so different. There was nothing wrong with Doris Flinkenberg, it was just a bit difficult to have the energy to deal with her after everything that had happened.

But from there, from the garden on the First Cape, you also saw other things. For example the great woods, which started behind the First Cape, the one the English Garden imperceptibly blended into. A way into the woods, the marshes. First, Second, Third, Fourth. And the only one of the marshes that had a real name, Bule Marsh, where the public beach was for a short while before it was moved to a lake west of the town center.

Farther north (out of sight but you knew they were there) the outer marshes where the frozen and beaten Doris Flinkenberg came from, the one who was found in the house on the First Cape wrapped in a blanket.

. . . But in the garden, there was of course the other direction. The Second Cape with the housing exhibition, it was the first year after it. The houses were sold but life on the Cape was still new. Bencku was crazy about the Second Cape and the houses there, he knew everything about them and it was important to him that it should be that way, that he was involved, that he was a part of it. But Solveig and I, we didn't bother about the Second Cape, the sea certainly, but as a body of water to swim in—that first year we mostly fretted about the public beach being moved from the bay surrounded by cliffs on the Second Cape to Bule Marsh because the area was now private. Though the fretting soon passed. Bule Marsh also had its good sides. It also became interesting later, when Miss Andrews came.

But so, it was one evening, a while after we had met Miss Andrews in the English Garden, and we looked around. Then Solveig out of nowhere yelled, "Look! There she is! Miss Andrews!"

It was in other words at the Glass House on the Second Cape, just outside. It was the baroness's house. And Miss Andrews—she was the baroness herself. She was the one who lived in the Glass House; it was a remarkable discovery. We became very excited about it at first.

But it was like this that it started, a bit earlier, this was how we met Miss Andrews at Bule Marsh's beach. It was an early summer morning and we had gotten up at five o'clock already to go swimming. We were going to become swimmers, that was our plan. Not a secret plan exactly, but certainly unofficial in such a way that neither of us wanted to talk openly about it. Not to mention how trite it would sound.

Training was required in order to become swimmers, training, and even more training, and a disciplined life. It was also a matter of not bothering about all the peripheral factors, like how the weather was and if it was cold in the water—in the beginning of the summer it was always needless to say ice-cold in Bule Marsh. It's deep and the current is strong. But you got used to the cold and the currents. We jumped headfirst from Lore Cliff, taught ourselves the high jump all on our own, me and Solveig, though Solveig was the better one. "It's just the two of us," said Solveig and she said it all the time, already back then.

We were well under way with our morning training when it happened. She came out of the bushes, hullabaloo, like an animal. At first we thought it was a moose or something, but before we had time to become really frightened she was standing there in front of us, didn't introduce herself but asked, almost harshly and strictly, who we were and what we were doing there.

We were quite surprised. This is what she looked like, Miss Andrews: She was maybe fifty–sixty years old, both of us thought old, Solveig and I, and light. Light hair, light skin, slender, thin, and tough so to speak like some women are who look good for their age, you know. She spoke quickly and nervously and didn't breathe between sentences. And sweat often ran down her face, her cheeks and forehead were scarlet. Because of the excitement of a game—an adult game.

We would also learn that Miss Andrews had another way of speaking. Not entirely different, but she had many different vocal pitches for different situations. When she was someone else in other places, the ones we didn't have access to. But we understood that later. Places where she wasn't what she said she wanted to be for us. Our godmother.

But then Solveig who had a highly developed sense of justice immediately became really irritated.

"As far as I'm concerned we still have everyman's right in this country."

"Well then, the public beach is HERE," Miss Andrews grunted happily in response. "Then I've come to the right place after all."

And that was how it started.

Our godmother. Miss Andrews. She said she loved water and water games but she couldn't swim. Would we have anything against teaching her? In return she would teach us what she knew and that was a lot, for example the English language. With Oxford pronunciation, besides.

"You must understand, girls," said Miss Andrews where she was standing in her bathrobe and her comfortable wooden sandals, "I am the only one here who speaks proper English."

And, good God! How that sounded in the silence of the marsh. It sounded exotic. It sounded crazy.

And how us girls stared at her and didn't know if we should laugh or be impressed. On the other hand, it was though a moose had called in the woods out of laughter, on the other hand the situation was simultaneously so tender, so devout. Miss Andrews was also a person who obviously wanted something from us, just us.

"What's that?" Solveig blurted out in the typical District dialect she rarely spoke otherwise.

"Now it is I in turn who has difficulty with my hearing." Miss Andrews tilted her head to the side and peered, eyes filled with humor.

"She says," I said full of laughter because we used the district dialect for fun, "that now she doesn't understand anything at all."

"In other words it means," said Miss Andrews, "that I am the only one here who speaks proper English. Though soon I do not need to be." And blinked. "If you want to, that is.

"The language of the future," Miss Andrews yelled and threw off her clothes. Seconds later she was standing in front of us on the beach cliff in an old-lady bra and enormous underwear.

"Come," she called to us and slapped her thigh. "Hop in the water."

And then—we didn't believe our eyes—she threw off her bra, jumped out of the enormous underwear *don't you say underswear here in the District*, and ran stark naked into the water with a scream that echoed wildly in the nature surrounding the marsh where also other eyes might be watching.

In the water with Miss Andrews. And Solveig after. And me. And then we splashed around along the water's edge and tried to methodically structure the teaching assignment we now had on hand.

"Tomorrow," said Miss Andrews when she left with the red towel in a turban on her head, "there will be a lesson again."

We understood right away of course that she was partly bananas. But it didn't matter. Besides, we were rather easily amused, Solveig and I. It wasn't every day that strange ladies showed up and wanted something in particular from you. We liked her. To put it mildly. Things would get worse in that respect. Unfortunately.

Cat is running after mouse. Mouse is running round the house.

And we studied. And giggle giggle giggle and giggle. The next morning she was back again. And the next. We carried on like that for some time and everything was good.

"And so, girls, conversation."

"And so, girls, hop in the water."

Miss Andrews. We taught her the breaststroke, freestyle, and the butterfly, in any case the basics and for the most part on dry land.

It became so messy in the water; when it was a matter of being in the water it turned out Miss Andrews had a hard time putting what she called "theory" into any kind of practice whatsoever.

She probably didn't try very hard either.

"The current is taking me," she joked. And up and showing her breasts.

But still, you could remember Miss Andrews this way when she was at her best:

"This is probably a hopeless undertaking, kids," Miss Andrews called to us from the water when she, oblivious to the learning process, was gesticulating wildly with her arms and legs and her naked butt stupidly popping up piggypaddle above the surface of the water between strokes. Miss Andrews insisted on swimming in the nude due to eurythmic principles.

As I said. It was crazy, she was crazy. But we were loyal to her, very loyal.

We got our own life. It was a life that spoke against so much of the life that existed in the cousin's house or in the District at all. It was meaningful. Too meaningful to be revealed to any outsider.

So she didn't exactly need to ask us not to tell anyone about her existence, it was for a time our most important secret.

"Seize the day," she also said. "You can do what you want."

She taught us we could break boundaries and do what we wanted. Anything.

And she told us, in English, about Ponderosa, that ranch where you and the others who were her nieces lived, her real goddaughters, she said. She spoke about her nieces, about you and Inget and Eddie, like a story, with that perfect Oxford pronunciation, and we listened, but actually not as devotedly as she maybe thought. I mean America, Ponderosa, it didn't mean anything to us. But maybe we were also a little jealous of you already back then.

It was completely clear that you, the real goddaughters and nieces, you beat us by horse lengths, we didn't doubt that.

"We didn't live on any ranch, Rita," Kenny filled in then. "Good God, Rita, how that woman could make things up. She just had a lot of ideas about us, from the beginning I mean. Her ideas, in other words. She was so filled with them that she didn't want to see. Well, keep telling now, I want to hear it to the end. Though I think that I know—"

But then later, Rita continued, it started going wrong. It started with us seeing her in the Glass House and we understood who she was. That she was the baroness. From the Glass House. That damned house. One of the Second Cape's very finest.

"She's tricked us," Solveig said when we saw her there where we were in the garden. "Has she Rita?"

"No," I said. "She just didn't want to tell us. Not yet. It's a game."

And the stupid thing was that, even though we knew, expectations were stirred in both of us so to speak. In other words that was when we started expecting things from Miss Andrews. Expected for example that she would invite us to the Glass House. Or reveal herself. Confess. We didn't know, but it hung in the air. Though Miss Andrews didn't notice anything. Maybe we even started imagining that was the whole idea of the game. That she would take us, show us—yes, shit. Who knows. The frog who becomes a prince, all of that.

"Welcome girls, to my lovely garden."

Her marvelous garden. That she would greet us there.

Then I made a mistake. It was one time not so long after. I ventured to say to Miss Andrews that Solveig and I knew something. That we knew that Miss Andrews wasn't really Miss Andrews. That it was a game. I said it like that, so to speak half seriously, as if I wanted Miss Andrews to understand that Solveig and I were rather clever children.

That in other words Miss Andrews could be proud over having chosen such clever children for her friends. "My godchildren," as Miss Andrews used to say.

So I continued talking and my intention was to invite Miss Andrews to go a step farther in this mutual confidence. It wasn't like that. Of course. Miss Andrews may have understood, maybe even more than calculated. But what happened? Well, she lost her head completely.

What did the girls think of themselves? It wasn't something she said out loud but it was certainly the essence of it all. She became so angry, angrier than we had ever seen her, ever been able to imagine her being.

The blood drained from her excited face, her lips turned white and quivered with indignation. Miss Andrews wrapped herself in her bathrobe and said with a tense voice that she had certainly not understood it was two ordinary snoops she had been dealing with the whole time.

Those words, how they fell out of the sky. They would never be forgotten.

And if she had known that, Miss Andrews continued just as tensely, while her hands impetuously tied the red towel in a turban on her head, and put her feet in her comfortable sandals—the ones she went on and on about how "feet friendly" they were (she was the only one in the whole world who wore real wooden clogs in the woods)—it wasn't at all certain that the trade between them had existed at all.

"You understand of course," she said finally, "that it was built on a trust that has now been forfeited."

And then she marched away, in the woods. We stood and stared at her back, how she disappeared among the bushes and the trees.

And we regretted it SO.

But what did the girls think of themselves, really?

And swish, like a suction in the water in the middle of the marsh, we were sucked down, how should I put it, but "figuratively" speaking, down, down into nothing.

Here we would be, by the muddy beaches—

"Welcome girls, to my lovely garden."

"Welcome girls, to my lovely garden."

Well. That would never happen.

And we certainly understood then finally how truly crazy Miss Andrews was—but it didn't mean anything. We were convinced it was the last time we would see a trace of Miss Andrews and it was terrible. The door to the garden had been pulled shut right in front of our noses even, once and for all, and besides it was nobody else's fault but our own.

"Look at what you've done now!" Solveig said to me, but weakly, where we stood alone by the marsh in our bathrobes because it was really so terribly cold this morning. And alone. Damned. Alone. Of course Solveig understood that she was just as much to blame. I had just been more precocious. With words. Like always. And we, we were two of course.

I said nothing.

The mosquitoes bit. Damn, actually. God, God damn.

But consequently there was no point in standing below the Glass House and looking up at the Winter Garden and imagining something marvelous would happen.

We didn't talk about it, but maybe it became a watershed between us, me and Solveig, in some way, I don't know.

Maybe Miss Andrews regretted it. I don't know. Because she came back. Already two days later. Then she was extra nice, had presents for us. New bathing suits. One blue, one green.

And everything was delightful again. But still. Not at all. Solveig put on the new suit and jumped in extra-high spirits around on the beach and then she took Miss Andrews with her far out into the water and tried to get her to do the freestyle back to land. It was almost a disaster. Both of us had to work to save Miss Andrews again.

"You should receive a lifeguard medal, girls. There's a strong current out there."

"We've noticed that. It's just a matter of being able to handle it. You have to have swimming experience. If you have that then you can manage. It's not that hard," said Solveig.

She said to me later that in the water with Miss Andrews then she had noticed Miss Andrews really was as good a swimmer as the next person, she had just been silly and pretended. Everything with the trade, it was a game.

Miss Andrews showed up one day and you could tell something had happened. She informed us grandly that she was going to travel, the location was so to speak implied . . . because when she came back she might have her own little niece with her. Next year. It was at the end of the summer, in other words, already then.

"I hope to see you again, girls," said Miss Andrews. "I have namely become very attached to your company. Same place, same time. I mean in the morning, here at the marsh, next year again. Shall we agree on that?"

We answered yes, of course. She was so silly that you still couldn't keep from liking her. In any case just a little. But something had changed after her rage. Consequently not just with our dreams, but between us, Solveig and me on the one hand, and Miss Andrews on the other. We didn't really trust her anymore.

Not in the obvious way, anyway.

And besides, she had effectively gotten us to stop hoping for something new, something different, something amazing.

And then we also started thinking about that, think if Miss Andrews had known someone was spying in the bushes, and maybe that was why she was carrying on clowning about so, demonstrating her "eurythmic principles." That maybe she didn't have anything against standing there like that in his field of vision and in that case all of it was REALLY sick.

Miss Andrews jumping on one leg on the cliff. Just another fleshy tantadara instead of the Queen of the Winter Garden we had painted for ourselves. Miss Andrews, who taught us the world was large and open and that you could walk out in it.

"Seize the day, girls."

. . .

"Yes, girls," Miss Andrews said at last. "It sounds like you will not be rid of me next year either. Don't mention it."

Miss Andrews bowed and curtsied on the beach.

"Don't mention it. It's fine with me. YOU are some of the funniest things I've experienced. In my life."

And then it was the next year, that was the year Eddie came and Eddie died. Drowned, sucked up into the marsh. And now I'm going to tell you right away. Kenny. That we saw it. That it was us.

But wait a minute, I'm going to finish telling the story. How it was. Well so. Summer and Miss Andrews again. She came early that year, already in June, and she had that girl with her. The "niece," in other words, whom she had talked so much about but you could see right away that everything was wrong. If we had been cheated out of our dreams then it was nothing compared to what Miss Andrews had been cheated out of. It really wasn't a "bright" girl from, one more of Miss Andrews's favorite sayings, "the great outdoors."

Eddie de Wire. The American girl. This was one of those real teenage girls, of the worst kind. She didn't come down to the beach either, just sat extremely reluctantly—you could see that at a distance also—there on Lore Cliff across from the bay with the small clump of reeds where we were swimming. And watched us. Listlessly, in other words. Swatted at mosquitoes and lit a match. When she did that Miss Andrews called to her, her face was unusually sweaty and she couldn't concentrate on the swimming at all, glancing up all the time, with anger and irritation, but it was also, we understood later, that she was scared—well in any case when Eddie on the cliff lit that match Miss Andrews called to her, saying that the first thing she did in the morning didn't need to be smoking a cigarette.

Then the girl called back that it was a match she lit, not a cigarette, because of the damned mosquitoes, fire was a way of getting rid of them, they were everywhere of course. The girl didn't look at us at all.

And when she spoke the very first times, she certainly spoke Swedish, but she had a funny accent. She would lose the accent pretty quickly, surprisingly quickly, later, with Björn. And Bengt. They were together of course, the three of them. Well that's a pretty ménage à trois or whatever it's called, she could have said that, Miss Andrews, before, but it was as though she wasn't inclined to hold that kind of exposition any longer.

Miss Andrews just snorted at Eddie and put on her swimsuit and now we swam a little, but nothing really became of that either because it was rather difficult to concentrate. She sat there on the cliff and lit matches, which she threw in the water, lit and threw. And suddenly we were freezing. We almost never froze but now we did and suddenly all the energy and desire had left all three of us, and then we just sat on the beach for a while and felt like we were being watched. It was time for a little English. But with the girl there, it was too idiotic.

And Miss damned Andrews quoted for us from her favorite quotations. Pico della Mirandola.

"This, girls," she said, "is Pico della Mirandola: 'I have placed you in the center of creation so that you will be able to plainly see and judge all that exists in the world. You are neither of heaven or earth, neither immortal nor mortal, but are your own sculptor, freely and nobly fashioning yourself as you would like to be.'

"What is he saying, girls?

"He says," Miss Andrews continued absentmindedly "that it is possible to make up your own life.

"But note carefully, girls, he says famously, 'One must live one's life with style.' And that is what so many people misunderstand. One thinks that style is how things look, or something that exclusively has to do with aesthetics. One can separate . . ."

And point point point. Because then Miss Andrews got going. The girl on the cliff across from them. Suddenly she was gone.

"I must go. She cannot be left alone . . ."

And we sat there alone, Solveig and I, at the marsh. It could have been rather comical, but it wasn't at all, not in light of what happened later.

Consequently Miss Andrews didn't come to the marsh very often that summer and when she showed up nothing was like before. There was rarely any swimming, mostly talking. Sometimes she didn't even get undressed. I mean, the bathrobe. She had entirely stopped swimming in the nude. All of that, the eurythmic principles, belonged to another time.

And one thing and the other was said, but nothing memorable. She didn't have the peace to concentrate on the English. Sometimes she just came to be sitting there on a rock while the words flooded out of her.

I couldn't help but feel sorry for her. Later came to understand that it was what it was: a person in dire need. Eddie was in the process of taking the spirit out of her.

"That girl is such a disappointment to me," she said once, but to the cousin's mama, not to us. That was during the very last time when she suddenly showed up at the cousin's house because she wanted to "warn" the cousin's mama about Eddie, "the American girl," she used that nickname willingly too, which she hadn't done earlier. Then Björn and Eddie were already in full swing of course. And Bengt and Eddie.

And maybe we also would have thought then, Solveig and I, when she came to the cousin's house, that we felt for her, but she didn't tell us who she really was this time either. As the one she was, with us. Miss Andrews, in other words.

One time, in the morning by the beach, Miss Andrews lit a cigarette. A cigarette, it was now seven o'clock in the morning, before it had been unthinkable. Though she put it out immediately.

"And now, out in the water with all of us," she carried on, Miss Andrews, but while she said that she was standing in the shadows hugging herself. "Out in the water, everyone, come come come."

But just sat there.

"Seize the day," she said. "That is what it's all about." And then she stopped again.

"That is one of my most important principles." She came to be staring in front of her at a loss when Solveig kindly asked what that meant—we had stopped with English a long time ago, it was actually completely quirky what we sat there and talked about in the mornings, the swimmers and their crazy godmother Miss Andrews.

The swimmers and their crazy godmother. You could also see it that way.

Well, this much was certain. The American girl had come into Miss Andrews's life and everything had changed.

She never spoke to us about her, never even mentioned her. And of course we didn't ask. We had learned not to ask too many questions and furthermore, that "niece," that was still a sensitive thing for us.

So we didn't know what Eddie was doing or what she was up to. Not directly.

"You cannot trust her," she said to the cousin's mama. And you could have thought then, who was it who said that Miss Andrews's version was the right one. It certainly was not easy to come and stay with a Miss Andrews with all her dreams about who you are and then be expected to be that and act accordingly with it so to speak.

But we saw how unhappy she was. For real, in need. And scared.

Later for example I understood that Eddie was stealing. Money and things. Big and small things. There was so to speak no logic in her.

And she had started picking up strangers in the city by the sea and bringing them to the baroness's house. Not just for parties, but otherwise also. People who came and went. Sometimes you couldn't get rid of them.

Above all you couldn't get rid of her, Eddie.

And maybe in some way the baroness still had some hope that Eddie would become different. She was so young also, nineteen. That she would come to her senses, grow up.

It probably felt quite insecure. The baroness was alone. She had no husband, no children—she had for the most part one friend, and that was a boarder. In other words one of those male students who had once lived as a boarder with her. The Black Sheep. It was just a type.

But still, he certainly helped her. She had a habit of calling him and asking him to come and empty the apartment of people, that sort of unpleasant thing. She also tried to get him to talk some sense into Eddie, but it didn't work at all, and so on.

It was him she called in desperation that last night, from the Glass House. When Eddie was still alive. She had locked Eddie in a room. Without clothes. So that she wouldn't run away. Now she was going to leave. And the baroness called the Black Sheep in a scattered state and he, yes, he came.

So she asked him to come and take her away. She never wanted to see Eddie again.

For alleged reasons. I happened to know a bit about it since my brother Bengt was extremely involved. It was together with him that she, Eddie, was going to leave. Together Bencku and Eddie had cooked up the world's intrigue; they were going to run away together and so on.

It actually could have been a little comical too. In some way. If now for . . . As said, Eddie was together with Bengt. Little Bengt in other words, and he was head over heels in love with her. But that was so to speak more unofficial than the fact that she was also together with Björn. She and Björn were the number-one turtledoves of the District for a while, where they hung out in the opening of the barn and made out and smoked and were going to get engaged and everything.

We weren't terribly interested in that, Solveig and I, but nevertheless what was a bit interesting was how different Eddie was with the two of them. With Björn she was one way, with Bencku another. Though he saw what Bencku and Eddie did when it was just the two of them. Björn that is.

Eddie, soft as a cat and purring. It was, when she was standing there in the opening of the barn, as if she were standing on a stage and playing her part as Eddie the lovely, so good.

It was like another side of her, one Miss Andrews never saw, but maybe it was the same thing.

Well, they were in other words going to go away, that night. Bengt and Eddie. Sat and swore immortal things to each other in the boathouse, while they were intimately entwined, and then comes Björn. He doesn't understand anything. Bengt. Bengt is five years younger, to start with.

Well, he understood later because he went and hanged himself.

He drank himself silly and thought ominous thoughts. Went to that damned outbuilding and was there almost the whole night. And Bengt and Eddie. Well. They didn't know anything about it.

That was probably also what made Bengt go insane.

And then it was that cursed morning. It was so, I don't know, stupid, shit, terrible. We had already really started losing heart, Miss Andrews, Solveig, and I. We were bored to death of her— also of her showing up and her nervousness. When we weren't even allowed to play a part, we had no part. We were just "the godchildren" at the beach, which she came to sometimes, I don't know why, but maybe because there was still something there that should be normal.

But maybe it was good we had lost interest then before everything happened. I mean, we already knew we couldn't expect anything from her.

I don't mean when Eddie drowned in front of our eyes and we didn't do anything, I mean afterward. It wasn't exactly a big surprise that she didn't acknowledge us in any way then either.

That in the future we would have to get along as best we could.

She certainly came, in some sort of inappropriate feeling of guilt, and put on airs for Bencku. Invited him up to the house so he could "practice his art there." She had seen his maps in the boathouse when she was straightening up there after Eddie's death. She invited him to the Glass House in other words, what for us had been and still was the most forbidden. Maybe she felt guilty, it's possible, thought that it was enough to "replace" us with him. We were siblings, of course.

Well, that terrible morning anyway. It was very early, we were at the marsh, Solveig and I. I don't remember why we had gone there so early, earlier than usual. Maybe it was the anxiety. We didn't know anything about what was going on. But maybe we felt it anyway. I'm thinking about Björn, what he did that night. And about Eddie, and about Bengt. What they were doing. And what they had been doing.

The one thing had led to another before Miss Andrews came. To us, at the marsh, in her wooden clogs and her bathrobe and her swimsuit. Well, if there was something you saw at a distance of a thousand miles it was that Miss Andrews had been pushed to the brink now. And therefore it would now be normal. So normal.

Well, first, before Miss Andrews came. We were going to swim, but we hadn't gotten around to starting that either, I mean Solveig and I, the two of us.

We were sitting on the rocks on the beach, trying to wake up, the motivation had probably started leaving us. What, swimmers?

What did we think of ourselves?

Well, there came Miss Andrews then.

As background for what happened later I can now tell you about what we didn't know then yet, Solveig and I, about what had been going on in and around the Glass House and the boathouse during the night. The previous night Björn, who would of course be the first lover in this tale, had surprised Eddie and Bengt in the boathouse, in an intimate situation that left no room for interpretation, or whatever it's now called.

Then he hadn't known what to do. And gone, somewhere. But no one had gone after him. Neither Bengt nor Eddie. Instead, when they had been surprised, they started putting together their own plans. I have no idea what Eddie was thinking, for her it was probably very much a game right now, well, that with Bengt, or what do I know. But I know that for Bengt it was dead serious.

He was going away, he was going away with her now, to the end of the world if that was the question.

And they agreed to leave right away; Eddie had enough of the baroness as well, which she had explained so many times to Bencku. But, well, they needed things. Money. And so they made a plan. Eddie would go up to the Glass House, to where she no longer had a key—that's why she had to stay in the boat-house because the baroness didn't want her in the house any-more—Eddie would go up there and arrange money somehow. And then she and Bengt would meet at a fixed place in the woods and she would have her things in her backpack and he would have his things in his backpack and then, away.

Bengt left to pack his things and get ready for the big journey, and Eddie, she went to the Glass House. That was the last time he ever spoke to her. Before she went up to the Glass House and Miss Andrews.

What happened there in the Glass House no one really knows. But in some way the baroness must have caught Eddie red-handed when she was rummaging among the baroness's things, or maybe Eddie was bolder than that. Quite simply said what she wanted, and was going to get it out of the baroness, so to speak by force. Money. But she failed in this.

And that was the important part, of course. The baroness locked her in a room in only her underwear, so that she wouldn't run away. And then she didn't know what she was going to do. She didn't come up with anything else except calling the Black Sheep. "Come." And he came.

Her friend in the white Jaguar, her former boarder. Take her away from here. Eddie was dragged out to the car, still, I assume, without clothes on.

Eddie was going away. Wherever, just away from there.

And Bencku, he waited and waited for her in that place in the woods where they had agreed to meet, but of course she never came. Then he became nervous and started walking around and that was when he was standing on the side of the road and the car drove past and there was Eddie. That he saw.

That was the last time he saw her.

How she was sitting there in the backseat, stiff and unrecognizable, as if she were vulnerable to a threat.

He saw her, and it came to nothing for him. And he realized a lot of alarming things as you do sometimes when you're really desperate. He understood that it was now a matter of finding Björn, where was Björn?

And he went to the cousin's house and saw that Björn still hadn't come home, and then he ran, filled with suspicions, toward the outbuilding.

But we, we were at the marsh, Solveig and I, like two idiots. First Miss Andrews came. Still to this day I don't know what in the hell she was doing at the marsh just this morning, but you can imagine she might not have wanted to be present when Eddie was taken away, or when everything was so horrible there would in any case be something that was like before, somewhat normal.

She came and tried to be like always. Though we saw immediately that something was wrong, but now there would be a game anyway, swim and splash and God knows what, and Solveig and I, we didn't exactly go into the show hook, line, and sinker, but we didn't do anything else either. We acted like nothing had happened. Strained in order to act that way too.

Now we were going to swim, according to Miss Andrews, really. She threw off her bathrobe. "Come now, Solveig, come now, Rita. Hop in the water." And out into the water with her. And out into the water with us.

And we carried on like that for a while, though nothing was normal. And then, suddenly, we saw her again. Eddie. The American girl. She was standing on Lore Cliff and what was special about her was that she had on a red plastic raincoat, a lady's raincoat, and she had only her underwear on under the coat (it was visible because she was standing and gesticulating wildly with her arms). For an absurd moment we might have thought she was going to jump in now, in her underwear. But no.

She stood there and was furious. Completely terrible, pitifully flying mad yelling at Miss Andrews. But actually also triumphant so to speak. What had happened? You didn't know. But it seemed as though Eddie, little Eddie, cunning Eddie, had managed to escape out of the car anyway. And she was wearing something she had found in the car.

In some way she had managed to trick the Black Sheep into stopping the car and then she had escaped, run into the woods. And come to the marsh, and found Miss Andrews there.

The Black Sheep couldn't be seen anywhere and why would he have been, actually? He had completed his task as best he could, that was it.

"Wait!"

When Miss Andrews caught sight of Eddie on Lore Cliff, she snapped so you could see it. "Wait!" That was how she had called to Eddie, but with an entirely different voice, a deep one, one with authority. And the strange thing was that Eddie waited.

Maybe she also understood in some way that she had gone too far. With everything. For her all of this was for the most part some kind, if not a game, then advanced hobby in any case.

Miss Andrews got out of the water. We did as well, wrapped ourselves in our bathrobes and stood there as if petrified for what felt like a million hundred years, an eternity. Miss Andrews put on her bathrobe and her wooden clogs. She said, "Wait!" to us as well, and then she started walking around the marsh up to Eddie on Lore Cliff.

And then the following happened. We stood there both of us, Solveig and I, as I said, and watched. Watched the whole thing like a play, Lore Cliff right in front of us. But there wasn't any safety in that theater, none at all. We were scared already then. Senseless, just about.

We were nailed in place, whether we wanted to be or not. We just were.

Miss Andrews had come up on the cliff. It started like an argument. An ordinary one, with two people who stand and yell at each other. It went on for a while, in English in Swedish in dialect in all languages.

Then it became a scuffle. It was Miss Andrews who started. And what you saw immediately—that was why we were so frightened also, maybe, Solveig and I, because we already understood something without so to speak really being aware of it—what you in other words immediately saw in Miss Andrews was that she now had a mission. Get Eddie in the water.

They fought. And the baroness, she was strong. And before we knew it, or, that was the worst, that was exactly what we knew would happen, Eddie was in the water.

"Note carefully," Miss Andrews had said and quoted Pico della Mirandola. "He says *nobly*. One must live one's life with style."

And blubb blubb blubb blubb immediately in the next scene, which wasn't any scene rather a really terrible awful reality, Eddie sank, "a disappointment," before our eyes in the marsh.

And we stood there and the years passed. Time passed.

Rita, the swimmer, Solveig, the lifeguard. And did, for the most part, nothing.

. . .

"Wait!" Miss Andrews yelled from Lore Cliff. "In a moment she'll come back up. I see her!"

She had in fact sunk immediately, Eddie. Like a rock.

But the current is swift in the middle of Bule Marsh. It is.

And we waited. Stood there and waited. But Eddie, she didn't come up again.

In some way it was something we had known the whole time.

And suddenly, we didn't really know how it had happened either, we were alone at the marsh.

Alone from Miss Andrews anyway.

Miss Andrews had left us. Without saying good-bye, which it so nicely is called.

And now it was for good.

But we would see her later, in the house on the Second Cape, the Glass House. We would see her in the Winter Garden, in its aesthetic and light secludedness. In the middle of its fantastic architecture she would, despite the minimal geographic distance, be far away from us. Unreachable.

She wouldn't see us. Never again. One time, it was on the way to the cousin's house when she was coming to get Bencku, she would walk past us on the cousin's property and hiss:

"Poor children. Poor wicked children. May God have mercy on you. This will have to be something between you and me and God."

"That I promise," said the baroness/Miss Andrews. "Life afterward is in itself a sufficient punishment to bear."

That was the last thing she ever said to us, Miss Andrews.

But maybe she was talking about herself.

She was so broken in some way. There was no energy left in her anymore.

We were alone at the marsh. Everything had happened. It was so surreal. Miss Andrews had left.

And it might as well not have happened. It could just as well have been so that Eddie, the American girl, had suddenly just been obliterated from the face of the earth. Or like in that pop song Doris played and played.

"Our love is a continental affair, he came in a white Jaguar."

That the Black Sheep had actually gotten her to stay in the car and taken her away.

But no.

Still, Kenny. Pico della Mirandola, all of that. In some way I missed her. Miss. Not her, the baroness. But that person. Miss Andrews. And it's strange, it's as if it still means something in some way. I don't really know what I mean by that. But that you *can* do something, so to speak.

Solveig. She would just inhibit me. In everything. When I wanted something. Something else. And she was capable of quite a lot. Setting fire to the woods. She was the one who did that. That terrible day when the American girl floated up again, in the marsh.

Then she set fire to the woods by the house on the First Cape where the Backmanssons lived. So that I wouldn't go away with the Backmanssons. Never ever away from there. From her, that is. It would be me and her in all time's eternity, together together, with our own terrible secret.

"Oh," Rita finally said to Kenny. "What do you have to say now? When you know?"

"I have certainly known," said Kenny, "quite a lot. But not everything. And I've wanted to know of course. And I've also suspected—but—"

"So that is why you came," said Rita. "I mean. Started calling me and so. Because you heard something and wanted to know how things really were."

"Yes, maybe," Kenny said softly. "But it's over now, all of that, Rita. And that's not why I'm here now.

"But I'm certainly terribly sad about Eddie. She was so young, so stupid. It never passes. But it's no one's fault. Or everyone's. Or however it is."

And Sandra, in the hall, among all of the shoes, she listened.

"Is that why you came?" Rita had asked.

"Yes," Kenny had replied. "Maybe. But that's not why I'm here."

And thought that it could have been that way for her, as well. With Doris. But it was not like that now. She would never be able to change anymore.

But now, looking it in the eye: it was the following that could not be kept quiet anymore. It had started in the fall, in Inget Herrman's work lair. During the time Sandra had been alone with all the material that would be sorted for Inget Herrman's thesis, material that definitely did not shrink with sorting.

Periodically it was an interesting job, but rather monotonous, especially if you did not have Inget Herrman's main topic, what it later happened to be: "This is interdisciplinary in the most genuine sense of the word," Inget Herrman herself had said and Sandra had nodded, though rather short. In some way Sandra was not very interested. She possibly lacked the enthusiasm that Inget Herrman used to say was the prerequisite for a successfully planned and carried-out research project. Sandra had in other words noticed that her thoughts and attentiveness had started to wander.

Instead of "have your thoughts purposefully concentrated on the task at hand," which Inget Herrman said was the alpha and the omega for successfully planned and carried out research, Sandra noticed her thoughts started wandering around, as if under their own power, in their own directions in this little apartment that consisted of a cooking corner and a room whose walls were lined with bookshelves cluttered with folders and notebooks and books and paper paper paper paper. In the beginning she was not interested in these bookshelves. She had enough paper with her sorting work. Every morning the desk was overflowing with paper, paper that was "the day's job assignment" for her, Sandra, as Inget Herrman so purposefully expressed it.

Later, little by little, Sandra started getting up from the chair at the desk and walking around the room. And since there were not so many things in the room on which her wandering gaze could rest, it had still moved in the direction of the bookshelf and the folders and the texts, written in black and red ink, on the spines of the folders.

Moved her fingers over them, pulled, in places, lines in the dust.

"Diary, minutes," and different years following.

There was, it seemed, just about not a single date in Inget Herrman's life for which there was not a record.

She looked at different years and pulled out books here and there. San Francisco. Sven Herrman (that was Inget Herrman's husband, a long time ago, "in another life," as she Inget Herrman had a habit of saying).

Gradually it had maybe struck her that she had so little interest in anything that had happened in Inget Herrman's life, who she was, where she came from, and so on. Considering how bewitched she had been by her sister, Eddie de Wire.

Maybe she was still bewitched. She could still evoke that voice inside her. The American girl's voice.

"I'm a strange bird, Bengt. Are you too?"

"Nobody knew my rose of the world but me."

Sandra had pulled out a few folders from that time, which had also been the Women's time in the house on the First Cape. Started reading. Record from "Us and Our Men"—study group in relationships the fall in the year Doris died. Record keeper: Inget Herrman; record adjuster: Anneka Munveg; that sort of thing.

"The meeting was about our relationships with men. We agreed that we are sooner objects of too much attention than too little. There are too many men in our lives. Not too few."

She had not been able to read any farther. But she continued rummaging in the apartment. And it was in the broom closet she found a few plastic bags that contained paper topsy-turvy. More "material." And she poured the contents out on the hall floor and by chance so to speak her eyes fell on a large brown envelope labeled "Women in a State of Emergency. Thesis material," and then the year when Doris died. In the envelope there was more paper, and another envelope. A thick letter, and it was unopened.

It read "To Inget Herrman" on the envelope. And a date, which was Doris's date of death. It was Doris's handwriting. She did not understand it right away. Then came the discomfort.

And the earth stopped spinning, for a while.

At the same time as it was not a surprise, not really.

"If you haven't said what you had to say during life then there's no point in getting verbal diarrhea just before your death."

That was how Doris herself had explained it to Sandra once and several times when they talked about whether you should leave a message behind if you committed suicide, or not.

Doris had really sworn it so many times.

Oh, Doris. You said that.

Still, it was a relief also, in some way. To see and understand that Doris was not so stubborn and consistent, so honest and so, which you had so to speak started seeing more and more after her death. Sandra, that is. Sandra created this image of Doris, who knew the truth, and also knew what Sandra had done.

This was namely nothing more than Doris Flinkenberg's good-bye letter, written to Inget Herrman. An appallingly thick, unopened envelope and an actual bricklike novel inside.

The other thing that was clear and maybe even more powerful, almost dreadful, was that the envelope was still unopened, the letter inside unread. Doris had put it in a place where she had been sure Inget Herrman would find it. And where else than among the material for Inget Herrman's thesis?

How Doris had gotten it there (though that was not the most difficult thing to understand; as said, Doris had, you had seen that, her head full of her own tricks).

Sandra and the letter. She had carried it to the desk and laid it on the table. Pushed away Inget Herrman's remaining "material" so that the letter would have room on the desk, lie there alone on the desk's empty surface.

Still unopened.

Then she sat down at the desk and pulled out the top desk drawer as far as possible. At the back, the very back, almost hidden, there was a small flat and unopened quarter-liter vodka bottle. She had discovered it a long time ago.

Now she took the bottle and screwed off the top and took a slug. Then she sat down to wait. She waited and waited.

When she was not able to wait for Inget any longer she stopped caring about any of it and opened the envelope, unfolded the letter, and started reading.

And there it said what she somehow the whole time had known would be there.

And some other stuff. Not much, but some.

What did Sandra do then?

She sat there as though petrified and tried to take in what she had read and relate to it and what she should do now. Should she stay, should she wait, should she leave? She finished the vodka and waited until it started growing dark.

Inget Herrman did not come. She put the empty bottle farthest back in the desk drawer, took the letter and put it in her bag, and left Inget Herrman's apartment.

The moment of opening was over.

The next day she had been in Inget Herrman's work lair as if nothing had happened.

Then Inget Herrman showed up in the middle of the second

shift and immediately took a small unopened bottle of vodka from her bag and placed it on the desk between them.

"As a little tip. If you pinch from other people's bottles you should preferably tell them. It can save another person's life."

Then she started laughing and screwed off the cap and took a gulp from the bottle.

Sandra said that she had a headache and needed to go home.

And later, the whole fall she had on the tip of her tongue—

But she had not returned the following days and when she had gone to see Inget Herrman again Inget Herrman had disappeared.

SCENES FROM A MARRIAGE

(Sandra eavesdropping among
the shoes, somewhat later)

———————

I HAVE TRIED SO MUCH," KENNY SAID TO THE ISLANDER AND Sandra listened. Their voices were low but could be heard well out in the hall where Sandra, another time shortly afterward, was sitting in her pajamas on the floor next to the telephone table, under coats, among the shoes in the middle of the night, listening.

"But it's like sand has run through my fingers," Kenny continued in the bedroom.

Kenny cried, a child's tears. Inget Herrman's words: "She hasn't had any childhood. She has a lot to make up."

The Islander consoled Kenny. Clumsily and with great benevolence. Fatherly. But it was not him, you could hear that. In any case Sandra heard it so clearly. Did Kenny hear it?

"It'll be okay, Kenny. Calm down."

With a voice that certainly wanted. Wanted to be someone who stood behind his word, every letter, an Islander, who still could not . . . the voice broke. And suddenly, in the middle of Kenny's exhaustion and tears, the Islander started sneezing.

"I love . . ." the Islander started as if he was also playing a part in a bad TV series. And *achoo*, he sneezed, as if to what, buy time?

"I've tried," Kenny sobbed in the bedroom. And no one could deny that. To the best of her ability Kenny had even tried to take care of Sandra. And the object in question understood that it was an undertaking, if she was in the mood to think along those lines. She had not been bad at it either, Kenny, not even after they had moved to the city by the sea and Rita had shown up—the trips to the Film Archive, the parties, "Sandra, come along," "Don't sit at home and stare in front of you," "What do you want to do today, Sandra?" "Should we do something really fun today just the two of us?" And she who had just shrugged her shoulders. "No. I have a lecture. I should study for an exam." And the attending to life's practical details, to manage them was almost automatic for her. This feat, of keeping everything afloat without anyone noticing. "A man's woman," as Inget Herrman had said.

"I don't know." Kenny sobbed now, sobbed and sobbed, in there in the bedroom, in the Islander's arms.

The house in the darker part of the woods for example. It was through Kenny that it had been made somewhat cozy despite the fact that Kenny, as she said, was not interested in home furnishing and the like. It had also been Kenny's idea to leave the house for the winter months. It would be more comfortable in regard to Sandra's studies, which was of course true. Though already in the house in the darker part the phrase "Sandra's studies" had evoked a smile in Sandra herself. Sandra's studies, was that not one of the silliest things you ever heard?

But it had impressed both the Islander and Kenny that Sandra had of her own accord applied for the entrance interview for the major aesthetics and philosophy with the Department of Philosophy at the university in the city by the sea. She was not exactly full of initiative, Sandra, and with Kenny who was so active and mobile and so honest and straightforward all of the strangeness and slowness in Sandra stood out.

Kenny had found and bought the apartment in the city by the sea, which was of course amazingly light, amazingly beautiful, and with a gorgeous location near the sea. Naturally you

needed a lot of money to live like that. And of course for the
Islander, which he still in various ways gladly explained, money
was a minor problem. But now so to speak moderated in a way
that embarrassed Sandra more than his impressiveness before.
Quite simply because it was not him at all.

But you also need a nose and luck and an eye; the apartment
was in a bad state at first, and Kenny put a lot of energy into
planning the renovation. Nose, luck, and eye: Kenny had THAT.

"It is your project," the Islander had said to Kenny.

What he had meant by that, Sandra if anyone knew, was also
that he personally was going to continue sailing boats abroad
and therefore be gone most of the winter. And, yes again, there
was such a contrast to the Islander who one day in the history
of the world had stood in front of the alpine villa in the Central
European Alps and spoken those magical, fateful, but yet so effective words: "Can be done!"

"You do as you think best," the Islander had said to Kenny. They
were still living in the house in the darker part of the woods
then and Kenny's two dogs had died. She had gotten two golden
retrievers, and two months later they were dead. It had turned
out they suffered from a hereditary illness. First one of the dogs
got an attack, which lasted half a day, it had lain frothing and
cramping on the bottom of the pool among the tropical plants
that withered away one by one despite the lamps and being carefully watered—it was in any case too dark and the wrong kind
of damp or whatever it was. The veterinarian advised Kenny to
have it put to sleep. Kenny decided to put the other to sleep as
well, even though it had not gotten sick yet.

"I'm not going to sit here and wait for him to get sick as well,"
she said.

And shortly thereafter she had gotten in touch with the real
estate agent and headed out to see apartments in the city by
the sea.

It was actually the only time, with the dogs, that Kenny had been discouraged.

In the fall Kenny and Sandra had moved to the city by the sea, the Islander had headed out to sea. He was not running away of course, or anything. He loved Kenny. No question about it. Could not do anything else. He said that, even to Sandra, one time when he had too much to drink and called from wherever he was in the world.

"You can't do anything but love her," he said.

He said it in an unfamiliar way. And furthermore, why would he say that to her, Sandra? And, Sandra had also thought: it was, as said, not at all his way of talking either. The Islander's way was not the humorless, serious way that had started spreading around above all on television and formed itself so that the words lost their meaning.

Loved and loved. Anyway. It was powerless. Meant nothing.

The embrace of powerlessness. One time Sandra surprised Kenny and the Islander in an intimate moment in the house in the darker part of the woods. She had been embarrassed, also because she had a hard time getting used to the Islander touching Kenny in that way, Kenny who was not much older than herself. But that was a small matter. It was something that could be lived with. It was not so bad. But this: they had stood at the window and embraced. By the little, little window and you could see a foggy day outside, you could see the jetty and the reeds; it was the time of year when the house in the darker part was at its best. Just before the snow fell, when all the vegetation had withered. Kenny had not been crying then, but her face was pale. The Islander buried his face in Kenny's shoulder and he was leaning toward her with what looked like all of his weight. They had clung to each other.

That had been what Sandra immediately identified as *the embrace of powerlessness.*

It was something Sandra was familiar with from her time with Doris Flinkenberg. They had watched *Scenes from a Marriage*. A thousand boring episodes after another.

Scenes from a Marriage consisted of a thousand embraces of powerlessness and fights and sweat in between. The real life. Welcome there.

Sandra had thought it was something that existed only on television or in movies, so conventionalized and well articulated in any case. When the Islander and Lorelei Lindberg had been mad at each other, for example, they had been so angry they had barely been able to formulate a single sentence clearly—instead they had *done* a lot: thrown things around, messed with the rifle, that sort of thing. And Doris Flinkenberg, her experiences . . . no, it was too awful, it was indescribable.

But here, exactly here she had that embrace in front of her and it had both moved her and embarrassed her and she really wished she had not come into the kitchen in that moment.

The Islander and Kenny in each other's arms in that strange, heart-wrenching way. Both of them resisting each other, at the same time as they were clinging to each other.

And then suddenly, in the ghostlike silence surrounding the embrace of powerlessness, a song could be heard. A single-pitch dimsong from the gray, untidy landscape outside, this November afternoon that was so like the afternoon that had been Doris Flinkenberg's last afternoon alive.

Sandra looked through the window behind the couple who were standing and hugging.

She was standing on the jetty in the fog singing, dressed in heavy, gray, rough homespun clothing. And the voice, it just got louder.

It was Lorelei Lindberg who was singing.

And she was singing the Eddie-song.

Look what they've done to my song.

And it was of course a kind of hallucination, something that only Sandra understood completely. But the Islander: that was when the Islander had looked up from where he was standing with his arms around Kenny and his chin on her shoulder. Yes. A moment. He heard as well. He definitely heard.

And now, the Islander who was holding Kenny who was crying in the bedroom in the apartment in the city by the sea. His helplessness. He could not do anything about it. She saw that now. So clearly. It was really a pity about both of them.

But everyone's helplessness. She could not do anything about that.

The Islander, who had come home in order to hunt for a while—he loathed missing a hunting season—was placed face-to-face again with everything he could not handle, everything he . . . could not do. That is how it was. However much he lov . . .

"Wherever you want, Kenny," the Islander whispered to Kenny in the bedroom in the apartment in the city by the sea. "You can go wherever you want. I'll pay." But that did not help at all of course. She just sobbed even louder.

It was the morning after when she saw clearly. As if the last piece of the puzzle lay where it lay and the picture was complete. The phenomenon had a special name, which Kenny could inform her about, in the theory of visual arts. That small piece of the image that could distort an entire painting. Make the entire image look different.

A few days after that day Sandra left the apartment in the city by the sea—and herself.

But first, it was also a decision, she would go to the house in the darker part in order to get the shoes.

Kenny had come into her room that same morning and woken her by asking if she wanted to go to Paris. Not a trace of desperation from the night before could be seen on her face anymore.

"We can go together. All three of us."

All three.

"You, Rita, me."

And was that not what she had been longing after too? To belong? Yes. In a way.

Sandra tried to feel how it felt. She felt nothing.

"No. I'm going to go hunting. And there's . . . my studies of course. I have a final exam in The Growth, Development, and Educational Possibilities of a Human Being. I have to study."

"Relax," Kenny said when she had listened to Sandra's breathless explanation. "You don't have to lie. I know where you're directing your thoughts. To the house in the darker part. Now you two want to go out and shoot. You and the Islander. The two of you are so alike."

Then she added, not with any undertone whatsoever, but like an open statement, in a Kenny way:

"And I don't really understand why it has the ability to hurt me."

"You do what you think is best," Kenny finally said.

"But it's too bad. We could have had such a damned good time together."

And it sounded like a sentence out of a Hemingway novel. It *was* a line out of a Hemingway novel. The last line in *The Sun Also Rises*. And this last line was also Kenny's last words directly to her.

But it was not Kenny but Sandra who went away.

A pair of hiking boots.

She was not going to hunt.

She was going to get them.

And yet, out again, in the sun: hopelessness, yes. But yet, Doris, if now everything was so hopeless why was it then so damned beautiful? So warm and pleasant in the air?

So sparkling?
Such damned beautiful weather?

From Doris's last letter to Inget Herrman:

. . . and they buried her under the house. There wasn't a swimming pool at that time. It wasn't finished, like it never really was. Not during the entire time they were there. When they moved into the house, mother, father, child, the basement was half finished, the most important thing was the house would be finished for her, Lorelei Lindberg's, birthday. He wanted to do everything for her. He loved her.

The pool in the basement was a hole in the ground. The intention was that it would be tiled as quickly as possible. But it didn't happen, nothing happened, it took time. They had so many other things to do. Also getting used to living in the house in the darker part of the woods.

And life, it fell apart so to speak. Withered just like the house. You know, what Bencku has always said. It's true. That house is porous.

She had a fabric store. Little Bombay. It went bankrupt. She became sad. Maybe there was something else too. Other men. Girlfriends. He—yes. He didn't recognize her anymore. He became insecure. Jealous. They fought often. They had always fought, but their fights had been different before. They always contained a moment of reconciliation. But now it wasn't there. One time he pushed her down the stairs, you know, the entire long staircase. She got stitches at the hospital for it, so it wasn't a secret. EVERYONE in town knew it.

He was terribly remorseful. And came home with a very expensive ring, which he gave her. One with a ruby the size of a tablespoon. She became happy at first but started fumbling, and suddenly she dropped that ring in the hole in the ground. There, where the pool is. Then everything left him again, all sense all reason anyway. He pushed her down into the hole and took away the ladder. And then he went and got the rifle. And the girl, she saw. That was Sandra. She had that bad habit of walking in her sleep. But she wasn't walking in her sleep. She wanted to see, maybe she was anxious too, for real. All of it was so strange. Everything that had been happy games, maybe a bit too wild, had now gone over into something else. Something that was serious. For real.

And Lorelei in the pool, while the Islander got the gun, appealed to her. "Sandra, come and help me. Help me out of here. Get the ladder!" And Sandra hesitated, but she still didn't do anything. Not until it was too late, in any case. She just pretended she was walking in her sleep again. She's good at pretending, Sandra, being inside her own fantasies. I know her like no one else. I know.

Before anyone knew it the Islander was back, with the rifle. He was just going to scare her a bit. But, suddenly, before you really knew what was happening, the rifle had gone off. And she lay dead at the bottom.

And then, well, they were alone, father and daughter. With that terrible thing in the pool. And there were things they could have done. Real things, gone to the police and things like that. But they didn't.

Instead they buried her in the hole for the pool, took up the old tile, and let new tiles be laid.

And Sandra, she watched. She didn't do anything. She watched.

And both of them, father and daughter, had this terrible secret to carry.

I have gone around and thought about it. I can't get away from it. I always and forever come back to it. Her in the pool, Lorelei Lindberg. And that *I was her*. In that game we played that one time. We played quite a lot of games.

So we've played. But now, now I don't know if I want to play anymore.

I went to Bencku later, in order to see something that was on the map he has. Perfectly visible above his bed. And there she was. I saw her there. She has been there the entire time.

The woman on the bottom of the pool. He saw it, he said so anyway. A man who aimed a rifle at someone in the pool.

And the shot that went off.

I hear that shot all the time.

And now I've started doubting everything. Now I don't know who she is, or him. I saw the red raincoat as well. The one that Eddie had on when she died. The one who never wore that kind of clothing.

It was a loan. Now I also know where the coat came from. It was Lorelei Lindberg's. She was wearing it in a photograph I saw.

And now I wonder about everything. And it's obvious. There are so many questions to ask, and so many answers.

But I'm so tired now. I don't want to ask. Because I'm afraid of what answers I will get.

I don't want to play anymore, I don't want to live. Sandra. She's the only one. So now, soon I won't know anything anymore.

Sandra Night/Doris Day, Doris Night/Sandra Day

THERE ARE PEOPLE WHO CAN TELL JUST ABOUT EVERYTHING about themselves, as colorful as life itself and with a richness of words that can get anyone to be taken aback. Such a person was sometimes, in certain moments, Doris Flinkenberg.

But there are also other storytellers, a special kind of mythomaniac who can serve versions of, above all, their own life stories, stories completely unlike each other, all just as false. And yet not lie. Such a person was, in certain moments, Sandra Wärn.

Lie far and wide without lying.

Lorelei Lindberg's back, her smiles, singing voice, and Little Bombay, the fabric. The jet-setter's life, the music, "I'm Waiting for the Man," the banana record, "Mr. Tambourine Man."

None of the stories were really true, but in all of the stories there was a grain of truth. A detail, a tone, a recurring theme. And threads of truth shot out from these. Like fireworks, with colors, like a rainbow.

And Sandra learned something about stories and storytelling.

That the fireworks, that the flip side of the mythomania was emptiness.

One, or many, holes in the day, a hole in reality.

And it was her.

The girl turned toward the window

"SO DORIS. WAIT NOW! THAT WAS ALSO JUST A GAME. EVERY-thing was a game. Don't you understand?"

That was how she should have said it. To Doris. While she was still alive. While there was time, and there were chances. You should have understood and the stupid thing was, actually, that you did understand. But that you just continued, anyway. Quite simply, in order to—well, you never could have imagined that she would . . .

No, enough words now, explanations.

This was how it was.

It was the girl at the window in the house on Åland, and it was in those moments Doris died in the District. Exactly in those moments.

The girl on Åland, she looked out over the sea that swelled toward her on the other side of the window. The girl, who in the moment Doris shot herself, was humming the Eddie-song. Really. She was.

Look, Mom, what they did to my song.

Suddenly, in the middle of the humming, she became afraid. The little harelip, Sandra-Pandra. She just could not stand there like that alone and look out over the sea anymore, she just had to turn around. She just had to turn toward "the aunt," who was always there, behind. With her low-voiced talking, about Åland, the sea, all the rest. *Also* all the rest.

Above all it was that which she had not been able to listen to, for a few years. It was above all that which had gotten her to turn toward the window and the sea over and over again—where it was also rather drafty, so that you got a cold and got all of the childhood diseases in the world.

"Sandra!"

She had shown patience, rare for her anyway, "the aunt."

But it started to drain off her now. One time during these days she suddenly impatiently grabbed hold of Sandra, shook her shoulder rather harshly, but certainly oh so familiar.

"What's wrong with you? You're like a dead person? You should at least cry a little if you are so sad for once. Think! That it would be so that I would long for you to start crying. I who used to loathe your tantrums. Do you remember?"

And yes. Sandra remembered. There was something sweet and sour about it. Bittersweet, suddenly. But still a while, a short while, Sandra held out. She shrugged herself free. But it was entirely easy. "The aunt" held her tightly, and suddenly she was not at all ready to let go.

And now "the aunt" changed her tone of voice. It was as if all of the floodgates in her had broken.

"I don't know what I'm going to do with you, Sandra. I've now had you here and I . . . well, you know, Sandra, how terrible it is to live without you. You know how much I would like you to want to visit me and be here with me. Not just now, but . . ."

But it was as if the courage had left her as soon as she started. And the resignation stepped in. It was as if she had suddenly given up right then, "the aunt." And quietly, slowly slowly, turned around. Turned away from Sandra, Sandra's back. And gone back and sat down at the table in the living room at the eternal puzzle that she was always working on. The one with at least half a million pieces, which never got finished—the one called "Alpine Villa in Snow."

Sandra remained standing, facing the sea. Standing and staring and staring so that tears had gathered in her eyes. And at the same time the song had flown up inside her again, the Eddie-song, stronger and more alarming than ever. *Look, Mom, they've destroyed my song.*

The song roared in her head. So that it almost burst. Was it exactly then, in that moment, that Doris raised the pistol to her temple and fired?

But in the air, on Åland, in the house, the room with the veranda facing the sea, the room with the window and the girl facing it, "the aunt's" words hung there, "the aunt's" resignation.

And then the following happened: Sandra at the window turned around. From the window, from the sea, in toward the room. In toward "the aunt" who had pulled back to her table where she was sitting puzzling and puzzling. And suddenly it was so cozy to see—especially after the gray and storming and great sea outside. So pleasant to see. Mom. So amazingly delightful wonderful. Tears in her eyes and in her throat, a crying that was hindering her from saying anything at all. But that now came.

"Mom," said Sandra. "Mom," she started. And that was what she should have said a long time ago, in any case to Doris Flinkenberg. Not "the aunt," not Lorelei Lindberg—which she had been called in a game. A name that Doris had made up once, which had matched perfectly. Which had been so important then, which had really been needed. Not only in a game, but as protection against everything hard in the soul from which stories could not be woven. Still not then, maybe never.

"Mom." Who had lived in the house in the darker part once but had left it and gone with the Black Sheep to Åland. "Managed to get over there," as she said it herself at the time when you really did not want to have anything to do with her. Neither the Islander nor herself. She might as well have been in Austria, or in New York.

Sandra had turned away from the window and looked at her mother who was sitting alone at the table with her puzzle: in front of all of the thousand million pieces of which all of them were snow or clouds and did not look like they fit anywhere. And her mother looked up, a little surprised, carefully. Almost shyly.

"I'm going to tell you something," Sandra continued. "About me and Doris Flinkenberg. We had a game once. We called you Lorelei Lindberg. Then we made up a man, Heintz-Gurt, who was a pilot and came from Austria where he lived and he came and got you with a helicopter. It landed on the roof of the house in the darker part . . ."

And so Sandra had told Lorelei Lindberg, "the aunt," her mother, the story about her mother, as Doris and Sandra had played and told it to each other, over and over again. And her mother, she had really listened for once. Not interrupted with her own comments, which she had a habit of doing before. "I was also interested in movie stars . . ." And all of her own anecdotes that later followed and always in some way were so much bigger and more fantastic than what you had to say yourself.

She had listened.

When Sandra finished Lorelei Lindberg had been so moved that she almost cried.

"So it was so terrible for you too," she said finally. "If only I had known."

But then she opened her arms and Sandra, little Sandra, rushed right into them.

"I never thought we would be friends again," she said. "I am so happy now, Sandra. And so sad. But now. Now everything will be good again. I promise.

"We've gone through so much, Sandra. We're going to manage this as well. Dear beloved child, I promise."

And the mother had rocked her little daughter in her arms.

And the small, soft silk dog, had wagged her tail.

"Everything will be okay again."

. . .

But of course it was not. Because it was exactly then, exactly in those moments, that—*PANG!* Doris Flinkenberg went up onto Lore Cliff with the pistol, fired.

And the world that had for a short moment opened itself, closed again.

The last hunt

HE CAME TO THE HOUSE IN THE DARKER PART OF THE WOODS. Sandra did not really know when, but it must have been sometime during the night when she was lying in bed asleep. He was not there during dinner, the long dinner that followed after the long hunt. Sandra had not taken part in the hunt but stayed in the house where she spent the entire morning alone.

The "catering girls" came in the afternoon. For real that is, which was news now since the Islander had married his "young wife."

And it was fascinating. Also the way the Islander spoke about Kenny in Kenny's absence. "My young wife," he said and sounded proud.

Otherwise the hunting league was the same. Men who in Sandra's childhood had been old men now stuck out in a different way, started having their own qualities and outlines, which they had not had for her earlier. It was Baron von B., who was Magnus's father whom Bencku was still like grease on bacon with, they lived in some kind of "bachelor pad" together in the city by the sea, you were told.

Then there were Lindströms from the District, Wahlmans from the Second Cape, and so on. And Tobias Forsström of course, like always. Who had now developed a truly sinister attitude toward the firearm and to the hunting in general. That was the main thing, not the party afterward. On that point the Islander and Tobias Forsström were in agreement. They spoke expertly about a lot of exciting things that had happened during the hunt, the one that had taken place earlier in the day, and other hunts. It got Sandra in the mood, in some way, to see the two men's understanding and suddenly the memory of Pinky in the Closet had also faded.

"How is it going with the university studies?" Tobias Forsström was also the only one who turned to Sandra especially and asked her anything.

And she lied so politely:

"Good."

Tobias Forrström became in some way, you could see it on him, happy to hear it.

That moved Sandra. She came to think that maybe you did not have to love Tobias Forrström, but he had his good sides. Him too. When he was in his element, it was to his advantage.

She almost laughed when thinking like that. Also Doris-in-her laughed.

Not a sick laugh either, but a perfectly ordinary one.

The Islander raised his glass to Sandra and said cheers. Sandra raised her glass. They clinked glasses.

It was such a splendid mood that was ruling in the house when suddenly a car drove up.

"*Our love was a continental affair, he came in a white Jaguar.*"

Not just any car. It was a Jaguar, a white one. An antique Jaguar from the thirties, the kind that you nowadays got to drive only a few days a year.

He had a habit of coming over to the mainland and driving it sometimes. The Black Sheep that is. From Åland. Where he lived. And had lived all these years. With her, Lorelei Lindberg, who was now his wife.

The two brothers, the two brothers.

The Islander might have stiffened for a microscopic moment at the dinner table. But not longer than that.

And he recovered immediately. Cast a glance out the window.

"I think we have company," he said. "It's my brother."

And then the doorbell rang. The Islander disappeared for a

while, might have been gone longer than usual, while Sandra and the other dinner guests remained sitting at the table.

There they came later, into the living room, both brothers. Not with their arms around each other now, but almost. And both of them were in a brilliant mood.

There you see it Doris Flinkenberg. Everything passes.

The Islander got another chair and set a place for the Black Sheep at the table.

And so they sat there, the Islander and the Black Sheep, like very good friends, ate and drank and talked about nothing.

They even talked about Åland.

Maybe the Islander would even travel to Åland again sometime. Now when the old stuff did not seem to mean anything anymore.

"Maybe I could steer the boat there sometime," the Islander said.

He did not say "with Kenny, my new wife." Because it did not belong there either.

And Sandra, little Sandra, she hid everything in her heart, and contemplated.

Little Bombay. A small unsuccessful store, with fine silk fabrics. Which no one wanted to buy.

While the days passed they were there, in the store, the little girl and her mother, and listened to music and just talked.

Sometimes the phone rang.

Sometimes they waited for the Islander.

"What time do you think he'll come today?"

And they guessed right. And they guessed wrong. But he always came, the Islander, when the day was over and took them home.

That was how it was, a long time. In the middle, as it's called, of passion's whirlwind.

In the middle of the beautiful, soft, like silk, really fine habotai, or silk georgette. Silk georgette, which when you were older you under-

stood it wasn't such an expensive fabric—but the girl, the little silk dog, thought the name was so beautiful.

Silk georgette.

The love. The passion. Whatever it should be called. Silk georgette. The beautiful, soft ground.

So one day, the Black Sheep came. It would be wrong to say it was a surprise. He showed up again, but had of course always been there somewhere in the background.

"MMMMMMMMMMMMM," he said when he stepped into the store. "It smells like MOUSE here."

And at first it was an unpleasant trespassing. It was. And maybe for a long time afterward. But there were also other things that changed.

Lorelei Lindberg who took hold of the lamp over the sink and shocks like lightning went through her, FSST. She turned around, completely unhurt.

"Brr. I must have gotten a shock," she said. Not happily, but rather anxious. It was unpleasant after all. Like an omen. "I could have died."

Because things had also started happening in the house in the darker part. Small shifts. Arguments that didn't always end with reconciliation as they usually did. Arguments that were fought without any thought of reconciliation. And the Islander, he wasn't a brooder, he was a doer.

Maybe he went too far.

It was like this: she couldn't live with the house. She couldn't be there, Lorelei Lindberg.

You didn't really know why. Maybe she didn't either because it should have been so good. It should have been.

And she loved the Islander, she did.

But it was as though a dissonance had come in somewhere, a poison. Maybe it was the Black Sheep.

"I was going to show you what your dreams look like. Not particularly good."

"A matchstick house for matchstick people. By the beach."

The last, "at the beach," he sighed with all the ironic authority that only someone from the sea and Åland can mobilize at the mere thought of a similar marsh environment.

He was an islander too. Lived in a nice lighthouse by the sea. On Åland. Where the relatives were.

He was the Older Brother.

And not a sympathetic person at all.

He hadn't completed a single project in his life, not least his architecture studies, which began chaotically.

But he would succeed in this game, he had decided that.

"We were two brothers," the Black Sheep said to Lorelei Lindberg in Little Bombay. "We had two cats. One cat and the other cat. But there was only one mouse."

And it really was, in some way, so sick what he was thinking.

And what the mouse was, at that stage in life—

It doesn't need to be said. It was so obvious.

Lorelei Lindberg didn't care about any of that, in the beginning. But gradually, when it started becoming so strangely lonely in the house in the darker part of the woods, with all of those dreams that now were realized that you were supposed to live up to, then everything changed. Slowly. Slowly.

That terrible staircase. "A staircase up to heaven," the Islander had said. But he did not see it himself, that which was so obvious, that it was a staircase up into nothing.

"I'm going to show you what your dreams look like."

He had not only drawn the house, the Black Sheep. He had also found the lot; told his brother the Islander about it.

The Islander, he was no thinker.

He had forgotten about that game a long time ago, the one with his brother. Now, with Lorelei Lindberg and their little daughter, it was so obvious that you played other games.

The Black Sheep had "contacts" in that part of the District. He had lived as a boarder with the baroness, a relative of Baron von B. who had once owned almost the entire District, while he was studying to become an architect in the city by the sea.

It was the baroness who had told the Black Sheep that there might be a lot to buy. And the Black Sheep, he knew what the District was. He had driven around on the small roads there in his old cars.

The baroness was his friend. But they were not close in any way. She was a relatively lonely person, and she helped him and he helped her, also when he no longer lived with her. Also with Eddie de Wire, the niece. When the baroness was at her most desperate. With that girl who sucked life and soul out of her.

Who stole, who swindled, who could not be trusted. Who was everything else other than what you expected of her.

The American girl.

"Come and take her away away away away," the baroness had screamed on the telephone to the Black Sheep that last night. "I have her in a room here! I've locked her up! And taken her clothes to get her to stay here for the time being! Now she's going!"

The Black Sheep had come. He happened to have a raincoat, which had been left behind in the car at some point. Lorelei Lindberg's red raincoat.

It was once, a rainy day, during the very last time in Little Bombay. The girl and her mother waiting for the Islander who was late. The Black Sheep showed up instead. He insisted on driving them to the house in the darker part. When they had come to the house the rain had stopped and the sun was shining again.

"I was going to show you what your dreams look like," the Black Sheep repeated in the car at the top of the hill just before they rolled down into the glen where the unlikely house was.

Their home. Lorelei Lindberg was so upset she forgot her coat in the car.

Lorelei Lindberg and the Black Sheep. He got her later. He "won" the game.

And no. There was no real plausibility in it. She was not "in love." You do not fall for the kinds of stupid things the Black Sheep was doing. Those games.

You do not. Actually.

But assume that something happens, something unexpected, something that makes you not be so sure of yourself anymore. Of anything. For example passion, love.

What was it? Lorelei Lindberg was standing on the landing and the Islander had come up behind her. Suddenly, there was a scuffle, so he had pushed her. Down the stairs, down into the mud.

"She fell like an angel, down from heaven." As it had once played in Doris Flinkenberg's cassette player.

But it was no longer beautiful. Nothing was beautiful. The warm, soft earth had become malicious.

She had to get stitches at the hospital with a stitch called a butterfly. When she came home again the Islander was remorseful. He had bought her that wretched ring, the one with the big red stone in it, "a tablespoon-sized ruby." But it went wrong again.

She was standing at the edge of the pool and fumbled with it. And before you knew it she had dropped it. Down into the hole in the ground that should have become a swimming pool a long time ago. And the Islander became angry and shoved her down into the pool to look for it.

He took the ladder away and walked off.

The mother in the pool, the girl also there, in a corner under the spiral staircase. The mother saw her and was quiet about the stone. "Quick," sure enough, Doris, you were right, the little girl did nothing. She was as though frozen. A sleepwalker again. Sleepwalker.

And furthermore. It happened so quickly. The Islander. With the rifle.

"It is so empty. I'm shooting flies with an air gun."

And fired.

But idiots. There was no ammunition in that rifle. An idiot who would shoot around in his own house.

It was an empty round and not straight at her in the pool, but to the side.

But it was enough.

After that shot, it was true, Bencku, nothing was the same.

. . .

IMAGINARY SWIMMING. If you were wondering what it was that you saw a little later, when you came back.

The girl who was running back and forth in the pool.

It was certainly Sandra. It was me.

Back and forth back and forth. Those were terrible times, you should know. Dry swimming in the pool without water. Then there was nothing.

No reconciliation.

There was no silk dog any longer, rather some kind of bizarre animal of an entirely different species, some kind of damp rat with nasty fur that shone and shone from one end to the other.

And when it was at its most difficult. Then he came, the Black Sheep. Then he was so nice.

She just cried then, that was in Little Bombay also. Afterward.

"Stoopp!! I want to go away!!!" She screamed to him and he did not need to listen for very long in order to understand.

"Away!" she sobbed. He took her at her word.

They came to Åland, to the nice house, to the sea.

Quite some time went by before I agreed to meet with her at all.

Because it was a betrayal. That's what I thought then. Now of course, I think so differently.

The last time, that was in Little Bombay.

"Are you coming, Sandra?"

They were standing in the door now, both of them, and he was quite impatient.

But Lorelei Lindberg did not want to, she was shilly-shallying. Starting to become unhappy again.

"Sandra?"

She did not answer. She disappeared. Became nothing. Plupp. A spot on the floor.

The silk dog, the invisible.

"Are you coming, Sandra?"

"Sandra."

But he did not have as much patience as her, who never had patience otherwise. Only just then—all the patience in the world.

But it was time.

Time time time time, thought the little silk dog who lay and pressed under the table.

And it was in Little Bombay, that too.

Among the fabric.

Silk georgette organza habotai taffeta and rasgulla hung down in whirling cascades, like a rain over the edges of the table. Flowed, flowed—

And that, all of that, belonged and would, under a long period of time, belong to that hard stuff in the soul from which stories could not be woven.

For both of them.

The Islander and Sandra Wärn.

For a while it was so, that everything that had been Lorelei Lindberg, and that is, was obliterated.

The girl, Sandra, left the dinner table after dessert. She was sleepy. It was nothing more than that. She was tired, she went to bed.

Also the hunting had lost its appeal. The changes in the party. The game. All of that.

A few hours later she woke up to a sound out in the corridor. She thought she could make out a familiar voice also, already then, but she fell asleep again anyway.

"It's just the boys who want beer," someone yelled.

And not a lot of imagination was required in order to understand who the two boys were who had shown up at the house in the darker part of the woods, in the middle of the hunting party, in the middle of the night, uninvited. Magnus von B. and Bencku, the two unmanageable ones who would never grow up.

Both of them lost sons, in their own ways.

But the fathers took them in now, and offered. And offered.

In the early morning the girl woke again, in the darkness. The electric alarm clock on the nightstand next to the enormous marital bed where she had rolled in a sweaty, deep, dreamless sleep, showed six thirty in clear, sharp orange-colored numbers.

Sandra was suddenly wide awake. She sat up in bed. The first thing she noticed was the silence. The deafening house-in-the-darker-part silence, which covered everything so to speak. The party was over now, an early, early Sunday morning.

Everything was over.

Sandra got out of bed, put her feet in the movie star slippers, and pulled on the silk kimono—though that had stopped meaning anything now, no scents left on the fabric. No reminiscence anyway, nothing.

She unlocked the door and went out into the hall. The door to the basement was open. Sounds could be heard from below, a sound she immediately recognized again—and it was a reminiscence.

Snores. Someone was sleeping down there.

Maybe for a moment she thought the fantastic. That Doris . . . that nothing had happened, that everything had just been a dream.

But it was just a brief moment.

Then she got herself together and went down the stairs.

The sound of the snores grew.

The whole house shook from it.

But she did not shilly-shally on the stairs but went down quickly, but still as quietly as possible.

And this was what she saw.

They were lying in the pool. Both sleeping, both snoring, as if competing with each other. It was actually comical too, though she did not laugh just then. One of the ones on the bottom of the pool was Bengt, the boy. Sure enough he had been one of the "boys" who had arrived intoxicated and uninvited to the hunters' party in the middle of the night.

The other, that was the Black Sheep. He was lying on his back and it was from him the true foghorns were coming.

He lay there with his shirt open. Someone may have torn it open while he was sleeping. So defenseless. The Black Sheep. The loose shirtsleeves without arms spread to the sides over the green tile like angel wings, loose. And just below, like under one wing, the other boy, in other words, Bengt was lying.

In just as deep a sleep, snoring almost as loudly.

Sandra stood for a while and looked at it all, also the entire desolation after the party, the knocked-over bottles, the entire disgust.

Maybe she also stood there and imagined, or expected a continuation. That someone would wake up. Bengt.

"Now I'm going to tell you about love," Inget Herrman said once. "You don't fall in love with someone because that person is nice or mean or even because of that person's thousand good qualities. You fall in love with someone who brings something inside you to life."

But she turned around. She went up again. Left them there, all of it. Showered and got dressed. Got the boots from the Closet, they had been there the entire time. They were the boots Doris left for her before she died (but Inget Herrman had put them away, by mistake, before Sandra had seen them).

They had been there the whole time next to Pinky's glitter shoes, next to above all those ice skates that she had with great effort one time a long time ago painted green and tried to skate on Bule Marsh.

And then there was not so much more with anything at all. Sandra put on these enormous boots and walked out into the world.

Rather she took the ferry over to the continent already the same day. Rather that is how she came out into the world.

"THE DAY THE MUSIC DIED. AND I STARTED LIVING."

(the return of the Marsh Queen, a few years later)

––––––––––

THE MUSIC DIES HERE. IT IS SO SIMPLE. ON CONEY ISLAND, America, sometime at the beginning of the 1980s.

Sandra likes to be there, leave the city for a while. Here there are beaches, parks, restaurants, an amusement park with old carousels.

She has a few dollars in her hand, she has asked for them.

She is hungry, she is thinking about buying some food.

That is when she catches sight of a recording booth, it is located at the edge of the amusement park, like a relic from another time.

Sing your own song and give it to your loved one.

She steps into the booth, mostly for fun, puts in a coin.

The red light comes on: record.

She starts singing. An old song. The Eddie-song, which it was once called.

Look, Mom, what they've done to my song.

They've destroyed it.

But it is so stupid. Suddenly she has forgotten the words. The words to THAT song, it is almost unbelievable!

She stops singing, stops completely. Suddenly sees herself from outside.

What in the world is she doing standing there in the booth howling, all alone?

It is absurd.

She looks around.

There are some people walking by.

A young woman is strolling last in the group; suddenly she turns around and catches sight of Sandra in the booth.

She raises her hand in a greeting. Sandra waves back. The woman hesitates a few seconds but then she leaves the group and runs over to Sandra.

". . . and that was A. And they stripped in Tokyo, in Yokohama, in Los Angeles (the day shift at the airport hotel; they were not the 'right type' for the more lucrative evening and night shifts) . . . and in Alaska. And that is where they found themselves one illustrious New Year's Eve just before everything started to happen and the music started for real. At the end of the world, Alaska, darkness, snow. And they made their New Year's resolutions, wrote them down in oilcloth-covered notebooks. A wrote like this: 'The Marsh Queen and I, in the month of August play in Wembley Arena.'"

It did not turn out quite like that.

But almost.

THE WINTER GARDEN, 2008

———————

T HE WINTER GARDEN, 2008, IN THE FALL, SOLVEIG AT A WINDOW.
"For thine is the kingdom, the power, the glory." Something in
Solveig Torpeson had broken apart. She is standing, as she so often has
a habit of doing, in the kitchen in the house where she lives with her
family, what was once the cousin's house. She stares out into the darkness, she is thinking.

When it is really dark the strong light from the Winter Garden can
be seen over the treetops so it looks like it is coming from a spaceship
that has landed in a crater.

"For thine is the kingdom, the power, the glory." Sometimes Solveig
Torpeson says it out loud.

It is Rita who has everything. She is the one who owns and runs the
Winter Garden.

"Mom. Are you standing there in the dark again? Where's my
phone?" It is her daughter Johanna who comes into the kitchen and
turns on the ceiling lamp and everything is normal again. Or should be.

The telephone, on the table between them, starts ringing. For a moment they are both frozen, out of surprise and bewilderment.

Solveig reaches out for the telephone. Johanna tries to stop her,
"Give it here! It's mine!"

But it is too late. Solveig has picked up the telephone—

Click. The one who is calling has hung up.

Johanna is furious. She tears at the phone, runs out.

Solveig calls after her:

"Where are you going, Johanna?"

"Out. I'm going out."

THE WINTER GARDEN, 2008

———————

THE WINTER GARDEN, 2008. RITA BUILT THE WINTER GARDEN, which was inaugurated in 2000, on New Year's Eve.

First she did away with the language: "adventure park," "water park," "recreational park," "amusement park," all of that. Which it was also going to be called. Because all of that, it is also in the Winter Garden. But that is not what the Winter Garden is.

There is the other, the other rooms, the other games, which are also played in there.

And all the rest.

Rita, she did away with the language and started giving everything her own names.

And brought her own images with their own meanings into the Winter Garden.

And it was also interesting, a bit like on her brother Bengt's maps once.

"In the middle of the Winter Garden there is kapu kai, the forbidden seas."

"Look, Mom, they've destroyed my song."

There are many familiar stories in the Winter Garden, like the ones told by the images on the walls.

The photographs.

The drawings.

The maps.

Even some of Bencku's maps.

The District then and the District now.

The Winter Garden is a place you love to describe. Exactly because you cannot.

Not capture it.

You know nothing of its secret.

Johanna found the red room by chance. It was the same night the Winter Garden was inaugurated, New Year's Eve 2000.

It happened at Bule Marsh, in the room.

The red room. She wandered in there by accident.

But when she was going to look for it again she did not find her way back.

She has never found her way back. But she knows it exists. She knows.

The red room. The Bule Marsh Room. And all the images on the walls.

The American girl, the one who died.

That morning.

The girl who is lying in the water, but no one helps her get out.

And yet, on the beach across it is as if there was a whole family there swimming.

And Johanna knows, she has already known for a long time, that she has to find her way there again.

Project underworld. Orpheus was going to get his Eurydice from the underworld. She was dead. The gods had taken her to them, but Orpheus loved her so much that the gods had mercy on him. Go down to her, she will follow you, but do not turn around in the underworld.

Project underworld. It is a project they had, in school, this semester.

And now suddenly she gets an idea. Maybe she can use it.

Because she cannot go alone. She needs a friend, an ally.

It happened at Bule Marsh. Everything is there. She has to get there again.

. . .

But she cannot do it alone. She does not dare.

So it is one evening, one of those dark and ordinary fall evenings in the District, when Johanna goes to the house in the darker part of the woods.

The Marsh Queen lives there, she has come home again. Her, and her son, the one whose name is Glitter.

She does not know him, but she does not bother about that now. She walks up the many steps and rings the bell, he is the one who opens. She says:

"Hi. I'm Johanna from school, you might know me. Now I want you to do a project with me."

It is so simple.

He says yes. "I'm coming." Then Johanna and Glitter walk out into the Winter Garden.

(to be continued)

Author's acknowledgments

The American Girl is the first of two books, the second being *The Glitter Scene*, which together make up one story.

The text is fiction through and through. I have at times taken the liberty of translating the lines from well-known musical pieces and from pop songs on my own, so as to be appropriate for the novel's plot.

I extend a thank-you to Pro Artibus in Ekenäs for the fellowship allowing me to stay in Villa Snäcksund 1999–2002 and to the Lärkkulla Foundation in Karis, which placed a workspace at my disposal several times during my work on this novel.

Also a thank-you to Merete and Silja for inspiration, ideas, and good advice; thank you Hilding. Most of all, thanks to Tua for your help and support that exceeded everything I could have dreamed of.

Translator's acknowledgments

I wish to thank Other Press for allowing me the opportunity to translate such a remarkable piece of literature, in particular Corinna Barsan for her commitment and insight during the editing process. I would also like to thank Monika Fagerholm for taking the time to answer my questions. Being able to work with the author herself was a wonderful asset. Finally, thanks to friends and family for their support and encouragement, and especially Gerald for his patience and love.